FOLLICLE FARM

Follicle Farm

A Novel Adventure

STEPHAN DE JONGHE

Ordering Information:
Special discounts are available on quantity purchases by corporations,
associations, and others. For details, contact the publisher at the email
address above.

 A catalogue record for this
book is available from the
National Library of Australia

ISBN 978-0-6453718-0-2 paperback)
ISBN 978-0-6453718-1-9 (ebook)

Cover art & design: Pickawoowoo Publishing Group

Interior Layout: Pickawoowoo Publishing Group
Printing & Distribution: Ingram (USA / UK/ AUS/ EUR)

Dedication

Bobby may be the hero of my story...
My wife, Deb, is the hero in my life.

Principle reference text:

Principle of Anatomy and Physiology by Sandra Tortora and
Sandra Grabowski. John Wiley & Sons, Tenth Edition.
(Apologies for Authors privileges)

AN INTRODUCTION TO FOLLICLE FARM: THE INSIDE STORY

For the most part, we human's take our hair for granted. Except of course, when it's growing where it's not wanted or, when it isn't growing where it is wanted, or if it's turning grey, when we don't like the colour or we want it curlier or straighter or it needs more body; or if it's too dry, too oily, too short, too long, and it should be shinier, have fewer kinks, less knots an no split ends.

Hair gets damaged by over-brushing, too much washing, chemicals, pollution, being pulled, heating irons, tight hair rollers and hair bands pulled too tight and of course, stress. It gets dirty and needs washing and conditioning as we try out the thousands of available products and we continuously struggle to decide which are the best and what truly works for us.

Actually, growing and managing our hair is very serious business!

This task is not easy. We wash; condition, blow dry, cut, detangle, colour, perm, bleach, pluck, electrocute, zap, comb, brush and braid our hair to the point of obsession. For many humans, managing hair is as important and deciding what clothes we're going to wear. It is a significant factor in the mating rituals, and we all know how vitally important they are.

But for all the time and money we humans spend managing our hair, do we ever consider the microscopic world of the organisation which grows our hair? Do we ever contemplate the millions of decisions our mind makes about where, when, and how much hair to actually grow? The truth is that we don't, and the reason we don't is because of people like Bobby. Bobby isn't a person the way we understand people, but Bobby exists. Bobby is a *Mitochondria* and works as a Follicle Farmer. He, with millions of colleagues, is part of the amazing organisation dedicated to growing hair for the man that they live inside off.

This man barely exists for Bobby. He doesn't know his name or really anything about him. Nor does he care. Bobby spends as much time and energy thinking about the man that he lives in, as the man spends time thinking about which hair to grow next.

On the left side of his man's face, which looks pink and grey to the human eye, Bobby and his team handle growing one hair follicle. Bobby is a Team Leader for a follicle in the beard. He, and his two workers, feed and nourish that single hair and encourage its growth.

They are a proud and noble force within the human body, responsible for growth, replenishment, and repair management for their man. They are a very dedicated team.

Their motto is *'If we don't grow, we don't grow'*, and they are Follicle Farmers!

This... is Bobby's story.

The easiest way to describe Bobby would be say that he is medium sized, middle aged squat mitochondria. Whilst he isn't technically a man and only a very, very small part of a one, it is common practice to refer to him, as a man. All the other men that work with him aren't technically men either, so therefore it doesn't matter. He is however, all male, and he lives and works in an all-male environment.

Bobby knew he'd never reach his ideal height. He accepted that he was generally shorter than most others. Often, as a Team Leader, he had taller workers reporting to him. He knew of other men in supervisory positions that were also squat. Some of them suffered 'small-man syndrome', but he didn't. He was very confident of his skills as a leader and as a mentor and trainer of others. He knew he had earned respect and he enjoyed it. His height had nothing to do with his skills or his professionalism.

Bobby knows how to grow hair. He is a Team Leader for the growth of a single hair and he lives and works on the left side of the man's face. He is literally under the man's skin. Bobby is a very successful Team Leader and an enormously proud to be a Follicle Farmer.

Follicle Farmers are basically human shaped with a head, torso, arms and legs. They wear a one-piece uniform that fits snugly and looks like coveralls. They don't wear hairnets because they themselves are completely free of hair. To us, apart from subtle differences, they all look alike. To see them, we'd need a very powerful microscope. Follicle Farmers are inside all of us, busily growing the hundreds of thousands of hairs that push out through the skin of our human body.

All the Follicle Farmers, workers, and leaders alike, that work in a male human body are referred to as 'he' or 'him'. Like all other parts of the body, they reproduce by division in a process known as *mitosis,* so they have no need for sexual organs. *Mitosis* is exhausting for a cell to do, so they only do it when more cells are really needed.

Follicle farmers therefore aren't distinguished by gender or colour. They have no religion, unless belonging to the Follicle Farmers Union is a religion. They are all members and follow the union position with religious fervour. Interestingly, this includes the entire management team also.

What they do have is politics. Lots and lots of politics. One of Bobby's former mentors had explained it him, *'Bobby, if you want to get ahead, you'll need to be good at growing hair. If you want to be a leader, you'll need to be good at teaching others how to grow hair. If you want to be a highly respected important leader, you'll need to become very good at politics.'*

Bobby hopes he'll get promoted to Team Supervisor one day. Then he'll be responsible for up to twenty teams. Bobby's current supervisor, Dan, knows that Bobby is a great Team Leader and there are many of Bobby's former subordinates that have been promoted to Team Leader because of his high standards. Bobby knows that Dan hopes that one day he'll be promoted to Area Manager, and so he plans of being promoted to Supervisor.

There are four areas in the beard. Bobby and Dan work on the left side of the face. The other areas are the right side of the face, the neck, and the moustache. Their Area Manager is Greg. His title is AMBLS (Area Manager Beard Left Side) and from all accounts he was essentially a nice guy before he got promoted, but now he gets very frustrated with the other three AM's. Between them they are responsible for all beard growth. Greg claims he enjoys his regular meetings with Pete, Shaun, and Bill to discuss out-put and staff rotations. Pete, Shaun, and Bill think he's an idiot and take sport in teaming up against him. Mostly they argue about where the borders of their areas on the face are. Pete is the AM for the moustache,

Shaun for the neck and Bill is AM for the right side of the face. Every manager in beard production, in fact in all of follicle production, has a fancy title.

Rumour has it, that if Greg doesn't improve his attitude soon, he'll be out. So therefore, all the supervisors in Greg's area are on their best behaviour and striving for excellent performance. They're all hoping for a promotion because of Greg's inevitable downfall. Dan included.

Steve is the Regional Manager of Beard Hair, or the RMBH. He doesn't care about his AM's hostilities toward each other. He cares about overall beard hair production and as long as this is happening according to his KPI's, then his four AM's can argue as much as they like. Steve is currently focused on the chin. He likes the idea of the chin being designated a separate area from the two sides of the face and the neck. It would mean he'd have five Area Managers reporting to him instead of four. More to the point it would mean less stress for him should another directive come from Head Office to grow a goatee. Steve believes this is a distinct possibility, as he heard a rumour from a guy, who knows someone, who overheard it from the *Testosterone* Factory Manager. Apparently, they heard that efforts were about to be made to bulk up in other parts of the body and growing a goatee would help the desired image that the Marketing Department was now looking to achieve. Steve has been saying on the Beard Network News that the current border disputes between his AM's needed to be properly resolved or he'll have problems co-ordinating growing a goatee of which they can all be proud.

It was generally agreed by union members of the beard region that they wanted the chin to be a separate area. Many cycles ago, Steve was given a directive that the hair on the chin was going to grow unhindered and they all made a special effort to exceed daily growth rates. This meant that the two Area Managers had to agree to cooperate on daily growth targets. The adjoining supervisors that worked on the point of the chin are rivals, so the whole goatee growing directive caused considerable tension between the two sides of the face.

The situation only sorted itself out when the directive from Head Office came through that the goatee was being removed. But it did leave many in the beard growing team, with a feeling that the animosity could have been avoided if only they had a separately recognised area for the chin. Steve has been very vocal about his support for this. Head Office is reluctant to ratify the fifth area within beard production until the negative politics have been resolved. This further frustrated Steve since ratifying the fifth area would resolve those issues.

Whilst Steve chairs the meetings for the Beard Area Managers, he rarely contributes much to them. These Beard Area Managers Meetings or BAMM's are scheduled by Steve's support staff. They also organise the meeting rooms, which rotate between areas, set the agendas, and arrange refreshments and protein packs. They record and issue minutes, document the proceedings and follow up on all the outcomes. They are very professional and totally organised.

Steve's Chief of Staff is Dave. Dave has only ever aspired to be Chief of Staff and all he wanted was to be, was the very best chief, and manage the best staff. Dave's title is, Chief Of Staff to Beard Assisting the Regional Manager or COSTBARM. Dave is living his dream which is to have a lot of power but no responsibility.

Dave is very happy about Steve's ambition and subsequent lack of power. Steve is very happy about Dave's role and his persistent lack of ambition. Steve is also very proud of one particular meeting where his entire contribution consisted of four words. 'Meeting open,' and 'Meeting adjourned'.

Steve asked Dave to arrange a meeting with the four AM's with just one item on the agenda. It was "The proposed separation of the chin from the other areas." Theoretically, it should work well. The only dissenter is Greg who is sensitive to the fact that size of his area will be reduced because of the additional new area. He is the only AM that utilises fear management to get results and he acts dissatisfied and angry most of the time. Greg is also a small man who generally resents being small.

Dan both fears and hates Greg. Dan openly supports the chin separation plans as it increases the number promotional opportunities and he wants to get promoted to AM. He secretly hopes that one day he'll explode and that he'll get Greg's job. Greg hates him for this and secretly hopes that one day he'll implode so that he can replace him with a more supportive subordinate.

Bobby has also been actively supporting the separation of the chin and has been reported saying so on the network news. He'd love to see a directive that focuses on growing the goatee hair on the chin. However, as all the support has been unanimous, Bobby's contribution is completely overlooked. As with all organisations within the body, ambition means you vie for promotion by being excessively agreeable.

Bobby enjoys contributing his thoughts on the *beard grower's network news*. Team Leaders and above can contribute news, ideas, and opinions on a public forum. Harry, the General Manager of hair came up with the idea and it has been very popular with the whole hair growing fraternity. To keep it simple, the network extends only to a specific region. Beard growers only get to share news with other beard growers.

Apart from the RM, beard hair growers don't hear much about follicle farmers in other areas. The RM's across the body do receive copies of each other's network news additions, but they rarely share details with their own Area Managers, Supervisors or Team Leaders.

'All is well in the beard,' Steve tells himself. 'The AM's will work it out, the supervisors will motivate the Team Leaders and they'll all carry on doing a good job.'

Bobby often feels the same way, but at this moment he has some pressing concerns. Recently, Bobby's team was split up. The two subordinates that he had trained were now promoted and had moved on to lead their own teams. They were part of the never-ending cycle of promotion and advancement within the follicle growing department of human activities.

Bobby is anxiously waiting for his two replacements, as the next growth cycle is about to begin, and he needs these workers to be able to complete the task.

Alone in a pinkish coloured room, Bobby is checking his computer terminal that sits on top of a small pedestal. He walks to the hair follicle and checks its temperature. He walks back to the computer and types in the result when he hears someone entering behind him.

Bobby turned to see Dan entering his area. He is unaccompanied.

'Ah Bobby, there you are,' he exclaimed. 'Let me...' he turned around to look behind him and stopped mid speech.

'What about my replacements?' he questioned Dan in frustration. 'I can't do this on my own you know!'

'They were right behind me,' Dan spluttered. He turned and looked down the passage to see if anyone was coming up behind him. 'I'll be right back,' he explained to Bobby, and he left back the way he had come.

Bobby stood firm, crossed his arms and began tapping his foot impatiently.

Dan re-entered with two bewildered workers behind him. 'Bobby. This is Shorty and this is Curly.' He indicated the two workers walking in behind him. 'These... are... your... replacements'.

Bobby looked at them and was unimpressed.

Dan placed his hand on the shoulder of one of the two. 'This is Shorty.' He pushed him forward. 'Shorty previously grew hair in the left arm pit.'

Shorty wasn't paying much attention and so Dan shook him. Shorty looked at Dan in annoyance. 'Shorty!' Dan admonished him. 'This is Bobby,' he said pointing at Bobby. 'He's your Team Leader. You now report to him.'

Shorty hopped one footed over to Bobby and offered his hand in friendship. 'I'm sure I'm very pleased to make your acquaintance,' he said to Bobby who returned the handshake somewhat bewildered by Shorty's behaviour. Shorty performed the handshake with exaggerated enthusiasm and Bobby was feeling somewhat underwhelmed by this new worker. He rolled his eyes at Dan.

'How you going, Team Leader?' Shorty asked Bobby loudly. 'It's a huge honour and an extreme pleasure to make your acquaintance. I'm so very happy and delighted to be assigned to your team,' he continued.

'Is there something wrong with your foot?' Bobby asked him.

Shorty lifted his food and examined it. 'No,' he answered as if puzzled by the question.

'You hopped, so I thought that maybe you'd hurt it,' Bobby explained.

Shorty said nothing.

Bobby took a deep breath, sighed and looked toward Dan appealing for some kind of explanation.

Dan shrugged his shoulders. He introduced the other worker who had been waiting patiently with his head bowed. 'This is Curly. He's the other one I was telling you about. Curly used to grow pubic hair.'

Curly looked up, smiled and came over to Bobby and delicately shook Bobby's hand. 'I'm so awfully glad that you consented to have me in your team,' he explained to Bobby meekly 'I think I'd rather overstayed my welcome in the public hair region.'

'Pubic hair,' corrected Bobby. 'You called it public hair.'

'Considering where our boy has been, we called it public hair.'

Bobby looked desperately at Dan once more but he just shrugged his shoulders.

Bobby reflected on how he felt when Dan first told him that he had been selected to supervise a trial worker exchange program. 'It's all part of a new experimental programme,' he explained. 'It'll be a pleasure for you,' he had assured. 'And very satisfying,' he concluded.

Obviously he'd said too much.

'Okay then...,' Dan was preparing a way to escape. 'The next growth push will start soon and you'll need to get acquainted and all that, so I'll leave it to the three of you to do what needs doing.' He moved to leave but turned back to look at Bobby. 'Call me if... you know...,' his voice trailed off.

Bobby knew that Dan didn't want to be called. He also knew that Dan knew that he wouldn't call, because Bobby was good at his job and they both knew that. Dan was being polite. Dan had left the room.

Bobby turned to look at his new subordinates. 'I really do appreciate the support management gives me...,' he explained diplomatically. 'Righty oh then! We don't have much time. I do insist that this team's work is spot-on.'

'Me too,' chipped in Curly. 'Dan said you were one of his best Team Leaders in the beard region and that we were very lucky to have you as our trainer and mentor.'

'That's very kind of Dan...'

'He also said you were a staunch union man,' Shorty added.

'I wouldn't say staunch as such, I just....'

The computer pinged as a new message arrived. Bobby crossed to the screen and read the message aloud to the others benefit. 'A *Kerion* builder has been spotted in the area. We need to be on alert and report any suspicious activity.'

'I don't like them,' said Curly. 'They gum up the *epidermis* and mess with production and it can be very painful.'

'We'll be all right,' comforted Bobby unconvincingly.

'What's a *Kerion* builder?' Shorty asked worriedly.

'It's a fungus worker,' Bobby explained. 'They invade and multiply quickly, cover everything in pus and they make the whole area stink and feel unwell. We have antifungal packs here in this locker.' Bobby walked over to the locker and opened it to reveal a blue spray can of antifungal agent. 'If we get it before it multiplies, we should be able to contain it'.

Shorty looked worried.

'I'll order in some more spray packs so that we're well armed.' Bobby moved to the computer terminal and typed in the request. The computer responded immediately with a ping. 'There. Our order is confirmed. They're very efficient, so don't worry,' he assured them. 'Right the,' Bobby continued. 'Here, we grow beard hair. Beard hair is tougher than most other hair.' Bobby walked over to the follicle and patted it with affection. 'Being a beard hair follicle farmer has a lot of responsibility...'

'Do we get shaved?' asked Curly.

'Yes we do,' answered Bobby, annoyed at the interruption.

'I ask you, why do we bother?' Curly continued.

'What?'

'If the beard gets shaved, why do we bother to grow it?' Curly persisted. 'If a beard isn't wanted, why do we go through all this trouble of growing one? It seems to me that it just creates work for other parts of the body. Why should they have to go through the trouble of removing it every day?' Curly lamented.

Bobby said nothing. He looked blankly at Curly.

Curly went red in the face. 'I just think that if we only grew beard hair when Head Office actually wanted a beard, which would be fine. We'd have a purpose.' Curly stared at Bobby for acknowledgement but Bobby said nothing. 'So..., why do waste effort growing beard hair?' Curly demanded.

'Because...,' answered Bobby.

'That's actually not a complete answer,' challenged Curly.

'Because we're told to...,' continued Bobby. 'It's our purpose, it's what we do'.

'I just wish we knew why,' Curly whined.

'Hey man, I just want to grow hair. Is that okay with you guys?' Shorty interjected looking wildly at the two of them.

'Growing beard hair is very different to growing armpit hair, Shorty.' Bobby appreciated the opportunity to move away from Curly's awkward line of questioning.

'Hair is hair. I can grow it in my sleep,' Shorty chided. 'There was this one-time...'

'I bet no one ever shaved the hair in the arm pit,' Curly said directing his comment to Shorty.

'Why would they do that? They only shave beards and moustaches, don't they?' Shorty looked at Bobby for confirmation.

'Yes,' confirmed Bobby.

'Not our boy,' Curly contradicted. 'He's been shaved down there as well!' Curly indicated the region that would be his groin, if he had one. 'Word came through from Marketing that it was going to happen, and then whoosh, off it came!'

Bobby and Shorty looked at Curly in shocked horror.

Bobby recovered his composure and walked to the computer. 'The next push is in fifteen beats,' he informed them. 'Let's get ready to grow this hair. We can discuss more about the logic of doing so, after the growth push is finished.'

Both Curly and Shorty nodded their agreement and moved to get ready to grow the follicle.

'Now...,' Bobby started to explain. 'Beard hair is very different to arm pit hair and public hair...'

'Pubic hair,' interrupted Shorty.

'That's what I said,' Bobby sighed.

'No, you said public,' Curly confirmed.

'See, now you've messed me up and I...' he paused and took in a big breath. 'I just want us to get on with growing this follicle. Agreed?' He asked with exaggerated enunciation.

Curly and Shorty nodded.

'Good. If I explain things that you already know well too bad. I need to know that you know, and I don't have time for twenty questions... This is the follicle,' he said patting the hair follicle. 'We're responsible for feeding the *matrix* via this *papilla*.' He then pointed to the tiny blood vessels that feed into the bottom of the follicle at its base. 'The *matrix* base is bulb shaped and it helps hold the hair in place, so despite the shaving…,' Bobby emphasised this point. 'The hair stays in the skin.'

Bobby looked at his team quizzically and they initially stared at him blankly in response. Curly nodded his head in understanding and he elbowed Shorty, who then nodded his head positively also.

Bobby sighed and continued. 'The follicle consists of the *medulla*, the *cortex*, the thin layer of *cuticle* and the inner and outer layers of the sheath. All of this is bound together by this connective tissue sheath which holds it firmly in place in the skin.'

'The *Dermis* and the *Epidermis*,' contributed Curly.

'Yes, Curly,' Bobby agreed and Curly smiled.

Bobby continued. 'Next to the hair root is this *sebaceous* gland.' He patted the gland. 'This is filled with oil and helps lubricate the shaft as it pushes through the *epidermis*,' he explained looking at Curly, who was nodding encouragingly at the correct word usage in discussing the skin. Bobby next pointed to a muscle near the top of the bulb. 'This is the *Arrector pili muscle*. It doesn't get worked much here in the beard and he's pretty well redundant.'

'That's not very nice,' chided Shorty.

'He's asleep,' replied Bobby. 'He's always asleep, so ignore him,' he added.

'It's getting warm in here,' Curly informed the others.

'So it is,' Bobby agreed. 'Heat comes from both internal and external sources…' Bobby started to explain, but both Curly and Shorty groaned loudly, and Bobby paused in introspective reflection. He decided that maybe he was giving too much information considering they were experienced follicle farmers, even if they were new to beard hair.

'I'll turn up the *apocrine sweat gland*, and that'll release some of the heat' he advised them, and Bobby went to the computer monitor and touched the screen. Moments later, the temperature decreased sufficiently for it to become pleasant again.

'Okay. I think that's about enough for now.' Bobby paused once more in thought. 'We have three beats remaining and we'll have a growth push to perform. Shall we, do it?' he asked rhetorically?

'Absolutely,' agreed Curly.

'Most defiantly,' confirmed Shorty.

Bobby ignored the word play error that Shorty made. Growing beard hair was serious work and he would soon train Shorty into a professional beard hair grower of the highest standard. He had done it before, and he'd do it again.

Bobby went to get the trolley that held the chemicals they'd need for the growth push. It was his habit to follow the manual and store the trolley in the trolley bay. He always fully replenished it at the end of each push so that it was ready for use at the next push. He would demonstrate the correct procedure for doing this to Shorty and Curly. Bobby knew that many Team Leaders were lazy and didn't restock or store their equipment and consumables according to procedure. He hoped that his new subordinates didn't have too many bad habits.

As he was about to re-enter the follicle room he overheard Shorty and Curly whispering. He paused. He felt guilty for pausing, realising that he wanted to eavesdrop on their discussion. He was momentarily saddened to realise that he cared about what they were saying, but that he didn't want them to know that he cared. He was about to move forward into the room when it occurred to him that they would be more revealing if they thought he wouldn't know the details of their conversation.

Bobby momentarily felt torn between wanting to clandestinely overhear what may prove to be candid dialogue between workers and the guilty feeling he got from actually doing it. It occurred to him that he was to be considered as management material, and maybe this is what he had to do to get promoted. Managers always seemed to know more about events, and other important facts, than workers did. Information was the key to power. Knowing what they knew, without them knowing that he knew it, may just be the path for him to take to future advancement. Maybe that was true for all management.

Bobby listened.

'Shush,' said Curly. 'He'll be back soon'.

'I hope he stays away forever,' groaned Shorty in a loud whisper. 'All this talk…, it's like a human biology lecture. We just grow hair,' he bemoaned some more. 'It's not difficult; we don't need to know what or why. We just do it.'

Curly disagreed with him. 'I'd like to know why we bother.'

'It's so boring!' Shorty moaned, 'But,' he added, 'as our RM's explained, 'If we don't help to make our trial transfer a success, then poof! We're goners.' He mimed with his hand the explosive event that would be their demise.

'I still don't accept that I was a difficult person to work with,' lamented Shorty. 'Working in the pits is emotionally, the pits.'

'At least here it's clean and bright and not too hot,' encouraged Curly. 'Let's make the best of it.'

Shorty nodded his agreement and even though Bobby couldn't see Shorty's reaction to Curly's advice, he sensed capitulation.

The red light started flashing on the top of the computer monitor indicating the growth cycle was about to commence. Bobby moved the trolley back into the room. He quietly positioned the trolley near the *papilla*. Shorty and Curly came up next to him and they each reached for a bottle. They each measured the required volume into a measuring cup. Shorty and Curly held theirs up for Bobby to inspect and he nodded his head in acknowledgement that they had the correct volume of liquid. Bobby opened the input valve in the *papilla* and they poured in the chemicals. Bobby closed the valve.

Bobby next did something that neither Curly nor Shorty had ever seen before. He reached down and stroked the *melanocytes*. He then started massaging them and did so for quite some time. He next removed a flask from an inside pocket in his clothing and poured a liquid from it into an opening at the *papilla*. When he'd finished he stood up, returning the flask to its hiding place. He smiled at them knowingly, but said nothing.

'What were you doing?' Curly asked curious.

'I was massaging the *melanocytes*,' Bobby replied with a wry smile.

'I could see that.' Curly wanted to expand the conversation. 'Why were you doing it?'

Bobby was pleased that Curly wanted to learn. It was always easier to teach workers who wanted to learn, as opposed to forcing them to learn. Was learning how to motivate others into wanting to improve, part of his journey? He decided that he'd find some quiet time to reflect on this.

'Do you know what the *melanocytes* are for?' he asked them both.

'They colour the hair,' Shorty answered.

'That's right,' confirmed Bobby. 'Massaging them stimulates the *melanin pigment* production and reduces the risk of the hair going prematurely grey.'

'That's not in the procedural manual,' Curly observed.

'No, it isn't,' agreed Bobby. 'But I hope that someday it will be. I just know we get a better result when the *melanocytes* are massaged, so I do it every cycle.'

'What was the liquid you added after you rubbed them?' Curly asked wryly.

'It's just a secret compound that I've developed. Nothing for you to worry about,' he explained without explaining.

'Is it in the procedures?' Curly pressed him for more information.

'No, but it should be,' Bobby assured him. 'Don't worry, all it does is harden the hair and enrich the colour. One day I hope it'll become part of the standard operating procedure, but at the moment I'm just running my own little experiment.'

'What is it?' Curly was curious.

'I call it "SCF Krox 20,"' replied Bobby. 'The twenty is because this is the 20th version since I've been testing the formula. This time I think I've got it right,' he stated proudly.

They were quiet for a time and then Curly laughed. 'There was this one time in the pubes, we convinced the boss to turn the *melanocyte* off; just to see what would happen.'

'What happened?' Bobby was astonished.

'We grew a long white hair!' Curly laughed some more. 'The Area Manager was worried that we'd all get into trouble but, well, you wouldn't believe what happened!'

'Tell us!' demanded Bobby and Shorty.

'Out it came, root and all. Marketing must have received a report about it and the grey hair was plucked from the skin.' He continued with laughter in his voice. 'It shook us up a bit but it sure was funny,' He sighed. 'Next thing all Team Leaders were told to watch the *melanocytes* against future failure so that it didn't happen again. The Regional Manager thought it was a faulty pigment thingy and, well, we never told him we had done it deliberately.'

Bobby was deeply shocked but managed a modest laugh accepting the humour. Shorty thought it hilarious and wanted to try it. 'We should do it!' he exclaimed.

It occurred to Bobby that Curly, and probably Shorty, knew more about growing hair than Dan had indicated. He accepted that they were both misfits, but maybe they were clever misfits, and just needed proper leadership to bring out their professionalism and full potential. Bobby had much to ponder.

'Is there anything else you want to learn about growing beard hair?' Bobby asked them. He decided he'd encourage them to ask, rather than just impose facts onto them.

'When do we eat?' Shorty asked. 'I'm hungry.'

'Let's eat now,' Bobby agreed.

The blood delivers *proteins* complete with *amino acids, sugars, albumins, globulins, fibrinogen,* and other important stuff required by the follicle farmers. They are delivered in manageable parcels.

Bobby went to the protein depository and collected the three food packs and distributed them amongst Curly, Shorty and himself. They sat and consumed their parcels in relative quiet and Bobby hoped that the three of them were now slowly becoming a team.

'You want to know something that I don't understand?' Curly asked between mouthfuls.

'Please,' Bobby invited.

'Ultimately, all Follicle Farmers report to the General Manager of hair production, right?'

Both Bobby and Shorty nodded agreement.

'And the General Manager reports to Grey Matter, right?' Curly continued.

'Why do we call it Grey Matter? I thought it was the brain?' Shorty joined in the conversation.

'Because it's grey?' chided Curly.

'It is grey, that's true and the organ that controls us all is the brain, but really the thinking, planning and decision making is done by the mind,' Bobby explained.

'What's the difference?' Shorty was intrigued.

'The brain is the organ at the top of the head.' He continued. 'Hence our jokes about head office...' Bobby looked about for knowing acknowledgement of what he was talking about.

Curly and Shorty both slowly nodded that they understood.

Bobby continued. 'The brain is the organ,' Bobby reiterated, 'and the work it does is called thinking. This is done by the mind within the brain.'

Curly and Shorty both said nothing. Bobby felt he may have lost them a little.

He continued. 'The mind is like where all the memories are stored...'

'Like a library?' Curly asked.

'I don't get it,' Shorty said.

'The mind is where the thinking is done and ultimately where decisions get made,' Bobby elaborated.

'Like when to grow hair?' Shorty wanted to know.

'Not exactly,' Bobby tried his best to explain. 'Follicle farmers know how and when to grow hair. The mind decides when it should be treated or altered in some way. Most of the body's activities are done automatically without the mind having to think about doing it'.

'You mean like shaving?' asked Shorty.

'No,' Bobby said patiently. 'I mean like us growing hair, like the Heart beating and the *Lungs* breathing and all the millions of other things the body just does because it needs to stay alive. It's all controlled by the *medulla oblongata* along with the *pons*. It controls all the messages. It takes about a trillion neurons to do it all,' he added in order to sound impressive. 'If the mind had to think about doing all that stuff, then it wouldn't have time to think about the interesting things.'

'Like what?'

'Like relationships and learning about leadership and training,' said Bobby triumphantly, pleased with his own level of awareness of what was happening.

'How do you know all this stuff, Bobby?' asked Curly.

'I do research on the computer,' Bobby explained pointing to the computer on the pedestal. 'It's all in there.' He turned to them and continued. 'I have a thirst for knowledge and the patience to look it up'.

'So, the mind decides when to shave the beard?' Curly asked tentatively.

Bobby groaned, realising where this was going. 'Yes,' answered Bobby. 'The mind decides about what is best for the hair we grow on the body.

'It still seems a convoluted arrangement to me,' Curly defended.

'The bigger the organisation the more complicated the decision making,' explained Bobby, knowingly. 'Often, we are working against each other, and one team doesn't know from the other, what is going on.' He looked down and continued. 'One day, I'll get to visit Grey Matter and learn more about it, but for now, we'll...' his voice trailed off and they were quiet for a while.

'Why did you call your previous department public hair?' Bobby asked Curly in an attempt to change the subject.

'We could tell from all the activity that our man met many other people. His pubic hair was very public. His privates weren't private. The smell was as ripe as... well you can imagine, and he is on heat more often than I have hot protein shakes. Our boy's sex is very sexy and he...'

'Okay! I think we get the picture!' Bobby cut him off when he decided he had had enough of Curly's crude explanation. Changing the subject once more, Bobby turned to Shorty and asked him 'What was it like in the left arm pit?

'Mostly dark and often smelly.' he reflected. 'We were mostly left alone to do our stuff in the pit. The whole pit has only one supervisor who reports to just one Area Manager,' he reported 'Apparently there is a Regional Manager for pit hair, but I've never met him,' he chuckled 'Word was that he didn't know the left pit from the right pit.'

'So how did you end up being transferred to the beard?' Bobby had heard it from Dan, but thought the time was right to hear it from Shorty.

'I may have been a bit too vocal about the smell,' he explained. 'One day, we'd be sweaty and horrible, the next day we'd be drowning in sweetness and aluminium'.

'Aluminium?' Bobby asked confused.

'They put it in the sweetness that marketing arranges to be sprayed onto the armpit hair. It comes from the outside world,' Shorty explained decisively and he seemed to know what he was talking about. 'The aluminium is toxic man. It shouldn't have been allowed'.

'Why, what does it do?' now Curly wanted to know also.

'The aluminium blocks the *sebaceous glands,* so they don't sweat as much. But we need them to sweat to get rid of the heat and other toxins!' he was getting excited recounting his ordeals in the pit. 'But it's poisonous to us follicle workers.'

'What did you do?' Bobby demanded.

'I bundled a whole heap of aluminium up and I sent it express to the brain with a message 'Suck on this!' he declared and smiled proudly. 'I guess I shouldn't have signed it with my own name' he laughed at his own mistake.

'Then what happened?' Bobby wanted to know.

'I guess my parcel reached head office and that grey matter wasn't happy about it. They must have told the GM and he complained to the RM, and he was told that I had done it, and the RM next instructed the AM to warn me and that I either agreed about being transferred here to you, or I'd be asked to *apoptosis*.' He looked wryly at them as they said nothing.

Shorty continued, 'I nearly told them to shove it... but I later learned that the mind had given it some thought, and ordered R and D to search for an aluminium free sweetness for the pits. I guess you could say that 'I gave them the shits and they now have aluminium free pits!" He laughed at his own joke. 'My pit brothers think I'm a hero and I got sent here to the beard because I'm a trouble maker! Go figure!'

They got back to work and for many cycles Bobby and his new team worked well together. Bobby felt that he'd achieved the routine of managing and growing their follicle with the professionalism and efficiency that he had built his reputation on.

Dan visited infrequently, and their routine was friendly chit chat and then on a quiet aside, well away from Curly and Shorty, he'd check with Bobby that his two workers were getting along well and were a good fit to the team. Bobby promised Dan that all was well and so he went away satisfied.

It was many cycles later that they discovered that they had an intruder.

Curly heard a rumbling behind him. He turned and saw a creature that frightened him, 'What's that!' he yelled gesticulating wildly.

Bobby and Shorty stopped what they were doing and turned to look where Curly was pointing. Near the opening to their work place stood a ghastly pus covered thing, it was the ugliest menace that Bobby had witnessed in all his time as a Follicle Farmer but he knew what to do. In his typical, take charge attitude, he yelled to the others, 'Quickly now, Curly! Call for back-up, Shorty! Get the antifungal spray packs!'

Curly moved to the computer and sent the distress code for a fungal invasion. Shorty reached into the work station locker and grabbed three spray cans and threw one to Bobby and the other to Curly. Bobby caught his spray can and in a continuous flow of the arc of his swing, he released the antifungal agent onto the beast. Shorty and Curly joined in and the three drenched the creature with liquid spray, disabling it where it stood.

They were soon joined by a pair of Natural Killers, who stood about guarding the creature and occasionally blasting it with a gas of their own, further neutralising any threat.

Dan arrived, looking worried.

One of the NK's recognising Dan's status as a Team Supervisor offered an explanation. 'We arrived to find that the *Keion* was neutralised by these three follicle farm workers,' he said in a deep resonating, almost monotone voice. 'We are now guarding the fungus should an unlikely resuscitation event occur. The clean-up crew will be here soon. Your men are to be commended for their quick action in preventing an outbreak,' he explained, totally devoid of emotion.

'Well done!' Dan exclaimed, relieved that the fungus was neutralised and that the team were all okay.

They smiled at each other, but said nothing.

Next soap bubbles began to fall from the roof of their work station and Bobby looked up and laughed knowingly at Curly.

~ 2 ~

'Is that...what...I think it... is?' Curly asked, drawing out his words. They all looked up as soap bubbles slowly descending from the roof of their work area. The bubbles glowed red, taking on the ambient light and drifted almost imperceptibly in a semi rhythmic dance as they descended toward the floor. Some landed on Curly's uniform and burst.

'What happening?' Shorty demanded clearly alarmed.

'Our beard is about to be shaved,' explained Bobby in a calming way. 'It happens often, nothing to worry about,' he continued. He walked to the computer station and pulled the cover over it.

'This is exactly the event I was talking about,' Curly began. 'If we didn't grow the beard hair then they wouldn't need to go through the trouble for it to be shaved.' He pointed upwards

Dan looked horrified. 'Curly! Reach up and catch a soap bubble,' he ordered.

Curly looked at him confused. A bubble came near him and he let it gently come to rest in his hand.

'Now wash your mouth out with it!' Dan instructed a very confused looking Curly.

'Wha...?' Curly wasn't sure that he should do what he was just ordered to do.

Bobby laughed. 'What Dan means is that you should wash your mouth out with soap. If we didn't grow beard hair, then we wouldn't have a beard growing region, and therefore we wouldn't be needed to grow hair. It'd adversely affect all the workers, team leaders, supervisors and managers in this region.'

Dan was very indignant. 'We'd all be told we were redundant, and ordered to self-combust!'

'Not again!' complained Shorty.

'And who'd be here to grow a beard when Head Office decided we wanted one?' Bobby continued.

'We need to grow beard hair, Curly. It's our purpose. Just because it gets shaved doesn't mean we shouldn't do our job,' Dan said clearly belabouring the point. 'What if marketing decided he'd look good with a very short beard? Not a proper beard, but just the beginning of one.'

'Stubble?' Bobby clarified.

'He'd look pretty rugged!' Curly Countered.

'Precisely! And maybe that's the image marketing decided was needed. We're not qualified so who are we to judge?' Bobby asked rhetorically.

They heard a dull roar that was getting louder. Suddenly, it became a deafening roar and for a brief moment the shaft of their follicle vibrated violently and then the roar grew fainter. This process repeated several times but the effect on the follicle was minimal during the second and third time.

'There,' Bobby looked about him. 'All finished.' He smiled cordially at his two colleagues.

Shorty took a deep breath and sighed.

Curly apologised. 'Sorry Dan, Bobby. I won't mention it again.'

'Well, okay then. You do need to keep your comments in check. Please remember that you're still on probation,' Dan acknowledged Bobby and left the room.

Bobby walked to the computer terminal refolded the protective cover. He then recorded the shaving event. After pressing a few keys he announced 'The next growth cycle will commence in three cycles. Curly, would you get the trolley please?'

Curly did as he was asked and the three prepared the items from the trolley. At the appropriate time they completed the addition of the growth chemicals and Bobby added his special formula and then vigorously rubbed the *melanocytes*. They replenished the trolley and Shorty offered to return it to the trolley station, which he did. Bobby fetched the protein packs and they settled themselves into their regular dining places and replenished themselves.

'Bobby, what are your thoughts on the union?' Curly asked sounding innocent.

'How do you mean?' Bobby responded cautiously. After all these cycles together he was beginning to recognise Curly's leading questions. He sensed a trap.

'Well, it occurs to me that the union really should count for something,' he continued.

'It does, and...?' Bobby wanted to draw him out before responding to the overall question.

'What do you mean, "And?" Curly replied trying to draw Bobby deeper into his discussion.

'Why don't you ask Shorty, why ask me?' Bobby countered.

'I'm a member,' offered Shorty.

'Of course you are. But, do you know why you're a member?' Curly demanded.

'No.' Shorty answered seemingly confused. Then he remembered. 'They told me that I was a member, but I can't remember when it happened,' he smiled. 'But also, I can't remember not being a member, so I guess I've always been one.'

'We're all members,' Bobby added. He was getting a little tired of this conversation.

'Exactly, that's my point!' Curly triumphed.

'I don't see "your point" at all, Curly,' Bobby sighed.

'If we're all members of the same union, and that just happens to include all of management, then who is the union actually representing? Who are we negotiating with? What is the union trying to achieve? How do we know that the union is doing its job, or how well it's doing it?'

'Our union is made up of all Follicle Farmers as we are a unique group of workers...,' Bobby started to explain.

'And that includes our Supervisors and our Area Managers and Regional Managers. Hey! I'll bet even the General Manager is a staunch union man,' Curly added.

'He is, and...,' Bobby confirmed.

Shorty snored loudly and the two turned and looked at him. Shorty was sound asleep.

'So we're all in the same union and we all share the same goals and have the same values. Why have a union when there is nothing for the union to fight for? If we're all on the same side, then there is no negotiation,' Curly concluded.

'The Union does a lot of things for us,' Bobby defended.

'Like what, run the annual picnic?' Curly stated sarcastically.

'Picnics don't happen. The union does assist in representing us to grey matter during important issues. It also gives us a forum to exchange ideas and make suggestions that are a positive for all Follicle Farmers. It also helps us with our identity. Don't forget, growing hair is only one very small aspect of human activities. It ensures that we maintain our place in the hierarchy of human functions.' Bobby was enjoying his long speech. He was on a roll. 'Without the union we wouldn't have a collective voice to protect our interests against outsiders who might want to do us harm...' Bobby stopped when he heard someone entering their work space.

Dan entered the room.

'Hello team,' Dan offered a cheerful greeting.

Bobby discreetly shook Shorty, rousing him from his nap.

'Hello Dan,' Bobby acknowledged. 'We were just discussing the benefits of the Follicle Farmers Union. Maybe you'd like to share your views with us?'

'You want my views on our Follicle Farmers Union?' Dan clarified.

'Yes, your views on the benefits of the union. Curly wants to learn more.' Bobby and Curly exchanged glances.

'Bobby is very well versed and I'm sure he's covered the basic advantages about our union. What he may not know is that the union was recently called on to facilitate the discussions between various regional managers on an important matter of contention.' Dan enjoyed appearing knowledgeable.

'What's happening?' Bobby wanted to know.

'It appears that marketing has convinced grey matter that all the chest hair should be removed by waxing!' He looked about them expecting a reaction.

Bobby and Curly were aghast. 'What? No! Never!' They chorused in mutual shock.

Dan continued. 'It's true. Our union, along with The GM for follicles, the RM for chest follicles and the GM for *Epidermis* made a deputation to the System Manager. Apparently, he readily concurred. They have collectively petitioned Grey Matter. At first, it didn't look we were going to prevail and the chest hair was going to be removed. But because they involved our union, they're quietly confident there'll be a change in the decision.'

'That's a relief,' Bobby sighed with relief.

'But still you never know...' Dan continued. 'I heard that those marketing types are very persuasive. I believe that our union have left delegates to lobby grey matter to ensure we retain chest hair.'

Bobby was still in shock. 'Why would marketing want to get rid of chest hair? That would be terrible.'

'Fashion, apparently. Having strong, abundant, healthy chest hair was once considered to be more important than scalp hair. Those days are long gone. It seems now that marketing is happier with us having less chest hair.'

'Less hair!' Bobby moaned, disturbed at what he was hearing.

'That's why our union is stepping in. There are strong concerns about the damage that waxing, or any extraction will do to the follicles and to the Follicle Farmers. The Skin Union was there also representing the *dermis* and *epidermis* workers in the chest region. Both unions are citing examples of probable infections, particularly if hot wax is used. Then there is a possibility of long term damage to the viability of regrowing hair on the chest, assuming this decision remains reversed. Preventing damage is better than repairing damage according to our union. We can only hope that Grey Matter is listening,' Dan explained.

'See,' Bobby told Curly triumphantly.

'You're saying that our management team couldn't dissuade Grey Matter into retaining chest hair but our union could?' Curly demanded.

'That's right,' Dan responded. 'The GM for hair is just one person and when they gang up on him he is only one voice. When he calls in the union, grey matter has to deal with all of us. With the union backing, it makes the GM's argument much persuasive.'

Curly said nothing.

'The debate continues,' Dan conceded. 'However, from what I can gather, mind debates rarely produce anything viable.

'Three cheers for our union!' Bobby offered. The others joined in as Bobby lead them through the Union Salutation.

'If we don't grow, we don't grow!' They sang in unison.

'Satisfied?' Bobby demanded of Curly.

'Sort of.' Curly sounded unconvinced. 'Do you think we'll ever go out on strike?'

'We never strike,' explained Dan. 'We just have a bad hair day.'

Bobby and Shorty burst into laughter. It was an old joke but still a good one.

'Do you remember that time when Grey Matter was planning to shave the scalp?' Dan asked Bobby.

'That's right!' Bobby replied brightly. 'The scalp became so affected by dandruff and Grey Matter overreacted and wanted all hair to be removed.'

'It was a dreadful scandal,' agreed Dan.

'The union convinced Grey Matter to get Research and Development on to it and after a time, they found an effective anti-dandruff shampoo. They managed to solve that problem without removing the hair,' Bobby continued with his explanation.

'The union ended up receiving a citation in excellence for its persistence. It read "For developing a sensible approach to deal with a community issue,"' Dan added.

'Our union, the Hair Follicle Farmers Workers Union is good for all of us,' Bobby reiterated.

'Speaking of citations, you're getting a team award for the way you dealt with the Keion. Well done you three.' Dan smiled cordially at the three who looked smug. 'The award is "For initiative and bravery in dealing with an invasive force."'

'Anyhow, this is just a quick visit. I wanted to let you know about the award and that all we're very proud of you.' Dan stood up and turned to leave.

'Thanks Dan.' Bobby offered his hand. 'That means a lot to us.' Bobby was smiling proudly.

Dan shook Bobby's hand and waved a farewell as he left the room.

'Wow,' said Curly, 'An award. That's never happened to me before.'

'Me neither,' added Shorty.

'I have some award,' Bobby told them. 'They're just performance awards and team citations for professional excellence.' He paused. 'I've never received an award for bravery before. This is exciting,' he sounded humble.

'Where are they?' Curly was curious.

'In my storage locker,' Bobby answered.

'Why don't you have them on display?' Shorty asked.

'Oh... they're not that important,' Bobby dismissed the notion.

'It's your job to inspire us,' Curly chastised his Team Leader. Properly displaying your awards will help achieve that'.

'You think I should?' He looked at them enquiringly.

Curly and Shorty nodded vigorously.

Encouraged, Bobby left to go down the passage to his personal locker and collect his prized awards. He stopped and reversed slowly back into the room, watched by a confused Curly and Shorty. Curiously, they watched him walk backwards into the room.

'Wha... What are you?' he demanded nervously.

Curly and Shorty tried to look past Bobby but neither could make out who it was that Bobby was talking to.

'Please, don't be afraid,' a deep voice boomed. 'I assure you, I mean you no harm.'

'But, what are you!?' Bobby demanded again loudly. He had reversed back to the others and the three stood there astonished.

Before them was a creature of frightening proportions. It was a giant round ball with short spikes and a small tail. The ball was yellowy orange and the spikes were orange from the base changing to a deep red at their tips.

Bobby yelled to the others. 'Get the antibacterial spray packs!'

'They won't have any effect on me,' the creature advised them calmly. 'I'm a virus, not a bacterium,' he added.

'A virus!' Bobby continued to yell, panic in his voice. His legs wanted to run but he had nowhere to run to.

'Yes. And, as I said, I mean you no harm,' the virus tried hard to assure them. 'Besides, I can't harm you as I'm a respiratory virus.'

Bobby, Curly and Shorty said nothing.

'And, I'm lost,' the virus explained.

'You won't harm us?' Curly asked the creature uncertainly.

'That's right, I won't,' the virus answered. 'Please understand..., I'm very tired and feeling rather fed up with being a virus.'

'Why are you here?' Bobby asked the creature with trepidation. He motioned to Shorty that he should go to the computer. Shorty seemed to understand and discreetly headed sideways toward it.

'I got separated from the others in my unit...,' the virus explained. 'We were launching our attack in the nose when a hair got in my way. I got confused as the prolific numbers of nose hairs weren't shown on the simulators that we trained on and I... I stopped to admire one,' he smiled and but quickly became serious. 'It was then that I realised that I was left behind...'

'Wait!' Bobby asked him cutting him off. 'What's a simulator?'

'They replicate the target area which we use for training for our invasion preparation.'

'Viruses do that?' Curly asked in amazement.

'Yes,' the virus replied. 'We achieve a faster and much higher infection rate when we train on the assault course simulators prior to our attack. The simulator didn't show enough nose hairs and I was temporarily confused when I saw them.'

'You had a close encounter with a nose hair?' Bobby asked smiling.

'It was more like I crashed head first into the hair. I wasn't expecting it and we were in a hurry to create the infection before your NK's could respond. I passed out,' he said looking embarrassed. The viruses' complexion turned a brighter red. He was blushing.

'What did you do?' Shorty asked meekly.

'When I recovered, I attempted to apprise my commander of my situation. That didn't work as I was out of communication range with my unit. So I sat still for a few moments while I contemplated my next move.'

'So, viruses have a command structure, disciplines and training?' Bobby was incredulous.

'Who would of thought?' Curly asked the others rhetorically, pointing to the virus. 'Those viruses were a structured force, planning and executing deliberate attacks on our body.'

'Then what happened?' Bobby wanted to keep the virus talking.

'I traversed down into the hair shaft and I encountered others like you. They panicked and fled. I tried to follow them, but... I became even more lost. I followed several passage ways and I saw a group of hair workers with NK's looking for me and so in my panic I ran. I wanted to get away from them. Eventually I came here into your area. I have decided I don't want to be afraid any more, and I don't want to spend the rest of my short life being an infector. So I've figured that my best option is to surrender to you.'

'You surrender?' Bobby asked in confusion. He'd never heard of a virus getting lost and he'd certainly never heard of a virus surrendering. He was suspicious. 'Why would a virus surrender?' He wanted to know.

'I can't take all the negativity. I live in a world where we plot to make others sick and miserable. It really gets you down, after a while.' The virus looked remorseful. 'I really don't want to have to do that anymore.' He added meekly.

Bobby, Curly and Shorty said nothing.

The virus looked up. 'I want to build things, like you guys. You grow hair, you're about life. You care about each other, you have friends...' he paused. 'I want to have friends; I want to be thought of as a contributor, not as a destroyer. I want to grow emotionally and feel good about myself.'

'But...,' Bobby was doubtful. 'You're a virus.'

'I know what I am..., but I can change, I can be good, I can be positive. I just need the right opportunity. I need the right environment.' He looked hopefully at the others and they returned his look with blank stares of bewilderment.

After an interminable silence Bobby finally spoke. 'So..., you surrender.'

'Yes,' the virus confirmed.

A virus was regarded as a threat to them, but this one wanted to change and that had to mean something. Bobby turned to the others. He looked into their faces and they nodded almost imperceptibly. Bobby understood from this that they were in agreement. They'd help this virus despite the obvious risks. They were farmers, they grew hair, they were positive and they could respond to a cry for help.

'Very well,' Bobby said softly. 'We'll accept your surrender and we'll help you.'

'Thank you,' the virus acknowledged also with a soft voice. He started to cry and Bobby and his team knew that it was from relief. They were tears of happiness of being safe and having found workers in the body that would help him rather than kill him. All of this had led to this deeply emotional state the virus now found himself in.

'We'd better give you a name,' Bobby offered.

'Oh, I have a name.' The virus looked up wiping away tears with two short spikes. 'I'm officially known as HRV-B69 – 117 of U245,' he explained.

They looked at him blankly.

'My commander calls me 117,' the virus added helpfully.

'What type of virus are you?' Bobby asked.

'I'm a Rhinovirus! I cause the common cold!' He said and then offered a meek smile.

The others weren't smiling.

'We'll call you Rhino,' concluded Bobby. 'It can be your name until you decide to change it.'

'Rhino, Rhino,' he said it several times trying it out, sensing how he felt about being called by this name. 'It's original, it fits, and I like it!' he concluded happily.

The computer pinged that the next growth cycle was about to commence and so Bobby indicated to Rhino to stand and observe them from a safe place. Rhino stood politely and discreetly to one side as the follicle farmers undertook their practiced routine of adding growth chemicals to the base of the follicle, checking temperatures and rubbing the follicle with affection. He marvelled at their synchronicity and professionalism. When they had finished and Bobby had recorded the event into the computer, Rhino cheered in sheer pleasure of being there with them, observing them at work.

Curly sided up to Rhino and motioned to hold his shoulder in a friendly manner. He hesitated and stopped as he realised that Rhino didn't have a shoulder. Rhino's spikes were intimidating. Instead, he looked deeply into Rhino's eyes and explained. 'This is new and wonderful for you, Rhino, but for us, this is our routine. This...,' he indicated about him, 'is normal for us and you'll soon get used to it and probably get bored with it as much as I am.'

'Oh no,' Rhino countered. 'I could never get bored with what you do. You have the perfect positive job and I already know that I'll love it here.'

'Good for you,' Curly smiled and went to get a snack. 'Are you hungry, Rhino?'

'Very,' Rhino answered after him.

The others received their protein packs from Curly and they motioned Rhino to come and sit with them. They ate in silence, not sure how to engage in small talk with their strange visitor.

'Have you had enough?' Bobby asked.

'Yes, thank you,' Rhino replied. 'It was very good.' he added politely. 'Much better than what I normally get.' He smiled.

Curly and Shorty laughed, and Bobby gave them a reproachful look.

Rhino was quiet while he contemplated his next move. As he looked about the working environment of the Follicle Farmers he felt an eerie sensation that he was being watched.

'It feels... like the walls are staring at me!' he exclaimed to no one in particular.

'What?' Curly responded.

'The walls!' he reiterated. 'They seem to have eyes,' he said as if it was really making him feel uncomfortable.

The three others chuckled. 'They're not walls,' explained Bobby. 'They're fat cells.'

'Fat Cells?' echoed Rhino.

'Yes,' he confirmed. 'They're all around us'.

'Why are they watching me?' Rhino demanded.

'They watch everything,' Bobby explained as he moved closer to a large fat cell and patted it affectionately.

'It's not like they have much else to do,' added Shorty.

Bobby indicated to the largest fat cell. 'Rhino, this is Fatty,' he introduced. 'Fatty this is Rhino'.

'Hello, Rhino,' responded Fatty in a deeply resonating voice.

'Err Hello..., Fatty,' replied Rhino hesitantly.

Whispering to Bobby 'Is that really his name?' he asked, trying to be discreet.

'Yes, it is,' Fatty answered for Bobby in a normal voice.

'Oh, sorry,' Rhino whispered, he blushed a deeper red.

'Don't be. That's my name,' Fatty stated as a matter of fact.

'And I'm Fatcey,' said another fat cell. 'And, this is Faticia.' he indicated to a neighbouring fat cell.

'You're not going to infect me are you Rhino?' Fatica asked, winking at him and smiling.

'No!' Rhino exclaimed in horror of the notion. 'Never...'

'Well, that's okay then,' Fatica confirmed.

'How many Fat cells are there?' Rhino asked Bobby.

'Heaps,' he answered.

'Millions and billions,' added Curly.

'We're as many as is needed,' Fatty explained.

'What does that mean?' Rhino asked, perplexed.

'We store fats and oils for the body,' He explained. 'If there is too much incoming fat, we soak it up. If there isn't enough, we release it back.'

'We store fat!' said another Fat Cell.

'We love fat!' added another.

'And..., you all have names?' asked Rhino astounded.

'Sort of,' Fatty tried to explain. 'I'm Fatty, that's Fatcey, and that's Fatica' He pointed to the two other fat cells that Rhino had already met. 'And that's Fatso, that's Fatimo, that's Fatra, Fathera,,.' He stared blankly, whilst pointing at a small fat cell. 'I'm sorry, but I don't remember your name?' He apologised.

The cell hesitated, seemingly embarrassed. 'I don't have one,' the small fat cell squeaked in a high pitched voice.

Bobby looked up at the squeaky fat cell and asked. 'You're new here aren't you?'

'Yes,' squeaked the tiny fat cell. The poor little fat cell was clearly embarrassed about all the attention he was receiving.

'Well! We'd better give you a name,' Bobby advised.

'Is it your job to name the fat cells?' queried Shorty.

'I made it my job,' Bobby replied. 'They don't get given names and it seems nice and respectful to refer to them individually.' He added. 'So, I give names to all the fat cells that work in our area'.

The fat cells wobbled vigorously in happy agreement.

Bobby moved closer to the new fat cell. 'I shall name you...,' he paused for dramatic effect. 'Fatzi!'

They cheered, 'Hooray for Fatzi!'

'We store fat' chanted a fat cell, 'we store fat... we store fat!'

The other fat cells joined in 'WE STORE FAT!' They chorused loudly and proudly.

The Follicle Farmers and Rhino joined in the song and after a few more repetitions they all ended up in laughter.

'Ah..., that was fun,' concluded Shorty.

Just then the computer signalled, and the follicle team set about to perform the next growth cycle. Rhino again stood back and once again marvelled at the precision and professionalism of the team in action. When they'd finished, they ate some more, and their conversation resumed easily.

'Tell us more about being a Rhinovirus, Rhino,' Bobby suggested.

'We attack the *Nose*, *Throat* and *Lungs* of a human. We attach ourselves to receptor cells in the *Nose* and *Respiratory Tract* and stop those cells normal functions. We quickly multiply and can duplicate ourselves many thousands of times. Before you know it, the victim is sneezing trying to dislodge us, but we have these spikes that dig in deep.' Rhino's spikes glowed by way of clarification. 'We're quite well anchored. Pretty soon were raising the body's temperature and the victim is coughing, sneezing, and blowing their nose. This is how we get about; you know,' he added by way of explanation.

'Your immune system cells are trained to catch and kill us. I never understood why we do what we do. I guess I could never really appreciate what it means to be a virus,' he paused, 'Inevitably your body's defences win, and we end up as combustive material.' He paused again in deep thought. 'Some of us are able to move on to another victim and repeat the process. We evade, train, and invade. We do it unthinkingly and we do it unquestioningly.'

Just then a massive *T-Cell* entered the room, and everyone stood still, frozen in shock.

~ 3 ~

Bobby was the first to recover. 'What are you doing here?' He demanded of the fierce looking *T-Cell* that stood before them.

The *T-Cell* is a *Lymphocyte*, a White Blood Cell or WBC. He's an antibody and part of the highly specialised team within the Immune System. This *T-Cell*, like all other *T-Cells*, was dressed immaculately. Everything about him was white, shiny white, including his armour and weaponry. His rank and numerous honour badges signified that he had lived a very long time and had been in multiple defensive campaigns.

As Bobby approached him, the *T-Cell* explained his presence. 'We've received a report that an infectious agent is in your workplace. I've been sent here to investigate and eradicate it.'

T-Cells independently roam the body, analysing and eliminating threats. They rapidly form termination squads that defend the body against serious pathogens. This WBC had insignia on him that showed him to be highly specialised in defending the body against viruses.

Along with B-Cells, *Phagocyte's,* and Natural Killers they're the elite of the elite and are therefore highly respected and more than a little bit feared.

Bobby attempted to assure the *T-Cell*. 'Ah..., the situation is..., all okay now.' He looked at him pensively but then thought he'd add a knowing, confident smile. 'We have everything under control, and you can go. Thanks for coming, it's really appreciated.'

The *T-Cell* said nothing. He stared at the *Rhinovirus.* He was trying to process the mixed messages he was receiving. Clearly, there was a report indicating a *Rhinovirus.* Clearly there is a *Rhinovirus* present.

He was trained in eliminating these invaders, even though he has never had to deal with one in the beard hair region before.

They are fewer in number with only about 35,000 *T-Cells* in the human body, and only about 700 of these are on patrol, at any one time. They are based in the lymph nodes or in the spleen where they are bathed in lymphatic fluid. There, they are either undertaking training, getting briefed on an assignment, or attending a lengthy debriefing after returning from an assignment. Others spend time recovering or receive minor rehabilitation after being wounded in battle. They don't like time wasters.

Bobby recalled asking Shorty to send that message. In the confusion of dealing with Rhino, and their subsequent acceptance of him, he had forgotten to rescind the alert.

'Er..., you can go now..., if you'd like,' Bobby suggested hopefully.

'We have an official log of this invaders presence,' the *T-Cell* explained.

When combating a serious threat posed by invading microbes, *T-Cells* can replicate themselves very quickly and in numerous quantities. Each *lymphocyte's* replication receives the originals superbly trained killing skills, the same highly developed analytical skills, and excellent identical memories. Each has access to the massive data base that contains highly detailed files on the various pathogens that the immune system has had to deal.

Rhino started to quiver in fear and Curly attempted to physically comfort their new friend, but found he was somewhat limited in what he could do due to the abundant sharp spikes emanating from Rhino's spherical body.

These Follicle Farmers were evidently trying to protect this Virus. That wasn't supposed to happen. His commander wouldn't like it or understand it. He would therefore ask his mentor about this.

Bobby reached up to comfort the *T-Cells* shoulder. This wasn't easy to do as his shoulder was at the full reach of Bobby's arm. Bobby felt it was important to act with an air of familiarity in an attempt to achieve a safe and satisfactory outcome for Rhino. He gently pushed his shoulder in order to steer him away from the area. The *T-Cell* didn't move. Bobby pushed harder but he still didn't move. Bobby pushed as hard as he could, but the T-Cell still didn't move. He didn't even seem to be aware of Bobby's efforts.

Bobby gave up and became exasperated. 'Look,' he started to explain. 'This Rhinovirus has surrendered to us. He isn't a threat, he's really a nice guy, a bit confused, but he wants to change and...' Bobby drew a deep breath. '...he's claimed sanctuary from us.'

The T-Cell reacted. He turned to Bobby and formed a questioning look on his face.

'I'm not joking!' Bobby burst out defensively.

He motioned his head in doubt.

'It's for real.' Bobby motioned to the others and they nodded rapidly in agreement.

'It's a virus,' the *T-Cell* said by way of an explanation. 'It is unreasonable to expect a virus to behave in any other manner, other than how a virus normally behaves.'

'But, it's true, he does want sanctuary,' Bobby tried desperately to explain it all to the *T-Cell*.

'Viruses do not ask for sanctuary. They infect human cells,' the *T-Cell* explained looking at Rhino. 'It has been targeted for termination'.

'But, he doesn't want to infect us anymore!' Bobby blurted indicated all about him.

'How do you know?' The *T-Cell* demanded.

'He told us,' Bobby replied.

The *T-Cell* looked doubtful.

'He did!' Bobby insisted.

'When did he tell you?' The *T-Cell* sighed.

'I told you. When we captured him and he surrendered to us,' Bobby explained.

'You... captured this virus?' The *T-Cell* asked in disbelief.

'Well...,' Bobby took a deep breath. '...not exactly captured..., but he did surrender.'

'Why?'

'This particular Rhinovirus no longer wants to be an infectious agent.' Bobby was becoming exasperated.

The *T-Cell* said nothing.

Bobby was getting desperate. 'Rhino come here and explain to...' He paused and looked at the giant warrior standing beside him. 'I'm sorry, but what is your name?'

'Lek,' the *T-Cell* answered.

'Please explain to Lek, what you said to us,' Bobby instructed Rhino.

Rhino stood up and took a few pensive steps forward and stood before his formidable adversary. Rhino was clearly very nervous. They could hear it in his voice when he cleared his throat before he spoke. 'Really, I'm not a threat,' he explained. 'As a Rhinovirus, I can only really infect the respiratory system. I'm no danger to these...wonderful...' his voice trailed off and he indicated the three follicle farmers. 'They're now my friends and I'd never hurt them,' he ventured.

'Friends?' Lek asked doubtfully.

'Yes,' Rhino answered. He looked at the others for confirmation and they all nodded.

'How did you get here?' Lek asked, wanting to know more.

'I got separated from my unit and took some wrong turns and ended up here. I've had time to think.' He paused thoughtfully. 'I don't want to infect anymore.'

Lek stood passively while he processed all of this strange information.

Rhino continued. 'The thought of a future in infecting others makes me feel sick. I'm tired of running and being scared all the time. I'm just tired,' he moaned and started to weep.

Bobby asked Lek. 'What are you going to do?'

Lek removed his weapon belt and dropped it noisily onto the trolley. Bobby shuddered but said nothing. Lek motioned Rhino to sit down again and when Rhino did, Lek sat near him.

'I'm tired also,' Lek explained. 'I've been a *T-cell* all my working life and I understand what it feels like to want a change.'

The others said nothing.

'When I get up and I'm either training to kill, actually killing or talking about a kill. Kill, kill, kill, that's all I do,' Lek lamented.

Bobby was about to speak but Lek held up his hand to stop him. 'Whilst...,' he pointed at Rhino. 'Rhino is here with you, he's no threat to the body. It true he's only a threat when he's in the respiratory system. So as long as he stays here, and doesn't make any move to leave, it is safe enough for everyone for him to remain.'

The others sighed in relief. 'Thank you!' said Bobby relieved. Bobby motioned for Rhino to thank Lek also.

Rhino stood up and said 'Thank you, Lek. I want to promise you that I'm one hundred percent going to change. If Bobby and his team will have me, I'd like to learn how to grow hair.'

Bobby, Curly and Shorty cheered.

'I suppose,' Lek nodded his head knowingly. 'There is a first time for everything.'

'Thank you for your understanding, Lek. I'll report to my manager just how professionally you handled the situation here. Don't worry; we'll call you if we should need any help,' Bobby advised the *T-Cell*.

'I'm not going anywhere,' Lek advised him.

'Oh,' Bobby was confused.

Lek pulled out a communication device from a hidden pocket in his jacket sleeve. He pressed a button and held the device to his ear. Momentarily he reported 'This is Lek, TC-WBC A19U34 follicle LF327. Situation normal,' he paused. He then added 'I'm taking a rest break and a sweet protein pack.' He nodded to no one in particular. 'Roger that.' He took it away from his ear, looked at the device and returned it to his pocket.

Bobby looked at Lek expectantly.

'I'm fatigued,' he said sounding exhausted as he sat down on a comfortable chair. 'I need a long rest and this is as good a place as any,' He explained to Bobby. 'Rhino is under house arrest and as long as he remains here, he'll be free to live and learn how to grow hair with you guys. I'll stay here and guard him for a time.'

Lek rested one leg above the other and he stretched out. He placed his hands behind his head and yawned. He looked like he was beginning to relax and was settling in. He turned to Rhino and explained. 'I feel for you man. I've done a lot of killing and it gets to you after a while. I think I either need a change of scene or maybe a different occupation.'

'Is it hard work being a *T-Cell*?' asked Curly sitting beside him, speaking for the first time since the Lek had entered the room.

'It's exhausting,' Lek told him. 'The physical training is brutal and there's a lot of reading to do. There seems to be endless lectures we have to attend. We have to pass exams you know?' He asked rhetorically. 'It really messes with your head. Every time one of these viruses mutate, we have to learn a new way of dealing with them.'

Curly said nothing.

'What are you?' Lek asked Rhino.

'I'm a HRV B69,' Rhino replied.

'Oh, you're easy enough to kill.' Lek nodded his head confidently. 'We wiped out a whole unit of yours just before I got sent here.'

'My Unit,' Rhino concluded head facing down.

Lek said nothing.

'How do you do it?' Curly wanted to know.

'It's my job,' Lek explained.

'I mean, how do you actually do it?' Curly asked again.

'Kill a Virus?' Lek clarified.

'Yes,' Curly answered.

'Out in the open like this, it's easy. Viruses are tough bastards but we can kill them. If we arrive after the virus actually penetrates a human cell and corrupts it...,' Lek explained.

'Corrupts?' Curly didn't understand.

'Yes, the virus burrows into the human cell, corrupts it into a pathogen and it replicates many times. This is how it attacks our body. This virus...,' he indicated Rhino 'is a respiratory system attack specialist.'

'So, how do you...'

'Oh, we surround the host cell with a hardener; make a hole in it with a chemical called *Perforin*. We then inject it with a pathogen specific toxin called a *cytotoxin* which explodes the infectious agent from within.' He paused and then pointed out. 'Death is quick... and we believe it's relatively painless.'

'What happens to the human cell?' Shorty asked timidly from across the room.

'Oh, it died as soon as his type infected it.' He nodded at Rhino once more. 'After we kill it, we give the all clear and issue a *chemotaxis*. Then *macrophages* clean up the debris.'

Curly got up and approached the trolley carrying the Lek's weapons. 'How many toxins do you carry?'

'Hey, keep away from that. It could harm you. Dangerous.' Lek cautioned.

Curly stepped away from the trolley.

Bobby stepped forward. 'We'll need this trolley soon, Lek. We have another growth cycle commencing soon,' he explained.

Lek stood up and retrieved his weapons from the trolley. He walked back to where he was sitting and arranged them neatly on the floor.

Shorty plucked up some more courage and asked Lek another question. 'Why do they call you a *T-cell*? What kind of name is that?'

'The T is for Terrific,' he smiled. 'Or perhaps it's for Terrifying!' he joked whilst putting on a scary face.

Shorty said nothing.

Lek set about making himself comfortable. He took a deep breath before he explained. 'We're born in the *bone marrow* along with all the other blood cells, but we're sent to the *Thymus Gland* for intensive training. The "T" comes from *Thymus*.'

The others gathered about Lek, fascinated by what he was saying. Lek enjoyed having an audience, his explanation gathered momentum. 'We train in groups of fifty, but usually only one of us graduates, sometimes two,' he told them. 'To graduate you need to be very smart, fast and the best of the best.'

'What happens to the other candidates?' Bobby wanted to know.

'*Apoptosis,*' he answered with a wink.

Bobby returned his wink with a blank stare.

He shrugged, 'You know. Programmed cell death. If a *T-Cell* doesn't cut it, they are out of the program, permanently,' he responded smiling.

'But in your case, they made an exception!' A voice behind them boomed.

They turned to see a heavily armed *Phagocyte Macrophage* cell saunter into their work area.

Bobby, Curly, Shorty and Rhino watched the *Phagocyte* approach them. He was aqua blue and shaped like two very large round balls. His skin was lumpy and scarred as if he'd been in many campaigns.

Rhino started quivering again.

'Fargo old buddy! Good to see you.' Lek, seemingly invigorated rose quickly and embraced the aqua blue cell he called Fargo. 'So, have you eaten?' he asked laughing.

They laughed together at a long standing joke that only they seemed to understand.

Then they sighed.

'So? What are you doing here old buddy?' Fargo asked Lek whilst studying Rhino.

'Chilling out,' he replied and they laughed some more.

'You deserve it man.' He paused. 'Is this piece of shit causing you any grief?' He asked looking at the very scared Rhinovirus.

'Nah, he's harmless. Wants to grow hair.'

'On himself? He asked smiling.

They burst out laughing once more.

'For us, would you believe?' explained Lek.

'In this job, I've seen everything and so therefore...' Lek joined in and they chorused. 'I believe in everything.' They laughed at what was apparently another in-house joke.

Lek turned Fargo to face the others. 'Guy's..., this is Fargo.' He looked at Fargo and then indicated in turn to the others as he pointed. 'This is Bobby, he's the Team Leader and he is in charge here.'

Bobby didn't feel like he was in charge of anything at the moment. These two military types were formidable and somewhat intimidating. Bobby had to remind himself that they were here to protect and serve the body, the same body that they grew hair for. 'Hello, Fargo,' he responded to the introduction.

'This is Curly,' he pointed to Curly. 'Curly is curious, so be careful as he'll bombard you with many questions.'

'Curly,' Fargo acknowledged.

'That good looking dude standing tall is Shorty. But, don't be fooled, because in real life he's very big.'

Fargo laughed and waved.

Shorty hesitantly returned the greeting.

'And the guest of honour has been named, Rhino,' Lek explained to Fargo with a hint of humour in his voice.

'A good name,' responded Fargo.

'A very good name,' agreed Lek.

'You mostly go by a serial number don't you?' Fargo asked Rhino respectfully.

'Yes,' Rhino answered.

Lek and Fargo began an animated but private discussion so Bobby decided now would be a good time to try to regain control of his work area. Bobby was feeling somewhat overwhelmed with the ever changing encroachments and impediments to their routine. As well as hosting a *Rhinovirus*, who now wanted sanctuary and training on how to grow hair, he now had to contend with a T cell enjoying a reunion with an old friend. His follicle work place was turning into a socialising cum rest area for the warriors. The next cycle was going to begin soon and he didn't need, or want, this distraction.

'Err, excuse me Fargo,' he wanted to sound authoritative but polite. 'Will you be leaving soon?' Fargo and Lek turned to stare at Bobby in annoyance of being interrupted, but Bobby wasn't going to be dissuaded. 'We,' he indicated his team, 'have another growth cycle to focus on, and it's getting a bit cramped in here.' He indicated the work station.

'We'll only be a moment,' Fargo explained and turned back to Lek. 'So what's happening here?' he asked of his friend.

The light on the computer monitor flashed red alerting the team that they had to prepare for the next growth cycle. Rhino stepped back, too frightened to participate knowing the two killing specialists were seated behind him. In truth, neither Lek nor Fargo was concerned about Rhino. They were however; somewhat interested in watching the team perform the growth procedure on the follicle.

Once their tasks were completed, they re-stacked the trolley and put it away. Bobby re-approached Lek and Fargo.

'That was fascinating,' Lek told Bobby without enthusiasm.

Bobby was a bit pleased that he had said that, but was modest. 'Oh. It's just what we do,' he told them.

'You must explain it all to us,' Lek continued. 'We'd really like to know,' he turned to face Fargo who nodded his agreement.

'Maybe later,' countered Bobby. 'Right now, I'd like to know what your plans are.'

'I need a place to rest, and this place is as good as any. Your new recruit needs to prove himself before I feel comfortable leaving him here under your charge,' Lek explained patiently.

Fargo added to the response. 'I'm tired too, so I'm going to rest here with my friend and enjoy some protein and some sanctuary also.' He smiled at Bobby.

Bobby left the two of them to their conversation. He went to the computer and recorded the growth event and prepared a report on Rhino's inclusion into the team and the arrival of the immune system warriors. Satisfied, he went to get the protein packs for his team which now included Rhino.

Fortunately there were sufficient seating places to accommodate the growing number of workers and visitors at Bobby's work area. The six consumed their proteins and amino acids whilst making small talk about texture, flavour and nutritional benefits. They learned that Lek and Fargo had unlimited access to protein and in unlimited quantities. This was due to their need to be correctly sustained, given to the extreme nature of their work.

'How did you get to be a *Phagocyte*, Fargo?' Curly asked out of curiosity.

'Same way as most cells, Curly. I was divided from my original cell many, many cycles ago,' Fargo answered reminiscing. 'I learned from my host cell, pretty much everything I needed to know on how to do my job.'

Curly said nothing. He nodded his understanding.

'I was invited to do some advanced training in the *Thymus* where I met Lek,' he continued to explain. 'We do our work a bit differently but we need similar skill sets to be successful.'

'He eats his prey,' Lek teased.

'What!' Curly was shocked.

'That's what it means, *Phagocyte*, eat cells, isn't it, contributed Bobby knowledgeably.

'Yes, that's true,' Fargo confirmed. 'It's more technical than just catching and eating baddies but it is what I'm designed and trained to do.'

'Can you tell us more?' Curly was fascinated.

'We receive a communication that there is an enemy combatant to deal with via chemical called *chemotaxis*. That tells us the what, where and who we have to deal with,' Fargo explained.

'Never the why,' Lek added. 'We just do what we're told, as soon as we're told do it.'

Fargo nodded in agreement and continued. 'Once we have cornered the enemy we bind ourselves to it. This is called adherence. We then extend these *pseudopods* to encompass the microbe.' He demonstrated by extending his outward.

'Wow!' Curly and Shorty were impressed.

Bobby and Rhino said nothing.

Fargo smiled and elaborated. 'When I've completed the engulfment, I fuse my *pseudopods* and commence ingestion.' He paused. 'The resultant sac is called a *phagosome*. I simply inject the baddy with chemicals in a process called an *oxidative burst*. And then they die.'

'Is it painless?' Shorty wanted to know.

Fargo looked at Lek who nodded imperceptibly.

'Of course,' he answered sincerely.

'Wow,' said Curly again. He was clearly impressed and somewhat in awe of these visitors. 'You guys are the best. You're... magnificent,' he gushed.

'Just doing our jobs,' Lek sighed.

Shorty asked uncertainly. 'How many have you... err?'

'Killed?'

Shorty nodded his head in confirmation.

Fargo indicated the notches on his weaponry.

'Wow,' Shorty responded in hushed tones.

Curly was about to ask another question but Lek interjected. 'Our body will die one day, but it's our mission to prolong his life for as long as we can. There is a whole team of specialists protecting our boy from a huge range of invaders.'

'It's you guys that are the true heroes.' He pointed to the follicle. 'You grow and build things.' Fargo was being gracious.

'You're just being gracious,' Bobby told him. 'All parts of the body are equally important. We're a team and we all have to work together to nourish, repair and protect our body. We grow hair, you kill baddies. We all do our part,' Bobby concluded.

'But it doesn't hurt to learn about their lives and task.' Curly almost pushed Bobby aside in his enthusiasm.

'We do need to rest a bit,' Lek told him. 'Then we'll share with you the fourteen principles that all *immunology* fighting units learn.'

'Wow, that's great guy,' Curly gushed some more. 'Thanks, thanks a lot,' he was clearly excited.

Lek and Fargo talked in hushed tones and Curly, under the watchful eye of Bobby, restrained himself from bothering them while they rested.

Things got quiet for a while at Bobby's follicle station. As Lek and Fargo snored in what seemed to be practiced unison, the team completed three growth cycles. Each time, Rhino was given more responsibility and was slowly becoming proficient at the tasks being demonstrated to him. He seemed genuinely pleased to be a part of the team and that pleased Bobby very much.

After a time, and during a meal break, the two warriors woke up. After some stretching, scratching and snorting they cleared their throats in a time honoured tradition.

Lek walked over to a protein station. Placed his hand on the dispenser, punched some numbers and received a massive ration of protein and amino acids. He brought them over and shared them with Fargo.

Bobby, Curly and Shorty watched in fascination, clearly impressed by the unlimited supply of food that these cells could receive. They had to share their small rations with Rhino and they looked at Lek's and Fargo's pile with hungry eyes.

Fargo threw Rhino a ration pack. He was smiling as he did so and Rhino indicated his appreciation.

'You see guys,' Lek began to explain, 'We protect the body.'

'Sometimes we have to protect it from itself,' Fargo added.

'I don't get that,' queried Curly.

'Tumours, cancers etc.' Fargo explained. '*T-Cells*, deal with those internal problems as well as killing infectious microbes.'

'*Phagocytes*, like Fargo here deal with microbes by ingesting them,' Lek patted his friends shoulder affectionately.

'Microbes are bacteria, mostly,' Fargo added.

'We know what microbes are,' Bobby retorted.

'Have you ever eaten something you didn't like?' Curly asked Fargo.

Fargo gave him a long hard look. He answered using softer tones. 'The bacteria that cause food poisoning are particularly hard on us. Many *phagocytes* die dealing with them. I have come close to perishing a few times myself. If only "he" was a bit more cautious about the food "he" ate we wouldn't lose so many good men.'

Curly said nothing.

'B-Cells can only kill microbes before they enter a cell,' Lek continued unfazed by the interruption.

'And *T-Cells*, like my good friend, Lek.' Fargo gave Lek's shoulder a mock punch. 'Specialise in killing the virus after they infect a human cell.'

'We do the dirty work when my colleagues fail to make the kill,' Lek teased Fargo.

'You guys are legendary,' Curly gushed.

'The thing is, despite our different killing techniques and our differing responsibilities, we all follow the fourteen principles of engagement.'

'Please tell us!' Curly begged.

Shorty and Bobby came closer to Lek and Fargo.

'We could tell you, but then we'd have to kill your new friend here,' explained Lek, and they all looked at Rhino who shook with fear.

'We can't have those secrets reaching enemy ears,' added Fargo.

Lek and Fargo burst into laughter. Rhino almost wet himself in fright.

'I won't tell...,' blurted Rhino. 'I promise!'

Lek laughed some more. 'Don't worry Rhino; you'll die of old age before you'll ever get to tell anyone any of our secrets.'

Fargo started to explain. 'The first principle is to never waste resources. We are few in number and microbes and virus can multiply very fast. We never send in the whole army to fight a single battle.'

Lek continued, 'The second is learning from all previous experiences. We remember an enemy and how we dealt with it. This saves much time and we counterattack quickly before the enemy numbers builds to an overwhelming strength.'

'The third is somewhat common-sense,' Fargo explained. 'It is accepting the truth. Deal with the situation specifically and never pretend it is something else.'

'The fourth is, never underestimate the enemy's numbers or capabilities,' Lek explained.

'Or overestimate your own numbers or capabilities,' Fargo added.

'True,' Lek agreed.

'The fifth is being decisive,' Fargo explained. 'Make the call and act swiftly. Replicate the resources required to do the job and just do it.'

'He who hesitates has already lost,' Lek lamented.

'Isn't that the truth,' Fargo agreed.

'The sixth is being persistent!' Lek explained. 'Never slow down and never surrender!'

'I really like that one,' Fargo added. 'After all if the enemy ever truly wins... we'll all ultimately die.'

'Kill or be killed,' Lek agreed. 'The seventh is push on with the attack until the enemy is defeated.'

'You can't stop for a rest half-way through a campaign,' Fargo agreed smiling.

'Plenty of time to rest and recover when it's over,' added Lek.

'The eighth,' Fargo took a deep breath, 'Is do the reconnaissance. Learn what you are up against'.

'I would have thought that should be one of the first things that you'd do,' Bobby countered.

'So do I,' Lek agreed. 'I've never understood why that one was number eight, do you Fargo?'

'Beats me,' agreed Fargo. 'But it is.' He confirmed.

'What is the ninth?' Curly asked. He was really absorbed in the details of the fourteen principles of *immunology* warfare.

'The ninth,' Fargo answered him, 'Never attack the enemy at their strongest point. Attack where they're at their weakest. Make a bridgehead; then attack some more. Weaken their moral, dissolve their resolve, and do so by systematically reducing their numbers.'

'The tenth is a bit of all of the others,' Lek explained. 'It is about being clever about the attack, rather than just charging in.'

'The eleventh is to use the element of surprise when that option is available,' added Fargo.

'That one should be obvious but it needs to be learned,' Lek explained.

'It does,' Fargo agreed.

'The twelfth is never play the blame game. We are a combined force dealing with the enemies of the body. We're all well trained, highly self-motivated and we're all team players,' Lek stated, sounding passionate about this principle.

'If someone makes a mistake they'll either learn from it, or they'll die as a result of it,' agreed Fargo.

'The thirteenth is, report the truth of the campaign. Never distort the news just because you think that your version is what command wants to hear. Future decision making is dependent on reliable, quantifiable reports,' Lek told them.

'And the last principle,' said Fargo.

'The fourteenth,' confirmed Lek.

'Is that there is no such thing as good luck when dealing with enemy bacteria and viruses,' Fargo continued.

'We win because we're good at killing the enemy,' reiterated Lek.

'Because we do our research,' added Fargo.

'And because we're well trained,' Lek Continued.

'We're highly motivated!' Fargo enthused.

'And, we have the best tools,' Lek patted his weapons.

'You guys are amazing,' Curly was clearly impressed.

'Yes! We are!' agreed Lek laughing.

'And modest also,' added Fargo smiling broadly.

Lek and Fargo burst into laughter once more.

'How do you learn all of this?' Bobby wanted to know.

'For *T-cells* it's our mentors that teach us,' explained Lek. 'Our mentors, better known as *Dentritic Cells*, reside in the *Thymus*. They gather newbie *T-Cells* into classes of fifty when they arrive from the Bone Marrow. Their job is to impart knowledge and wisdom into us and then select the one in fifty that graduate.'

'We, *phagocytes* are part of the system,' Fargo explained.

'We're part of the system also,' Bobby added.

'That's right!' Fargo agreed. 'I have more in common with Lek from the Immune system but I'm part of the system that grows hair, skin and nails. Go figure,' he chuckled.

'And, you shouldn't be here!' Dan's voice boomed from across the room.

The six looked up as Dan strode into the work area.

Lek rose and loomed over Dan. He started to explain. 'We were invited here by Bobby. He had a situation with a Rhinovirus and we came to deal with it.' He pointed at Rhino who stated quivering again.

'Did you?' Dan asked.

'Did we what?' Lek countered.

'Deal with the *Rhinovirus.*' Dan was now standing next to Rhino, clearly aware that no one had "dealt" with the Rhinovirus as he was standing right there with them.

'Sort off, we...,' Lek started to explain to Dan.

Bobby interjected. 'We asked them not to!'

'Why?' Dan wanted to know.

'We like him. His name is Rhino and he wants to be a Follicle Farmer, just like us. Lek and Fargo said it was okay. He's really a good guy; you just need to get to know him a little and you'll see that it'll be okay.'

Dan looked doubtful. He looked at Lek who nodded his approval.

'Can he stay? Can we keep him?' Bobby was panicky.

'If it's okay with these two...' He looked at Lek and Fargo. '...Then I suppose he can stay,' Dan responded slowly. 'But, you can't keep him, Bobby'.

'Why not?' Bobby wailed confused.

'You're being promoted to Team Supervisor, Bobby. You're about to be transferred to the moustache,' Dan answered smiling. Congratulations and well done.'

~ 4 ~

Bobby was somewhat taken aback. 'Please say that again?' he requested meekly whilst taking a step backwards.

Dan was smiling broadly. He was pleased to be able to bring this news to his best Team Leader. 'You... are... being... promoted!' he started to sound out each word dramatically and then paused. 'You're promoted to Team Supervisor!' he blurted it out, nodding his head in exaggerated enthusiasm.

Bobby said nothing. He was overwhelmed. Finally, his dream of advancement was being realised. He never doubted it, and never wavered from the goal. He kept going despite the prolonged despondency of watching less qualified Team Leaders being promoted before him.

Shorty became emotional and teary eyed. He came over to give Bobby a congratulatory hug. 'Well done boss,' he told him. 'That's fantastic news.'

'Wow,' he returned the hug. 'Thank you, Shorty,' he responded.

Curly came over to shake Bobby's hand. 'I have to hand it to you, Bobby; you are destined for great things. I remember thinking that about you when we first met. Congratulations'

Lek and Fargo, realising that important follicle events were happening, decided to move away. They indicated to Rhino that he should follow them to the seating area. He hesitantly followed them and they sat down and discreetly observed the follicle farmers meeting.

Dan continued to apprise Bobby of what was happening. 'You'll be managing about forty Team Leaders growing hair in the moustache. Specifically your area is the centre of the moustache at the *philtrum*.'

'The *philtrum?*' Bobby was unaware of that location.

'It's the groove under the nose. It extends from the base of the nose down to the upper lip. It doesn't do much, in fact it doesn't really do anything, but it is pole position for moustache follicle production,' Dan explained.

'Why do we have one?' Bobby questioned.

'Marketing said it may have something to do with facial muscle control. Apparently the manager of Muscular System Marketing Department was unhelpful when our research team made the inquiry.' Dan replied.

'Too busy promoting the *pectorals*, *triceps* and *biceps*,' Curley commented flexing his arms.

'The Muscular Marketing Department deserve a swift kick in the *Gluteus Maximus*,' Dan agreed.

Bobby sighed. 'Wow! I'm going to the moustache.' He looked about him.

'It won't mean much. The moustache area gets shaved at the same time we do,' Curly observed, smiling knowingly.

'In this case, that isn't correct. The big news is that the moustache is now to be fully grown along with a fully grown goatee,' Dan advised.

'That'll be problematic,' Bobby concluded. 'Greg has never worked well with the other Area Managers on agreeing where the left side of the beard ends. A goatee will create all sorts of friction between the beard growing Area Managers. Steve will be busy with border disputes,' Bobby observed.

'It's already sorted,' Dan advised him. 'Steve finally got permission from Harry to segregate the chin from the neck and both sides of the face. A colour coded map is being prepared and this will be issued to the five Area Managers showing where each area starts and finishes...'

'That's awesome,' Bobby interjected.

'...and as the newly appointed Area Manager for the Chin, I get to grow a goatee...

'Area Manager!' Bobby interjected again.

'...as you get to grow...'

'A moustache!' Bobby enthused.

'...a moustache. Yes, that's right. I'm the new AMBGAC or Area Manager Beard Growing Area Chin.' Dan was now positively beaming.

'Congratulations! Well done!' They chorused.

'It's a brand new position and I'm honoured to be the first to hold that title,' Dan sounded proud.

'How did Greg handle all this news?' Curly wanted to know.

Dan looked at Bobby and spoke in a slightly hushed tone. 'Greg has also been transferred. He's moving from the left side of the face to manage the moustache. Greg is still your boss, Bobby.' Dan explained almost apologetically. 'You'll be reporting directly to him without having me to protect you.'

Bobby was excited to be promoted but anxious about reporting directly to Greg, given his reputation for being difficult to work with. He gave a brave smile at the news.

'At least it's easy to determine the boarders of a moustache,' Bobby concluded.

'You'll be fine,' Dan encouraged.

'That's great news about you being made an Area Manager, Dan, you deserve it.' Bobby shook the hand of his mentor and leader.

'Thank you.' Dan was smiling broadly, evidently very pleased with his own promotion. 'The transfers will take place after an award ceremony here at your follicle station,' he advised them.

'Dan. Who will be taking control of this follicle?' Curly wanted to know. Shorty nodded his concern also.

'You will be Curly. You're being reinstated as a Team Leader. Congratulations,' Dan said to him.

'Reinstated?' Bobby was confused.

'Yes, didn't Curly tell you? He was a Team Leader in the pubic hair region before he got demoted and transferred to you for retraining.' Dan looked at Curly questioningly. 'From Bobby's positive reports, we concluded that you're ready. Am I right, Curly?'

'Yes sir, you are. I have learned humility and respect from this man,' he explained looking at Bobby. 'I'd be delighted to take responsibility for this follicle,' he added.

'What about me?' Shorty wanted to know.

'I've been reading great reports about you also, Shorty.' Dan was pleased to tell him. 'Are you okay staying here and working for Curly?'

'Yes Sir!' Shorty performed a salute to Dan followed by one to Curly.

They laughed.

'Will we be getting a third?' Curly asked.

'Not for the time being. We're a bit short staffed given the excitement of the moustache and the goatee. We are being re-organised into four person teams in both the moustache and the chin areas due the push,' Dan was apologetic.

'I think it is time that you met Rhino,' Bobby signalled to the very worried *Rhinovirus* who had been sitting nervously with Fargo and Lek during the Follicle Farmers discussion.

Rhino stood up and slowly approached the group.

'Dan, this is Rhino,' he introduced the quivering amber ball with red spikes that slowly walked toward them. 'He's a *Rhinovirus* that wants to give up a life of infecting humans and he now wants to learn a trade'.

Dan awkwardly extended his hand in greeting which Rhino clumsily accepted.

'Trade?' questioned Dan.

'Yes,' Bobby replied. 'Rhino became lost during a mission in the nose. He was part of an invading attack team when he became separated from his unit. He avoided capture and found himself here, with us. He's asked for sanctuary and a chance to change his life.'

Dan said nothing but motioned for Bobby to continue. He was fascinated with what he was hearing, having never heard anything like it before.

'We've been teaching him how to grow our follicle.'

'I see.' Dan clearly didn't. He looked about the follicle unconvinced.

At this point both Lek and Fargo decided to join in the discussion. They raised themselves from their seats and the Follicle Farmers and the virus watched them as they re-equipped their uniforms with weaponry and communication equipment. When they were both satisfied they were properly attired, they nodded to each other and walked over to the others.

Bobby introduced them to Dan. 'This is Lek and Fargo. Lek is a...'

'I can see what they are, Bobby,' Dan cut him off coldly.

'We came in response to a reported threat,' explained Lek.

They all looked at Rhino who quivered some more.

'I see,' Dan still clearly didn't and he looked at the Virus unconvinced.

Lek continued, 'I have now assessed the situation, and as long as Rhino remains at this follicle station, he is no threat and we'll allow him to remain here. He wants to learn how to be a Follicle Farmer.'

Dan looked at Fargo.

Fargo cleared his throat, nosily. 'I agree with that assessment,' he added.

'Fargo, I don't mean to sound rude or appear ungrateful, but what is your role here? Your mission parameters don't cover dealing with Viruses,' Dan asked.

Fargo took a deep breath. 'Lek and I have known each other for quite some time. When I heard he was here, I thought I'd pop in and say hello and I offered to lend a hand.' He then shook hands with Lek and they smiled at each other at an old joke they had just shared.

'I suppose you need to get going now,' Dan suggested. 'I'm sure you have more important work to do.'

'That's true,' Fargo nodded in agreement. 'Thank you fellows,' he said looking at Bobby, Curly and Shorty in turn. 'I really appreciate the hospitality. I wish you well with all your various promotions and transfers.'

'Thanks Fargo,' Bobby replied for all of them. 'It was a pleasure to meet you.'

'I'm sure we'll meet again,' Fargo told him. 'It's a small body.'

Fargo turned to speak directly to Rhino. 'Don't go causing any *otolaryngo-logical* events my friend,' he advised.

Fargo waved a cheery goodbye to Lek. He came to attention, saluted, turned and marched away.

Dan turned to look at Lek once more. 'Oto...lar...logical?' he questioned.

'It means "a sneeze", Fargo's just showing off by using a big word that he's recently learned,' Lek explained.

Dan smiled.

'Rhino will be monitored. He can't leave this area. As long as he is welcomed by this Follicle Farmer's team, we'll allow him to live here and he can learn how to grow hair,' Lek explained.

'You said we're all going to be short staffed and we could do with a third,' Curly added hopefully.

'Can Rhino stay and become a part of the team?' Bobby asked Dan.

Dan hesitated considering. 'Fine by me,' Dan eventually replied. 'I'll make a record of it and file it with the personnel officer responsible for staffing in left side of the beard. Ultimately it'll be up to your new Area Manager, Curly.'

'Who's that going to be?' Curly asked.

'Look,' Lek interrupted. 'I'm going to get back to work myself.'

They looked at him.

He turned to Bobby and offered his hand. 'Thanks for having me. It was a genuinely new experience. That's getting to be rare for me,' he said shaking Bobby's hand. He turned to Curly. 'Keep asking your questions, Curly. Good luck Shorty, Rhino. Goodbye.' He waved and walked out of the follicle work area.

They watched him leave and then they turned toward each other.

'Those guys creep me out,' Dan said to know one in particular.

The others said nothing.

Dan continued. 'I don't know yet. Steve hasn't made the announcement,' he answered Curly. Then to everyone he added. 'We may find out during the award ceremony.'

Just then the computer alerted them to the next growth cycle. Dan watched them as they proficiently completed the growth task. He was impressed with Rhino's contribution and noted that he worked well with the follicle farmers. He made a mental note to question Bobby privately about the extra chemical that he was adding after the stipulated tasks were completed. When the trolley was restocked and put away, Bobby dutifully recorded the growth details into the computer.

They next returned to Dan to continue their discussion.

'When will the award ceremony be held, Dan,' Bobby wanted to know.

'I'll see if I can find out.' Dan walked over to the computer. He keyed in his own unique identifier and was able to access information reserved for Area Managers and above, his new status having been updated.

'It'll be in fifteen cycles from now,' he told them. 'Meanwhile, you four continue your work with this follicle. Perhaps Bobby you should take a step back and assist Curly's preparation for Team Leader and Rhino's training as a Team Worker.'

'Delighted,' Bobby assured him.

Dan waved his goodbye and left the work station.

Life for the three Follicle Farmers, and the now sanctioned Rhinovirus continued uneventfully for the next fifteen cycles. They grew the hair, replenished the trolley, fed on protein and amino acids and talked positively about growing beard hair despite it being regularly shaved.

Bobby was confident that Curly would make a good Team Leader. He liked the patient way he dealt with Shorty who really wasn't a truly capable Follicle Farmer, but at least he was trying and was working well for Curly under his direction. He wondered about the prolonged effect the aluminium exposure had had on Shorty when he worked in the arm pit.

Rhino's enthusiasm made Bobby smile. He was going to miss the yellowy orange blob. He reflected that he may go down in history for being the first follicle Team Leader to give sanctuary, and subsequently a career, to a virus that was an enemy of the body.

Bobby reflected on his own promotion to the moustache. He was finally a Team Supervisor, and at a time when the moustache would be allowed to grow. He wondered about the decision process that made these things happen.

Did someone in marketing really evaluate the benefits to the body by sporting a fully grown moustache? He also wondered if the goatee added to the moustache or if it were the other way around. He speculated that a goatee without a moustache would look silly and marketing wouldn't want that. He hoped he'd get the opportunity to discuss it with Dan someday. He had much to ponder.

For the remaining cycles they worked, rested, ate and joked about. All times they were very aware that this team would soon be split up. Bobby would shortly be on his way to start his new appointment. During one of the rest breaks, Bobby decided to ask Curly about his time as a Team Leader. They were seated in the rest area and were having a mini-siesta after a meal of proteins and amino acids.

'Curly,' Bobby started.

'Yes,' Curly responded.

'What happened when you were a Team Leader in the pubic hair region?'

Curly said nothing.

'If you don't want to talk about it, I'd understand.'

Shorty opened his eyes and looked at Curly in anticipation.

Rhino snored. He seemed happy and content to be well fed and looked after.

Curly looked from Bobby to Shorty and back to Bobby as if considering a response. He then answered. 'You know how I'm always on about shaving?' he asked in reply.

'Yes,' Bobby acknowledged.

'You see, it happened once in the pubes.' He looked at them both for a reaction.

He didn't get one.

'You see, that never happens in the pubes. It doesn't get shaved, so when it did, it was a big deal,' he explained.

'I never read about it in the Follicle Farm news service,' Bobby countered.

'Me neither,' added Shorty.

'It was big news for the pubes,' Curly reiterated.

'What happened?' Bobby asked.

'It seems it was a once only event. I gather shaving didn't get the response that marketing thought it would, so the hair was immediately allowed to re-grow.' He paused. 'In fact, they were persistently going on about maximising re-growth stratagems.' He added

'And?' Bobby invited Curly to continue.

Bobby and Shorty glanced at each other. They were both curious.

'Well,' Curly paused. 'My follicle got pulled when it was shaved. When it started regrowing we couldn't penetrate the *epidermis* and it became an ingrown.' Curly looked down, downcast from the memory. He continued. 'The area became infected and some NK's had to come and clean up the mess. My Supervisor got angry and the Area Manager and the Regional Manager needed someone to blame and that someone was me.' He looked at the two expectantly.

'Oh,' said Bobby.

'Oh indeed,' Curly agreed. 'So now you know,' he said accompanied with a mock brief smile.

They heard noises of others entering the work station area. Shorty shook Rhino awake and they stood up to greet the visitors.

Fifteen Cycles can seem like a really long time when you're waiting for something to happen but Dan had finally returned. Steve was with him as the Regional Manager for Beard Hair. So was Greg, the former Area Manager for the left side of the beard and now the designated Area Manager for the moustache. There was also a Follicle Farmer that Bobby hadn't met before. Judging by his insignia, Bobby concluded that he must be the new AMBLS.

Steve was tall for a Follicle Farmer. He was wearing a magnificent robe that looked like it was worn only during important occasions. The robe was attached under his chin and Bobby thought it looked uncomfortable and therefore impractical to wear. This didn't seem to diminish Steve's desire to wear it and he did look resplendent in the cloak as he strode purposely and confidently into the work area. Following Steve were two assistants. He usually had two or three wherever he went. One of them was burdened with files and folders and the other was carrying a small container.

Dan did the introductions. It turned out that the new guy was named Sean and he confirmed that he was the new AMBLS. After introductions Sean took Curly over to the seating area and became engaged in a lengthy discussion, clearly for their ears only. Bobby observed them looking at Rhino and hoped that all would be okay for him.

Steve came close to Bobby and offered his hand. 'Congratulations, Bobby,' he told him. 'I hear great things about you,' he added.

'Thank you sir,' Bobby responded. 'I'm very glad that you do and that you should say so'.

'Steve,' Steve invited.

'Thank you, Steve,' Bobby reiterated.

'On top of your promotion you have been recognised for a bravery award,' Steve continued. 'Promotions happen all the time,' Steve explained. 'I'm here as a result of your bravery,' he smiled.

Bobby said nothing. He looked at Dan who nodded.

Greg also said nothing.

Sean and Curly returned to the group.

One of Steve's assistants passed on to him a typed report. The letterhead revealed it was from the *Immunology* System. Steve cleared his throat and read from the page. '*NK's* arrived to find that the *Keion fungus* had been neutralised by the three Follicle Farm workers at this work station,' he said in a deep resonating, almost monotone voice. 'We kept guard of the fungus should an unlikely resuscitation event occur, but it didn't. The clean-up crew cleared away the remnants of the *Keion*. Your men are to be commended for their quick action in preventing the outbreak. It has been signed by the Manger of the *Immunology* System. I can't pronounce his name.' Steve turned to one of his assistants who whispered in his ear. 'Osvaldo,' he said loudly. The assistant whispered some more and Steve said 'Osvaldo' for the second time and the assistant tried to whisper some more but Steve gestured him away.

Steve flipped the page and satisfied himself that the back of the page was blank. He next returned the page to his assistant who efficiently returned it into a folder.

'On behalf of the Follicle Farmers Union, the *Epidermis* department and the *Immunology* System, we present you with this bravery award.' The assistant provided Steve with a medallion that Steve draped over Bobby's head and down onto his shoulders. He patted it down neatly onto Bobby's chest and clearly Bobby was humbled by the experience.

Bobby turned to show the team the bravery award. It was made of the finest cartilage and was attached to a transparent ribbon so that it appeared to float on Bobby's chest. Bobby smiled proudly and the others clapped and cheered.

Curly called, 'Speech, Speech!' several times and Bobby held up his hands in capitulation.

'Steve,' he started with the most senior Follicle Farmer present as was correct protocol. 'As our Regional Manager for Beard Hair I'm honoured that you should visit in person to present me with this award. It is appreciated and I'll wear it with pride.' He then paused, gathering his thoughts. 'Our action and response to the *Keion* threat was a combined effort. It would not have concluded successfully had my team not responded when needed. Thank you, Curly and Shorty, for being there when it mattered.' He looked at the two of them with great affection. 'We did well,' he concluded.

They all clapped their acknowledgment.

Bobby continued. 'Dan. Thank you for being my role model and mentor. We have been colleagues for many cycles. We have worked well together and trained many follicle farmers in the art of growing beard hair.'

Dan nodded his appreciation.

'Greg, I'm pleased to be transferring with you to the moustache. I appreciate your endorsement and I'm excited to take up my new role as your Team Supervisor. I'm looking forward to meeting the Team Leaders that will be reporting to me and I'm certain, in conjunction with the other Team Supervisors, that we can produce a moustache of which all Follicle Farmers can be proud.'

They all clapped in acknowledgment.

'Sean,' Bobby made eye contact with Sean. 'You're getting a good team here. With Curly in charge and Shorty and Rhino supporting him, they will make history as the first interspecies follicle growing team.' Bobby smiled at his soon to be former team members.

It occurred to Bobby that he didn't know who the new Team Supervisor was for Curly. Sean was the new AM but who was the new TS. 'As I wrap up my short impromptu thank you speech, I would like to ask, who's the new TS replacing Dan now that he is going to the Chin?' Bobby asked no one specifically.

Steve answered for them. 'That role is still vacant Bobby. What with the push on there are still some vacancies we need to fill. We may need to transfer senior people in from other parts of the body.'

'We have a long history of promoting from within. Given the changes that our body experiences as it ages, we will be taking a long examination in the benefits of moving Follicle Farmers across all regions.' He took a deep breath and continued, 'Harry's current thinking is to embark on long term training, development and information sharing about hair growing techniques and practices. He has the full support of our System Manager,' Steve announced.

'Great,' Dan and Sean acknowledged together. The others nodded in support to the initiative.

'That's about all I can tell you for the moment. We'll be posting formal announcements on the network news.'

At that point one of Steve's assistants took a close-up image of Bobby with his award hanging from his neck.

'The image is for the network news Bobby. We want to inspire others with your bravery and promotion,' Steve explained.

The assistant looked at his boss and indicated Rhino, questioningly.

Steve shook his head. 'Let's leave that news for another edition,' he ordered.

The assistant nodded his head.

'I think we're done here.' Steve looked at the two AM's and his staff. They all nodded in agreement.

'We wish you all the best, Bobby. We'll be watching as we expect great things from you,' Steve concluded.

Bobby and Steve shook hands.

Dan turned to Bobby smiling.

Bobby returned the smile, but said nothing.

Bobby indicated to Curly that he, Shorty and Rhino should go and rest up before the next growth cycle. He watched them while they fetched some protein packs and amino acid bottles and went to the rest area to enjoy a meal.

'Dan did you notice that Greg and both of Steve's assistants look identical to Steve?' Bobby asked his former boss.

'They are identical,' Dan agreed. 'Steve replicates all his own staff from himself. He feels comforted knowing that they know what he knows and that he is still in charge.'

'Oh,' Bobby acknowledged.

'Greg is an exception. He's a former assistant that Steve promoted to Area Manager.'

'That's... well. That's a bit unusual,' Bobby was surprised.

'I'll say. He is the only Area Manager in the whole body that hasn't been promoted through the ranks. It does rankle others in the management team somewhat,' Dan added.

'It doesn't seem fair,' Bobby agreed.

'Rumour has it that Greg knows something about Steve and has threatened to report it to Harry if Steve doesn't support him in his career.'

Bobby looked at Dan blankly.

'I'd watch out for Greg. He's never grown a hair in all his life. He doesn't know a *medulla* from a *cuticle*,' Dan advised.

Bobby continued to look at Dan blankly.

Dan laughed. 'Don't worry my friend. Just do your job properly and you'll do great.' He slapped Bobby's shoulder with familiarity. 'Hey I tell you what we'll do. We'll organise a celebratory moustache and goatee party when the hair reaches target length. What do you think of that idea?'

Bobby smiled nodding.

'One day Greg will rupture his *cytoplasm* and it will all be over for him,' Dan concluded.

Bobby sniggered and then laughed.

'That's better. Now go say goodbye to your friends and then I'll accompany you to the *Philtrum*.'

Suddenly, Bobby's life at this follicle was over. This chapter was drawing to a close. He walked to the follicle and patted it with affection. He looked at it and then gave it a prolonged hug. As he looked about the work area, Fatso called out. 'Bye Bobby.' He was a Fat Cell that rarely spoke, but he was the spokesperson for the Fat Cells in that area.

'So long, Fatso, give my best wishes to the others,' Bobby responded. The Fat Cells silently observed everything and co-habituated the area without comment or curiosity.

He walked over to the others and wordlessly hugged Curly and Shorty. Hugging Rhino was a problem because of the spikes, but they managed an awkward handshake.

Bobby waved a final farewell to his team, and then he and Dan left the room.

Bobby followed Dan into the blood stream. They had linked arms and were carried with the current. Bobby marvelled at Dan's confidence and Dan returned Bobby's admiring gaze with a knowing smile. Bobby thought they were traveling fast, even though they were in a minor blood vessel. The area was crowded but there were only a few other travellers, such as themselves. The bulk of the others present were red blood cells busily providing sugars, proteins and amino acids to the never-ending resupply stations that lined the *capillary*.

Bobby knew that all *mitochondria*, such as him-self, drew on the energy provided by these sugars, proteins and amino acids, so that they could continue the growing and regrowing functions seamlessly for their human body. He didn't have very long to marvel at the process as presently, he and Dan arrived just outside the moustache area. They exited the stream and Dan pointed out some blue panels on the walls.

'Bobby, do you see these blue squares?' Dan asked Bobby.

They were easy to see. 'Yes,' he answered.

'They're new. To the Follicle Farmers that work here, they indicate we're in the blue zone, which is the left side of the beard.' Dan explained. 'These blue panels are being erected along the border of the left side of the face and Follicle Farmers working for the beard production on the left side of the face will be issued with a blue arm bands.' Dan indicated his upper arm. 'That'll show everyone that they work for Sean.'

Bobby said nothing.

'The moustache area has yellow panels and there the teams will have yellow arm bands,' Dan continued to explain.

'What about the three other areas?' Bobby asked out of curiosity.

'The neck is red, the right side is green and the chin is black,' Dan answered with a smile.

'Green beard, red beard and blue beard. You're black beard and I'm in yellow moustache,' Bobby summarised.

'Yes,' Dan sighed. 'I know it does seem a bit immature, but Steve went along with the idea to keep Greg happy.'

'It's a good job they are an internal delineations, and not the colour of the hair we pumping out. Those colours would look ridiculous to the outside world and marketing would have an apoplectic fit,' Bobby observed.

'That would look pretty funny,' Dan agreed.

'Where do I go from here?' Bobby asked.

'There are five Team Supervisors working the moustache. You're the middle one,' Dan started to explain. Bobby nodded his understanding. 'You'll have to pass through far left and middle left to get to your part of the moustache. You're bound to meet Greg somewhere in there and he'll..., well..., I'm not sure what he'll do.' Dan paused. 'You'll be fine. Just figure it out for yourself.'

'Thanks, Dan,' Bobby meant that to mean 'thanks for everything'. Dan seemed to know. They hugged. Dan turned and re-joined the stream to go to the chin.

Bobby left the 'Blue Beard' region and entered the Yellow Moustache growing region. Moustache Follicle Farmers, with yellow arm bands, acknowledged him as he progressed passing the numerous follicle stations that made up the moustache.

A Team Supervisor came up to him and introduced himself. 'Hi, you must be Bobby? I'm Jack and we're neighbours.' He extended his hand in friendship.

'I am,' Bobby confirmed. 'Good to meet you, Jack,' he said as he returned the handshake.

'You'll be issued one of these,' Jack informed him. Jack showed Bobby his yellow arm band. In the centre of his yellow arm band there was a bold black number two on it, which was underlined.

'The blue area Follicle Farmers are having blue bands issued,' Bobby observed.

'The numbers identifies which part of the moustache we're working in. One through to five. You're a three. The underlined bold number and three means you're a Team Supervisor. Team Leaders are in bold but are without the underline,' Jack explained.

'Let me guess, another Greg initiative,' Bobby surmised.

'You got it in one,' Jack agreed. 'I believe you used to work for Greg in the left side?'

'The blue side,' Bobby corrected with a wink and a smile.

Jack laughed.

'I did, but only as a Team Leader. I had a Team Supervisor to protect me from direct contact with Greg.'

Jack laughed again. 'Well, congrats on your promotion. Now you'll have to deal with him as your Area Manager all on your own. Let know if you need any assistance settling in,' Jack offered.

'Thanks, Jack. I'd better get going and meet my Team Leaders and their workers. I wouldn't want them to start growing the moustache without me.'

They laughed and then Bobby continued with his journey to the centre of the moustache.

Soon Bobby was at a follicle where the workers had the number three on their yellow arm bands. A Team Leader came up to him and introduced himself. 'Hello, I'm Richard. You must be Bobby?'

'Yes I am,' confirmed Bobby. He was pleased that they knew about his transfer. It made it easier not having to explain all the time who he was and why he was there.

'Welcome to the centre of the moustache. We've been expecting you.' They shook hands. 'Greg said you'd be here soon, and he asked me to give you this.' Richard handed over an envelope.

Bobby acknowledged the Team Leader and found a seat at a work station to sit down and read the note that accompanied the yellow arm band that was imprinted with a clearly underlined, bold number three. The first page contained a list of the names of Team

Leaders and a map of their locations within yellow three. The second page had some instructions for Bobby which he read and sniggered. He looked about Richard's follicle station. He and his three workers were busily replenishing the trolley after a growth cycle. They appeared competent and clearly knew what they were doing. Bobby hoped that all the teams were equally capable. Bobby corrected himself. He hoped that all his teams were equally capable. He paused in his thoughts. This wasn't about him. He changed his mind and adopted a "we're all professionals" approach. All teams should do well. This wasn't a competition between Team Supervisors. It was about growing the best moustache they could.

Bobby thanked Richard and his team and started to explore yellow three. He used the map that Greg provided and, as it transpired, it was laid out logically. He followed it to visit his teams. Introductions were brief and name learning would come later. Bobby wondered if name tags would be a future 'Greg' initiative. He might suggest it himself at the Team Managers meeting.

'Excuse me, Sir,' a voice asked from behind him. 'Are you, Bobby?'

Bobby turned to see a smallish, smaller than even he was, Follicle Farmer standing before him expectantly.

'Yes,' Bobby replied, curious to learn who this person was. His yellow arm band had a circle around a normal sized number three.

'I'm Banjo,' the worker informed Bobby.

'Ahh. So you're responsible for all these arm bands?' Bobby teased, indicating their yellow arm bands.

Banjo didn't react. He didn't even have a glimmer of a smile. In fact, Banjo said nothing.

'I'm sorry Banjo.' He now wanted to find out why Banjo had sought him out. 'I don't know who you are and I don't know what a circle around your number three means.'

'It means that I'm your TSBMEA three,' Banjo informed him.

'TSBMEA?' queried Bobby.

'Yes sir,' Banjo acknowledged.

'I'll bite,' Bobby said and Banjo took a step back. He looked concerned. 'No, No!' Bobby assured him. 'It's just an expression. I won't bite you; it just means that I'll ask the obvious question as I have no idea what a TSBMEA is.'

'I'm your Executive Assistant,' Banjo explained dryly.

'Did you say you're my Executive Assistant?' Bobby sought clarification.

'Yes sir,' Banjo acknowledged.

Bobby was a bit taken aback. Only Regional Managers and the General Manger got to have EA's. He was only a Team Supervisor and now he got an EA?

'Do all the Team Supervisors in the moustache area get EA's?' Bobby asked incredulously.

'Yes sir,' Banjo replied.

'Why?' Bobby was mystified.

'To assist you, sir,' Banjo explained patiently.

So now I have a trained at stating the bleeding obvious, Executive Assistant, thought Bobby. 'Do we have a work area for the two of us to call home?' Bobby decided he may as well get used to the idea.

'Yes, sir,' Banjo answered.

'Would you like to take us to it, please?' Bobby asked. 'Now,' he hastily added .

Banjo wordlessly turned and headed away. Bobby followed him and they presently arrived at a work station comprising of a meeting room with tables and chairs for six people, a lounge area and two work stations, each with a computer link up to the main frame. Whilst it was sparsely decorated, in true follicle farm tradition, Bobby acknowledged that it was functional. On one wall there was a larger version of the map Greg had prepared. Adjoining it was an electronic board indicating growth per hair. Bobby had read about these. They were used during significant growth events. He examined the board and recognised all the follicle teams under yellow three's control.

'Impressive,' he said to Banjo who said nothing in response.

It then occurred to Bobby that his assistant was waiting for some activity to assist him with. He also realised that he was hungry and then figured that sharing a meal would be a great way to ease the tension that may, or may not, exist between them.

'Banjo,' he said to the assistant. 'Would you please fetch us both some protein and amino acid packs please?' Bobby asked realising he had said please, twice.

As Banjo did what he was asked, Bobby wondered if he was being overly polite in order to compensate for his lack of experience in having an assistant. Silently, Banjo returned with the food for them both. Bobby invited Banjo to sit and he did so. They ate their food silently. Bobby decided that it would be up to him to initiate conversation.

'Tell me a little about your-self, Banjo?' he asked.

'Sir, there isn't much to tell,' Banjo started.

'Please call me, Bobby,' Bobby invited.

Banjo explained. 'I was once Greg's EA for the left side of the face. I was demoted from Area Manager Executive Assistant to transfer here as your Team Supervisor Executive Assistant. Greg told me it was because of all my administrative experience and your … pardon me for saying so, your lack of experience, I was appointed to you.'

'I see,' Bobby acknowledged.

'Bobby, you need to know that I have never grown a follicle in all my life. Oh, I've it seen it done and I know all the steps and the chemicals they use, but I've never been a follicle growing team member.' Banjo seemed relieved to get that information out.

'I see,' Bobby acknowledged again.

'I was duplicated from another EA. The process saves time on training and such, but it means I had no practical experience,' Banjo continued, almost excitedly.

'You seem to be labouring that point, Banjo. Why?' he asked.

'Because,' he hesitated. 'If you're not happy with me..., I'll be demoted to Worker.' Banjo looked down, crestfallen with this admission.

'We'll just have to make sure that that doesn't happen,' Bobby reassured him.

Banjo looked up and smiled. It was the first time Bobby had seen his EA smile and he decided he liked it. Bobby decided he'd get used to having an assistant and hoped this emerging relationship would work out well for both of them. He also decided he didn't want to know why Greg demoted him. He'd evaluate Banjo for himself. Bobby mused, "Bobby and Banjo, the dynamic duo of yellow three".

The computer pinged, indicating there was a message. Banjo logged onto the system and reported to Bobby. 'Greg has scheduled a meeting. It's in this meeting room in five cycles.'

'What do we need to do to prepare?'

'I'll ensure adequate food supplements are available. Oh, by the way we qualify for an unlimited supply,' Banjo explained. 'I'll also print out the current growth rates for each follicle in Yellow three and have them ready for you.'

Yellow three, Bobby mused. He'd prefer it if it was known as moustache mid-section. He'd have to get used to this new terminology.

'What do I need to do?' Bobby asked his assistant.

'Well...,' Banjo hesitated. He was thinking. 'From experience, I know that Greg really likes it when a Team Supervisor has a new idea that assists the whole area being more efficient,' Banjo suggested. 'Perhaps you could have a positive suggestion that you could put forward during the meeting?'

'I'll think about that, thanks,' Bobby acknowledged.

After five cycles, the management team of the moustache arrived at Bobby's work station.

As each one introduced himself, Bobby invited them to food supplements and to make them-selves comfortable. As well as Jack, Bobby met John, Johan and Jimmy. He knew that Jack was Yellow two and he learned that John was Yellow one and Johan was Yellow four and that Jimmy was Yellow five.

Bobby smiled at the realisation that his colleague's names all began with a 'J'. He wondered if it was a coincidence. He smiled, thinking that in order they were "JJBJJ". He kept the thought to himself.

'Greg likes to make a grand entrance,' Jack advised the others.

Bobby looked up at Banjo who nodded, affirming the statement.

Greg's assistant arrived and was followed immediately by Greg. He wore yellow arm bands on each arm, each with the letters AM in bold and underlined befitting his status as Area Manager.

'I was half expected him to be wearing a cape,' one of the Team Supervisors had muttered under his breath.

'Yes, a bright yellow one,' someone else agreed. This was followed by suppressed chuckles.

Bobby was focused on his boss's entrance and didn't see the two who made the comments, but he smiled inwardly, pleased that he was in good fellowship with the other Team Supervisors.

Greg addressed the five supervisors. 'I'm glad you are all here. Punctuality is a sign of good leadership.' He sat down at the head of the table. Bobby and the others had automatically left it vacant for their leader.

'Please, in turn, introduce yourselves and give a detailed report on current growth statistics,' Greg commanded.

Over the next ten cycles each supervisor went through the motions of explaining who they were and how their teams were averaging. The results were posted on an electronic score board. Greg's assistant was busily imputing the data and the TSEA's were busily scrutinising the results, just in case anything was incorrect and therefore reflecting badly on their respective supervisors.

At the end of that part of the meeting, Greg asked his own assistant to graph the data. The result was a wavy line, displayed for all to see.

'That gentlemen, is how our moustache appears to the outside world,' Greg advised them.

Clearly, Greg already knew the situation. He didn't react to the graph other than to point out that the graph showed a moustache that was ridiculously uneven.

'Fortunately, the General Manager and the Marketing Manager both realise that we are a new team and still have some growing problems in getting it right. Our regional Manager, Steve, has been very supportive and also somewhat defensive, as the moustache has been shaved daily over the course of many human years and is therefore bound to have inconsistencies now that the shaving has terminated,' he paused. 'However, gentlemen, we are professionals and we have advanced technology to measure what is happening to the moustache, our moustache, and we have the skills to fix the problem!' Greg emphasised the last bit.

They said nothing.

Greg looked at them and asked. 'Do you agree?'

They nodded affirmatively and murmured yes's.

'Good,' Greg concluded. 'Now is there anything to report about your teams that we should know about?

They all shook their heads indicating 'no'.

'How about you, Bobby?' Greg asked.

'Greg, I've only just arrived. I have done a quick tour of all the teams in Yellow three and they seem to be getting on with the job. I have some tweaking to do in improving growth objectives across the board.' Bobby indicated the board for Yellow three. 'I've prepared a schedule of where I need to focus on training and development...'

'You've only just arrived and you have already done all of that?' Greg was trying to sound impressed, but if sounded as if he felt threatened.

Bobby realised the potential threat and chose not to answer.

Greg decided to capitalise on the moment. 'See supervisors. We can do this. Learn from Bobby's professionalism,' he advised without enthusiasm.

Bobby sank in his chair. He hoped that the others would forgive him.

Greg stood up. 'Gentlemen, we have a moustache to grow! Get back to your teams. Here are your individual growth objectives.' He then handed each supervisor an envelope; they opened them to read the contents to themselves.

Greg continued. 'By our next meeting, we should have achieved even and consistent growth across all follicles in the moustache,' he decreed. After a pause he added. 'Don't let me, or your colleagues down,' he cautioned.

Greg left the room immediately followed by his EA.

The others stood and said respective "thank-yous" and "good-byes". None seemed perturbed by Greg's focus on making a big deal out of Bobby's activities since arriving. Bobby was very grateful for this. They were professionals, and Bobby hoped that despite having Greg as a leader, they'd all work well together and produce a magnificent moustache.

Over the next thirty cycles, Bobby and his new EA, Banjo, visited each Team Leader. He showed them his techniques for growing hair. The experienced ones were fine, but some of the younger, less experienced leaders benefited from Bobby's lessons and were grateful for Bobby's caring teaching style.

Banjo logged the growth activity on the electronic scoreboard for Yellow three and Bobby and he agreed that the results were within the tolerances that Greg had established. Bobby concluded that by the next meeting their human would be sporting a fully recognisable moustache. It would be interesting to get feedback from the Marketing Department.

Those thirty cycles seemed to go by very fast. They were soon preparing for another meeting which Bobby found himself once more hosting. Banjo had the reports ready, the scoreboard updated, and the refreshments prepared well before the others arrived.

Greg went through each supervisors report and found that both Johan and John's teams were falling way behind in their objectives. Greg wasn't happy and told them so.

'I'm not happy,' he told the meeting. 'If you follow standard operating procedures we should be getting consistencies in growth across the whole moustache.'

John was the first to be defensive. 'As I get closer to the blue area, I find that the rate of growth is slower,' he confirmed.

'I have the same problem with the teams close to the red beard area,' Johan added.

'Do you have a blood supply issue near the border?' Greg offered a possible explanation as a question.

'We don't think so,' answered John for the two of them. 'I learned that there has been some pilfering of chemicals from the trolleys of the follicle teams close to the blue beard border,' he advised the meeting. 'But it has been insufficient to affect growth,' he concluded.

'Sean has been a bit jealous of the fact that we get to grow our follicles whilst his part of the face still gets shaved,' Greg mused.

'If you think elements of Sean's team are sabotaging our efforts, we should report it to Steve,' Jack suggested.

'We'll need proof,' Greg told them.

'I could...,' Bobby started to suggest.

'Not you, Bobby.' He cut Bobby off before he could offer. 'They know you on the left side. You wouldn't learn anything.'

'They don't know me,' Jimmy explained stripping his yellow arm band off his arm to show his disguise.

'Good,' Greg acknowledged. 'You see if you can find out what they are up to. Can your assistant manage yellow four without you for a short period of time?'

'Certainly,' Jimmy answered Greg.

'Good,' Greg said again. 'You'd better get going.'

Jimmy nodded at the others and left the room. The others looked about at each other but said nothing.

'Everybody back to work,' Greg told them.

The visitors left the room.

Bobby turned to Banjo. 'It would really surprise me if Sean or anyone else would sabotage our moustache. We're all Beard Hair Follicle Farmers and we all take pride in doing the best work that we can. A bad result for the moustache is a bad result for all of us, including the left side.'

'What do you think it might be?' Banjo asked.

'It can't be the blood. The circulation system doesn't work that way.'

'I agree,' Banjo said.

'It can't be the immune system retarding growth and we'd have heard if there were any *epidermis* problems.' Bobby continued.

Banjo looked at him.

'I wonder if there is a problem with the electronic scoreboard,' Bobby speculated.

'Boss?' Banjo queried.

'What if the data is wrong and the moustache is actually doing well in all sectors!' Bobby exclaimed.

'So from the outside world the moustache looks good, but to us it looks bad?' Banjo sought clarity of Bobby's claim.

'Exactly!' Bobby confirmed.

'We could ask Marketing for an opinion on the moustache from an outside perspective,' Banjo suggested.

'That may lead to awkward question,' Bobby countered.

Banjo went quiet.

'What if the results we're seeing are wrong? What if these electronic gadgets have been tampered with?' Bobby asked.

'I could scan the input data....,' Banjo offered.

'What would that do?' Bobby asked.

'It may be that the errors only appear in the accumulative data. The EA's check the accuracy of data as it is being inputted, but if there's an aggressive regressive algorithm, then it wouldn't show until after all the totals were tabulated. You'd need to be really good to spot that,' Banjo explained.

'Can you?' Bobby asked.

'If I had access to all the input data, I could,' Banjo confirmed.

Bobby explained 'It'll look like I'm sending you on a mission to confirm statistics from the yellow three Team Leaders,' he paused. 'But actually, you'll penetrate Greg's EA's workstation.'

'How will you distract Greg and his assistant?' Banjo wanted to know.

'I'll tell them I have an efficiency idea that I need to discus with them,' Bobby answered. He continued. 'Greg doesn't go anywhere without his... what's his assistants name?' he asked Banjo.

'He has a really weird name. He's called, Pierre,' Banjo informed him.

Bobby went to his workstation and keyed an invitation to Greg to come to discuss a plan to improve productivity. He was surprised when he received an immediate positive response.

'He'll be here in two cycles,' Bobby informed Banjo.

'I'd better get going,' Banjo replied and left the room.

In less than two cycles Greg and Pierre entered the room. 'Where's your EA?' Greg asked.

'Banjo is gathering some data for me, on the specific gravities and bulk densities of the growth chemicals used on each follicle.' Bobby knew that Greg knew Banjo because he used to work for him. Greg was just being, Greg.

'Specific gravities?' Greg looked puzzled.

'Yes Sir.'

'That's good.' He paused. 'Keep me apprised of the results,' Greg demanded.

'Yes Sir. I'd be happy to,' he responded.

'Now, what is this great idea of yours?' Greg wanted to know.

'I think we should all have name tags,' Bobby suggested. 'In that way we'd all get to know each other better and we'd all feel more accountable.'

'Accountable?'

'Yes'

'How would we feel more accountable?' Greg didn't follow.

'Well. As we're all anonymous we're less likely to take ownership of outcomes,' Bobby informed him.

Greg looked at Pierre who said nothing.

'If we know who each other are, then we'd become more accountable to each other, and therefore more motivated to contribute to a positive outcome.' Bobby hoped Greg would be impressed with the way he explained it. He hoped it sounded "Managerial".

'Why not bring this up at the next Team Supervisors meeting?' Greg asked.

'I thought it would gain more traction if perhaps you suggested it, sir,' Bobby answered bluntly. 'I really like the idea and if you do too, then with you taking control of it, I believe that we really could actually achieve something meaningful,' he concluded.

Greg thought about this. He was struggling to have a new idea to present to the next Area Manager's meeting and this might just be the idea he was looking for. Name tags. He liked it.'

'Thank you, Bobby. It's not a bad idea and so we'll do some numbers on it and see if it could be done. I won't make any promises, but I like your style and I'll remember your initiative.' He smiled at Bobby. 'Let's just keep it to ourselves for now, so we can introduce it properly to the whole team.'

'Of course, sir,' Bobby agreed.

Greg patted Bobby on the back. 'We ex-lefties make a good team, here in the moustache, Bobby.'

'My sentiment also,' Bobby agreed.

Just then Jimmy arrived at Bobby's work area. 'They said I'd find you here. Greg.'

'Did you learn anything, Jimmy?' Greg demanded.

'It would seem that the blue team is having similar pilfering problems as we are. There is speculation that members of yellow teams are raiding the blue team's equipment and supplies. They say that it is due to the enormous pressure we're under to get results with growing the moustache,' Jimmy reported.

'Rubbish!' Greg exploded. 'Our teams would never raid fellow beard workers. Follicle Farmers are trustworthy and united.'

'Err, you sent me to investigate the suggestion that the blues were raiding us, sir,' Jimmy retorted.

The look on Greg's face indicated that Jimmy had possibly just said the wrong thing.

'Besides, when Steve saw me, I had to tell him...,' Jimmy started to explain.

'What!' Greg was definitely angry now. His face flushed. Bobby had never seen that before.

'Steve was doing a tour and he spotted me. He asked why I was 'off station' and wanted to know who sent me. I had to tell him, sir.'

'How did he recognise you? You were in disguise.' Greg asked angrily.

'Oh, I've known Steve for a very long time. We started out on the same follicle together as workers...'

'What did you tell him?' Greg demanded.

'Just the truth, sir,' Jimmy replied as Greg buried his head into his hands.

Pierre was comforting his boss and Bobby give Jimmy a quizzical look.

Jimmy winked in reply.

Bobby said nothing.

Greg looked up and Jimmy added. 'He's coming to visit you, Greg. He wants a report on why there are varying lengths of follicles here in the moustache. Apparently, the chin is doing magnificent work with the goatee and...'

'Enough!' Greg exploded.

Jimmy stopped.

Bobby hadn't realised that Jimmy had had it in him. He was really pouring it on thick. Bobby thought Greg might self-combust at any moment. He certainly hoped so and he hoped that Pierre would go with him.

'We'll discuss this further at my office,' Greg told Jimmy. 'Please report to my work station in three cycle,.' he added, coldly but very politely.

Jimmy nodded his acceptance and turned to leave. He paused and turned to Greg. 'I'll just duck by yellow four and see how my EA is getting on. I'll be with you in three cycles,' he confirmed as he left the area.

Bobby looked at Greg and Pierre in turn but said nothing.

'Damn, it's hard to get good staff!' Greg erupted. 'I wish they were all like you, Bobby!' he exclaimed.

'Thank you, sir.' Bobby couldn't think of anything else to say.

Greg turned and left with Pierre close behind him.

Moments later, Banjo returned. He had an enormous smile. 'You were right boss. The numbers have been tampered with. I'd bet that from the outside world we'd have a magnificent moustache on display. One that all yellow would be proud of...,'

'How did you find out?' Bobby cut him off.

'All the raw growth data is there. All I had to do is re-tabulate the data,' Banjo explained smiling. 'It's only internally that it would look like we're in a mess.'

'Do you think Pierre is sabotaging Greg?' Bobby wanted to know.

'Oh no, sir. It's Greg that is sabotaging Steve. I've forwarded the communications to our terminal. Greg is conspiring for the moustache to fail and for Steve to get the blame. I wouldn't know why...'

'Greg want's Steve's job as Regional Manager! All eyes are on the moustache and goatee and if we do a bad job its Steve that is ultimately responsible and he takes the blame,' Bobby concluded.

'We should get to Greg's work station and be present when Steve arrives,' Banjo suggested.

'We should also make sure it happens whilst Jimmy is still there!' Bobby added.

'Send Steve a message and invite him,' Banjo suggested.

Bobby walked over to his computer terminal and started keying in the urgent invitation. He smiled as he pressed send. Bobby nodded to Banjo and they hurriedly left the room and made their way to Greg's office. It wasn't far and they arrived at the same time as Jimmy.

'Let's let them know we're here, but not go inside just yet,' Bobby suggested to Jimmy.

'Okay,' He agreed.

Steve arrived hurriedly. He acknowledged Bobby and Jimmy and went into Greg's office.

'I wasn't expecting Steve so soon,' Jimmy said somewhat surprised.

'I invited him,' Bobby started to explain. 'Let's go in now.'

'Good idea,' Jimmy agreed and he and Banjo followed Bobby into the office.

'What is all this I hear about you accusing the left beard area workers of damaging and stealing your equipment and supplies?' Steve demanded.

'I wanted an investigation carried out...,' Greg started to explain.

'We're Follicle Farmers. We grow hair. We're not saboteurs or thieves,' Steve admonished.

'I was concerned for your reputation...,' Greg continued.

'My reputation! It's the reputation of the whole beard region you should be concerning yourself with,' Steve told him.

'There were also issues with circulation...,' Greg tried to move the problem on.

'The blood supply is fine. The *Cardiovascular* System Manager found out about your accusations and he is angry that we accused them of being incompetent. So far I've managed to isolate the problem down to one bad Area Manager. That's you,' he said accusingly.

'A bad..., Area..., Manager..., me!?'

'Look at the data. It shows the moustache growth is all over the place. Hair lengths vary by as much as fifty percent!' Steve held up a sheet of paper covered with number and graphs.

'I'm not a bad Area Manager,' Greg stammered.

'What good things have you achieved whilst you have been here?' Steve demanded.

'We're now colour coordinated with rank signifiers,' Greg suggested.

'Pus!' Steve retorted. 'We're going back to having no colours. Everyone knows their place without these silly colours being plastered everywhere.'

'We're introducing name tags,' Greg offered hopefully.

'There are over fifteen million follicle farmers in this body. Do you know how many resources it would take up to name tag all of them?'

Greg said nothing.

'I'm waiting,' Steve demanded.

Greg had a flash of inspiration. He glared at Bobby to remain quiet. 'I've initiated a study of the specific gravities of the chemicals we use in relation to the growth achieved.'

'What?' Steve queried.

'It's quite technical....,' Greg tried to explain.

'It's not. Specific gravities are the same as saying 'how much it weighs in relation to its volume'. You're making something simple, sound complicated. You're a bad Area Manager,' Steve concluded.

'He was trying to make you look bad, sir,' Bobby offered. 'Here are his communications to Pierre instructing him to make the moustache look bad and in doing so, it would implicate you. Greg also started the rumours about the blood supply and about the theft of supplies and equipment.' Bobby handed him a copy of the communication.

Greg said nothing but his body language indicated his guilt. Pierre also looked guilty.

Steve drew in a deep breath. 'I should now insist that you both perform *apoptosis*.' He told them calmly. The two reasons why I don't are that we are short staffed and that Harry is big on giving everyone a second chance. You're going to be retrained. I want you to report to personnel for reassignment as I'm transferring both of you to the arm pit.'

Greg and Pierre looked devastated as the slowly left the room.

Steve turned to Bobby. 'That Follicle Farmer has been the bane of my existence. He was a terrible Executive Assistant. I thought making him an Area Manager might turn him into a responsible Follicle Farmer. Clearly I was wrong.'

Bobby, Banjo and Jimmy said nothing.

'When I got your message that there was an opportunity to be rid of Greg, I came straight away. Thank you, Bobby,' Steve told him.

'Is that what you wrote?' Banjo queried whispering.

Bobby nodded.

'Bobby, you and your fellow Team Supervisors are doing a great job despite having a bad Area Manager,' Steve told them.

'Thank you, sir,' Bobby and Jimmy chorused.

'Bobby, would you mind being acting Area Manager and completing this moustache?' Steve invited.

'I'd be delighted, sir,' Bobby accepted and Jimmy slapped Bobby on the back congratulatory.

'And get rid of these stupid coloured bands,' Steve added as he shook hands with all three of them and left the room.

Smiling at each other, they removed the yellow arm bands.

'Right then, let's grow this moustache. We can't let Dan's chin win with the goatee!' Bobby told them.

Over the next fifty cycles the former yellow team, aided by Bobby's special, but secret additive, grew the moustache to a magnificent full length. It was strong, full of colour and even in length.

Steve came to visit Bobby during that time and in a quiet ceremony he made Bobby's appointment to Area Manager for the moustache officially permanent. He was now the AMBRM. (Area Manager Beard Region Moustache). Banjo remained his EA. They made a good team.

As Bobby and Banjo were studying the electronic scoreboard examining the growth reports from the five Team Supervisors, the computer pinged.

Bobby went over to read the communication.

Bobby looked distressed as he informed Banjo. 'The moustache is going to be shaved.'

~ 6 ~

Bobby was devastated. He felt traumatised and ... gutted. Tears welled. He couldn't think. The moustache was going to be shaved. That's what the message stated. No reason given and no apology offered. No consideration for workers morale. There was nothing in the message that would ease his overwhelming feeling of pointlessness.

'Think!' He silently commanded to himself.

'Can we protest?' Banjo asked meekly. He was acutely aware of his boss's stress as he felt the same way.

'Protest?' Bobby queried.

'Tell them to reconsider,' Banjo added hopefully.

'I've never thought of protesting before,' Bobby said speculating on the proposition.

'It's sort of the same as objecting, only, it's more forceful,' Banjo added trying to be helpful.

'You're a good man, Banjo,' Bobby complimented his assistant. They had become quite close over these past cycles.

Bobby had come to learn of the power of praise. He restricted its use to only when it was clearly deserved. He tried hard to equate the praise to the accomplishment. He and Banjo researched the recipient, or recipients, prior to applying the praise. They wanted to ensure that the correct team members were recognised, and that the praise would come over as sincere. It must be well received, appreciated, respected and therefore desired.

Banjo regarded his boss's praise for him as more special than the others, here in the moustache. As he fully understood and worked the process, he knew that Bobby's praises for him were spontaneous and seemed, more genuine.

Bobby looked at Banjo. Banjo looked back grinning. He sensed his boss was onto something.

'I have a plan forming, Banjo,' Bobby told his EA.

'Excellent,' Banjo acknowledged.

Bobby briskly walked to his computer terminal. He looked at it. Then he typed. He continued doing this for some time, occasionally looking up at Banjo, who he realised, was studying him intently. He couldn't help grinning at his assistant.

Banjo said nothing.

Bobby finished his typing and re-checked his words. He next pressed send. He closed the lid on the terminal and smiled again as he walked over to Banjo. Before he could speak however, Steve walked into the room, startling them both.

Whilst it wasn't unusual for Steve to visit, it was almost unheard of for him to visit without advising them first. Steve didn't do surprise visits. It was also unheard of for him to visit without one or more of his executive assistants in tow. This time, Steve was alone. His naturally pale complexion was even paler than normal. He cleared his throat before speaking.

'The boss wants to see you,' he told them flatly.

'Harry?' Bobby queried.

'No. I mean George,' Steve answered.

'Who's George?' Bobby queried again but this time looking at Banjo.

Banjo shrugged.

'George is Harry's boss,' Steve answered for Banjo.

'Err..., Harry is the General Manager for hair. I didn't realise he has a boss,' Bobby countered looking at Banjo once more.

Banjo shrugged once more.

'Of course, he has a boss. I'm your boss. He's my boss and he too has a boss. His boss has a boss, although I don't know who that is. It's on a need to know and I don't need to know. When I do need to know, they'll tell me,' he paused. 'Why would you think that our boss's boss wouldn't have a boss?' Steve was rambling.

'I thought that being the General Manager of hair meant that generally he managed everything to do with hair,' Bobby countered flippantly.

'He does, but he reports to a System Manager,' Steve explained.

Bobby looked at Banjo who shrugged again.

'You're no help at all,' Bobby told his assistant.

Banjo said nothing. He didn't even shrug.

'Our System Manager is named George,' Steve explained patiently. 'When you wrote the message to Harry, he forwarded the message to George. George responded to Harry and Harry got on to me. I was told to come here and ask you what you meant.' After a pause, Steve continued. 'What did you mean?'

'I thought that hair follicles were a system,' Bobby seemed confused.

'No, we're all part of the *Integumentary* System. George is the *Integumentary* System Manager. He wants to know what you mean about strong full coloured hair,' Steve was sounding agitated.

'I want to protest about the decision to shave the moustache, so I thought that if I offered up my research on how to grow strong full coloured hair, that marketing would agree to us keeping the moustache intact. We've all worked so hard, and it isn't fair on the others,' Bobby started to explain, pointing in the general direction of the others.

Steve held up his hands indicating that Bobby should stop explaining.

'I'm just trying to protect the morale of the workers who...,' Bobby continued.

Steve interrupted him. 'Our System Manager has a problem with greying hair and hair loss,' he explained. 'You claim to have a solution to that problem; therefore, he wants to know about it,' he continued.

'I do,' Bobby responded meekly.

Bobby was confused. He couldn't fathom if by him figuring out the solution to greying and thinning hair was going to get him rewarded or in serious trouble. Was this a good thing or a bad thing?

'You're to report to the System Manager immediately,' Steve ordered.

'I'll look after the moustache while you're gone,' Banjo assured Bobby.

Steve turned to Banjo. 'Banjo, you're going with him.' He turned back to Bobby. 'Bobby, please take your fancy chemicals, their formula and any research notes you have with you,' Steve explained.

Bobby and Banjo shared a glance.

'I don't know how to get to the System Manager,' Bobby told Steve.

'I'm to take you part of the way. Someone from Head Office will meet us and take you to see George.'

'Head Office!' Bobby exclaimed. 'I never thought I'd ever be visiting Head Office.'

'Gather your materials and we'll get going,' Steve instructed.

'Steve. Are we...? I, me. Am I in trouble?' Bobby queried.

'Trouble!' Steve blurted. He shook his head as he pondered. 'With you luck you'll probably get an achievement award!'

Banjo arranged the documents and Bobby packed vials of his special formula into a carry pack. Apart from Bobby's awards, *Mitochondria* don't have any personal items.

A Follicle Farmer's focus was always about growing hair. They didn't get paid in money and they were highly self-motivated. They were paid in compliments. Their rewards were often advancement up the hierarchy that Follicle Farmers belong to. Performance awards were common, but achievement awards were rare and therefore highly prized, but then, events that created award winning situations were rare also. Steve's assertion that Bobby may receive an achievement award was almost unimaginable.

Bobby and Banjo hoisted their bags onto shoulders and looked about their work station. The significant difference between being an Area Manager and a Team Leader was the absence of follicles. Instead of monitoring hair growth they monitored the hair growers. Bobby hoped they would be back soon. He was proud of his role as Area Manager for the moustache, even if it did get shaved. Banjo nodded to Banjo that he was ready and they in turn motioned their readiness to Steve. He returned the nod. He led the way to the blood stream that would take them up to the brain.

'This stream is very fast by facial standards,' he cautioned. Steve went to a recess in the wall and pulled out several strands. He passed one to Bobby and another to Banjo. They followed his example and they lashed themselves together.

'Entering is easy, but the exit is tricky,' Steve explained. 'If you over shoot, it's hard to go against the current and we'll have to go the long way around. Just follow me.'

Steve entered the blood stream and Bobby and Banjo followed. They were initially buffeted by the swirling current. Bobby was amazed at how busy this artery was. The quantity of red blood cells, white blood cells and other workers that he didn't recognise was astounding to him. He didn't have long to think about this as Steve pulled on the connecting safety line and guided them into a smaller artery. The three moved into it and the current was slower. Steve pointed to an exit point and they left the artery completely. The area was entirely unremarkable other than for the volume of commuters that entered and exited the artery at this point. They all looked purposeful and showed no interest in Steve, Bobby or Banjo at all.

They detached themselves from the tethers and Steve placed them into an identical recess in the wall. 'Ready for the next group,' he explained.

Steve found a computer terminal and keyed in his password and was granted access. He selected from some drop down menus until he found what he was looking for. He type in another passcode and was again granted access to what he was looking for. Bobby and

Banjo watched him and were clearly impressed. Steve smiled at his two admirers in acknowledgement.

'Okay,' he started to explain. 'This is as far as I can take you. You'll soon be met by one of George's Executive Assistants. Don't let them intimidate you. They are *mitochondria*, just like we are,' Steve assured them.

'Thank you for bringing us here,' Bobby said for both of them. 'We'd never have found this place.'

Steve waved his farewell as he returned to the artery that took him away.

'You must be the Follicle Farmers from the moustache?' a voice from behind them queried.

Bobby and Banjo turned to face a tall assistant standing before them. He held an electronic clip board. The tall assistant looked impassively at them down the shaft of his long nose.

'We are,' Bobby confirmed.

'Follow me,' He instructed and turned and walked into a passageway.

Bobby and Banjo had to hasten to keep up with him. Being that there were no proper introductions, they had assumed that this was one of the Executive Assistants that worked for George.

The passage seemed remarkably long and quite dull by *epidermis* standards. They were deep into the head region and there were no recognisable features to observe. They passed other assistants equally burdened with electronic clip boards.

'Are they portable computers?' Bobby asked, trying to make conversation.

'Yes,' he replied.

'Where do you plug them in?' Bobby queried.

'We don't,' came the stilted reply.

Bobby looked at Banjo and was acknowledged with his customary shrug.

They continued in silence until they came to another and even larger assistant that sat on a chair behind a desk. He also had an electronic clip board. On his desk were remnants of protein packs and amino acids that he had recently consumed.

'Which one of you is Bobby?' queried the larger seated assistant.

'That's me,' Bobby replied offering a smile without receiving one in return.

'Your assistant can go with, Ramus.' He nodded to the assistant that had escorted them to this location. 'He'll be given a place to freshen up, eat and rest whilst you are in with George,' the assistant advised him.

Ramus turned and briskly walked away. Banjo shrugged once more, waved a goodbye and hastened after the now named assistant.

Bobby studied the seated assistant. These assistants looked very different from Follicle Farmers and from *epidermis* workers that he was comfortably familiar with. Their height was impressive and Bobby assumed it was due to the unlimited access to protein, amino acids and sugars that this department must have access to. Bobby assumed zero restrictions in Head Office. It was only the best for these guys.

The assistant also studied the Follicle Farmer standing before him. He hadn't met many and had only had conversations with Harry, the General Manager for Hair. He had met representatives from their union before but wasn't on a 'know their names' basis with them. He scoffed inwardly at the notion of a Follicle Farmers Union. He regarded it more as a club as they had no significant influence and System Managers pandered to them as a means of mass communication. The Union seemed to get the ear of its members faster than official communications. The assistant observed Bobby for quite some time. Such a small *mitochondria* he thought. It might be dangerous to underestimate him. A trap he wouldn't fall into.

'Bobby. Do you have your research material and a sample of the chemicals you developed with you?' the assistant asked.

'What is your name?' Bobby asked extending his hand in friendship.

The assistant looked at it and decided to reciprocate. 'My name is Erastus,' he explained shaking Bobby's hand.

'Yes, Erastus. I do have all my notes and some of the chemicals with me,' Bobby confirmed.

'Please give them to me. The boss has a research team ready to study and test your work,' he stated bluntly. 'I hear it shows great promise,' he added forcing a smile.

Bobby handed over the bags to Erastus who took them without ceremony.

Erastus reached under his desk. Momentarily, another assistant came through a doorway that Bobby hadn't previously noticed. The entry was camouflaged by the sameness of everything. Having seen someone come through it, the entry was now obvious to him, but it was invisible to him before. The assistant took the bag from Erastus without a word and without acknowledging Bobby.

Bobby sighed. Just like that, his pet project was being whisked away from him.

'Please sit,' Erastus invited.

Bobby looked about him and noticed a chair that he hadn't seen before. It too blended into the room and until he looked directly at it, it was seemingly invisible. Cautiously he sat on the chair.

Erastus didn't speak and Bobby found himself bemused by the absurdity of it all. He sat in silence. He realised he was hungry and thought of Banjo being refreshed and fed.

After an age, a tall, expansive *Mitochondria* wearing a long grey robe entered the office emerging from yet another invisible entry point. Bobby wished they'd stop doing that.

'Bobby? I'm George. Welcome to Head Office and to the Office of the *Integumentary* System.' George smiled broadly and offered a hand in friendly greeting.

Bobby rose and returned the smile and the handshake. 'Thank you Sir,' he responded.

'Follow me,' George invited and he turned. As Bobby stepped forward he almost crashed into the wall. The entry was tricky, even when he know knew where it was.

Bobby followed the System Manager into his office. He expected it to be very grand and in keeping with his esteemed position with the human body. It wasn't. It reminded Bobby of his own office in the moustache. It was functional with a desk, computers and monitors displaying production and growth results from all parts of the body. There were assistants checking these results, extrapolating and graphing them. None of them looked at George or himself. They were either too busy to notice or didn't care.

George indicated a chair to Bobby and he sat as George sat on the chair behind his desk.

Neither spoke.

Bobby felt himself feeling fidgety under George's scrutiny. Why didn't the man say something? George's computer pinged and George looked at the screen and smiled. He turned to Bobby and smiled even more broadly. Bobby figured a smile was better than a scathing comment, so he tried to relax. He couldn't, so he decided to break their silence.

'George.' He hoped he wasn't being too familiar. 'I'm embarrassed to say that until just recently, I didn't know we had an *Integumentary* System Manager.'

'I'm not surprised. We at the system level prefer to keep a very low profile,' George acknowledged.

'So apart from hair and skin what does the *Integumentary* System look after?' Bobby asked.

'We look after the *modalities cutaneous sensations*,' George answered.

Bobby said nothing. He stared blankly at George. He heard the words but didn't have any idea what they meant.

'Ah,' George concluded. 'Tactile, thermal and pain sensations,' he explained.

'I've heard of pain.'

'Tactile is a touch sensation. These include the pressure felt, vibrations experienced, and itchiness, irritations and tickle sensations,' George explained and then added. 'By that we mean when we use a crude form of touch we inform the brains touch receiver's specific information about the shape, size and texture of the thing or things being touched.'

'Oh,' Bobby responded.

George continued. '*Thermo-receptors* in the skin detect the temperature of what the skin comes in contact with. If the object is colder than the skin temperature, we call it cold. If it is hotter than skin we call it hot.' George smiled at the simplicity of it. 'It becomes more important as we also measure, very quickly, the significance of the difference as a defensive mechanism.'

Bobby nodded his head meekly.

'If the temperature is really very cold or very hot our *nociceptors* tell us of the danger and pain is transmitted to the brain putting it onto high alert so that damage prevention measures can be rapidly activated.' George drew a breath and then continued. 'The *nociceptors* also detect chemical and mechanical tissue damage so that the body can rapidly respond.'

'I guess that would also include bacterial and viral infections,' Bobby contributed.

'Very good, Bobby,' George complimented. 'Well done.'

Bobby nodded and smiled gratefully.

'There are also *proprioceptors*. We have some interest in them as they affect the balance follicles in the ears.' George explained. 'These fall outside of our jurisdiction but I do find them fascinating.'

Bobby shook his head slowly.

'Oh! We also look after the nails,' George explained smiling.

'Sir, no offence intended, but I think you may have a bit of an image problem.' Bobby was feeling brave.

'How do you mean?'

'If Follicle Farmers don't know about you and the very important work you do here, then your PR department isn't doing a very good job of promoting itself.'

'We don't bother with things like that, Bobby,' George responded kindly. He clearly wasn't offended. 'The Hair Department has a wonderful Marketing Department that works on proving itself on knowledge of hair style, colour and length of scalp hair. It was them that decided, along with the marketing boffins in head office, to grow the moustache and the goatee. I believe they have announced its removal?'

'Yes Sir,' Bobby acknowledged. 'By shaving!' he hastily clarified .

'The Marketing Department for the *epidermis* is equally productive. They concern themselves with the best products to hydrate and moisten the skin to keep it smelling good and feeling soft and smooth,' George explained.

George continued. 'There is a marketing person for nails, but he is only interested in keeping them short by lobbying for the trimming of the nails and overall cuticle management. We don't go for nail hardeners and fancy nail colours on this man's body,' he laughed.

Bobby smiled politely but didn't get the joke.

'The Marketing Departments within our System do enough work for those departments to keep me satisfied.' George smiled. 'The GM for Hair, the GM for Dermis, Epidermis and the GM for Nails report to me. They each keep their routine functions well managed and under control,' he explained.

Bobby said nothing.

'The *Integumentary* System is the largest within the human body. Your department alone has approximately five million hair follicles. There are 100,000 of these on the scalp alone. Hair grows at the rate of 10 mm per month. On average we lose and replace a hundred hairs per day through natural attrition.' George was on a roll.

'Did you know that a hair can remain in place for up to six human years? Hair doesn't grow on the soles of the feet, palms of hands, on the sides of fingers and toes or the lips. Only the root of the hair is alive, and the rest are just dead cells,' George continued to explain.

'Yes Sir. I knew that last part,' Bobby acknowledged.

George continued. 'In our adult male body there are approximately ten million Follicle Farm Workers, five million Team Leaders, a hundred thousand Team Supervisors, one hundred and twenty Area Managers, sixteen Regional Managers and each of those has up to twenty support staff.'

Bobby blinked rapidly. For the first time he felt overwhelmed at the extent of the Follicle Farmer network.

'And,' he paused. 'There is one General Manager, and his name is Harry.'

'Yes sir. I have heard of Harry, but I haven't met him,' Bobby offered.

'I'm sure you will. Did you know that Harry has over thousand support staff?' He asked rhetorically. 'They manage human resources, communications, monitor production, liaise with the other systems and run the union. They also lobby the marketing department in Head Office about issues affecting hair management. Harry's closest support staff attend to his well being and arrange his travel plans. They also plan and run the regular meetings that he has with the sixteen Regional Managers.'

'I didn't,' answered Bobby unnecessarily.

'Including himself, Harry has a combined work force of approximately 15,101,457 workers that are directly involved in hair follicle production,' George concluded. He studied Bobby for a reaction.

'We're certainly a big team,' Bobby agreed.

'And judging by these results we're seeing from your research notes, and the analysis of your chemicals, you're about to become a very important part of that team, Bobby. How do you feel about that?'

Bobby didn't know what to think. This was happening so fast. It didn't seem all that long ago that he was just a Team Leader, dealing with recalcitrant workers, a *Kieron* attack, a *Rhinovirus* intruder, and a disillusioned *T-Cell*.

'Tell me about your research. Explain how you came to use the chemicals you developed for use in the moustache,' George invited.

'I actually came across them when I was in the left side of the beard as a Team Supervisor,' Bobby started to explain.

'Oh,' George responded.

'Yes sir. I guess it didn't get noticed because it was just managing one hair in one part of the left side of the face. I was happily experimenting. I didn't do it for any other reason other than the fact that I wanted my follicle to grow healthy and strong,' Bobby explained.

George invited Bobby to continue. 'I understand. Go on.'

'Well sir. I discovered that massaging the *follicle medulla* at the base of the follicle helped keep it healthy. It seemed to me that it responded to my touch. I then wondered about the chemicals that we add during each growth cycle, so I started thinking about what could be done differently to produce a better result.' He drew a deep breath. 'Eventually, I succeeded. When the awkward managerial situation within the moustache was resolved, I decided to apply the chemicals to all the moustache follicles in order to achieve the quality moustache that the Marketing Department was after.'

'Bravo!' George pronounced. 'You did well,' he added. 'Now back up just a bit with your explanation and tell me about the actual chemicals you developed,' George requested.

'Yes sir,' Bobby acknowledged. 'At first I started using a mixture I named *Minoxidil*. I found it helped widen the blood artery thereby increasing the blood supply to the follicle directly into the *matrix*.'

'Very impressive, yes my Research Team acknowledges that'd work. I must impress on you that its use must be restricted. If used in large volumes it could be very dangerous to the whole body,' George explained.

'Yes sir,' Bobby agreed. 'They'll have seen from my notes confirming the very small quantities I was using.'

'We'll need to document all of this, Bobby,' George sighed. 'You must understand Bobby that these drugs, in unrestricted use, can cause fainting or an irregular heartbeat, and can even adversely affect the Respiratory System. We have a broader responsibility,' he continued.

'I'm sorry sir,' Bobby apologised.

'Don't misunderstand me. I applaud your initiative; however there can unexpected consequences,' George tried to explain this in a fatherly fashion.

'Yes sir,' Bobby acknowledged looking at his feet.

'How did you come up with that name?' George queried.

'Minoxidil? Oh um,' he hesitated. 'Mine oxide dilates. My idea, it's an oxide and it dilates the blood artery.' Bobby exclaimed, looking a bit embarrassed.

'Very original,' George seemed impressed. 'Please continue.'

Bobby went on to explain how he figured a way to grow strong, long full colour hair. In the beginning it started with an idea that he got from a worker repairing nerve tissue near where he was a Team Leader. The worker had a chemical that repaired frayed nerves. He added it in varying quantities until he had a compound that worked on the follicle. He documented these trials and had brought the optimum result with him when he was summonsed to meet George. He called the chemical Krox 20 because he thought it sounded sciencey and because it took him twenty trials to get the perfect combination of nerve chemical and follicle growth chemical that achieved the best results.

He next tried it on a few of his colleagues follicles and they all reported stronger follicle growth. He hadn't had the opportunity to try it on a dying follicle but he thought that it might work on them also. By chance, the chemical caused a reaction with the added benefit of the hair shaft becoming darker in colour. Some of the beard hairs were turning grey or white. Bobby discovered a connection between his chemicals and a protein he found in fat cells that contained stem cells. When he combined these, they made a powerful chemical that produced a long, fast growing, and full coloured, hair follicle.

It wasn't until he was the Area Manager for the moustache that he was able to seriously test these chemicals and procedures. When he did, they produced a fully grown, healthy, full coloured moustache. He heard that the goatee was a combo of black and grey hairs. He was about to share his research with his colleague, Dan, in the chin when the announcement came that both the moustache and goatee were to be shaved. Bobby admitted to being devastated by the news. The healthy follicle was important to him but it was only significant to the man if the hair was allowed to grow. He wanted his manager and the Marketing Department to be pleased with how well they could grow a moustache.

'Tell me more about the stem cells within the fat cells,' George invited.

'We have a number of the fat cells in the face. I know there's not as much where we are compared to other parts of the body, but they are with us. Mostly, Follicle Farmers ignore them and as they are mostly very quiet and don't do very much, so ignoring them is the natural thing to do,' Bobby explained.

'But you don't?' George queried.

'No sir,' Bobby confirmed. 'I've given names to all of mine... I mean the ones in my area.' He hesitated. 'I like being nice to them and they appreciate it. They are actually very shy, sir.' Bobby paused gathering his thoughts. 'They're also ticklish.' He smiled, remembering how they responded to his affections.

'Ticklish?' George was surprised.

'Oh, they love being tickled.' Bobby explained. 'I noticed that when I tickled them, they excrete a small amount of liquid. I gathered it up and used it in a trial to make my other growth chemical and it worked! I called it *Mesenchymal*, sir. They are stem cells and they produce the most magnificent hair.'

'How did you come up with that name?' George was curious.

Bobby blushed. 'At first I thought they were making a mess.'

'The Fat Cells? When you tickled them?' George qualified.

'Yes sir. My first name for their secretions was 'messy chemicals', but I quickly changed it to 'Meschem' and much later to Mesenchymal.'

'You did very well Bobby,' George told him. 'Please continue.'

Bobby looked about the room. 'I'm actually quite hungry,' Bobby informed the System Manager.

'How very thoughtless of me,' George admonished himself. He went to a computer and sent a message. Presently two assistants came in with a tray of proteins, sugars and amino acids that they spread out on George's desk. George indicated to Bobby to help himself and the two ate in relative silence. George looked in wonder at this Follicle Farmer turned scientist.

When they had finished and Bobby was sated, he stared about the room. He wondered what was going to happen next.

George spoke as the two attendants returned and cleared the desk. 'You're probably wondering what's going to happen next,' George said to him.

'Yes sir,' Bobby acknowledged.

'As I explained, The *Integumentary* System doesn't concern itself with marketing and self-promotion. The Department Managers do a good job with that. You indicated that we have an image problem. We don't, because our focus is on repair. My department mostly concerns itself with adverse issues affecting skin, hair and nails. When you bravely dealt with that *Kieron* attack I acknowledged your actions with a bravery award,' George explained.

Bobby was stunned. To imagine that his actions would have come to the attention of the System Manager was difficult enough, but to learn that the award that he received was actually from the System Manger, really impressed him.

'When the actions or in-actions of other parts of the body, or more specifically, when other systems cause aspects of the *Integumentary* System to become adversely affected, we set about repairing that damage. Do you follow?' George asked.

'I think so sir. Like repairing a surface cut, scratch or rash for example?' Bobby responded.

'That's correct, Bobby. I was certain that you'd understand. We also concern ourselves with sun-burnt skin, bacterial and viral skin infections and would you believe premature baldness?' George smiled at this.

'Sir. You mentioned bacterial and viral skin infections. Doesn't the Immunity System deal with that?' Bobby queried.

'Yes, you have had some experience with that too, Bobby.' George smiled some more. He was clearly very impressed with this Follicle Farmer. 'The Immune System does deal with infections and invaders. Because the *epidermis* is so large and so vulnerable we also have our own defences. These are managed here in the Integumentary system, quite distinctly by both the *Dermis and Epidermis* General Managers.' George paused. 'They are called *Phagocytes*. I believe you met one?'

'I have!' Bobby confirmed excitedly. 'His name is Fargo.'

'We have so many and I actually haven't met many of them personally. They do a great job and to the man they are brave and true and protect our body at considerable personal risk,' George explained. 'We are proud of them and grateful for their efforts,' he concluded.

Bobby said nothing. He pondered the fate of their protectors in humbled silence.

'I mentioned that we investigate baldness,' George said pressing on with his discussion.

'Yes sir,' Bobby agreed.

'You see our body, our man, is now entering a phase where this is starting to happen. The Marketing Department isn't too happy about it and so we're pressing for a solution. You follow?' George queried.

'I think so, sir,' Bobby responded.

'It looks like you have that solution, Bobby. You're the solution. Your discoveries are to be put to use all over the body. How do you feel about that?' George asked smiling.

Bobby stared at the System Manager. 'I'm pleased that I can contribute, sir,' he was finally able to respond.

'Contribute!' exclaimed George. 'I'm putting you in charge of the whole project,' George told him beaming with delight.

Bobby went pale.

'I'm promoting you to our newly created position of 'Quality Assurance Manager. You'll be reporting to Harry, of course.'

'Yes sir,' Bobby mumbled. He was staggered by what he was hearing.

'Are you happy with Banjo remaining as your Executive Assistant?' George asked.

'Yes sir. Banjo is very efficient and totally trust-worthy,' Bobby assured George.

'Good,' George agreed. 'My researchers say he has been very helpful, knowledgeable, a quick learner, and professional.' George smiled.

George continued. 'You'll have the rank of a Regional Manager, but your region will be the whole of the body. You'll work with the other Regional Managers to produce the finest, healthiest hair and you'll work to reduce the incidence of hair loss.'

Then George told him. 'Harry is planning a tour of the whole body. You and Banjo will accompany him. I first want you to conduct a needs analysis. Do you know what that means, Bobby?' George asked hopefully.

'Yes sir. I'm to look for where we can improve hair growth, hair colour and which areas are more prone to hair loss and work out what needs to be done, depending on the situation,' Bobby responded.

'Perfect!' George was delighted.

Bobby smiled broadly.

'There is just one more step to take before you start the job,' George explained. 'You'll need an endorsement from Percival. You'll be going deeper into the brain to meet my boss, Bobby. How do you feel about that?' He asked rhetorically.

Bobby was stunned.

~ 7 ~

Bobby was once again puzzled. He tried to look knowledgeable and confident. The pained expression on Bobby's face must have been very evident to George as he was smiling broadly and in a kindly way.

'Bobby, are you okay?' George asked sympathetically.

'Yes Sir,' Bobby answered unconvincingly.

'What is it Bobby? I thought you'd be pleased about your promotion,' George asked hopefully.

'Oh, yes sir, I am,' Bobby exclaimed rising to his full height. He took a few steps toward the System Manager and stopped. 'You see George; until just recently I didn't even know we had a System Manager..., I didn't even know we were part of an 'Integumentary System'. I thought we were the Follicle System. We grow hair..., and...'

'Bobby, we're all part of a wonderful creation. There are many, many systems and trillions of workers. Collectively, we all do our part. All parts integrating with each other. Our very survival depends on it.' George was being kind. 'We require organisational structure to manage the two hundred and ten different types of human cells that are required to grow and maintain this one man we call home.' He paused. 'I believe you understand that?' He asked hopefully.

'Yes sir,' Bobby acknowledged. And then he asked after a thoughtful pause. 'Trillions?'

'Yes, we number approximately thirty seven trillion according to the last census.' He smiled letting that sink in. 'So we all have report to someone. In my case, I report to an administrator named Percy. He's the Operations Manager for the *Medulla Oblongata*. I've advised him that you'll be visiting soon, so you'd better get going,' George suggested.

'Do I take Banjo with me?' Bobby asked.

'You'd better do this visit without him, Bobby,' George answered. 'Banjo is getting some intensive training on his new role in assisting you with quality assurance. We'll look after him.' George smiled.

'Thank you, George. When do I leave?' Bobby queried.

'Now,' George informed him with a smile and a conspiratorial wink.

Erastus entered the room. 'Follow me,' he ordered Bobby.

Bobby nodded a quick farewell to George and hastily followed a rapidly departing Erastus. Bobby wondered what all the rush was for. It seemed that only moments earlier he was congratulating himself on perfecting the moustache, only to learn that it was going to be shaved off. He suggests a trade of information and within a heartbeat he is summoned to the System Manager. It was all happening so fast... Bobby was perplexed. He sped up to maintain pace with Erastus whose long strides were leaving him behind.

Bobby pondered. He had only just offered his advanced growing and colour retention techniques when Steve turned up. It seems like Steve knew to come and get him even before he sent the message. It was all happening too fast. Steve knew. He had to. It's the only way he could have been there so soon after he typed his offer. Was it a way of getting him out of the way so that they could start shaving his moustache without him being there to protest! Was meeting George a ruse to get him out of the protest zone! 'Why would they do that?' Bobby mumbled to himself thoroughly distressed and confused.

'Erastus,' Bobby yelled to the speeding executive assistant. Bobby didn't understand the command relationship between the System Managers Executive Assistant and his own position as a Regional Manager for Follicle Quality Assurance. The cell turned and faced him.

'Yes sir?' Erastus asked without expression or interest.

Good, I'm higher up the chain of command than he is, Bobby concluded. 'Could you please tell me if the moustache is still intact?' he asked hopefully.

Erastus managed a glare down the shaft of his nose before he consulted his electronic note pad. 'It is,' he responded and turned and continued leading the way.

Bobby smiled inwardly. Outwardly he was showing signs of stress and frustration. Abruptly Erastus stopped and motioned Bobby to precede him into a room. Bobby did so and stared into the very long room. It was a massive room with thousands of workers, monitoring giant colourful screens that covered the walls and half the ceiling. He turned to ask Erastus another question only to discover that he was gone.

An Aid came up to Bobby and extended a hand in friendship. 'Welcome to the *Medulla*,' the man said. 'My name is William and I'll be escorting you to your appointment with the boss.'

'Thanks,' replied Bobby returning the handshake. 'My name is Bobby.'

'Of course you are,' William responded in a perfunctory voice. He smiled congenially. 'Follow me.' William turned and walked at a half pace, almost reverently, passing the technicians stationed at the numerous computer terminals that displayed statistics on parts of the body that Bobby never knew existed.

Presently, they came to a transparent cubical at the centre of the room. William nodded and indicated that Bobby should sit on one of the chairs that suddenly materialised from the wall of the cubical. When Bobby did so, William nodded once more and walked away.

Bobby waited and waited. He occupied himself by trying to make out what the activity was all about. The room, despite having so many workers was very quiet. Conversations between computer operators and the roaming, Bobby thought they must be supervisors, were minimal. Communications seemed to be by gesturing and pointing to information on a computer screen or one of the giant monitors that seemed to be everywhere.

Bobby tried to identify what was on the screens. He stood up to get a better look and then took some pensive steps forward to get a better view. Everyone was ignoring him and so he took some more steps closer to the action. He stepped lightly so as to not get in anyone's way, or disturb the work activity.

Presently a large work trolley was moving soundlessly toward him. Workers left their stations and helped themselves to the sugars, proteins and amino acids that were stacked high on the trolley. Evidently they ate on the job. Bobby wasn't peckish himself, but reached over to the trolley for a protein pack that he recognised and started to eat it. He suddenly felt self-conscious and worried if anyone had noticed him helping himself. He looked about, but quickly concluded that they didn't care.

He followed some workers and as they sat at their stations, he stood behind them and read what was on the displays. This part of the room seemed to focus on the *epidermis.* There were details about surface temperature, surface tension, friction, pressure gradients and current sweat levels. Bobby realised there was even a section on cuts, abrasions, burns, inflammations, corns and infections.

Bobby moved farther and was reading some of the details of a management plan for fighting an infection on the abdomen, when a hand rested on his shoulder. Bobby jumped in surprise. He turned and saw a smallish, lean faced man standing before him. He sported a deep scowl and his expression indicated deep displeasure at Bobby's presence.

'My name is Bobby. I'm a Follicle Farmer and I have an appointment with Percy,' he tried to explain to the man.

'It's Percival.' the man corrected impatiently.

'I was waiting outside of his office, but I found myself somewhat curious about what was happening. Sorry,' Bobby explained, indicating the room and all its activities.

'Yes, we heard you were curious,' the man replied.

'I suppose I'd better go back and sit and wait for..., Percival,' Bobby suggested.

'I'm, Percival,' the man explained. He turned and walked to his cubical. 'Follow me,' he ordered over his shoulder.

Bobby followed Percival into his cubical. As the door closed soundlessly behind them, Percival indicated he should sit. A chair suddenly formed where Percival had indicated and so Bobby sat. He felt tense and unable to relax. Percival looked like an angry man. He looked as if he might pounce on Bobby. They stared at each other for a minor eternity.

'George informed me that he wants you to head up a newly created position within the Hair Farmers hierarchy,' Percival spoke at last.

'Yes sir,' Bobby agreed. 'We prefer to be called Follicle Farmers, sir,' Bobby corrected.

'Hair, Follicles, it's all the same to me,' Percival concluded.

Bobby said nothing.

'Do you think we need a Quality Assurance Manager for growing hair, Bobby?' he asked Bobby taunting him.

'I know George does, and he's my System Manager so if he wants me to do a role that improves the quality and quantity of the follicles we grow, then that's sufficient enough reason for me to be enthusiastic about the role.' Bobby tried to be both polite and firm with his response.

'Well said,' Percival responded. He drew in a deep breath. 'However, I don't agree.' He looked at Bobby for his reaction.

Bobby sat pensively, all whilst trying hard to maintain a neutral expression on his face. Percival was George's boss and if he didn't approve of this appointment, he'd have the authority to deny it. He wondered if he could get his old job back as area manager for the moustache. Shaved or unshaven, he'd rather have a job to go back to.

'Your lack of response indicates you agree with me and that you'll accept your fate,' Percival suggested.

Maybe this was a test of Bobby's resolve. He could be trying it on to see how much Bobby wanted to be a Regional Manager for quality assurance for follicle growth over the whole of the body.

'No sir, I don't,' Bobby responded firmly but politely. 'I want the job and I'm excited about the prospect of completing the needs analysis and then improving hair density, strength and colour,' Bobby explained.

'Why?' Percival demanded. His voice was becoming slightly elevated in pitch and volume.

'Because I'm a Follicle Farmer and growing hair is what we do,' Bobby explained.

'It's a waste of human resources!' Percival exploded. 'Over fifteen millions of you lot growing and nurturing hair. It's a poor use of time and energy. Hair does nothing. Its piles of dead skin poking through the *epidermis* doing nothing. If it all fell out, no one would notice or care,' he sad sounding menacing.

Bobby said nothing.

Percival continued loudly. 'Hair contributes nothing to the human body. It's a redundant *Integumentary* function and I for one, wouldn't miss it if it stopped happening.'

Bobby didn't counter this man's opinion. There was no point. Bobby figured that he'd try to go back to growing hair in some remote location on the body. Even if he was just a worker it'd be better than *apoptosis*.

'Look, I know you're just a Follicle Farmer. You've been taught since the day you were created that your role was to grow hair. I understand that your mantra has been about how strong and how long and the deep rich beauty of the colour you can achieve. But I've been a Senior Operations Manager of this department since time began and I can't yet work out the benefits of having a hairy body,' Percival said almost yelling.

Percival was obviously on a pet topic. He clearly didn't like hair or want hair and had spent a great deal of time thinking about how much he didn't like or want hair. This was his opportunity to tell a

Follicle Farmer how he truly felt. Maybe, Bobby was just a sounding board. He was the recipient of many, many cycles of Percival's pent-up frustration.

Silence was golden and right now Bobby was being a golden Follicle Farmer.

'I'm sorry, Bobby.' Percival was now visibly trying to calm down. 'It's not your responsibility. Let me explain. Thousands of generations ago, man was literally covered in hair. It used to have an important role in human affairs.'

Bobby looked perplexed.

Percival continued. 'When I say covered, I mean covered. Externally, you couldn't see the skin. There were hundreds of times more hair than now. Hair used to protect the body from the sun. Now we wear clothing or external chemical applications to do the same thing. Clothing is abrasive and chemicals weaken our skin so they're not a great alternative.'

Bobby nodded his head in understanding. He hadn't experienced clothing on the beard, but he'd heard of the effects it had had on other parts of the body through the Follicle Farmer's network news. He had experienced sun protection creams on the beard. No one he knew, including himself, liked them.

Percival was unperturbed by the one sided conversation and readily continued. 'Hair was so dense that it protected the skin from abrasions, cuts and insect bites. Those events are less frequent now,' he informed Bobby.

Bobby nodded his head in understanding.

'Somehow, over the years, hair density decreased and skin took over as the dominant external barrier.' Percival was well versed in this topic. 'Skin isn't as strong as hair, but it is the way men have evolved. Do you know why?' Percival asked him. His face was uncomfortably close to Bobby's and it made Bobby hesitant to respond. Percival withdrew. 'I'll tell you why.'

Bobby looked Percival in the eye inviting him to continue.

'*Testosterone*,' Percival announced.

'*Testosterone*?' Bobby queried.

'It's a chemical, a hormone made in the testes. It's what gives males their sex drive,' Percival tried to explain to a very bewildered Bobby.

'You know what the testes are, don't you Bobby? They're the balls in the *scrotum* sack. They make *testosterone* and the more we have of it the more hair men grow. You're a Follicle Farmer, didn't you realise that the chemicals you use to grow your hair come from the *Reproductive* System?' Percival taunted him.

Bobby said nothing.

'Now as I was explaining, men are now producing less testosterone than what they were producing thousands of generations ago. The levels keep falling and the amount of hair we're growing keeps decreasing.' He smirked as he paced the room. 'In about a thousand more generations, all humans will be bald.' He turned to Bobby and scowled. 'Not only are Follicle Farmers redundant, one day you'll become extinct.' He laughed nastily.

Bobby was taken aback by this assertion. He was the newly appointed Quality Assurance Manager for follicle production. He was an award winning representative and role model for all Follicle Farmers. Now he learned that he was going to be redundant and soon extinct. This wasn't the outcome he hoped to achieve.

Percival looked at the distressed Follicle Farmer. He could see his words had affected him deeply. Perhaps over the ensuing generation's, Follicle Farmers could be redeployed into more meaningful functions. He decided he'd lighten up on the poor man.

'Bobby, I'm a manager, an administrator. I ensure that the primary functions within the human body are performed professionally and punctually,' he explained.

Bobby nodded his head in acknowledgment.

'Bobby, let me give you a tour of the *Medulla*. It's an interesting place and we do a lot of important work here.' Percival walked to the door and exited.

Bobby followed.

Percival walked over to a section and pointed to the floor. 'You'll see that the floor is colour coded according to the functions being performed.'

Bobby hadn't noticed the colours before and he smiled remembering the colour codes used in the beard for a brief period.

Percival hadn't noticed Bobby's smile and he started to explain the role of the *Medulla Oblongata*. 'You must understand that we perform numerous functions, Bobby,' he informed him. 'I'll try and explain some of them in layman's terms.' He smiled.

'I'd appreciate that,' Bobby replied, unsure if he'd been insulted.

'The *Medulla Oblongata* is primarily the Head Office of the *Nervous* System.' Percival knew that Bobby knew this and didn't insult him by seeking confirmation. 'As well as the *Integumentary* System Manager, who you know, all the other System Managers report to me,' Percival explained with a tight lipped smile.

Bobby nodded his understanding, unwilling to interrupt.

'The Nervous System Manager has an office here in the *Medulla*,' Percival continued as they slowly walked the length of the room.

He continued. 'Here we control the pumping station.' He turned to Bobby and smiled again. 'Its role is to push blood throughout the body. It's called the *Heart*.'

'Do you decide if it pumps or when it pumps?' Bobby inquired.

Percival stared coldly at him. Finally he asked, 'What do you mean by that?'

Bobby felt he may have touched a sensitive topic. Everything seemed sensitive here. He had better be careful.

'Well...,' Bobby cautiously tried to explain. 'From what I understand the *Heart* is part of the *Circulatory* System and as the System Managers report here..., to you,' Bobby paused.

Percival said nothing.

'So... that means you ultimately make decisions about the *Heart*.' Bobby decided to press forward. 'It's you who decide if it pumps, and you have the power to end us all. You have the ultimate power over everything...'

'What!' Percival was shocked by the assertion. 'Our whole mission is to keep the *Heart* beating. It's vital to all parts of the body. Everything functions because of the blood providing food and removing waste. Hormones travel via the blood. That pump keeps everything working,' he was almost yelling.

Calmly Bobby responded. 'So, here you decide when it pumps.' He nodded his approval and understanding. He continued to look at the *Heart* monitors that were on display in front of them.

He saw that they monitored *Heart* beats, pressure, blood pressure, temperature, blood volume and the consistency of the blood. The area was appropriately colour coded a pale red and workers had reddish uniforms.

'What does that tell us?' Bobby inquired pointing to one of the screens.

The overly flummoxed Operations Manager replied coldly. 'It tells us about any blood leakage.'

'Including wounds in the epidermis?' Bobby asked showing interest.

'Yes, among other places.' He replied.

They moved on to a brown colour coded area. Bobby turned to Percival and asked. 'What do they do here?'

'This is the digestive system. Here we monitor the foods as they progress through the mouth, stomach, digestion, and bowel. When the bowel is ready to purge, we inform the brain that they need to locate a suitable receptacle. We tell the anus to maintain a hold pattern. We confirm that we have informed the brain to instruct perambulation toward a defecation receiving station.'

Bobby said nothing.

Percival continued. 'We consider it bad form to just let out waste material from either the urinary section...' He pointed to a pale-yellow area within the *Medulla*. 'Or the digestive system...' showing the area they were now in. 'to spontaneously purge due to an internal pressure build up.'

'Oh,' Bobby responded fully unaware of the ramifications.

'It took us about three human years to perfect this procedure.' Percival was obviously proud of this achievement. He smiled knowingly.

Bobby smiled in response.

Percival moved off to a pale white colour coded area. 'Over here we monitor the respiratory system. These measure volume and quality of the air breathed in, the release of carbon dioxide, oxygen absorption.' He smiled. 'We also monitor hiccupping, coughing, sneezing and wheezing.'

'What happens when they occur?' Bobby asked thoughtfully.

'We send a message to the brain. They interpret the information and decide what measures are needed.'

'Such as?' Bobby wanted to know.

Percival was finding himself impressed with this Follicle Farmer. He assumed they were all dim witted and purely hair brained. He was warming to the intelligent questions, and responses to answers, that Bobby was exhibiting.

'For a sneeze we may need a receptacle to deal with waste material from the nasal passage. It can get quite messy you know,' he asked rhetorically.

'I've heard,' Bobby replied without elaborating.

'For hiccups we recommend an intake of water via the *oesophagus*,' Percival continued.

'What is happening over there?' Bobby asked with enthusiasm.

It was a small area and colour coded blue.

'This is where we monitor temperature,' Percival explained, realising that he wanted to tell Bobby more. 'We record the temperature and initiate a counter measure. If it's too cold, we shiver,' he smiled. 'By the way, we sometimes instruct the hair follicles to stiffen and erect. Certainly, a redundant response but it is still in the programming,' he smiled.

'Why?' Bobby wanted to know.

'Why do we send the response instruction or why is it redundant?' Percival asked confused by Bobby's question.

'Why is it redundant?' Bobby clarified.

'As I explained earlier, the human body was once covered in thick lush hair. The cold response was to erect the hair follicles to trap more hair between the hair strands. The trapped air became heated by the heat release via the *epidermis* thus warming the body. It was for survival,' Percival explained happily.

Bobby nodded his understanding.

Percival continued. 'Now, when we send a hot or cold message to the brain, their response is to either change location, change the environment or alter the clothing amount or type.'

Bobby only had a vague idea what clothing was, so he said nothing.

'The brain calculates the optimal response, given the variance in temperature to what is desired, and the estimated time it'll take to return to the desired temperature. You follow?' he asked a puzzled Bobby.

'Sort of,' Bobby responded. 'What happens if the temperature change is dramatic and sudden?' he queried.

'You mean a burn risk or a cold fluid immersion risk. When that happens, we don't wait for the brain. We have an overriding authority to protect and preserve the body from all external and internal dangers. We react faster than they can.' He smiled at Bobby. He found himself wanting to explain some more. 'You see the mind works like a committee. They want to know all the facts, read reports, call for expert opinions, debate the issues and assess both the risks and the benefits of each potential option. They then send out flowery messages of support and recommendations without serious commitment. If we waited for them to decide anything we'd either die from the lack of nutrition in the blood, or from exposure, or from injury.'

Bobby said nothing.

Percival continued. 'The body needs quality food to digest and supply it with sugars, proteins and amino acids. Thousands of generations ago, as a gatherer, our diet was limited, but now we have more food options than we can properly assess. We tend to eat any-thing that is convenient, without properly understanding the con-sequences to the body. That's the mind for you. Don't ever trust a committee with your life. That's what I always say.'

Bobby could tell that Percival was warming to him. He wished he fully understood what he was talking about. He thought the mind, AKA Head Office, AKA Grey Matter, knew everything. Percival was the Operations Manager and clearly he didn't trust them. Bobby de-cided to continue to say nothing.

'This body should be run with firm, decisive, intelligent and ra-tional leadership. That's my mission Bobby. To run this body as ef-ficiently as possible. All *Mitochondria* need food so that they can continue the work of maintaining the structural integrity of the body,' he stated proudly.

They had been slowly walking as Percival had been delivering his speech. He now stopped and indicated a crimson colour coded area. It was very small. There were four operators working on the two computers. There was also a supervisor.

Percival explained. 'This is where we monitor the aspect of folli-cles that interest us here in the *Medulla*.'

He pointed to the first screen. 'That's where we measure rogue hair growths. We check for unwanted outcrops of hair such as those spurting from the top of the nose, the space between the eyebrows and out of the ear lobes,' he said using an elevated voice. 'We issue pluck recommendations to the brain.'

Bobby went pale.

'That monitor is for when your eye lash team loses a hair onto the eyeball. We initiate an immediate response to that; I can tell you. A detached hair on the eye is not desired at all!'

Bobby felt faint.

'You look faint,' Percival observed.

'Sorry,' Bobby responded. He didn't feel well. Perhaps being a Follicle Farmer wasn't all that he'd believed it to be. He missed feel-ing proud and feeling united by the unity of all the Follicle Farmers, their union and the fraternity of brothers that grew hair. His brain was rambling as he tried to make sense of all that had been happening to him. He'd learned a great deal and he decided that he didn't want to know Percival's version of reality. He wanted George's version. He wanted to feel important to the body.

Here in the *Medulla*, the only things about hair that they cared about, was what to do with rogue hair growth and hair loss into the eye.

Bobby sighed.

'So, you see Bobby. I'm not going to approve your promotion. Follicle production doesn't need a Quality Assurance Manager. You can go back to growing hair in the beard region if you like,' he said uncaring.

Bobby felt deeply saddened.

William, Percival's Executive Assistant approached them with an electronic note pad. He handed it to his boss who read it. Percival went pale.

He turned to Bobby and in a gentle voice explained. 'I may have been a bit hasty in my decision. It seems that you're to report to my boss deeper within the brain so he can congratulate you on your advancement to Quality Assurance Manager. Also, the Marketing Department have prepared a ceremony to celebrate your promotion and they are presenting you with an "Advancement in scientific achievement' award".' He stared at Bobby. 'William will show you the way.'

Percival then turned and walked toward his cubical.

8

William looked at Bobby. Bobby noted that his smile was absent from his eyes. He was experiencing that a lot of lately.

'Please, follow me,' he instructed Bobby in a deep semi-hushed tone.

William turned without Bobby's acknowledgement and walked purposefully to the side of the room. Bobby followed. They were passing the green coloured area and Bobby noted that it was the section that handled messages to and from the respiratory system. Everything seemed calm and relaxed in this department and workers and supervisors were taking meal breaks, talking in hushed voices, whilst keeping an eye on the monitors. Bobby assumed that their man's body was resting.

Where it seemed that there wasn't an opening, William turned and stepped through one. An almost invisible opening was there for all to use when you knew about it. That too was happening a lot.

William led Bobby deeper into the brain. He was grateful that William knew the way as he was totally lost and disorientated. Working near the epidermis you experienced a pinkish red glow, and you always knew where you were in relation to the outer skin. Here, deeper within the body you had to rely on the light that emanated from the walls of the passage.

He was just about to ask William about it when he abruptly stopped. Bobby almost bumped into him. He mumbled an apology which William ignored. He had been plodding along behind him in a semi-autonomous obedient numbness, lost in confused thought about the speed of all the events that were occurring to him. They were out of his control, and well beyond his imagination.

William smiled. 'Go through into there. Jeremiah is expecting you,' William said pointing to a wall. Bobby looked and assumed there must be another invisible opening. He wished he could figure them out.

Bobby turned to thank William, but he was gone.

Lacking confidence, he studied the wall that he had to pass through. He was just a humble Follicle Farmer, who until recently was in charge of growing one hair on the left side of the face. He was about to meet his boss's, boss's, boss's, boss's, boss's boss.

Suddenly, a face appeared through a gap in the wall. 'Bobby?' It asked. 'I'm Jeremiah. I've heard a lot about you, and I've been very much looking forward to our meeting. Please come in.' His eyes were smiling in conjunction with his mouth. Bobby felt relieved and walked happily towards the face.

Bobby followed Jeremiah into his... work area? Bobby couldn't tell. The floor was littered with soft colourful bags that looked comfortable to rest on. There weren't any monitors or computers or even technicians. It wasn't a place of activity. Was this the main room, the Head Office, the famed *Grey-Matter*? It looks more like a place to relax than the central decision-making room of a massive and complex organisation.

'It must look a bit informal to you Bobby. I hope you weren't expecting anything too grand?' Jeremiah asked him almost laughing.

Bobby said nothing.

'This is my office where I meet with other Mind Managers,' Jeremiah explained.

Bobby took a deep breath. 'What does the mind actually do?' he asked hoping not to sound impertinent.

'What do you think we do?' Jeremiah was curious.

Jeremiah indicated that they should sit, and they both did so. The bag took on Bobby's shape and he was instantly comfortable.

'Gather information, talk about problems, make decisions and issue directives...,' Bobby answered hopefully.

'It's more than that...,' Jeremiah explained patiently. 'The official textbook version goes like this, **"the mind actively processes the flow of information, through elementary drives and complex motives to set out important information about reality. It relates bits of information, synthesises them to construct plans and programmes of behaviour. These are expressed by vocalising thoughts or by transmission of these thoughts into action throughout the body"**.'

'Wow,' Bobby was impressed. At least he thought it sounded impressive. He wished he knew what it meant.

Jeremiah continued to explain. 'At least that's the official answer.' He smiled. 'It sounds more complex than what it is, but when you break it down, you see, really quite simple.'

Bobby nodded, trying to seem as if he was achieving a level of understanding that suited the circumstances.

'It starts with **'Actively processing the flow of information.'** He smiled again. 'That is only true when information has a perceived value or a perceived threat. I assure you we are constantly experiencing information overload and so we have devised filters or tests. We try to actively block the flow of information unless it passes those tests. If it doesn't then we generally dismiss it.'

'Tests?' Bobby queried.

'The first test is that we ask all the managers within the mind is, "do you have any interest or perceive a benefit?" The second test is we ask, "is there any angst or any perceived threats?" The third test, "is there any possibility that this information may have some value, or threat, in the future?"' Jeremiah sighed. 'Sadly, most managers respond slowly and often benefits are missed, threats often get through and information that may have had some future benefit becomes forgotten or misfiled.' Jeremiah smiled. 'We're simply not as efficient as we'd like to think we are.' He laughed. 'Although if you believed any of the propaganda the Marketing Department issued, you'd think us infallible.' He laughed again.

'We all look up to you,' Bobby informed Jeremiah.

'Of course you do!' Jeremiah seemed pleased. 'That's what we're here for. Instill confidence and lead by example.' Jeremiah was smiling again. He smiled often, Bobby observed. He seemed genuinely happy.

Bobby said nothing. He sat still and smiled.

Jeremiah continued with his explanation. 'The next part is **'through elementary drives.'** that just means all of the mind managers get asked those three questions...'

'How many managers are there?' Bobby queried.

'I have no idea. Someone tried to count them once. We even discussed doing a census, but if we did do one, I never got to see the results. It seems that we're forever getting new ones and the older ones don't seem to retire, they just reduce their efficiency.' Jeremiah looked at Bobby without expression as if lost in a deep thought. He burst into a smile once again. 'I'm sure there are more than two hundred, but I think it is less than five hundred.' He informed Bobby.

'Mind Managers?' Bobby queried.

'That's right,' Jeremiah confirmed looking pleased with his assessment. 'There are two types, voting and non-voting.'

'Oh,' Bobby acknowledged. He had hoped that the mind was better organised and he now felt somewhat disappointed.

'Say, a friend takes our man fishing for the first time, and despite our initial misgivings, we realise that we actually like doing it.' Jeremiah was trying to counter the disappointed look on his new friend's face.

Bobby looked thoughtful. He had no idea what fishing was but grasped the fundamentals of the explanation.

'This new experience creates a whole new department within the mind that becomes responsible for current and the future planning of fishing expeditions. It builds a data base of experiences, constructs tests one, two, and three, that are specifically fishing related. A new mind manager position is created to manage that department and speak about it knowledgeably. A whole infrastructure is put together so that fishing is learned in terms of the types of fish, the regulations about catching them, where they are, what equipment is needed and of course what to do with the catch. That manager also liaises with other relevant managers.' Jeremiah looked at Bobby to see if he was keeping up.

'Do we...,' He looked about indicating the collective we. '...like fishing?'

'No we don't. We tried it once and we overwhelmingly felt sorry for the fish!' Jeremiah paused as if in thought. 'The point I'm making is that is how a new mind manager is created. Even if we did like fishing but stopped doing it, that manager, and his department would go on to exist, forever.'

'Forever?' Bobby was puzzled.

'Until death do us part,' Jeremiah explained.

Bobby knew about death and thought he understood what Jeremiah was saying. 'Do you mean *Apoptosis*?'

'No, I mean overall bodily death. Once created, we have a job for life.' Jeremiah smiled.

Jeremiah next returned to explaining the brains primary function. 'The next part is **'complex motives to set out important information about reality.'** He took a deep breath. 'You see, much of what we do here is deciding what is real, and what level of importance should be attributed to it. We can spend a great deal of time learning, discussing and evaluating fiction simply because of the pleasure it gives us. We need to constantly remind ourselves that it is entertainment, and not at all real. This is truly an important aspect of the brain's activities and we do seem to spend a great deal of time pondering over it.'

Bobby was about to ask another question but Jeremiah dismissed him with a hand gesture.

'I know it seems silly to spend time treating fiction as if it was real, but you could say the same about dream interpretation and prolonged fantasies.' Jeremiah paused. 'It is perhaps true that fiction is more satisfying than reality.' Jeremiah looked at Bobby and sighed. 'It's perhaps not the reality that you, a simple *Mitochondria* from the follicle growing team, would like to hear that when learning about the mind, but there it is.' He sighed again.

Bobby had forgotten his question and they were both quiet for a moment.

Jeremiah spoke. 'The next part of the official explanation of mind activity is **'It relates bits of information, synthesises them to construct plans and programmes of behaviour.'** Jeremiah paused in deep reflection. 'This is only partially true, you see for most of the time when we talk or debate about the thing for so long that the opportunity is often lost or wasted.' He looked glum.

Bobby looked disappointed.

'Is procrastinating something you do?' Jeremiah asked rhetorically. 'Are you actually doing something when you avoid doing?' He drew in a long breath. 'I'll have to get our philosophy team onto that one,' he chuckled.

'Our human body seems to be doing a lot of things,' Bobby offered.

'Yes,' he agreed. 'Particularly Percival's part of the brain does many, many things. Truly remarkable, but here within the White and Grey-Matter we seem to spend a lot of time avoiding doing things.' Jeremiah sighed again.

'I thought it was all Grey-Matter?' Bobby queried.

'That's a common misconception. As a guide, the closer you are to the centre of the brain, the whiter the matter.' He answered matter of factually. 'However, when we do decide to do something, we construct plans and alter our behaviour. The stronger the commitment and the more managers that are involved, the more expedient the progress and we sometimes we achieve an optimum result. We do love a great idea, especially when we came up with it all by ourselves,' He smiled triumphantly.

'I see,' Bobby acknowledged.

'Or, if we're sufficiently motivated,' Jeremiah added.

Bobby nodded his head in understanding.

'Or, if the consequences of not doing it put us at immediate risk,' Jeremiah said as an afterthought.

Bobby said nothing.

'We can be motivated,' Jeremiah concluded.

'The same applies to Follicle Farmers,' Bobby observed.

'The last part is relatively easy,' Jeremiah went on explaining. **'These are expressed by vocalising thoughts or by transmission of these thoughts into action throughout the body.'**

'Why vocalising? Bobby wanted to know.

'You see Bobby, humans are social beings. We typically enjoy the company of other humans and given the choice we like to work with them in a team environment. We like to make plans, share goals by voicing them with other like-minded people,' Jeremiah explained.

'Oh,' Bobby said.

He continued 'We next set about achieving them as a team, drawing on the skills and experiences that they have, contributing our own, which in turn is benefiting everyone.'

'It really does sound a lot like how Follicle Farmers think and work. Except that we have supervisors.' Bobby felt good being able to contribute more to the conversation.

'Oh, humans have supervisors and managers too. How we fit into that structure is often talked about here in the mind. Some managers feel that too much of what we do, is to please others, and not enough about what pleases us. However, the majority view is that what we're currently doing is what is ultimately what is best for all of us under the current circumstances. It's an ongoing discussion.'

'Why not just go it alone?' Bobby asked. 'Why bother with other humans?'

'Bobby, we prefer to work in a group. We exchange our thinking power and physical energy for media of exchange that allow us to procure the items that we need, and want, in order to live the life that we as an intelligent human expect to achieve. As an individual, it would be more difficult for us to gather enough resources to live a completely satisfying independent life. As a Management Team we discuss this a great deal,' Jeremiah explained patiently.

Bobby felt that the Mind Management Team did a lot of talking and not a lot of deciding. He was now sorry that he was invited to meet Jeremiah. It seemed that the mind lacked focus and a proper management structure.

'Our mind is much like a democracy without political factions. Certainly, we have cliques, but when we vote, it's an individual's vote, and each manager is entitled to express an opinion before the decision is made.' Jeremiah clearly enjoyed this topic. He continued after a laugh. 'Often they continue to express their dissension after the decision is made, and if ultimately they're proven to be right, then there is much soul kicking and "I told you so" and "I knew it." He laughed again as if being wrong was funny.

Jeremiah speculated murmuring to himself. 'Maybe, we're more like a commune...?'

Bobby didn't comment. Follicle Farmers didn't like democracies. They preferred the benefits of a benevolent hierarchy.

After a deep breath Jeremiah continued. 'A clique, in case you didn't know, is a group of like-minded people that share values and ideas. In our case the leisure focused managers form a persuasive group who have exaggerated influence over the others.' Jeremiah continued explaining but slowly became aware that Bobby had stopped responding or asking questions.

Bobby appreciated the fact that Follicle Farmers knew their place, their role and were generally praised for their efforts. If visiting here was part of his reward, he wasn't impressed.

They were both quiet for many moments and Bobby became more aware that he was uncertain of what to say or do.

'What did you think of the *Medulla Oblongata*?' Jeremiah asked seemingly at random.

Bobby responded thoughtfully. 'It was both frantic with activity but also demure at the same time.'

Jeremiah smiled once more. 'That is a reasonable summary,' he agreed. 'Percival keeps his team well trained and highly disciplined.'

'I was a little disappointed that the follicle growing functions occupy such a small amount of consideration given the importance placed on it by the marketing department,' Bobby added trying to sound important.

'Percival is a busy man. He has to distribute resources to where he feels it is required in relation to the overall needs of the body,' Jeremiah offered by way of an explanation.

'Percival said you're his boss. Does he report to you personally?' Bobby queried.

'He reports to this part of the mind and therefore we are his boss, yes,' Jeremiah answered. 'But no one manager is anyone's boss. We're a harmonious community and we seek to maximise desirable outcomes and minimise undesirable outcomes,' Jeremiah sighed once more.

'But Percival sends you communications concerning the body?' Bobby challenged.

'You have no idea,' Jeremiah sighed again.

Bobby wondered if perhaps Jeremiah was getting tired and needed a rest. He thought that he had better leave, but he had no idea how to get to marketing from here.

'We do get some messages about exfoliation and epilation.'

Bobby winced.

'You may well wince, Bobby. Sometimes I think if Percival had his way, the majority of the hair follicles on our body would be subjected to electrolysis,' Jeremiah said dryly.

Bobby felt a tear form in his eye. Jeremiah continued. 'Percival messages us about many bodily functions. We receive constant updates about respiration and perspiration. We get bombarded with requests for urination, defecation and ejaculation.'

'Ejaculation?' Bobby hadn't heard of that one.

'You know, from the groin..., err sex,' Jeremiah tried to explain. 'It does help counter hormone imbalances. If there isn't a willing female human with which to..., you know..., then he..., err, Percival wants us to perform masturbation.'

'Oh.' Bobby hadn't heard about a mass debate. Bobby was confused about how a group discussion could solve a hormone imbalance.

'Percival is persistent and often annoying, but we do listen. Sometimes his timing is off and his need for our body to perform ablutions is horribly inconvenient. It's not like we can perform these activities in public. We need to find the appropriate location and vessel with which to receive our purges. That may be easy to achieve when we're in a familiar environment, but when we're out and about; we can't always easily locate a receiving facility expediently. I can tell you it does cause some consternation between the *medulla* and the mind!' Jeremiah hoped Bobby understood as he didn't desire him going further into the explanation.

Bobby said nothing so Jeremiah continued. 'Did you know that Percival is responsible for issuing *endorphins* and *encephalin*?'

Bobby shook his head. 'So, when do you meet as a group, the Mind Managers I mean?' Bobby asked wanting to change the subject.

'Rarely,' Jeremiah answered. 'It's just too hard to co-ordinate as we're all so terribly busy, gathering, disseminating, examining, identifying, adjudicating and allocating within our areas of expertise that we agreed it improbable that we'd ever be together at the same place at the same time.' Jeremiah paused.

After a moment he continued. 'We communicate constantly via a specialised network that is both chemical and electrified which is called *neuron transmitters*.' Jeremiah moved forward and went to a wall and depressed an invisible switch.

The wall became transparent, and Bobby saw a lightening show that both amazed and dazzled him. He was stunned and he realised he was privileged to see these pulsing lights flashing through the brain.

'How many...?' Bobby started to ask.

'At any one time approximately 300,000 light impulses carrying information to over one hundred billion brain cells. It depends on what we're thinking about and how urgent the decisions are.' Jeremiah smiled. 'But don't let these statistics impress you, we often get it wrong.'

Jeremiah pressed the wall again and it changed back to its non-transparent state.

'Bobby, I don't want to seem ungrateful to you. It was nice of you to come to visit, but you must realise that I'm very busy and that we'll need to terminate this meeting soon.' Jeremiah wasn't smiling.

Bobby was confused. He was told that he was here at the bequest of the mind. He didn't want to impose and was happy to leave this place as soon as Jeremiah dismissed him. Bobby then decided to take the initiative. 'Jeremiah, I want to say how grateful I am that you were able to spend the time explaining about what happens here.'

'Nonsense young man. I've enjoyed your company. It was a pleasure.' Jeremiah smiled again.

'I especially appreciate you explaining it to me in terms which I, a humble Follicle Farmer, could understand.' Bobby returned the smile.

'You may be humble, but I know you're a clever Follicle Farmer. That work you did with the *stromal vascular fractions* was very impressive. Who else but you would have thought of stimulating the fat cells to release *mesenchymal* in that fashion?' he said grinning.

Bobby understood that it was a compliment but didn't really understand what Jeremiah was talking about. He smiled and nodded his head in appreciation.

'Er, how do I...?' Bobby started to ask indicating that he sought a direction to travel. 'Leave here?' Bobby asked hopefully.

'Oh, I'm supposed to send a signal to the Marketing Department when you're ready.' He typed something into a palm device sending the message. 'Apparently they have organised a photo shoot and some press coverage of your promotion which will be followed up with an award ceremony.' Jeremiah looked up at him. 'I'm sorry I won't be attending, but I have quite a bit of work to catch up on, you do understand?' Jeremiah looked at him expectantly.

'Of course, sir. Thank you again for having me.'

'Nonsense young man. I enjoyed your company, and it was a sincere pleasure.' Jeremiah smiled again.

Just then, a very tall, youngish, and ruggedly handsome looking *Mitochondria* walked into the room. He extended a hand to Bobby who took it, and they shook hands in friendly greeting. 'Greetings, Bobby. My name is Roscoe and I'm from the Head Office Marketing Department.'

'Glad to meet you, Roscoe.' Bobby returned the smile.

'If you've finished, sir, I'll take Bobby with me,' Roscoe confirmed with Jeremiah.

Jeremiah held up a hand in a single wave and turned, now focused on his palm device.

'Follow me Bobby; I hope you have your appetite as we've put together quite a banquet for you,' Roscoe explained as they left the room via another hidden exit.

Bobby realised he was very hungry and that he hadn't eaten since leaving the *medulla*.

'We've also managed to arrange some surprise guests for you at the reception,' Roscoe explained with a smile and an over exaggerated wink.

Bobby wondered who they could be.

9

Bobby observed that this passage was broader than most. He also noticed that it felt warmer than normal as he could feel heat radiating from the walls. He wanted to ask Roscoe what it meant.

Roscoe seemed to be aware of Bobby's confusion and probable interest. 'We're very close to the BBB, the *"brain blood barrier,"* Bobby,' he explained as they walked.

'The wha...?' Bobby confirmed his confusion. He was also struggling to keep up with Roscoe's long strides.

'The BBB is where the brain protected from potentially harmful substances. The brain uses up a lot of blood. It needs huge amounts of oxygen and glucose to keep it functioning. But it doesn't like harmful pathogens and some of the other rubbish that finds its way into the blood,' Roscoe explained. 'The BBB workers are a border control unit. They check the suitability of everything that the *cardiovascular* system sends its way. It's also why it is warmer here. All that activity generates a lot of heat and we're a long way from the skin.'

Bobby said nothing. He was reminded that he was a long way from his old home.

'You do understand that brain security has to be very rigorous?' He asked without expecting an answer.

'Of course,' Bobby agreed nodding.

Roscoe continued. 'Perhaps we need an additional *Liver* here in the brain to clean the blood before it is allowed to enter into the brain,' Roscoe laughed. 'What we have here is what marketing would call 'A design fault." He laughed some more.

Bobby had never considered the body as having design faults before. *Mitochondria* have faults but not the body.

'Anyway the BBB is managed by the *Astrocyte's* who look after the *Capillaries* that control the flow of blood into the brain.' Roscoe was nodding his head to Bobby to illicit an understanding response.

Bobby nodded his head in reply.

'Interestingly, the *Astrocytes* are star shaped so when they call them the stars of this place, they are being quite literal.' He smiled broadly at the little in-house joke.

Bobby returned the smile.

'Because it gets warmer here, than in other parts of the brain, we get priority on food and refreshments.' Roscoe continued smiling as he explained as they walked expediently through the lengthy passage. 'Rubbish removal is also very efficient.'

Bobby was about to say something when Roscoe stopped abruptly. He turned and walked through another seemingly invisible door.

Bobby followed and found himself in a wide, very large, comfortable looking room. It was well appointed with soft furnishings, replenishment stations and it had a wide array of technologies. It was similar to the *medulla* but it was much more like a place to relax. Workers and their supervisors observed him as he followed Roscoe deeper into the room, but they didn't stop talking. He heard laughter, but he didn't feel it was directed at him.

Roscoe slumped into a soft bag and stretched out to reach a glucose protein pack. He indicated to Bobby to do the same and Bobby hungrily accepted. As they relaxed and ate, Bobby continued looking about the room. He saw that there were standard monitors detailing various functions of human activity. They were also measuring *endorphin* levels and some other things that Bobby didn't recognise.

Presently, two other *Mitochondria* joined them. They were equally tall and ruggedly handsome and Bobby wondered if that was part of the marketing department's selection criteria. They stood when Roscoe did the introductions. 'This is Roderick and this is Ralph.' They in turn shook hands with Bobby.

Roscoe explained. 'Roderick is the Senior Manager in charge of Marketing. Ralph is the Marketing Manager for External Affairs and I'm the Marketing Manager for Internal Affairs. You are in the presence of some much esteemed company, Bobby.' Roscoe was smiling as was Roderick and Ralph.

Bobby returned the smile, bowed and spoke cordially and carefully. 'I am very pleased to meet you all. I'm a little overwhelmed at the opportunities being offered to me as I'm experiencing events that were previously beyond my conception.'

'Well said.' Roderick was the senior and spoke for the three. 'Bob, we're very pleased to have you here.'

'Thank you, Rod,' Bobby responded.

'It's Roderick.' He was smiling but the annoyance of having his name shortened was obvious on his face.

'And I'm Bobby, not Bob!' Bobby countered determinedly.

'We thought you might consider a name change,' Roscoe said hopefully. 'Bobby sounds a little... juvenile, don't you think?' He asked.

'No,' Bobby told him flatly.

'Bobby it is,' Roderick capitulated for them. He wasn't smiling. Roderick indicated that the four of them should sit down and they did so.

Bobby was relieved that he didn't have to fight them about his own name. The gall of it all left him with a bitter feeling.

'Bobby was once the ambam,' Roderick explained to his colleagues.

They smirked.

'Explain what that is please, Bobby,' he asked in mocking tones.

'It's actually A.M.B.R.M. Area Manager Beard Region Moustache,' Bobby corrected dryly.

'Did you know that the follicle department is the only department that uses those abbreviated titles?' Roscoe asked Bobby.

Bobby wasn't aware of that, so he said nothing.

'What are you to be called now that you're the QA Manager?' Ralph asked expectantly.

Bobby wasn't sure as this hadn't been discussed with him. 'Quality Assurance Follicles.' He speculated.

'Q.A.F. Qaf!' Ralph abbreviated. He then did a mock announcement. 'We have an emergency on hair 9-9-9. Quick! Call the Qaf!' he teased.

The others burst into raucous laughter.

Bobby wasn't enjoying this.

'Tell us, Bobby...,' Roderick had started to ask a question but paused for dramatic effect. He looked at the other two. 'What is the Follicle Farmer's motto?'

Without thinking Bobby replied. 'If we don't grow, we don't grow.'

They again burst into laughter. After they settled, Roderick asked. 'What does that actually mean?' He shook his head in mock bewilderment.

Bobby felt a bit embarrassed. He'd worked among Follicle Farmers all his life and he'd never had to explain the motto before. It was their motto and they'd just lived and worked by it. 'Well...,' he hesitated.

They laughed some more.

Trying not to be put off, he stated boldly. 'To us it means we are united! We're a team! We're proud, and we have a tradition of growing hair together! We have a common bond and a common purpose!'

They looked at him blankly.

Bobby added calmly. 'Growing follicles is what grows us as a team.' He felt like adding "so there" but refrained.

Roscoe looked over his shoulder and summoned one of the Senior Supervisors over to where they were seated. He hastily joined them, but he didn't sit down.

'Bobby, this is Ronny,' Roderick explained. 'He'll orientate you whilst we complete the final touches to the promotion ceremony. Next you'll formally receive your award.'

Bobby stood up and shook the man's hand. 'Hello, Ronny.' Ronny returned the handshake but looked both surprised and pleased. His smile seemed very genuine.

Roderick, Ralph, and Roscoe all got up. Without another word, they left Bobby standing there with Ronny.

Ronny smiled cautiously. 'Congratulations,' he gushed. 'It's not often that we get someone from the Follicle Farmers System for a promotion ceremony as well as an award.' His words seemed sincere, and he was clearly in admiration of Bobby.

Bobby thanked him with a slight bow. 'Follicle production is part of the *Integumentary* system,' Bobby explained.

'I didn't know that,' Ronny acknowledged. 'Thanks.'

'Anytime,' Bobby responded. He liked this one.

'I was told to give you a quick overview of what we do here and then to prepare you for the ceremony,' Ronny explained.

'What do we have to do to prepare?' Bobby queried.

'There's speech preparation, which we'll take care of, a photo shoot and you'll contribute to the press release,' Ronny explained.

'Why are we doing all of this?' Bobby was confused. 'I'm just one humble *mitochondria* doing his job.'

Ronny explained. 'We know that there are a lot of promotions that happen in the various systems throughout the body. Mostly they go unacknowledged by us. They're making a big deal out of you because it's a promotion and an award. We need to boost morale.'

Bobby nodded in understanding.

Ronny continued. 'They feel that in your case, we have the opportunity to capitalise on the positive effect that your advancement has on your career. You're now a role model to the broader community, and we're going to publicise that.'

It all sounded a bit scripted to Bobby, but he still didn't comment.

Ronny started to explain further. 'Your System Manager..., I'm sorry, I forgot his name?'

'George,' Bobby offered.

'George is very keen for us to make your advancement to Quality Assurance Manager for Follicle Production a big deal. So is Jeremiah,' Ronny informed him.

'Percival didn't think so.' Bobby remembered his experience in the *medulla*.

'Percival doesn't get a vote, despite being the manager that George reports to.' Ronny was smiling at the irony. 'Roderick does get a vote because he's the Marketing Manager and he is the department's representative to the mind.' He smiled.

'What about Roscoe?' Bobby queried.

'I've never seen Roscoe so excited. He was happily advocating this wonderful opportunity. He insisted on escorting you here personally. He wanted to make sure you were safe and that you felt good about what was happening.'

'Oh,' Bobby said.

'He's the Marketing Manager for Internal Affairs, so a big promotion and a significant award is a public relations bonanza for him. He'll use it to boost internal morale. That's how he gets measured, by the way,' Ronny explained.

'You seem to know a lot about this,' Bobby observed.

'I'm Roderick's Executive Assistant,' Ronny explained. 'I hear things. Lots of things.'

'I have an EA... somewhere.' Bobby suddenly pondered Banjo's fate.

'Oh, he's here already. They've been interviewing him and he's been very helpful, filling in some of the information gaps we had about what happened in the moustache.'

'Oh,' Bobby said.

'Ralph was so pleased when you were able to get the moustache growing properly. Of course we didn't know that that was your doing at the time, but it was Ralph's idea to grow the moustache and the goatee. He was furious when it wasn't growing the way he expected it to,' Ronny explained.

'I thought the Follicle Farmers had their own Marketing Manager?' Bobby queried.

'You do, but it's very minor now.' He paused. 'Cut-backs,' he added by way of an explanation. '*Mitochondria* morale is part of Roscoe's responsibilities. External appearances are all up to Ralph. He was sure glad you sorted out the moustache.'

'It was a frustrating time for all of us in moustache growth,' Bobby agreed.

'And, it was you who fixed it!' Ronny complimented Bobby on his success.

'Only temporarily.' Bobby was saddened by the memory of the announcement to shave to the moustache.

'Banjo has told us all about it,' Ronny explained. 'We're on our way to see him.'

'That's great.' Bobby was both relieved and happy that he'd be seeing his young friend again. During their time in the moustache he'd become quite fond of him and he appreciated his assistant's loyalty and efforts.

Ronny led Bobby through the various work stations in the marketing department. He pointed out some more interesting functions being undertaken as they wound their way to the media room.

'This group of people are monitoring external inputs,' Ronny explained. 'They have live feeds from the senses and they filter out what isn't important. Only if they see an opportunity will they inform Ralph.'

'Senses?' Bobby was puzzled.

'Mostly we deal with audio and visual, but we get continuous feeds from olfactory, gustatory and of course the epidermis,' Ronny explained as if it should be common knowledge.

Bobby said nothing.

'Ralph has developed a large number of rapid responses, should the stimulus from the live feeds prove interesting. They have become second nature and are almost instinctive.'

Bobby wanted to know more, but Ronny was already explaining another unit's function.

'Here they monitor achievements verses expectations. When the mind decides on an activity, it has to work out how to do that activity successfully. Thankfully, that's not our problem. We measure the actual success against the expectation. If it works out better than expected, we capitalise on it. If it meets expectations, we simply file the experience and give it little further regard. If we achieve below expectations we then go into damage control,' Ronny explained.

'Do you have to go into damage control often?' Bobby queried.

'More than you'd realise.' Ronny was sullen.

'Why, what happens?' Bobby urged.

'It often results in sadness. Disappointments can be countered by resilience measures, but not always. That's especially true if there is an oversupply of hormones involve,' Ronny continued.

Bobby only understood part of what Ronny was trying to explain. He figured that local knowledge was a powerful thing and that you had to work here to properly understand it all.

'This team researches ideas on what will improve overall morale. They study everything from relaxation techniques to self-improvement and even entertainment options. They make recommendations and sometimes put together a proposal for Roderick to make a formal presentation to a Mind Committee.' Ronny was smiling, remembering some of his boss's successes.

'Do they listen?' Bobby queried.

'Yes, they do,' Ronny answered. 'As a Marketing Manager, Roderick has considerable influence on the mind's overall decision making.'

Bobby believed him.

Ronny stopped. He had a very serious look on his face. 'The reality is that we have fears, inadequacies, self-doubts and insecurities. We don't like admitting to them externally and we're often reluctant to admit them to ourselves.'

'I have fears and doubts also,' Bobby countered.

'But here we deal with that on a whole of body and mind level. We have to be honest to ourselves and when you do that during a self-appraisal journey; we often learn things about ourselves that we didn't want to know... or want to have to deal with.' Ronny was very serious.

Bobby didn't know what to say.

Ronny continued. 'A lot of mainstream *Mitochondria* feel that we in the marketing department are just a bunch of happy go lucky, entertainment chasing, feel good junkies.'

'How would you know what *Mitochondria* think?' Bobby questioned.

'We do a lot of surveys,' Ronny answered.

'Oh,' Bobby responded.

'The more we learn about our unique personal traits and characteristics, the more insight we'll have when dealing with others, when dealing with ourselves, and especially when dealing with unusual or unknown situations,' Ronny declared. 'We try to get it right. But it isn't easy.'

Bobby didn't comment. Ronny turned and they continued the rest of the way to the media room in silence.

They first arrived at a rest station. There were comfortable bags to rest on and there was a table filled with colourful protein shakes, glucose in interesting shapes and amino acids. Bobby stared at them in wonder.

'The Marketing Departments R and D team put these together,' Ronny explained. 'Help yourself. They'd love to hear what you think of them.'

Bobby picked them up and studied them. He was interrupted by a familiar voice.

'Hi Boss. Long-time no see,' Banjo said by way of a friendly greeting.

Bobby turned toward his friend's voice. 'Banjo!' He hadn't quite realised just how much he'd missed Banjo until that moment. 'It's so good to see you. Where have you been?'

'Why don't you two to catch up with your news while I'll go see if the media room is ready,' Ronny informed them.

'They are,' Banjo confirmed. 'They have been waiting for both of you.'

Ronny left them standing before each other. They smiled and they simultaneously embraced. They pulled away from each other and studied each other.

Bobby spoke first. 'Have they treated you well?'

Banjo smiled. He was pleased that his boss was concerned for his welfare. 'Yes,' he responded. 'Here, in this place, I've been answering a lot of questions, but in the QA department, I just had to do a lot of listening.'

Bobby sat on one of the seating bags and indicated that Banjo should do the same.

After they were comfortable, Bobby invited Banjo to continue. 'Go on.'

'Here, it's all been about our lives as Follicle Farmers, your promotion to the moustache, some of the difficulties that we encountered and how we overcame them,' Banjo explained. 'They do have some questions for you, but to be candid, I don't think they really care all that much,' he added in a hushed voice.

'How so?' Bobby queried.

'Our solving moustache growing problems was news worthy for internal morale. But this place is mostly about external marketing, not internal,' Banjo explained.

'Have you met Roscoe?' Bobby wanted to know.

'Nice guy, but Roderick and Ralph have most of the power. Those two have a huge mandate to make decisions that influence mind judgements.' Banjo leaned closer to his boss and whispered. 'It seems their biggest fear is being embarrassed.'

'Oh,' Bobby nodded in understanding. He could relate to that.

Banjo continued to whisper. 'They'll say almost anything to avoid it. Or they'll avoid doing things to avoid it.'

Bobby moved backward into his bag and pondered. 'This place freaks me out,' he confided to Banjo whispering.

'Me too,' Banjo agreed continuing in a hushed voice.

'Tell me about the Q.A,' Bobby invited Banjo in a return to normal voice levels. They looked about the room and were relieved to see that everyone was ignoring them.

Just then, Ronny returned. He motioned them to get up and they did so. Ronny turned and they followed him as he led the way into the media room.

'This is Richard,' he introduced the tall, ruggedly handsome, *mitochondria* that had an electronic tablet in his hands. 'He'll be doing the interview.'

Richard extended his hand in greeting. Bobby returned the hand-shake. Richard and Banjo nodded to each other. They had met previously during Banjo's interview.

'I only have a few questions, Bobby,' Richard informed him. 'I already have the specific details from George's department and Banjo has filled in most of the gaps.'

'What would you like to know?' Bobby queried.

'How did you feel when you were appointed to Area Manager of the moustache?'

'I really don't remember,' Bobby pondered. 'I guess I felt bad that the moustache wasn't going well and when I was given the opportunity to fix it I felt relieved, but also excited.'

'Okay, so how did you feel when you perfected the moustache, and they told you it was going to be shaved off?'

'I was initially angry. The team had gone through a lot to get the moustache colour and length perfected. I added some of my own special chemicals to assist in this and well... we achieved it! We were celebratory… and then we're told it was all for nothing,' Bobby explained.

'You were quite rightly indignant,' Richard agreed. 'We feel the same way when similar things happen here.' He smiled halfheartedly.

'So I offered a deal to my bosses. I'd tell them about my secret chemicals, if they'd agree to keep the moustache,' Bobby continued with his explanation of what had happened.

'How did that work out for you?' Richard asked as he started to type onto the tablet.

Bobby hesitated, not wanting to interrupt the typing as he spoke.

Richard looked up at Bobby. 'Don't worry about me. I can listen, talk and type simultaneously.' He laughed. 'I've been doing this job all my life and I'm very experienced.'

Bobby took a deep breath. 'It didn't. The orders for the moustache removal came from this department. It had nothing to do with the Follicle Team or the *Integumentary* System. I was trying to influence the wrong people.' Bobby laughed at the irony as he was recounting it all.

Bobby continued. 'The next thing we knew we were collected by my boss, Steve and sent on a summons issued by our System Manager.' Bobby laughed. 'It all happened very fast, didn't it Banjo?'

'It certainly did. I was worried we were in deep trouble for being insolent, but as it transpired, we ended up being congratulated.' Banjo was smiling broadly.

'Just one more question,' Richard told them. 'Is there anything that worries you?' He asked.

'Electrolysis.' Bobby had answered with a smile. It was an in-house joke which he didn't expect Richard to understand.

'Seriously,' he responded dryly.

'I.P.L' Bobby looked at Richard nodding his head in affirmation. 'Even the thought of tweezers upset me,' he added.

Richard typed.

'Excellent,' Richard informed them. He turned to Ronny. 'That's all I need.' Then he said to Bobby and Banjo. 'Thanks chaps. Congrats on the promotion and your award, Bobby. I hope you both have a wonderful time in your new roles.'

Ronny motioned the two to follow him and they entered a room that was set up as a photographic studio. It had bright lights reflecting off shiny screens that gave the room and evenness about the light. There were no shadows. The operator didn't introduce himself and Ronny didn't offer to. He indicated that Bobby and Banjo should step onto a marked part of the floor. He adjusted the equipment. They heard a faint click. The operator indicated they should smile, so they smiled, and they heard another click. He then indicated that they should shake hands, and so they shook hands and they heard yet another click.

Roderick, Roscoe and Ralph entered the room. They said nothing and the operator repeated the process with Bobby, Banjo and Roderick. Then he directed it to be with Bobby, Roderick, and Roscoe, then Bobby, Banjo and Roscoe and finally with all four of them. They smiled, back slapped, and shook hands all under the careful ministrations of the operator.

Ralph wasn't in any of the photos, but he was holding two certificates. He gave the first to Roderick. Roderick showed it to Bobby, and he read **'Congratulations Bobby on your appointment to Quality Assurance Manager for Follicle production at the rank of Regional Manager.'**

'Wow!' Bobby was delighted and impressed.

The operator motioned Bobby and Roderick to pose with the certificate for a photo, so they did. Click.

As Roderick handed over the certificate to Banjo for safe keeping, Ralph gave his boss the other certificate. Roderick showed it to Bobby. It read **'This science Achievement Award is presented to Bobby, Follicle Farmer within the *Integumentary* System for his contribution to the improvement of natural hair density, hair strength and hair colour.'**

Bobby and Roderick repeated the process of having their photos taken with this certificate.

When they finished, Roderick spoke. 'Congratulations Bobby. We'll be circulating these photos and a brief, but detailed, news story about your promotion and your award. What you have done is a great thing for hair growth, as well as being a great morale boost for all cells in the body.'

'You mean the Follicle Farmers News Network?' Bobby queried.

Roderick smiled. 'I mean all networks. Every news service for every system will learn of your promotion and science achievement award. You're officially a role model for all living cells in this body.' He chuckled. 'And in your case, the dead cells also.'

The dead hair joke wasn't lost on Bobby or Banjo, but they didn't respond.

Without waiting for a response, Roderick, Roscoe and Ralph filed out of the room.

Ronny spoke. 'We now have a small banquet and some special guests waiting to help you celebrate. Follow me.'

Bobby and Banjo acknowledged the operator who returned the nod. They followed Ronny into a small room and there they found, Dan, Curly and Fatso waiting for them.

The four Follicle Farmers and the one very slim fat cell began enthusiastically greeting each other. There was much laughter and back slapping and hugging. Bobby felt teary and noticed that Curly was also overwhelmed by the reunion.

Ronny announced. 'I'll leave you five to get reacquainted. I've arranged a banquet and I'll go check where the food is. I won't be long.' He turned and left the room.

Banjo hadn't met Curly or Fatso before so there were formal introductions.

'How did you three get here?' Bobby finally demanded after the ritual hellos and how are you, were dealt with.

Dan replied for the three of them. 'We were collected by one of Roscoe's assistants. He took us through some capillaries until we joined the left facial *artery*,' Dan gushed. 'What a wild ride. I'm glad we were all linked as it would have been easy to get separated and miss the *arterial* departure point into the Marketing Department's *systemic capillary*,' he explained excitedly.

'Did it take long?' Bobby wanted to know.

'Hardly. One cycle we were in the stream and the next we were exiting,' Dan replied.

'How are things on the chin?' Bobby asked Dan.

'Good,' he answered. 'It's clean shaven daily, as is the moustach,' he informed him.

'I expected it would be,' Bobby acknowledged.

'Dan is now the acting Regional Manager for the Beard,' Curly announced.

'Really! Congratulations Dan,' he said a and then paused, thinking. 'Where's Steve?' Bobby was pleased for Dan but his concern was for Steve.

'He was injured.' Dan looked down, saddened by the memory of it. 'He was in the middle of an invasion by a squad of *herpes* viruses and some Natural-Killer cells aggressively repelled them. Steve was badly wounded,' he explained and hesitated before continuing. 'They don't think he'll survive.'

'Oh.' Bobby was lost for what to say.

'How about you?' Dan asked of Bobby.

'I've been through numerous passages. The place is a maze. I've walked for ages.' Bobby was pleased the subject had changed.

'Where have you been?' Dan asked.

Bobby recounted his meeting with their System Manager, the *Medulla* Operations Manager and his meeting with Jeremiah whose title, Bobby didn't find out, but he seemed to be generally in charge of a lot of things. The four listened with avid fascination and were particularly disappointed when he explained Percival's disdain for follicles and his predicted future for Follicle Farmers.

They were quiet for a while, when it occurred to Bobby that he didn't know why Fatso was here and that he hadn't yet asked. 'Fatso, how did you get to be included in our little band of brothers?'

'After you left, they came to interview me about our relationship,' Fatso explained. 'They wanted to know how often you extracted the stem liquid stuff from me. At first, they made it sound horrible, but I told them it wasn't like that.'

'That's good. Go on,' Bobby invited.

'I explained that your interest in the stuff that came out of me was only because you were caring enough to clean me up after I leaked when you tickled me.' He then smiled at the memory of being tickled.

'I've been informed that most scientific discoveries are as a result of an accidental occurrence,' Bobby nodded in agreement.

'They did tickle me a fair bit, Bobby,' he said sadly. 'I don't think I'd have much stem stuff to leak out for you, if you need any right now,' he explained looking glum.

'Don't worry my friend. I'll hug you, I won't tickle you,' he said smiling and they embraced once more.

Bobby turned to Curly. 'How are things at my favourite follicle?' he asked.

'It couldn't be better.' Curly explained. 'Rhino is pink and healthy. He's a good operator and it wouldn't surprise me if they make him a Team Leader soon.'

'Wow!' Bobby was pleasantly surprised. 'I'm glad to hear that.' He then looked at Banjo. 'Remind me to tell you about Rhino, Banjo.' He instructed.

'Oh, I've already heard all about that legend, boss,' Banjo informed Bobby grinning happily.

Curly continued to explain. 'Shorty is doing well also. He's happy being a worker. I don't think he's that ambitious or curious about the world. He does his job, eats and rests.'

'That's fine,' Bobby agreed. 'We'll always need workers and we can't all be ambitious,' he laughed. 'There just isn't enough room at the top.'

Just then Ronny entered the room. He was pushing a trolley loaded with tasty treats, colourful protein shakes, glucose and amino acids, similar to those Bobby had seen outside the media room.

The five ate hungrily and noisily. The five friends were happy and content and Ronny had found them some bags to rest on after they had finished eating. Ronny didn't join in the meal or the revelry. He was a dutiful host and saw that his guests were happy.

Presently, the camera operator came in and he took some photos of the friends relaxing and then got them to pose for a group photo.

After he left, Ronny advised that an assistant would be there very soon to escort Dan, Curly and Fatso back to their areas.

The friends mumbled "good byes" and "good lucks" as they embraced each other.

The assistant came to fetch them and after waving farewell, the three followed him out of the room.

Ronny sat down and invited Bobby and Banjo to sit also. They did so heavily.

'Soon, you'll be escorted to the training centre to start your QA training,' Ronny informed them.

Bobby nodded his understanding and acceptance. He then asked. 'Do you like working in the Marketing Department, Ronny?'

'It's a job,' he replied without enthusiasm.

'You don't seem very pleased with it,' Bobby observed.

'Not particularly,' Ronny agreed. 'It used to be more fun in the early days. Before it was called the Marketing Department we were known as "Ego."' Ronny smiled at the memory of it.

Bobby and Banjo shared a knowing glance.

'We were much more impulsive in those days, and we worried much less about the consequences,' he continued. 'This was before Roderick became the manager,' he explained.

Bobby and Banjo said nothing and Ronny seemed to want to talk.

He continued. 'Roderick is very good at his job, but he seems more focused on damage control these days...' He paused thinking and then continued. 'Ego is about the person's self-esteem, self-worth, self-respect, their self-confidence. Now we've turned it into something that is supposed to be more practical and more socially responsible.' He paused again but then continued. 'I agree we'd profit more from a well-managed self-esteem, but sometimes I wish we were more impulsive and spent less time considering all the consequences. I don't want us to get into any trouble. I don't propose to go about breaking society's laws or becoming the bad boy. I just feel that we should worry less about what other people think and more about what makes us happy.'

Bobby didn't know how to contribute to the conversation. He looked at Banjo who replied with his customary shrug.

Ronny was on a roll and expanded his explanation. 'Roderick is all about 'If you don't like your self-image, change it,' and 'If you don't like yourself, it is absurd to expect others to like you."

Ronny sighed.

'I think if you see your life going well then it has a chance of becoming true. If you see it going badly, then that will come true,' Ronny said after a lengthy silence.

'Did you know that there is more research currently being done on self-doubt than there is on improving self-confidence?' Ronny asked Bobby and Banjo.

Bobby and Banjo shook their heads, agreeing that they didn't know.

'I agree we'd all be much happier if we learned to like ourselves and it's absurd to expect others to like us if we don't even like ourselves,' Ronny repeated.

'All of us are guilty of being all too willing to think about what is wrong with ourselves and are too reluctant to think about what is right about ourselves.' Ronny had clearly given this a lot of thought. 'Remember that,' he advised Bobby and Banjo.

That sat in silence for a moment.

Then Bobby ventured. 'I think we'd all like to feel good about ourselves and have a feeling of high self-worth.'

'Unfortunately, that only becomes true for a small percentage of us,' Ronny explained. 'Some of us are at ease with the world, so the world is at ease with us. What keeps the rest of us in our place is our own fear.'

'Test yourself,' Ronny advised them. 'Test your self-talk. You know... that conversation that you have in your head. The one you keep to yourself. Is it positive and advancing your position. Or is it negative and slowly tearing you apart?' He asked rhetorically.

Bobby was silent. He reflected on Ronny's words. Ronny was experienced. He'd worked in the Marketing Department long before it was even called the Marketing Department. Ronny seemed to know what he was talking about. Bobby decided he'd heed the advice.

Banjo looked at Bobby and shrugged. Bobby gave him a quizzical look indicating that he didn't get the silent message.

'I think Ronny may have other things to do...,' Banjo ventured.

Bobby couldn't believe his ears. How could Banjo be so ungrateful? Ronny was giving them heartfelt wisdom. Words they could learn from, and grow, and become stronger from the greater level of understanding that they... then Bobby realised that Banjo had observed that they were being scrutinised. From across the room, Roderick was staring at the three of them. Almost imperceptibly they both indicated this situation to Ronny. Ronny caught on and promptly changed the subject.

'As I was saying...,' he said in a loud voice, 'The photos will be ready for your approval before you leave.'

Ronny headed towards the media room and Bobby and Banjo dutifully followed.

'Thanks guys,' Ronny said when they were in the room and out of sight.

The operator that had taken their photos approached them. 'They came out pretty good,' he concluded as he set about laying them out on a previewing table. Bobby and Banjo saw photos of themselves with the marketing hierarchy but were puzzled by the number of others that were also in the photos. If you were to believe the photos then there were hundreds of others gathered to celebrate Bobby's promotion and award.

Their perplexed expressions said it all, so Ronny assisted. 'Photo shopped,' he explained. 'We upload the images into our computers and they…,' He indicated the operator and the others working in the room. '…edit the images so they'll appear exactly as we need them. It's done all the time,' Ronny explained.

'But… it's a bit deceitful,' Bobby admonished.

'Not really,' Ronny defended. 'Don't get me wrong, we do use a lot of borderline ethical techniques to better represent our internal and external marketing functions, but this isn't one of them.'

Bobby and Banjo looked at Ronny disbelievingly.

'It's true,' he reiterated. 'In a perfect situation, we'd have wanted this many supporters here to help celebrate your achievements, but it doesn't work like that. The logistics involved in bringing in that many *Mitochondria* and that much food into this department would make it impractical. We have to take short cuts.'

'We understand,' Bobby said and looked at Banjo who was nodding his agreement. 'We're just a couple of Follicle Farmers a long way from the hairy part of the body. There's a lot that happens here, that we don't need to understand.'

'Are you teasing?' Ronny queried cautiously.

'Nah,' Bobby slapped Banjo's shoulder and they laughed. 'Not much anyway.' They laughed again. 'I'm sure you all know what you're doing,' he concluded. Banjo nodded his head in agreement.

Ronny joined in the laughter and as it subsided, he added. 'I'm glad that you don't think worse of us,' he said seriously. 'For all the techniques we use, they're all for a good cause.'

'I'm sure they are,' Bobby acknowledged.

'When do we move on to…,' He hesitated as he thought. 'Where do we do our training?' Banjo asked.

'The body has an extensive quality assurance program,' Ronny explained. 'You'll do your training in the training centre.'

'Will someone come and show us the way?' Bobby queried.

'I'll send a message and ask them what the plan is,' Ronny assured them both.

They exited the media room and Ronny left them by the refreshment table. While Bobby and Banjo had something to eat, Ronny was at his desk typing. They assumed it was to the QA Training Department.

Banjo explained. 'I've done some initial training with the techs at the *Integumentary* System office.

'Good,' Bobby acknowledged.

Banjo continued. 'But as we've never had a QA Manager for Follicle Production before, they were embarrassed about how lacking in information they were. They know a lot about skin, but not as much about hair.'

'I'm sure we'll figure it out,' Bobby said confidently.

Ronny returned to them bearing a smile. 'They'll be here shortly,' he informed them. 'They are sending someone to escort you.'

'Great,' Bobby acknowledged. 'Thanks for all your help and in particular your valuable words of wisdom.'

'It was a pleasure,' Ronny bowed briefly. 'I will add one other thing,' he said seriously. 'You'll both face many challenges in your new roles, and sometimes you'll fail. The thing to remember is that making a mistake, or even just not knowing something, is not a true failure unless you give into it. True failure is refusing to get back up after you fall down.'

'That's deep.' Banjo looked at Bobby who agreed with a nod of his head.

'We will take your advice, my friend, and we will use it wisely,' Bobby promised. 'But, sorry to change the subject, I do have one question that will niggle at me unless I ask.'

'What is it?' Ronny was intrigued. Banjo looked on with interest as he had no idea what his boss was going to ask.

'Everyone that we have met in this department has a name starting with R.' He said more as a statement than as a question.

'We do to...,' Ronny agreed, startled at the realisation. 'Although it never occurred to me until you said it. I wonder why that is?' Ronny mused.

'I was just making an observation.' Bobby added.

'I'm curious also,' Ronny replied. Just then a colleague walked passed them. Ronny called to him and asked. 'Raymond, do you know why all our names start with an R?'

Raymond shrugged as if it was of no importance to him. 'Maybe because we're in the maRRR keting department,' he said with a smile as he carried on walking.

Ronny shook his head in disbelief while Bobby and Banjo chuckled.

Roscoe, appearing from seemingly nowhere, came over to them. He said sternly 'Percival has asked that both of you go to see him, you're to leave here immediately.'

Then William came up to them and stood before them. He nodded acknowledgement without smiling. 'Please follow me,' he instructed Bobby and Banjo. He next turned and hurried away.

With a brief wave to Ronny and Roscoe, Bobby and Banjo chased after William.

10

Bobby and Banjo followed William through a doorway and found themselves in a very narrow passage. It wasn't a long passage, and they walked its length quite quickly. When they stepped through yet another doorway, Bobby realised that they'd returned to the *Oblongata*.

'This place is a maze,' Bobby muttered to no one in particular.

Banjo nodded his head in agreement. He said nothing and was clearly fascinated with all the activities that were going on. Banjo hadn't been in the *oblongata* before and Bobby was about to point out some of the things he'd learnt from his previous visit, when William abruptly stopped. Bobby and Banjo nearly bumped into him. When they recovered, they noticed Percival was standing in front of them.

'Bobby, I've been expecting you,' he stated coldly. He looked fidgety and impatient.

'We came as soon as we were told that you wanted to see us...,' Bobby replied defensively. He couldn't tell if they were in trouble, though he couldn't think of a reason why they would be. In the Marketing Department, he'd just got promoted and had received an award. But here, now, Percival seemed annoyed with them.

Bobby continued. 'This is Banjo, my assistant. He's...,' Bobby started to introduce Banjo, but Percival cut him off.

'I'm aware of Banjo and they inform me that he'll be an adequate assistant to you,' he stated coldly without looking at Banjo. 'I hope that you are both up to the task.' Percival expressed himself using a tone of voice that might have indicated that he didn't think they were.

'Ah, err..., what did you want to see us about?' Bobby queried. 'We're about to commence our training and I think they're waiting for us,' he added.

'They're waiting for me to be finished with you,' Percival countered.

'Oh,' Bobby responded. He looked at Banjo and Banjo replied with a one shoulder shrug.

'After your induction and training you'll be accompanying Harry on his tour of the body.' Percival informed them. 'As he is the General Manager for Follicle Production, and as he does the tour of the follicle growing regions on a regular basis, it makes perfect sense to do the tour of the body with him.'

'I understand,' Bobby responded. He looked at Banjo again and he nodded his head. His assistant was smiling and seemed happy.

'As you know, you now report to Harry. He's your boss and the managerial position up on your chain of command.' He paused. 'I also want you to submit a report to me. I want details of what you see and do. I want regular updates on what is happening in other parts of the body. Do you understand?' Percival was curt and to the point as always.

'What about George?' Bobby clarified.

'I'm sure that George will want a report also, but it is up to him to explain to you what he wants you to report on.' He paused deep in thought. 'George is really only interested in *Integumentary* activities, so the information he'll need will probably be limited to those activities. What I want is a very comprehensive report on all observations that you make. Clear?' Percival looked at Bobby for a response. The coldness exuded from him.

'Yes sir,' Bobby agreed returning the cold stare.

'Good.' Percival concluded looking at Bobby and Banjo in turn and at length as if soaking up the image of them. 'You may go,' he said dismissing them.

Percival turned and walked away. He stopped before a workstation and gestured to one of the supervisors. The supervisor began explaining an anomalous event in hurried hushed tones. He now had Percival's full attention.

William cleared his throat. 'Ahem,' he said interrupting their curiosity. 'This way please,' he said politely inviting them to follow him once more.

'Yet again, we enter one of the numerous passages of human life.' Bobby sighed as he said it to Banjo as they hastily followed William out of the *oblongata*. They stepped through yet another hidden doorway and went down another short passageway, through another door and found themselves in the training room.

'This is where I did my training!' Banjo whispered to Bobby. He was smiling and clearly happy to be back in this environment.

William turned and faced them.

'This is where you'll complete your training on quality assurance protocols,' he explained. 'Before you can commence your tour of the body, you'll also need to undertake one of the occupational health and safety courses,' William added.

'Why?' Bobby wanted to know.

'They don't like mishaps when there are passengers on the Zodiac's,' William answered.

'Zodiac's?' Bobby didn't understand.

'They're a powerful and highly manoeuvrable craft that transport managers to designated locations within the body. It's faster than using the barges as their speed is limited to the blood flow current of the vein or artery,' William explained. 'Harry is very experienced. I'm sure he'll espouse the benefits. You'll need to complete your training on how to properly use, and be safe, whilst within the Zodiac. Next the transport manager will allow you to board and be transported.'

'We understand,' Bobby responded. Banjo was nodding his head in agreement. 'When do we do the training?'

'After you graduate from the QA course,' William answered.

Bobby and Banjo looked at each other nodding in agreement.

'I want to give you both some advice,' William said unexpectedly.

Bobby and Banjo looked expectantly at him. He had their interest.

'Intelligence relates to how fast you can learn to do a thing properly. Ability is how well you perform in doing those things that you have learned. Any poor attitude will separate you from achieving what you are truly capable of,' he explained. 'You appear to have intelligence; ability and a positive attitude, so don't mess up this wonderful opportunity.'

'Thank you William,' Bobby responded for the both of them. 'We will apply what we learn with enthusiasm.'

'I'm confident you'll do well,' William concluded. 'Be safe and good bye.' He then turned and walked off, leaving them to stare at his back. He stepped through the doorway and was gone.

'Well. I'd never have expected to hear that uttered by William,' Bobby said to Banjo.

'I didn't know him that well,' Banjo observed.

'Neither did I,' Bobby explained. 'He just led me to places. Just now was the most he's ever said to me.'

'He's a *Mitochondria* of few words,' Banjo offered.

'Yet, they were powerful words. We will remember them,' Bobby concluded.

'Banjo!' A squat thick set cell approached them. 'I'm so glad you've returned. Now we can complete your training,' the *Mitochondria* declared loudly. He was chuckling and clearly happy to see Banjo.

'First, let me introduce you to Bobby,' Banjo suggested to the new comer. 'This is my boss, Bobby. He's the new head of the Follicle Farmers QA Department.' Banjo indicated his boss, smiling proudly. 'Bobby, this is Frank. He's our QA trainer,' Banjo completed the introductions.

'I'm very glad to meet you, Bobby. We've heard so very much about you. Banjo is a wealth of information and a quick study. I'd hang on to him, if I were you,' Frank advised.

'It's a pleasure to meet you also.' Bobby and Frank shook hands in friendly greeting. 'And I intend to,' he added assuredly, looking at Banjo.

'Now, before you can be officially titled 'QA Manager for Follicle Production', you will need to graduate,' he smiled as he explained. 'Don't worry; we have a very high graduation rate. I'm certain they wouldn't have selected you, if you didn't have the right stuff.' Frank rubbed his hands gleefully.

'That's comforting,' Bobby replied. He didn't know that he had to pass anything. He had just assumed they'd show him what he needed to do, and he'd get on with figuring out the rest for himself.

Frank turned and pointed to various features in the large room. It was mostly filled with desks and benches fitted with taps and sinks. There were numerous computer terminals. The trainers wore white coats that were held closed by a Velcro type of material. Their coats had names printed on them, whereas the student coats only had the letter L and a number.

'You'll each be assigned a desk and a bench. We tutors have a desk although we don't really need one anymore.' He smiled and held up a computerised tablet. 'We're now totally online for assessments,' he explained proudly.

'Can I please have the desk and bench that I was using before?' Banjo asked politely.

'Yes you can, Banjo,' he agreed. He explained it to Bobby. 'That's a popular desk. The desk and bench that Banjo was using whilst he was here last is close to the refreshments.' He patted his waist. 'As you can tell, we don't have restrictions on our intake in this department.' He smiled happily.

'I am peckish,' Banjo wasn't being subtle and he and Bobby looked at Frank expectantly with slight nodding of their heads in encouragement.

'Very well, let's eat,' Frank agreed offering no resistance. 'I can explain some things whilst we replenish our energy levels.' He smiled happily at his own joke.

They followed Frank into a cafeteria. It had comfortable chairs that were placed around round tables that could easily accommodate ten diners or more at any one time. There they helped themselves to a buffet of amino acids, protein shakes and a colourful glucose solution that was served in cups with curly straws. Bobby and Banjo followed the heavily burdened Frank to one of the tables. They had to unload their hands and arms before they could sit down.

As they ate, Frank began to explain about the role of a quality assurance manager in general terms. He next focused on Bobby's role. 'We will have to customise the procedures and protocols specifically to growing follicles, you do understand?' Frank queried.

'Why hasn't there been a QA Manager for follicle growing before now?' Bobby queried. 'It feels like we're doing something that should already have been in place.'

'I really don't know. It could be that no one thought of hair as being that significant as to require quality assurance. I believe the unexpected early onset of alopecia and greyness has prompted this response from the Marketing Department.' He lowered his voice to a whisper. 'They're a bit vain, you know'.

Bobby and Banjo nodded their heads conspiratorially.

Frank continued. 'Hair loss and greyness has always been an accepted aspect of aging. We may hide the hair grayness with artificial colour, or cover the loss with fake hair, but we've had to accept that these changes are an expected outcome of getting older.' He paused and took a deep breath. Neither Bobby nor Banjo interrupted him.

Frank resumed his explanation. 'Your discovery has led many in the QA Department; the Marketing Department and the scientists within the *Integumentary* System to believe that with proper procedures, and clever management, we can reduce the visible aspects of aging. This is from an outside perspective of course,' he added hastily.

'We've never experienced that,' Bobby informed him.

'Oh, but you must. A visit to the *Ocular* Department is a must for all senior managers. It puts everything into perspective.' He was insistent. 'I'll arrange a visit for you,' he offered.

Bobby nodded his gratitude.

Bobby and Banjo shared a glance.

They sat in silence for a while as they chewed their food. Frank was tempted to get some more and indicated a return visit to the buffet. Both Bobby and Banjo declined, but Frank accepted the outcome without regret. He would visit again later. Perhaps, sooner than later. He smiled magnanimously.

'Collectively, the mind has agreed to pursue an improvement in hair strength, hair colour and hair growth output. All because you tickled a fat cell and thought cleverly about what to do with the ooze that seeped out of him.'

'I was lucky,' Bobby admitted modestly.

'Yes, you were,' Frank agreed. 'But then, most of the great discoveries come about that way. What separates the greats from the mediocre is the intelligence to understand what is happening, the skill to apply it to a real opportunity and the positive attitude to see it through.'

Bobby and Banjo did a double take.

Frank rose from the table and Bobby and Banjo followed. They walked to two desks where Frank issued lab coats to them. Bobby was L4 and Banjo was L6.

'We only have twelve students here currently,' Frank explained. 'We can accommodate up to fifty, but we're a bit quieter than normal.'

'Any reason why?' Bobby queried.

'Mostly we train replacements for Quality Assurance Managers and workers that have reached their life span. Many of the individual systems have on-the-job training programs of their own. Often, they utilise replication to replace an aged QA Manager or QA staff member. The problem with that of course is that the replacement is identical to the original, so any bad habits or incorrect procedures are replicated within that replacement.' Frank smiled. 'Beating out an incorrect procedure of a replicated quality assurance person isn't an easy task.' Frank thought that the presumption of physically beating a QA person into a greater level of understanding was funny, so he laughed.

Neither Bobby nor Banjo understood the gist of the joke, so they nodded their heads almost imperceptibly to be polite.

'Before we begin your training, I want to ask you a few questions,' Frank explained. He pulled out an electronic notepad and opened it to a form. He had a stylus ready to record Bobby's and Banjo's responses. 'This will be loaded into the computer mainframe, and we'll be able to print out a draft SOP for growing follicles'.

'SOP?' Bobby queried.

'Standard Operating Procedures,' Banjo explained.

'Oh,' Bobby responded.

'From the SOP's we'll be able to tailor your WS's,' Frank added.

'Work Sheets,' Banjo explained.

'All electronic, of course.' Frank smiled. 'Banjo is ahead of you in the training. He's a quick learner.'

'He is,' Bobby agreed.

'The primary benefit of this is that you'll receive meaningful, and in real time, data that has variable parameters,' Frank stated.

'I have often thought that was important,' Bobby replied with a faint smile.

Banjo gave his boss a look of remonstrance.

Frank gave no indication of noticing.

'Let's begin,' Frank suggested. He sat down and Bobby and Banjo pulled their chairs closer and sat also.

'Do you have a layout of where the follicles are located?'

Bobby responded. 'Follicles are all over the body. They are everywhere but the palms and soles.'

'And lips,' Banjo added.

'And lips,' Bobby reiterated.

'But they are mostly extending outwardly from the *epidermis*?' Frank queried.

'That's right,' Bobby agreed.

'Anywhere else?' Frank queried.

'In the inner ear, the olfactory chamber and...,' Bobby hesitated, trying to remember. 'No, I can't think of anywhere else.' He looked at Banjo who nodded in agreement.

'Is there an organisational chart of the responsibilities within the Follicle Farmers Department?' Frank asked.

'Yes,' Bobby replied. 'I'm sure George or Harry would have that,' he added.

'Both of them,' Banjo agreed.

'I'll request a copy,' Frank mused. After a pause he continued. 'What records are maintained by Follicle Farmers presently?'

'We record the follicle temperature when a growth chemical has been applied and in what quantity,' Bobby responded.

'Who does this?' Frank queried.

'The Team Leader,' Bobby answered.

'Who gets the information?' Frank wanted to know.

Bobby and Banjo looked at each other and they both shrugged. 'We don't know,' They chorused.

'I'll ask George,' Frank said as he typed.

'What do you use to measure the temperature?' Frank queried.

'There is a gauge that measures temperature. We record what we read when we apply the growth chemicals,' Bobby explained.

'How do you know if the gauge is accurate?' Frank asked quietly. He knew the response.

Bobby and Banjo said nothing.

'What formal training is provided?' He asked with a deep sigh.

'The Team Leader trains workers. Team Supervisors train Team Leaders and so on,' Bobby answered.

'Is this documented?' Frank questioned.

Bobby looked at Banjo who shook his head. 'I don't think so,' he replied cautiously.

'If it isn't documented then it didn't happen. That's an important aspect in QA management, remember it!' he advised.

They nodded their heads in understanding. Frank was busy keying in notes and didn't see it.

He continued. 'At the follicle stations, is there a cleaning regime?' he asked.

'We're very clean,' Bobby assured him.

'Is it documented?' Frank asked.

'No,' Bobby answered. 'But you can see that it is clean, just by looking at it,' he lamented.

'Then you can't prove it, can you?' he asked rhetorically.

'If it isn't documented then it didn't happen,' Banjo stated melodically.

Frank smiled.

'We're doing all these things,' Bobby countered. 'Why the big deal about documenting them?'

Frank put down his tablet and looked at both of them studiously before responding. 'Quality assurance is about having a set of instructions, which all management and workers learn, understand and work by. It relates to specific tasks to prove that they are completed consistently to a minimum required standard. The emphasis here is on the proof.'

Frank's smile appeared genuine, he continued. 'Until just recently, hair hasn't been important. We weren't worried about the standards achieved and we allowed follicle growing standards to be self-regulating. Now that there is a formal position of Quality Assurance Manager, all Follicle Farmers will need formal, documented, training on correct procedures and record keeping. Without that as a minimum, the whole purpose of quality assurance will fail.'

Bobby said nothing and Frank took that as an acceptance.

'We shall continue,' Frank asked a now subdued Bobby.

'HACCP stands for Hazards and Critical Control Points,' Frank explained. 'Before you graduate, we'll identify the important steps to grow and maintain follicles at their optimum strength, thickness, colour, length and temperature and we'll document all of it. We'll set out which chemicals are to be used, when to use them and what quantities and we'll document it all. We will set out who receives training and who does the training and we'll document that. We'll set up cleaning rosters and we'll document those also.' Frank then paused.

Bobby was about to ask a question but Frank forestalled him by holding up his hand showing his palm.

'Your job will be to monitor the efficient implementation of these procedures and record keeping. You'll monitor the data as it comes in and you'll report on improved outcomes, investigate weakness in implementations and design and construct methods to further improve outcomes. It'll be a lot of fun for you both,' Frank concluded.

Bobby and Banjo looked at each other for support.

'You were going to ask something?' Frank invited.

'Oh, err..., yes.' Bobby collected his thoughts. 'What about the follicle rejuvenation chemicals that I developed. How does that fit into this?' He queried using hand gestures to indicate the QA training room.

'As soon as they have been approved for use, they'll become just another chemical on the list of additives that each team will apply. We'll need to work out a priority list for where the new chemicals will be used first and establish feedback protocols so we can monitor before and after results for comparative analysis,' Frank answered.

'But, they won't be needed at every follicle,' Bobby informed Frank.

'Oh, I didn't realise that. We were led to believe that the new chemical was to be applied to all follicles and that they would be phased in over time over the whole body.' Frank looked puzzled.

'I think you'll find that the Marketing Department will want to restrict its use to where more hair is beneficial to its marketing initiatives,' Bobby started to explain.

'Certainly the scalp would benefit,' Banjo added.

'True, the scalp would look better with stronger hair that is also richer in colour,' Frank agreed.

'They may restrict its use on facial hair,' Bobby then added. 'Specifically to when there's a moustache or a beard growing directive,' Bobby explained.

'For the rest of the body, it seems that less hair is actually desirable,' Banjo added to the explanation.

'I see,' Frank said. 'You have a brilliant discovery with limited application,' Frank concluded.

'So it would seem,' Bobby agreed.

'We'll need to document which areas of the body may have your chemical for possible use, and those workers will need the additional training,' Frank concluded.

'Okay,' Bobby agreed.

'Does your chemical have a name?' Frank was curious.

'Minoxidil,' Bobby answered.

'Interesting,' Frank murmured as he typed it on his pad.

Bobby and Banjo watched Frank type. They grew restless and started to fidget. Bobby looked over at the desk that he was allocated, but there wasn't much to see. He noticed an electronic notepad and picked it up and examined it.

'That's yours,' Frank informed him. 'It's your QA ledger. You'll use that during and after your training.'

Bobby smiled. He'd only ever used hard wired computers before and only ever dreamed of having a portable one with remote access. And it was brand new! He guessed all equipment had to be brand new at some point of its usage cycle.

'Banjo has one also.' Frank then indicated to the device on Banjo's desk.

Banjo restrained himself from going over to it and picking it up. He nodded appreciatively.

'The last thing we need to incorporate is the list of participants and the frequency of documented QA Management Review Meetings,' Frank told them.

'How can that be the last thing?' Bobby questioned.

Frank put down his tablet and stared at Bobby.

Bobby took the initiative and explained himself. 'These SOP's and WS's relate to normal follicle growth functions, but shouldn't we also document what we do when things go wrong?'

'Such as?' Frank asked.

'Follicles and the epidermis are really part of a team. Anything that happens to the skin may affect follicle growth,' Bobby started to explain.

'There are also negative events that reduce hair growth only,' Banjo added.

'Ingrown hairs,' Bobby agreed.

'Hair extraction,' Banjo added.

'Tell me about negative epidermis events that affect follicle growth,' Frank requested.

'Skin infections such as a rash are pretty bad,' Bobby replied.

'Sunburn,' Banjo contributed.

'Insect stings and bites,' Bobby said.

'Eczema!' Banjo announced.

'Yes, that is a bad one,' Bobby agreed.

'Cuts, bruises, abrasions, grazes...,' Banjo was rattling them off.

'You see if the layer of skin is broken in any way, fully grown hair can be trapped in the wound during repair and healing. If the hair is dirty it can seriously infect the wound,' Bobby explained to the now fully captivated Frank. He seemed fascinated.

'It can more than triple the recovery times,' Banjo added, supporting his boss.

'Does hair get dirty?' Frank queried.

'The epidermis is actually very oily and the oil leeks out onto the surface. It would coat the external part of the follicle,' Banjo added.

'Once it penetrates the skin we lose control of what happens to the hair,' Bobby explained. 'There is a process that initiates outside body layer cleaning. It incorporates the use of water and artificial chemicals.'

'In the beard some of the chemicals would form into spheres on the roof of our work station and drift down to us,' Banjo said reminiscing.

'I believe that was the external cleaning chemical applied to the outside skin area to remove dead skin tissue and extraneous waste products,' Bobby concluded.

'What was it like?' Frank was curious.

'Everything smelled better, for a while,' Bobby mused.

'I tasted the chemical once. It's very bitter,' Banjo explained.

'I have also,' Bobby confirmed. 'I guess we all try it, at least once.' He smiled.

'I knew a guy who loved the taste of it,' Banjo informed them. 'He couldn't get enough of it.'

'That's disgusting,' Bobby recoiled.

'What happens if the cleaning chemical stays on the outside layer of the skin?' Frank queried. 'Does it burn? Some chemicals can burn you know?' he added.

'This isn't pleasant, but it doesn't burn,' Bobby answered.

'We'd better add all of this to the procedures.' Frank had accepted the requirement for additional SOP's and SOPWS's.

Bobby and Banjo chorused there agreement.

For many cycles they continued discussing the operating procedures that would be taught to all Follicle Farmers throughout all parts of the body. They worked determinately, sometimes as a team and often on their own, preparing drafts of how the procedures would read, discussing its merits and identifying potential traps and pitfalls. Each SOP had accompanying SOPWS's. Each procedure was read and reread. Mock forms were completed and scrutinised. They tested the procedures for fallibility, ambiguity and used as simple a language as was possible without being condescending to the intelligence of the average Follicle Farmer. When they were satisfied that they had completed the tasks they celebrated in the dining room with a feast.

'My friends,' Frank began. 'We have done well. Instead of training you both, I have found myself working alongside you as your collaborator.' Frank smiled appreciatively at both of them.

Both Bobby and Banjo returned the smile and held up their refreshments as a salute.

'I do feel that we have explored the hazards and critical control points thoroughly,' Frank continued.

'We have,' Bobby murmured in agreement nodding.

'Your next mission is to implement what we have accomplished here,' Frank announced.

'Do we need to get it signed off?' Bobby queried.

'Yes, apart from my approval, which you already have, we'll need to get Georges and Percival's approval,' Frank informed them. 'A formality, I assure you.'

'How long will that take?' Bobby was concerned over the possibility of a lengthy delay. He was keen to get moving again. They had spent too much time talking and not enough doing. He was getting very restless.

'I'll submit the completed documents whilst you do your Health and Safety course.' Frank advised them. 'We should get the approvals before your departure through the body.' Frank smiled. He was aware of Bobby's restlessness.

'Good.' Bobby relaxed.

'You should write your own executive summary outlining the purpose of the HACCP documents and the anticipated benefits of their implementation,' Frank suggested.

Bobby tensed. 'More paper work?' He asked querulously.

'I'm afraid so,' Frank smiled.

'If it isn't documented, then it didn't happen,' Banjo stated melodically. This had been quoted often during the course of preparing the QA manual for follicle growth.

Bobby and frank laughed.

'We should contact the Union,' Banjo suggested.

'Good idea,' Bobby agreed.

'Why?' Frank questioned.

'The Follicle Farmers Union is the best way to gain support for any changes,' Banjo advised Frank.

'Surely the Follicle Management Team would be better positioned to implement changes. They're in charge after all,' Frank asked concerned.

'There is often push back... a resistance to management initiated changes,' Bobby explained.

'If it comes from the union, then it seems that the workers themselves have already decided that these changes are okay. Therefore there is often less resistance,' Banjo added, agreeing with Bobby.

'But who convinces the Union?' Frank was concerned.

'We do,' Bobby answered.

'I'll put this to you gently, Bobby.' Frank smiled at the irony. 'You are management.'

'I know,' Bobby acknowledged. 'The Union basically works for the Management Team. The Management Team uses the Union to implement what management wants. In this way everyone wins. Workers aren't ordered to do a thing. They are agreeing to a change because they know their Union Representatives have negotiated in their best interests before accepting the decision.'

'It's an arbitration process,' Banjo added.

'Follicle Farmers feel empowered when it comes from the Union. They feel uncertain when it comes from management. It's just the way it is.' Bobby smiled.

'Do management always succeed using this method?' Frank was puzzled by the process.

'Of course they do.' Banjo chuckled. 'That's why it works. That's why it suits so many Follicle Farmers.'

Frank said nothing.

After they rested, Bobby wrote his executive summary which he gave to Frank to proof read. Frank made a couple of corrections and they wrote the final version for inclusion into the HACCP file for follicle growth.

They then ceremoniously dispatched the electronic file to Harry, George and Percival. Bobby was given the honour of pressing the enter key on the computer that sent their hard work off for formal approval.

'Congratulations Bobby,' Frank told him. 'You are now officially the QA Manager for Follicle Production.'

'Thank you,' Bobby responded.

'After your tour you'll need to recruit your QA team...,' Frank began to explain

Harry entered into the room and interrupted them. 'Follow me boys! They're ready for you!'

After collective handshakes, the two fell into line behind Harry and with a farewell wave to Frank; they walked out of the training room.

~ 11 ~

Harry held the door open that led into the safety training room. Bobby and Banjo hadn't realised that it was in a room adjoining the QA training room.

'How did you know that we were ready?' Bobby questioned his boss.

'You sent me a message with all your finalised HACCP documents attached, so therefore I knew you had completed the training,' Harry smiled.

Bobby chuckled.

'Also, I read that you had signed your covering letter as 'QA Manager. Frank wouldn't have allowed you to do that if you hadn't yet graduated,' Harry explained.

'We have,' Bobby acknowledged.

'Not too challenging for you?' Harry teased.

Bobby laughed. 'I like learning new things. They can seem a bit daunting at first, but with focus and the right attitude, you move quickly past the fear barrier and get on with learning the job,' Bobby explained proudly.

'How did you go, Banjo?' Harry asked.

'Yes fine. I'm all good,' Banjo confirmed.

'That's good,' Harry concluded.

They had entered a room that had a large *Plasma* pool in it centre. There was a walkway perimeter, and it was extra wide on the side that they were standing. Within the pool there were activators that swirled the plasma, keeping it moving to prevent the *Platelets* from clotting. Bobby noticed that there weren't any blood cells present in the plasma and he wondered how they had separated the cells from the pellucid liquid. A graduated scale rose from one side of the pool to indicate how deep the pool was.

The floor of the *Plasma* pool room was stained with repeated splashing of the sticky liquid. Even though he had travelled within it, Bobby realised for the first time what strong odour *Plasma* actually had. He'd never seen it in such a large quantity before. It felt homely. On the walls of the pool room were coloured large scale diagrams of the *Cardiovascular* System. They were protected with a transparent glass like surface enabling them to be easily cleaned should *Plasma* splash onto them.

Harry left them staring at the charts and went into a side room. It had transparent walls and Bobby and Banjo could see Harry talking to the two others within that room. One was seated behind a desk and the other was standing. Harry pointed to Bobby and Banjo. The one that was seated stood up. He then preceded Harry and the other man out of the room, and they walked directly toward them.

'Fellows, this is Bobby and his assistant Banjo,' Harry did the introductions. 'This...,' he indicated to the larger of the two *Mitochondria* standing before them, '...is Philip. Philip oversees the Zodiac's Transportation Department.'

Philip extended a hand which Bobby accepted as did Banjo. 'Please call me Phil.'

Harry smiled as he stepped back to present the other *Mitochondria*. 'And this ugly chap is, Skip.'

'Hang on,' Skip said mocking admonishment as he extended his hand in greeting to Bobby and Banjo. 'You're not exactly Mr Handsome yourself, you know,' he said to Harry, smiling.

Harry laughed 'We've known each other a long time, Bobby,' he said explaining the banter.

'We should therefore plan to retire both of you,' Phil suggested. 'You can keep each other company,' he teased.

They all laughed.

'Skip will be responsible for your training and he'll be your Captain for your jaunt around the body,' Phil explained.

Banjo nodded his head in understanding. He was excited and it showed. 'When do we start?'

'First I'll show you over some maps of the *Cardiovascular* System,' Skip explained. 'That'll help you better understand why it is important to remain within the Zodiac at all times except when embarking or disembarking the craft.'

'Phil. Could I have a private word with you whilst Skip starts their training?' Harry asked Phil.

'Certainly,' Phil agreed and led Harry back to his office.

Skip took them to the charts. He started with the overview of the *Cardiovascular System*. 'These charts show us where we are in relation to the rest of the body,' Skip explained.

He pointed to a chart. 'That is the control room for the entire system.' He was pointing to the *medulla oblongata*.

'I've been there,' Bobby explained. 'Twice. The second time Banjo was with me but that visit was a very brief,' he added.

'I'm surprised they even let you in,' Skip told them. 'It is probably the busiest department of the whole body,' he paused reflecting. 'And it's probably one of the most important also.'

'I thought the brain was the most important,' Banjo interjected.

'The brain can think what it likes.' Skip clearly wasn't impressed. 'It's the *Oblongata* that does the vital work.'

Bobby looked at the maps of the *Cardiovascular* System that were spread across all the walls. He was specifically looking at the map that showed the blood vessels at the base of the brain.

'Which one are we in?' Bobby queried.

'We're in a small artery adjacent to the *Basilar*,' Skip replied.

Bobby could see the *Basilar* on the map. He pointed it out to Banjo who nodded.

'There are approximately 120,000 kilometres of arteries, veins and capillaries in the human body,' Skip informed them.

'What's a kilometre?' Banjo asked.

'It's a very long distance,' Skip answered hesitantly. 'I had the privilege of transporting a guy from marketing once, and he said he'd heard it from a Mind Manager, who knew about such things. If you linked the arms of a half a billion *Mitochondria* in a single straight line, it wouldn't be as long as one kilometre.'

'Wow!' Bobby and Banjo chorused. Clearly, they were impressed.

'So, it's vitally important that you don't get separated from the Zodiac whilst we are out there. It'd take me forever to find you again,' Skip cautioned.

Bobby and Banjo nodded their heads in total agreement.

Skip pointed to the maps. 'We'll be traversing across to the *Superior Vena Cava* and then we'll proceed to the *Heart...,*' he was explaining.

'The *Heart!*' Bobby and Banjo yelled. 'Isn't that dangerous?' Bobby questioned. 'I hear the turbulence...,'

Harry cut in. 'We do it all the time, and besides from here it is our only way to access the rest of the body.'

Bobby and Banjo were sceptical, but they remained quiet.

Skip continued. 'After the *Heart* we'll be in the left pulmonary artery.'

'Doesn't that go to the *Lungs?*' Banjo queried.

'It does,' Skip confirmed. 'We'll be taking the perimeter route. The blood vessels are slightly wider and therefore easier to navigate. It's tricky traveling internally within the *Lungs* so we prefer not going directly into them unless we really need to.'

'Oh,' Bobby acknowledged.

'From there we exit via the left pulmonary vein, back through the *Heart* and out into the aorta. That'll take us into the left *subclavian* artery.'

'Who are we seeing there?' Bobby asked.

'Harry said you'll be meeting the Follicle Farmers in the left arm pit,' Skip replied. 'He mentioned you had an interest in someone who works there or use to work there?' Skip clearly wasn't sure.

'I had a worker transfer to my follicle from the pit. It would be nice to meet some of his former colleagues,' Bobby explained.

'Greg and Pierre got transferred to the left pit after the moustache incident,' Banjo reminded his boss.

'That's right!' Bobby chuckled, amused at their fate. 'Perhaps we shall learn what happened to them.'

Skip said nothing. He grunted and continued explaining. 'All these charts have now been digitalised. There are screens on-board the Zodiac and we'll use those whilst we are traveling. We keep these ones here for introduction and training purposes. Also, I guess we're a bit sentimental.'

'We'd better learn all about the Zodiac's,' Bobby suggested.

Harry and Phil stepped out of Phil's office and came over to where the three of them were standing.

'Phil is going to give you some background info on the cardiovascular system before Skip shows you the Zodiac,' Harry informed them. 'Which Zodiac are we using, Skip?'

'The Taurus,' Skip answered.

'Good. I like that one,' Harry said. 'It feels like it has that bit of extra grunt when needed.'

'I'm sure they are all the same,' Phil countered.

Skip and Harry laughed.

'Well, technically, they all should be the same,' Phil defended his fleet.

'They're not,' Skip informed him. 'Each has its own characteristics. Despite numerous overhauls, Pisces is still hard to get started from a cold start, Aquarius still leaks even though it has been patched, Gemini's steering is off, Leo's throttle sometimes gets stuck at full speed...'

Then Harry added. 'And no one will ride in Cancer. You've got to agree that's an inappropriate name for a boat.'

'Don't blame me. Naming them this way was another wonderful Mind Manager's initiative,' Phil lamented sarcastically.

Skip explained. 'Cancer isn't really a good boat as it tends to drift sideways.' He paused in thought. 'The Virgo is okay.' Skip paused and then added. 'Although the controls can be a bit stiff.'

'Okay, okay. I get it. More maintenance needed. I get it,' Phil capitulated.

'Bobby, while you and Banjo complete your orientation, I'll be visiting George. Is there anything you want me to discuss with him?' Harry offered.

Bobby was almost about to inform Harry and through him, inform George that Percival had instructed him to provide a detailed record of everything he observed during the tour.

He didn't.

'No, no, it's all good,' he replied and then added. 'Tell him we're excited to get going, we're ready to learn and we want to make a positive contribution.'

'Okay, I will,' Harry acknowledged and smiled.

With a casual wave of his hand, Harry left the room.

'Let me explain a little about blood,' Phil started. 'The red blood cells are made in the bone marrow at the rate of about 200 billion per day.'

'That certainly puts our one and a half million Follicle Farmers into perspective, hey Banjo?' Bobby said.

Banjo nodded.

'Follicle farming is a very small function in comparison to the enormous scale of other systems,' Phil agreed.

'We're not even a system in our own right,' Banjo lamented. 'We're only a small part of the *Integumentary* System.'

'Harry gets to use the Zodiac's a fair bit because of the wide distribution of follicles,' Skip informed them. 'You guys are busy all over the surface of the body.'

'The *cardiovascular* system handles delivering oxygen, proteins, amino acids and glucose, to keep all the cells happy, healthy and functioning properly. It is also responsible for removing carbon dioxide and general waste to filtration points for ejection out of the body,' Phil explained.

'Unless we really need to be there, it's better for us to avoid those areas,' Skip added holding his nose.

'And unless you need to be there, it is best to avoid any small capillaries or filters,' Phil agreed.

'Especially the *Kidneys*,' Skip added.

'Is the Zodiac too big to get through?' Bobby asked, getting the gist of what they were explaining.

'It's an unknown. We might get through.' Skip smiled. 'It'd be slow going, and we wouldn't want to be responsible for causing any blockages.'

'Blockages would be bad,' Phil agreed.

'Very bad,' Skip reiterated.

'I'm sure that Harry has a routine circuitous route for us to take. We'll go where he wants to go,' Bobby concluded.

'We're just interested in follicles,' Banjo added.

'Oh, I'm curious about the other systems, also,' Bobby was addressing Banjo.

'You'll see plenty on the route that Harry regularly takes. Just let me know if there are any particular body locations that you want to visit and we'll do our best to accommodate,' Skip offered.

'It takes about seventy beats for the *Heart* to pump the blood through the body,' Phil continued with his part of the briefing. 'The Zodiac's can do it in half the time, so you'll be moving quite fast. They are highly manoeuvrable as we can use the Zodiac's to traverse the flow of blood.'

'We can steer where we want to go, instead of just going with the flow.' Skip smiled as he simplified his boss's explanation.

'That's what I just said,' Phil countered.

'Sorry boss,' Skip apologised with a crooked smile.

Phil continued. 'Because of the speed and the manoeuvrability of the craft, it is vital for your safety, and ours, that you learn all about the Zodiac's. Do you understand so far?'

They nodded their heads in agreement.

'It is also vital that you follow Skip's orders at all times. Do you agree?'

'Yes,' Bobby answered.

'Absolutely,' Banjo acknowledged.

'That's good. It's a formality and I'm required to ask it,' Phil explained. 'I think it's time that you introduce the boys to the Taurus,' Phil suggested to Skip.

'Absolutely,' Skip agreed mimicking Banjo.

Phil headed back to his office and Skip went to a computer terminal near the wall. It had a transparent plasma splatter cover over it and Skip typed on the keys without having to remove it.

'I won't be long,' he informed them.

Bobby and Banjo nodded in understanding.

'Are you boy's hungry?' Bobby looked at Banjo who nodded enthusiastically.

'We are,' Bobby replied.

'Let's eat while they bring out our Zodiac,' Skip suggested.

He invited them into the staff room which had tables and chairs, some with plasma stains. The room looked messy. On a crude bench were crude platters of amino acids, glucose and proteins. They helped themselves and sat whilst they ate.

'How long have you been a Zodiac's captain?' Banjo asked Skip between mouthfuls.

'Gee. A long time, I guess,' he paused reflecting. 'I started out in maintenance. We all do. There are two maintenance workers and one Captain for each boat.' Skip explained.

'Where are the boats kept?' Banjo asked.

'In a dry dock, not far from here. They get cleaned after each trip. Platelets can get claggy and if they aren't washed down regularly they can cause us grief,' Skip informed them.

'How many Zodiac's are there?' Bobby asked.

'Twelve,' Skip answered. 'Twelve boats, twelve captains.'

'Where are the others?' Banjo asked looking about the room as if he could spy the secret of their location.

'Two are in dry dock. The Captains of those two boats will be resting. We have a mandatory rest period after each tour. The others will be out on assignment. We carry all sorts of managers in the

Zodiac's. Up to now there's only been the one Manager from the Follicle Farmer's Team, but there are at least four managers from the *Epidermis* that use the Zodiac's regularly.' He paused. 'There was once a nail guy who needed to get from the fingers to the toes in a hurry. He's one of yours, isn't he?' Skip queried.

'He's part of the *Integumentary* System, but I've never met anyone from the nails,' Bobby replied.

'Two of the Zodiac's are permanently assigned to the *Cardiovascular* System. They do routine work checking the integrity of veins and arteries.' Skip continued. 'It's important, but at the same time very boring work,' he lamented. 'We captains do a rotation for that assignment.'

Before Skip could continue with his explanation, they saw a panel open, and a Zodiac being manoeuvred into the plasma pool. The worker next lashed the boat to the dock and alighted. The three had finished eating. Skip rose from his chair and the two others rose and followed him to the boat. Skip thanked the maintenance worker for delivering the Zodiac and he left through a service door, presumably to go back to the dry dock.

'This..., is Taurus,' Skip introduced the boat. It had the word '**TAURUS**' in bold gold lettering on each side of the boat.

Bobby and Banjo stared at the craft. It was about the length of seven *Mitochondria* end to end. It was black and sleek. It had twin motors at the back that were gurgling contentedly. Bobby hoped it would be safe and Banjo couldn't wait to get going. He started to get into the boat, but Skip stopped him.

'Hang on young fellow.' He held Banjo's shoulder before he could step into the boat. Banjo stood upright and murmured an apology.

'The first thing I like to do is tell you a little about the Zodiac's. It'll help you understand better when I explain the features of the boat. Then I'll show you how to get in and out of it safely,' Skip informed them.

He continued. 'The boats hull is made from redundant cell fibres, using the highest standards of engineering, materials and workmanship. It is a one-piece hull, meaning that there are no seams. It is made from organic, natural materials that work with the blood and not against it.' He took a deep breath and continued. 'It is relatively light in weight. This means it can turn very quickly. When we get into the boat I'll show you how to strap yourselves in, as we only want planned and not sudden exits from the boat.' He laughed at the memory of a past experience.

'The tube like structure of the hull is filled with a lighter than *Plasma* polymer, which is designed to keep the craft stable during turbulence. You'll feel the benefit of that when we traverse the *Heart*. The floor of the boat isn't that thick so...' He looked at their feet. 'You guys are okay. You have the standard issue foot wear. We can't have sharp objects in the boat. It is puncture resistant, but we don't take unnecessary risks,' Skip explained.

He continued. 'The hull and the floor are triple bonded so despite the thin feel, it is tough stuff.'

'How does...,' Banjo began a question.

'Best to let me finish, then I'll ask you if you have any questions,' Skip cut him off politely.

'The thick yellow line you see on the circumference of the boat is a rub rail. If we come in contact with another boat or any hard surfaces, the rub rail is reinforced and will give us additional protection from impacts,' he reassured them.

Skip saw the look of concern on their faces. 'Don't worry. It hardly ever happens and I'll look after you.'

'The front of the boat is called the bow, the back is the stern. The left side is known as the port side and the right side is always known as the starboard.' He took a deep breath. 'I didn't invent those names, I just teach them,' he smiled.

Bobby was about to ask a question, but he refrained.

'The boat is designed to be tip proof and I haven't capsized one as yet,' he stated proudly. He then gave them a mischievous wink.

'Has anyone?' Banjo asked.

Skip replied using a deep mournful dramatic tone. 'One Captain did, but he isn't a Captain anymore.'

'What happened to him?' Banjo asked wide eyed with concern.

'They promoted him!' Skip exclaimed. 'It was, Phil!' Skip laughed at the irony of it.

'Oh,' Banjo responded and he and Bobby joined in the laughter.

Skip continued with the instruction. 'There are two seats. Each seat has straps for three passengers, but as there are only four of us we'll be quite comfortable. When I'm carrying five passengers plus me, it can be a bit of a squeeze.'

'Where do we sit?' Bobby asked.

'You and Banjo will be upfront. Harry will be at the back of the boat with me. Despite it being tip proof we should always balance the weight distribution,' he answered.

Bobby and Banjo nodded their understanding.

'There is the drain plug.' Skip pointed to a plug on the floor of the boat. 'Don't touch that. You need to be trained in its use and you won't need it. It's a potential trip hazard so I'm pointing it out.'

'Sure,' Bobby agreed.

Skip pointed to the boat. 'Those are boarding and disembarking handles. Hold onto them when getting in or out of the boat. Only do that when I instruct you to and only do so from the port or starboard sides of the boat.'

'There are two oarlocks for oars which we carry on board. I've never had to use them, but if we do, then leave it to me to install them and I'll row us out of difficulty,' Skip explained.

'Why would we use oars?' Bobby queried.

'Total engine failure,' Skip answered. 'We have two motors, so the only way it could happen, is if we run out of fuel or both motors get coagulated.'

'What fuel do we use?' Banjo asked.

'These beauties use 100% epinephrine,' he purred. 'We'll fuel up at the adrenal gland.'

Bobby and Banjo nodded in understanding.

'We'll have to fuel up soon as we don't have enough for the whole journey.'

'When will we be leaving?' Banjo asked.

'Soon enough laddie,' Skip answered with a smile. 'We have to complete the training and we mustn't leave without hairy Harry.'

Bobby and Banjo burst into laughter.

'What..., haven't you heard him called that name before?' Skip asked chuckling.

Bobby caught his breath. 'That's a new one to us. We have a few names for him but that's the best.'

'We'd better not use it to his face,' Banjo suggested still smirking.

'No!' Bobby agreed emphatically.

'Oh. I don't mean it in a hurtful way,' Skip defended.

'We know,' Bobby conceded. 'You've been friends for a long time. I'm sure he has a nick name for you also.'

Skip went quiet.

'Tell us more about the Zodiac's,' Bobby suggested.

'Within your seats are storage compartments for notepads etc. We also have emergency food rations, but we pass via numerous food stations so we won't go hungry,' Skip explained.

'I suppose we could reach out and help ourselves from the boat if we're desperate?' Bobby suggested.

'That wouldn't be polite.' Skip admonished.

Bobby said nothing and Banjo giggled.

'You see those D-rings along the bow and stern of the boat?' Skip asked them.

They nodded that they did.

'They are hand holds if we have to get out and manually pull the boat. They are also towing points. We carry tow ropes should we need to tow or be towed.'

Bobby and Banjo looked concerned.

'It won't happen,' Skip explained confidently while shaking his head.

Bobby and Banjo relaxed.

'Okay. Now we board the boat,' Skip told them.

Skip fitted them with their harnesses. He next demonstrated the safest way to board the boat. He showed them where they'd be seated and how to fasten the safety harnesses to the seats. They joked and teased as they fitted themselves properly into the boat. Bobby was on the starboard side and Banjo was on the port side. They smiled happily.

'Okay,' Skip said when he was satisfied they were in properly. 'Detach yourselves from the seat and come and look at these controls.'

They did as instructed and turned to face Skip. Skip pointed to a large flat screen that was positioned in front of the Captain's chair. 'This is the latest technology in boat handling.'

'This is a finger touch screen. The left side is a map of the whole body. The blinking blue dot shows where we are. We move the screen by sliding a finger on it.' He demonstrated. 'We can zoom in and out using two fingers sliding inward or outward across the screen. If we want to plot a course we can use a 'look up' function and request an optimum route solution. The on-board navigation computer has all the body locations and blood pressures, flows and hazards programmed into it. It quickly calculates the best and safest way to get to the programmed destination.'

Bobby and Banjo were impressed.

'On this side we control the steering and speed of the boat. There's also a touch screen so be careful not to touch it or bump me when I'm using it or we could end up in trouble,' he cautioned.

Bobby and Banjo looked worried again.

'Don't look so worried,' Skip gently scolded. 'I'll look after you,' he added reassuringly.

'We believe you,' Bobby conceded, but he didn't look entirely convinced.

'The screen also has a proximity alert so if we're too near to something, it not only warns me, but it will steer away from the danger.' He looked at them then continued. 'If I depress here, it shows me the location of all twelve boats.' He pressed the button and the screen of the whole body showed and there were twelve blue blinking lights. Three of them were in very close proximity. The others were spread out over the body. Skip was smiling, pleased with this aspect of the technology. 'Phil loves this feature,' Skip told them.

'If the computer screen stops working for any reason we still have the manual steering and throttle controls. During the refit, the Captains insisted that they remain. We also have a map book of the body so if we need to plot a course without the computer we can. It just takes a lot longer, that's all.' Skip took a deep breath.

Bobby and Banjo looked at each other but said nothing.

The three saw Phil coming toward them. 'How's it going?' He asked to no-one specifically.

'Good,' Skip replied for the three of them and Bobby and Banjo nodded their agreement.

'Just a few points that I'd like to contribute. Skip's probably already covered them, but indulge me,' he requested.

They looked at him expectantly.

'First. No more than six of you on the boat at any one time. If someone asks for a lift to somewhere and you're going their way, you can take them. Just don't exceed the boat's capacity,' he paused. 'Second. No additional luggage. Don't exceed the weight carrying capacity of the boat. I don't care how important or vital their stuff is. Don't exceed the weight limit.' He then took a deep breath. 'Thirdly. Never jump into or out of the boat. Use the hand holds and climb into or out of the boat. Fourth, when the boat is moving, hold on. Don't rely on your safety harnesses. The harnesses are for backup only. Hang on as if your lives depended on it.' He paused. 'Lastly, stay in your seat and never sit on the tube. Clear?'

'Yes sir,' Bobby answered.

'Yes, me too,' Banjo agreed.

'Skip. Get it all documented and then when Harry gets here you're clear to go,' Phil instructed. He nodded to them, turned and walked back to his office.

'Documented?' Bobby queried.

'If your training isn't documented, it didn't technically happen,' Skip explained.

Banjo giggled.

Skip looked at him but said nothing.

Bobby explained. 'The same applies to QA. Everything must be documented. We heard that repeatedly during our QA training.'

'Life use to be a lot simpler, once,' Skip lamented.

'I need to send a message advising that we've completed our Zodiac training and that we are about to leave,' Bobby informed Skip.

'While you do that I'll get the induction forms ready for you to sign,' Skip acknowledged. 'We can then grab a bite to eat whilst we wait for Harry.'

They climbed carefully out of the boat and Skip went into Phil's office to get the forms and Bobby and Banjo went into the staff room. As Banjo ate, Bobby sent a detailed report to Percival and a brief report to George with a CC to Percival and Harry. He had informed them that they had completed their training and were about to leave.

Skip entered the room. The forms, complete with their details, were ready for signing. Both Bobby and Banjo read that they had completed their training and that they agreed to follow the instructions issued by their Captain for everything and anything to do with the boat. Satisfied that everything was in order, they both signed the forms. Skip then signed as their trainer.

Skip took the completed forms back to Phil and returned to join Bobby and Banjo for a meal before departure.

'Phil got a message from Harry. He'll be here in two cycles,' he informed them as they ate.

Phil came into the room and reached over and took a helping of protein from Skip's plate. Skip said nothing. Phil sat down.

'The Aries is in trouble,' Phil said to Skip.

'Is it serious?' Skip asked concerned.

'It ran out of epinephrine,' Phil answered dryly. 'He's now coasting.'

'That's his third time. What are you going to do?' Skip asked.

'I've asked Sean to take the Capricorn and tow him to the adrenal gland to fuel up,' Phil answered.

'I meant what are you going to do about, David?' Skip asked as he pushed his plate of food away from him.

'I don't know,' Phil sighed. 'We installed low fuel warning alarms on all the boats. We installed long range tanks, we gave him additional training.' He paused taking a deep breath. 'I don't know what else we can do,' Phil lamented.

Skip said nothing and the room went silent. Bobby and Banjo had stopped eating also.

Harry walked into the room. 'Okay boys. Let's get this show into the flow,' he suggested enthusiastically.

Skip stood up and readily agreed. 'The Taurus departs in one cycle,' he told them. 'It's time to say your fond farewells and strap yourselves in.'

Bobby and Banjo looked about them and chuckled at Skip's joke as there was no one, apart from Phil, for them to say goodbye to.

Everyone was now up and busily clearing the remnants of their meal. Phil indicated that they should leave it and that he'd tidy up. He was businesslike and assisted the Captain of the Taurus to prepare for departure. The two of them completed the check list. Bobby, Banjo and Harry were securely in their safety harnesses and properly attached to the boat.

Skip released the lines that had secured the boat to the platform and they self-rewound into their storage devices. Skip started the inboard motors and they purred a gentle throb that sent a slight vibration through the boat.

Bobby and Banjo looked at each other. They were grinning in excited anticipation of the journey before them.

Skip waved to Phil that they were ready and Phil walked to the wall of the room, opened a panel and depressed a switch. A door slid open and the plasma pool was now reconnected to the *Cardiovascular* System. The four gave Phil a goodbye wave which he returned.

Skip gently increased the revolutions of the internal screws and the Taurus moved forward toward, and then through, the door. The door closed behind them and they entered the blood flow.

Bobby hadn't been in such a large vein before. He studied the red blood cells that appeared to dance in the plasma as they flowed. Interspersed within the red blood cells were white blood cells. Bobby hadn't seen so many types in one location before and he pointed them out to Banjo.

Banjo nodded excitedly. He too was fascinated and marvelled at the smaller platelets and how everything seemed to flow out of the Taurus' path as they sped through the current.

Bobby could identify four distinct white blood cells and he named them to Banjo. 'That's an *Eosinophil*, there's a *Basophil*, a juvenile *Neutrophil* and that's a...' He hesitated trying to remember.

'A *Monocyte*,' Banjo offered.

'That's it!' A *Monocyte*!' He agreed happily.

'The first one to spot a *Lymphocyte* is the winner,' Banjo challenged.

Bobby nodded his acceptance they both excitedly looked for a *Lymphocyte* to claim the title.

As they looked, the other thing that was apparent was the sound of the Heartbeat. All cells and specifically the *Mitochondria* live with the sound of the main pump beating rhythmically. It is a great source of comfort, and its absence would be quickly noticed. Now that they were in the *Superior Vena Cava*, the main vein into the *Heart*, the sound was almost deafening. The QA Manager and his Executive Assistant had to shout at each other to be heard.

Another Zodiac passed the Taurus at high speed. The Captain and passengers of the Capricorn waved and hooted in triumph as they sped passed and very close to the Taurus as they navigated the plasma flow.

'Idiot!' Skip yelled at the irresponsible behaviour of the Capricorns Captain.

Suddenly the *Heart* beats became more frequent. The blood flow increased in speed and the Taurus was buffeted by a dramatic increase in the swell.

'Hang on tight!' Skip instructed. 'Something has caused the *Heart* to beat harder and faster!' He yelled over the noise. 'This is going to be a very rough ride!

~ 12 ~

'I should have explained that there are two significant features that we don't have on the Zodiac's!' Skip had to yell to be heard above the noise of the rapidly pounding Heartbeat. 'Firstly, we don't have much in the way of reverse thrust. The second thing is that we don't have a brake...,' Skip's voice trailed off as he left his three passengers to contemplate the significance of this.

The Zodiac was now bouncing on the stream as the blood pressure pounded the craft and its occupants. Skip was increasing the throttle to improve the manoeuvrability of the craft as they dodged the red and white blood cells as politely as they could. They bumped a few and Bobby murmured feeble apologies, but clearly being bumped was just a fact of life in the plasma flow.

'We're now entering into the *Right Atrium!*' Skip yelled. 'We're going a bit faster than I'd like but this is the only way to smooth out the ride!'

Bobby turned and looked at Harry. Harry was holding on for dear life. His eyes were shut tight, and he looked very pale. Bobby nodded to Banjo who followed Bobby's gaze. Banjo returned the nod indicating that he understood.

'We're now coming up to the *Tricuspid* valve!' Skip informed them.

Bobby marvelled at Skip's commentary as they sped toward the flickering valve. Bobby hoped they wouldn't be pulverized by its pounding action.

'Look over to your left!' Skip yelled.

They spotted the Capricorn. It had been caught in a fold on the wall of the *Heart* and they appeared trapped. Skip eased the throttle and steered the Taurus closer to the Capricorn. The turbulence became more pronounced, and they were buffeted and bombarded by plasma and platelets.

'Leave them!' Harry ordered. 'We have to save ourselves!'

'No! We have to help them!' Skip responded.

Bobby and Banjo nodded in agreement. Harry buried his head in his arms. He was clearly very frightened.

As they got closer, they could see the captain of the Capricorn and his two passengers frantically waving for their assistance. They were pinned into the *Myocardium* by the blood pressure.

'Bobby!' Skip yelled. 'Can you pull out the hitching rope from that…,' he was yelling loudly over the pounding of the *Heart* and pointing to the self-winding rope receptacle.

Bobby understood what he had to do. He pulled the rope out to its maximum length. As they drew close to the Capricorn, he skillfully rotated the rope above his head and flung it into the out-stretched hands of the Capricorn's Captain.

The captain looped the rope through the bow eye just as the rope gained tension. As the current pulled at the Taurus, the rope held, and they pulled the Capricorn free.

The Taurus was now flowing backwards into the *Tricuspid* valve. The Captain of the Capricorn released the tow rope, revved his motor, and pushed the Taurus cleanly through an open phase of the valve. They were now in the right *Ventricle*. Skip did a hard turn returning the boat into the direction of the blood flow and they were headed for the *Pulmonary* valve.

The Capricorn's Captain waved in a forward motion vigorously, indicating they should accelerate, and that the Taurus should lead. Skip gunned the motors and the *Epinephrine* kicked in. The Taurus sped through the *Ventricle* with the Capricorn closely behind them.

When they were clear of the second valve and comfortably in the *Pulmonary* artery, the *Heart* rate was decreasing, and the blood pressure dropped noticeably. It seemed that the *Heart* was returning to its regular rhythm.

The Capricorn's Captain navigated his boat next to the Taurus. The two Captains wordlessly exchanged ropes and they lashed the two Zodiacs together before speaking.

'That was close,' said the Capricorns' Captain.

'That was fun!' Banjo yelled. 'Let's do it again.'

'After we circumnavigate the lung, we will,' Skip laughed as he responded to Banjo's suggestion.

The two Captains looked at each other. They smiled, laughed, and shook hands then loudly sighed.

'That was unnecessarily reckless!' Harry yelled at the two Captains. 'I'm going to report the two of you for dangerous conduct!' he threatened.

'It was a bit scary,' Skip agreed. 'But it wasn't dangerous,' he said contradicting his passenger.

'It was!' Harry reiterated loudly. 'I can't believe this, this, this...,' he spluttered.

The Captain of the Capricorn extended his hand in friendship to Bobby. 'I'm Jack.' He said introducing himself to the Follicle Farmer.

'Bobby,' he responded returning the handshake.

'Thanks for pulling us free, Bobby.'

'You're welcome,' Bobby smiled. 'This is my assistant, Banjo.'

'I'm very pleased to meet you, Jack,' Banjo told him.

'He should be disciplined. There should be an inquiry,' Harry insisted.

'That's our boss,' Bobby informed Jack. 'His name is Harry. He's the General Manager for Follicle Production.'

'Oh, a big wig?' Jack smiled. He waved to Harry who didn't return the greeting and appeared to sulk.

'When it comes to hair, he's the biggest,' Skip informed Jack.

'I have a couple of head office types myself,' Jack advised them. 'These two are from the *Cardiovascular* System. They are QA Officers checking structural integrity of veins and arteries.'

'QA!' Bobby exclaimed. 'That's what we do. We're QA.' Bobby looked at the two *Cardiovascular* System QA Officers with some expectation, but they looked away, clearly disinterested.

'We'd better get back to work,' Jack said to Skip.

'Us also,' Skip agreed. 'We're going to the pits.'

'Lucky you,' Jack chuckled. 'I've been there and I'm not in any hurry to do so again.'

'It's part of our job,' Bobby explained.

'I'm sure it is,' Jack agreed smiling. 'Thanks again for pulling us free. It was very courageous.' He then added after a pause, 'I should nominate you for a bravery award.'

'Not another award!' Banjo rolled his eyes in mock shock.

'Just doing my part,' Bobby responded graciously to Jack's gratitude.

'We're in a bit of a hurry,' Harry coldly informed them all. 'If you'd please unleash your rope as we really need to get going,' Harry added.

'We got to go, Jack,' Skip confirmed.

The two Captains undid the ropes and stowed them away. The Zodiacs drifted apart.

'We're not in any hurry Skip, so if you want to go first...,' Jack offered.

'We are. Thanks,' Skip replied. 'Shall we catch up for a drink soon?'

'Sure,' Jack agreed.

Skip increased the motors revolutions and the Taurus pulled away from the Capricorn.

Before they rounded a bend in the artery, Harry stood up and yelled back at Jack. 'I'm going to report you!'

'Bye hairy Harry!' Jack waved as he yelled his response and the Taurus sped away from the Capricorns' view.

Harry sat down. He very looked pale... again.

Bobby and Banjo restrained urges to laugh.

As they travelled along the relatively wide circumference artery of the left lung, Harry slowly regained his composure.

'You risked our lives for that idiot,' Harry accused Skip.

'I didn't,' replied Skip.

'He shouldn't have been speeding through the *Heart* during a *Heart* rate acceleration event,' Harry remonstrated.

'I agree with that, but we were never in any danger. Nor was anyone on the Capricorn.' Skip smiled at him, restraining his annoyance at having to explain.

'I thought they were pinned to the wall of the *Heart*?' Bobby questioned.

'They were,' Skip agreed. 'And we were obliged to help them if we could. But they were only temporarily trapped. As soon as the *Heart* rate returned to routine pumping, Jack would have been able to pull free and return to the blood flow under his own power.'

'So you risked our lives unnecessarily,' Harry reiterated his remonstration.

'There was no risk,' Skip assured them. 'We had to help them and we did. It's all part of the code of the flow.'

The four sat in silence as they sped through this part of the body. Bobby started to take an interest in what was happening. Newly oxygenated red blood cells were returning to the artery, having left carbon dioxide cargo in the *Lungs* for respiration to the outside world. Bobby preferred the colour of the bright red blood to the darker blue tinged blood. The redder the blood the more food and oxygen it carried and that was essential for all cells. It occurred to Bobby that food was becoming important to him again. He was hungry.

'Are we going to eat soon?' He asked Skip.

'I wasn't planning to stop for food until we got to the pit,' Skip replied.

'How long will that take us?' Banjo asked. He was getting hungry too.

'There is a ration pack in your seat, if you're really hungry,' Skip offered.

'We can wait,' Bobby looked at Banjo who nodded his agreement.

'We have to go through the *Heart* once more, and then we take the direct route to the pit,' Skip explained.

The Taurus' engines purred as Skip steered the Zodiac along the outer *Pulmonary Artery*. The four sat in silence. Skip was navigating; Bobby and Banjo were marvelling whilst Harry continued sulking. Bobby and Banjo shared numerous excited glances. They were seeing re-oxygenated blood return from the lung into the artery that they were travelling through. It was exciting and wondrous and they felt alive and part of what was happening.

'We'll be entering into the left *atrium* soon,' Skip informed them. 'The *Heart* rate is back to normal so getting through the *Bicuspid* valve and the *Aortic* valve will be easier than what we experienced before,' he assured them with a smile.

Harry said nothing. Bobby and Banjo nodded their understanding and thanks.

'I'll next steer us up into the *Arch of the Aorta*,' Skip continued. 'Then we left turn into the left *Subclavian Artery*.'

'How far from there is it to get to the pit?' Banjo asked. He and Bobby were looking at Skip expectantly.

'Not far,' Skip answered. 'The *Subclavian* becomes the *Axillary* and that's where we exit.'

Banjo and Bobby turned once more and sat in silence as they progressed through the *Bronchial*. They heard the *Heart* beat getting louder and its comforting rhythm was now much gentler than before. As they entered the *Heart*, they felt the burst of pressure in the blood flow as they were pushed through both valves and into the arch as Skip had told them.

The rest of the journey was peaceful, the roar of the *Heart* was behind them and they carried on their journey to the left pit. They each sat silently contemplating the next part of their mission.

The Taurus progressed relatively calmly as Skip professionally positioned them for the required exit.

'Remain seated until I fasten the tie ropes,' he instructed.

'The Taurus bounced gently into a smaller *Capillary* where the blood flow was gentle, and they were able to hold the boat in position whilst Skip fastened it to the mounts on the receiving wall.

Two *Mitochondria* were standing on the dock, looking at the new arrivals with genuine pleasure and they beamed their welcoming smile to the group.

'We've been expecting you,' one of them said.

'We're so very glad you could visit us,' the other one informed them as they disembarked from the boat.

'Do you know who I am?' Harry asked them indignantly.

'Yes GMH!' They chorused.

'GMH?' Skip queried Bobby in a whisper.

'General Manager Hair. It's one of his many titles,' Bobby whispered in reply.

'He has a lot of titles,' Skip agreed sotto voce.

'Yes, he does,' agreed one of the two Pit Hair Manager's as he leaned in very close towards them and also spoke in hushed tones.

'I want exclusive access to a fully equipped office, and I don't want to be disturbed!' Harry demanded.

'Yes sir!' The pit managers stood to attention and executed a snappy left turn and they marched away from the unloading platform.

Harry looked at his three travelling companions, shrugged his shoulders and followed them. Banjo did the same shrug, turned, and followed Harry. Bobby and Skip smiled and copied.

Harry was shown to a room which he entered. Without a word he closed the door, shutting out his hosts and colleagues.

'He'll be in there a while,' one of the two, Arm Pit Hair Managers explained.

'I think you should introduce yourselves,' Bobby suggested.

'We agree,' one of the two responded whilst looking over his shoulder. 'Let's not do so in a passageway.'

'We'll go the lunchroom,' suggested the other.

They followed the two hosts down the passage.

Bobby and Banjo became acutely aware of the unusual odour. It was acrid and sweet at the same time.

'Not exactly a sweet-smelling environment, is it?' Skip asked rhetorically.

'No. It isn't,' The first agreed.

'We're due for a wash,' the second added with a nod and a smile.

'Overdue, I'd say,' Skip muttered almost inaudibly.

They entered a lunchroom and their hosts invited them to help themselves to refreshments and seating. The furnishings were hard and worn. They seemed to Bobby to be the bits of furniture that had been passed down the chain of seniority and they had reached the level from where they'd be permanently discarded.

'My name is Sean,' the first said.

'And my name is Shane,' the second added.

'I'm pleased to meet you Sean and Shane,' Bobby responded citing their names. 'I'm Bobby, this is Banjo my assistant and this is Skip, the Captain of the Taurus.'

'Oh, we know who you are Bobby. You're famous. We've seen all about you and Banjo on the Follicle Farmers Network news,' Sean gushed.

'Congratulations on your promotion,' Shane added. 'We are soooo proud that you decided to visit us here in the left arm pit as part of your whole-body hair tour.'

'We're following Harry's itinerary,' Bobby tried to explain.

'Yes, and now you're here. In the pits with us pit bosses.' Sean and Shane laughed loudly.

Bobby responded with a smile. He then asked. 'How many workers are in your team?'

Before they could answer Skip held up a drink and some protein packs that he'd grabbed from the food dispenser and interrupted the Follicle Farmer's discourse. 'I'm heading back to the Taurus to check up on a few things.' He waved his goodbye and exited the room.

Sean answered. 'I'm the Area Manager for the whole of the left arm pit hair. I'm the AMLAP. Shane is my 2IC,' Sean explained.

'That's second in charge,' Shane clarified smiling.

'That's what I said,' Sean scolded Shane.

'You said 2IC. They might not know what that means,' Shane retorted indignantly.

'We do,' Bobby acknowledged. He next asked. 'How many Team Supervisors, leaders and workers do you have?'

'We have eighteen Team Supervisors, 216 Team Leaders and 432 workers,' Shane told them triumphantly.

'I was going to tell them that,' Sean scolded his 2IC.

'Well, you didn't so I did,' Shane retorted.

'And how are things going here for you?' Bobby asked.

'Good!' Sean replied.

'Apart from the odour,' Shane added.

'The smell is... very off at the moment,' Sean continued.

'Very bad,' Shane agreed.

'We're due to be washed soon!' Sean said smiling and they both took a deep breath to signify their relief at the prospect of a wash.

'Where is the stench coming from?' Banjo asked. He had an e-pad ready to make notes.

'From the bacteria,' Sean answered.

'From their pee pee,' Shane added as if clarifying it for the two guests.

'There are over 200,000 bacteria living on the skin of our pit at this very moment,' Sean told them.

'And they're all pissing,' Shane said, clearly enjoying the aghast looks on Bobby's and Banjo's faces.

'When the wash happens, the urine is cleaned away and the bacteria numbers are reduced to just a few thousand,' Sean assured them.

'For a short while it'll smell good again.' Shane smiled and took another deep breath.

'We may even get some sweetness,' Sean said to them.

'AHHHH,' Sean and Shane said loudly and in unison.

'Sweetness?' Banjo queried, pausing his note taking.

'It's a body odorant that soaks in to us through the *Epidermis*,' Sean informed them.

'We don't know where it comes from but it mostly happens after a soapy cleaning event.'

'We really appreciate it because it slows bacteria growth and masks the urine stench.'

'It makes us feel wonderful.'

'And most of all... we feel loved,' Sean said. He raced forward and gave Bobby a hug and then turned and hugged Banjo.

Shane was about to follow his boss's lead and hug them also, but Bobby held up his hand to indicate no. Banjo did the same. Shane's face changed expression into disappointment but his smile held its shape.

'We'd better check with marketing to see if external request are being repeatedly made to artificially decrease the level of offensive odours in the pits,' Bobby explained to Banjo who added it to his notes.

'Oh please don't make them stop it. We love it and it makes such a difference to morale,' Sean pleaded.

'We won't stop it, but it is important that we know what it is, that causes the... ah sweetness,' Bobby explained. 'We need to understand it so that we know that it isn't causing you or your team any harm.'

'It isn't aluminium!' Sean yelled teary eyed. 'Shorty got rid of the aluminium problem. It's all good now.' He sniffed.

'I know Shorty and I remember him telling me about the aluminium.' Bobby was elated. That experience was now becoming a full circle in his knowledge. 'Aluminium within the sweetness is a bad thing?' He asked them.

'That's what Shorty said. He pushed Head Office to change the sweetness away from the aluminium sweetness,' Sean replied.

'Now we have organic sweetness,' Shane told them.

'How do you know that? I never told you that. How would you know that?' Sean demanded from Shane.

'Pierre told me. So there!' Shane leered at his boss.

'Pierre!' Bobby looked at the, two Pit Managers. 'Is that the Pierre that was formally from the Moustache?' Bobby asked excitedly. 'He's here, working for you?'

'Yes. That right,' Sean answered. 'He's a Team Supervisor now.'

'He's one of the best Team Supervisors we've ever had,' Shane agreed.

'He'll go far,' Sean stated happily.

'If we let him,' Shane tee heed and Shane laughed loudly.

Bobby and Banjo looked at each other and Banjo rolled his eyes.

'Can we speak with him?' Bobby asked.

'Sure,' Sean answered. He turned to Shane and asked. 'Could you please fetch Pierre, and bring him here to meet Bobby?'

Shane got out of his chair and wordlessly left the room.

'You're not going to transfer him, are you?' Sean asked in a menacing tone. He was shaking his head as if using body language was going to get him the answer he wanted.

'No!' Bobby assured him. 'We used to work together in the Moustache,' Bobby explained. He then added. 'We both did,' now indicating toward Banjo. 'It would be nice to say hello before we start our formal tour.'

'Okay.' Sean visibly relaxed but then he stiffened. 'Formal tour?' He queried.

'Relax. We're not management. We're QA. We're on your side,' Bobby consoled the Area Manager.

'We're here to learn how you grow hair and perhaps assist you in growing it better,' Banjo added.

'Oh, we grow good long strong hair here in the pit,' Sean explained. 'It might smell a bit off, but we do our job properly,' he reiterated proudly.

The door opened and Pierre entered.

Sean rose and indicated to Pierre that he should take his seat. Pierre did as he was told. He didn't look happy to see Bobby and Banjo. He looked pensively at them. Sean wordlessly left the room.

'Hi Pierre. Remember us?' Bobby asked him.

'Of course I do,' Pierre admonished. 'What are you two doing here? What do you want?' He demanded defensively.

'We wanted to say hello,' Bobby responded, somewhat taken aback by Pierre's aggressive posturing.

'Hello Pierre,' Banjo waved his hand in greeting.

'I've served my punishment. I've been a team player. I fit in here!' Pierre laid it out for Bobby and Banjo.

'We know that,' Bobby explained. 'Both Sean and Shane speak very highly of you.'

'They do?' Pierre queried.

Bobby nodded 'We just wanted to say hello and learn how things are in the arm pit from someone we're familiar with.'

'So, I'm no longer in trouble because of what happened at the moustache?' Pierre speculated.

'We know you didn't have any choice and that you were following Greg's orders...,' Banjo contributed sincerely.

'Greg's not here!' Pierre blurted.

'Oh!' Bobby was surprised as they were both sent to this pit for rehabilitation. 'Err..., where is he?' He asked pensively.

'They transferred him to be a worker growing hair around the *Anus*,' Pierre answered bluntly.

'Oh!' Bobby exclaimed. He looked at Banjo and snickered. Banjo chuckled. Bobby laughed. Banjo laughed and Pierre laughed also. The three laughed and their bellies wobbled. As they calmed down they took a deep breath and they collectively sighed.

'He must have really upset someone,' Bobby suggested.

'He upset everyone!' Pierre answered. 'All he did was upset workers and Team Leaders. He hurled abuse at everyone. He complained about the smell all the time and was frightened of the sweetness.'

'What is the sweetness?' Banjo had been typing in his observations but paused to look at Pierre.

'It's similar, but different to the stuff they sometimes put on the face after a shaving event,' Pierre explained.

'I remember,' Bobby agreed.

'Look, they are a bit slow here. Most of them were impaired by the aluminium, before that got stopped. I guess the effects on them are permanent.' He paused. 'They're a good bunch and a good team,' Pierre defended his colleagues. 'I like it here.'

'I'm sure they are,' Bobby agreed.

Banjo queried. 'Do you get shaved here?'

'No. There is no point. Arm pit hair isn't a concern to Grey-Matter or to Marketing. Body odour is, so they wash us and sometimes splash sweetness onto the epidermis to mask the smell good for a while. They love it here. I'd go as far as to say they're addicted to the sweetness as they don't seem to function very well if they have to go a long time without it.'

'Oh,' Bobby responded.

'And Greg didn't like it?' Bobby questioned.

'Nah. He just complained about everything, especially about the odour, although you do sort of get used to it,' he assured them.

'So what happened?' Bobby queried.

'Well. Sean couldn't take it anymore. He wanted Greg to *Apoptosis,* but he couldn't get approval, him being on rehab and being monitored and everything,' he paused but then added. 'Next thing we knew he was on a slow raft to the end of the digestive tract.'

'Why do you call it that?'

'That's the words Sean used to explain it to Greg, just before they marched him down the passage and put him onto the raft,' Pierre explained with a chuckle. 'By the time the raft had pulled away and was into the flow, he'd figured it out and started yelling abuse. I guess he didn't want to work near the arse hole even though he was one,' Pierre smiled at this.

Bobby and Banjo exchanged a glance.

'We're the QA Department and we're doing a tour of the body,' Bobby explained.

'We have a QA Department?' Pierre was impressed. 'Is that because of the Moustache incident?'

'Partially,' Bobby answered.

'Oh,' Pierre responded. He was downcast.

'It might be better if we explain why, we're here to Sean and Shane,' Bobby told him. 'Would you mind getting them for us?'

Pierre got up and wordlessly left the room.

'He's probably spent enough time here for him to be reinstated to the Moustache,' Banjo suggested.

'No point. He's happy here. I think we should leave him with his new friends,' Bobby countered.

'He's still miserable about the Moustache event,' Banjo added.

'Write a communication to personnel explaining about Pierre's exemplary performance in the arm pit,' Bobby commanded.

'Nice one,' Banjo complimented.

'Also write a communication recommending that his record for his part of the misconduct in the Moustache incident be closed and that he is now deemed rehabilitated,' Bobby instructed.

'What will that give him?' Banjo was confused.

'It'll allow him to apply for a transfer if he ever wants it. It'll also allow him to advance his career beyond Team Leader if he's good enough,' Bobby explained.

Banjo murmured his support for the planned report when Sean and Shane entered the room.

'Thank you for allowing us to meet with Pierre,' Bobby told them. 'He seems to be doing well. We'll include your support for him on his personnel records.'

'Do you have the authority to do that?' Sean questioned.

'I'm graded a Regional Manager, so yes I do,' Bobby confirmed.

'Oh,' Sean replied.

'I should explain why we are here. We're the Managers of the newly formed Quality Assurance Department. Banjo is my 2IC.'

'We're here to measure your effectiveness using newly established quality assurance protocols,' Banjo added his contribution to the explanation.

Bobby went on to explain further. 'The body is aging and starting to exhibit aging symptoms. Gray matter has given its support to marketing initiatives to make the exterior of the body look younger. Increased follicle production and a return to natural hair colour are two of the objectives.'

'The main aim of our tour of the body is to learn how well each area is performing, despite these ageing conditions,' Banjo added.

'What do you want from us?' Sean was clearly overwhelmed by all of this.

Shane said nothing. He just stared at his boss. He looked worried.

Just then the door to the staff room opened and Skip walked in. He stood in the door and addressed Bobby and Banjo.

'How are you going?'

'We're about to start our tour of the follicles growing here,' Bobby answered.

'So you'll be a while?'

'I suppose...?' Bobby wasn't sure where Skip was going with his question.

'Harry is asleep in that office. If you two are going to be busy here for a while, I'll nip down to the *Adrenal Gland* and fuel up,' he informed them.

'Sure. Good plan,' Bobby agreed.

Skip waved goodbye and was gone.

Banjo looked at his boss in concern. 'Do we need to check on Harry?'

Bobby shook his head. 'Let's leave him be,' he answered. He looked up at Sean and Shane. 'The sooner we start the quicker we'll be out of your hair so please lead the way.'

No one laughed.

They followed the two Arm Pit Managers for the tour of the pit. For the next 200 cycles or so, Bobby and Banjo interviewed supervisors, leaders and workers under the watchful eye of their managers. Banjo made numerous entries into his e-pad. Both Bobby and Banjo asked questions about growth rates, temperature checks, the chemicals they used and dosage rates all in line with the protocols they had established within the QA Training Facility. As they were coming to the end of the inspection, they drew Sean and Shane aside.

Bobby informed them. 'We're pleased to note that you are doing a satisfactory job. We'll leave you with some added steps in documenting what you're doing. Banjo will explain how to use these and how to log the actual results into the new QA software on your computer monitor.'

'It's really easy...,' Banjo started to explain when Harry burst into the room. Skip was close behind him.

'Have you finished here?' Harry demanded.

'Err, just about,' Bobby answered. He looked at Banjo who nodded.

'Good! We have to leave now!' Harry informed them.

'What's happened?' Bobby queried.

Harry explained. 'There is a serious infection on the *Abdomen*. It's very bad and a lot of Follicle Farmers and their follicles are injured. We've been ordered to go there, take charge of things and set it right.'

Banjo turned to Sean. 'I'll email you those steps.'

The four waved their goodbye's as they hurriedly headed for the Taurus.

~ 13 ~

When Skip was satisfied that everyone was properly secured in the Taurus, he untied the ropes and stowed them properly away. Harry gave him an impatient look which Skip chose to ignore. He strapped himself into his own chair before starting the two, now fully fuelled, inboard motors. They purred into life. Skip gently eased the throttle forward and they commenced their journey to the abdomen.

'Sorry boys, but the only way to the abdomen from here is back through the *Heart*. I hope it's a more comfortable ride this time,' Skip advised them.

Harry looked concerned, Bobby nodded acknowledgment and Banjo grinned happily.

'We have to take this capillary through to the left *Cephalic Vein*, into the left *Axillary*, then into the left *Subclavian*,' he explained. 'We'll go through the *Heart* and *Lungs* as before and exit the arch, down the *Thoracic Aorta* and exit via the left *Gastric Artery* which will take us close enough to the trouble for us to work out where to go from there.'

'How long will it take us?' Harry demanded. He was clearly in a hurry.

'Two or three cycles,' Skip answered.

They were already nearing the *Heart*. Fortunately, it was beating in its regular steady beat so they passed through without any severe turbulence. They completed the circuit and accelerated through the wide *Aorta Arch* and sped along the busy *Thoracic Aorta*, just as Skip had described. Skip navigated by watching his touch screen. Their own vibrant blue dot was drawing ever closer to the planned exit.

Harry wanted to explain the situation occurring in the abdomen to them, but the noise of the motors and the rush of the very huge volumes of blood in this major artery made an understandable explanation improbable. He decided to wait until they were closer to the *epidermis* on the *abdomen*.

They rushed toward the exit and entered the left *gastric* artery at high speed, without bouncing of the walls of the artery. Skip was a good Captain. The Taurus immediately slowed as the reduced blood pressure in this smaller *artery* reducing the effect on their speed. Skip trimmed the motors revolutions to match the flow of blood. He zoomed in on the navigation chart on his digital display and looked for an appropriate exit.

'We'll take the *External Iliac Artery*,' Skip informed them.

Skip set the motors to idle so that they could manoeuvre with only minimal thrust. They turned left into the *Inferior Epigastric Artery* and then right into the *Internal Thoracic Artery*. Skip manoeuvred the Taurus into smaller *arteries* and then into even smaller *Capillaries*. He found a docking bay and held the boat in place with side thrusters whilst he lashed the boat to extended *Capillary* anchors. Harry disembarked first, followed by Bobby, Banjo and lastly, Skip.

The Follicle Farmers' Area Manager of the *Abdomen* was there to greet them. He introduced himself. 'Hello and welcome to the *Abdomen*. My name is Simon and I'm in charge of the follicles in this area.' He spoke in a disheartened, almost pathetic, voice. Clearly, he was shattered about what was happening. He held out his hand to Harry. Harry looked at it, saw that it was filthy, winced, and didn't move to return the offered handshake.

'Where's your meeting room?' Harry demanded rudely. 'I'll conduct our strategy briefing from there.'

'Um, follow me,' Simon offered. He turned and led them down a short passageway and into a large staff room. There were injured Follicle Farmers occupying all the seats, some were prone on tables and still more were resting on the floor. They were being attended to by a few able-bodied Follicle Farmers who looked equally filthy and stressed.

Bobby, Banjo, Skip, and Harry looked upon the devastating scene and were appalled. None of them had seen such horrific burns and injuries before and the sheer numbers of victims made the spectacle even harder to comprehend.

'I'm sorry, but I don't have anywhere private to take you. My office is being used as an advanced triage room. We're bringing the probable's into this room,' Simon explained.

'Probable's?' Bobby questioned.

'Probably survive,' Simon answered.

The four continued to survey the room and were shocked at what they were seeing. There were burnt *Mitochondria* and others with lacerations, and some others with dazed vacant expressions of shock and dismay, but without any apparent physical injury.

Harry regained his composure. He turned to the others as he spoke. 'Right, this is what I know so far. I'll do my best to explain. Simon, please feel free to fill in any gaps.'

'For some inexplicable reason, this part of the body was exposed to an extreme UV radiation event. The *Dermis* and *Epidermis* Builders, the Follicle Farmers and the *Adipose* cells were the worst affected. Their burns, as you have seen, are quite shocking. The *Epidermis* Manager for the *Abdomen* requested an external assist. Head Office immediately authorised it and an external lotion was applied to reduce the pain for the workers and improve recovery time.' He looked at Simon who nodded his agreement.

Harry continued. 'That particular lotion has a chemical in it that... well it turns out that our skin has a severe allergy to it. The chemical is known as MI, the long name is unpronounceable. Just trust me on this. The UV burn was bad enough, but the reaction to the MI has caused significant additional swelling and blistering.'

Harry studied their faces. Skip was pale. Bobby and Banjo were very solemn. Simon was teary. 'Neither of the Managers for the *Dermis* or the *Epidermis* survived.'

They said nothing.

'The *Nervous* System has been wonderful. They have been keeping the powers that be appraised of the pain we're all suffering…,' Simon blurted.

Harry nodded his head and then added. 'Now here comes the crunch.'

'You mean it gets worse?' Bobby questioned.

'Yes.' Harry looked solemnly at them.

'The allergic reaction to the chemical also caused an itchy *Epidermis*,' Harry said gravely.

'So we scratched?' Bobby concluded.

Simon nodded his head. 'Yeah, we did.'

Harry continued explaining. 'The nails on the fingers are long and sharp. They had also recently been used to excavate the nasal cavity. They therefore held large quantities of *Staphylococcus Aureus* under the nails. The weak and tender *Epidermis* was highly susceptible and the perforations the nails caused, introduced a full scale *Staph* attack on the skin of the abdomen.' Harry studied each face in turn. Next, in a deeply grave voice he said, 'Gentlemen…, we are at war.'

They were all silent for a moment whilst they absorbed this shocking news.

'What can we do?' Bobby eventually asked.

Simon spoke. 'NK's arrived soon after the MI reacted. They are exhausted and many didn't survive. I heard they've been given a temporary withdrawal from engagement. They couldn't cope with arrival of the *Staph*.' He drew in a deep breath and continued. 'Now *T-Cells* have arrived and they have begun to replicate. The Officer in Charge is preparing to surround the infected area with as many defenders as it takes. The *B-Cells* are also under his command.'

'What is the name of the Officer in Charge?' Bobby asked out of curiosity.

'His name is Lek,' Simon answered.

'I know him,' Bobby informed the group.

They looked at Bobby in surprise.

'He's a friend of mine,' Bobby explained.

'Also...,' Simon continued, 'I've learned that George, he's the *Integumentary* System Manager, has authorised a massive deployment of the *Phagocytes*. I believe they are mobilizing just outside the perimeter. The Officer in Charge of the *Phagocytes* is familiar with Lek, and they appear to be working well together.'

'Fargo,' Bobby said.

'That's right.' Simon looked impressed. 'You know him also?'

Bobby nodded his head.

'I'm not impressed,' Harry told them. 'The *T and B-Cells* and the *Phagocytes* will fight the *Staph*, but they won't help our wounded.'

'What should we do?' Bobby queried.

'Do you want me to arrange a medivac?' Skip offered.

'There are too many wounded and besides, where would you take them?'

Skip shrugged.

'Banjo, could you set up a communications room? We need to co-ordinate with all the other systems and get their immediate assistance with winning this battle. We need help healing the wounded, and the sick Follicle Farmers and *Dermis* and *Epidermis* Builders alike.' Harry looked straight at Banjo for his response.

'I'm on it,' Banjo replied as he turned to try and find some able-bodied workers to assist him in organising the items he required.

Harry next turned to Bobby. 'Bobby could you please interview these wounded? Learn about their experiences and then record the nature of their injuries. A comprehensive report will assist in the recovery of these workers and will also form the basis of the inquiry that I'm initiating as a result of this catastrophe.'

Bobby nodded his head. He was amazed that even at this early stage of the disaster recovery, Harry was already trying to work out who to blame.

Harry turned to Skip. 'Could you contact Phil and see who else has booked transport to this area? Try and find out if the other systems are sending any significant managerial support.'

Skip murmured his agreement to do so. He turned and left for the Taurus.

Harry spoke to Simon. 'Simon, could you arrange to bring all your functioning Supervisors to the briefing room. I think we should address them as a group to boost morale a bit.' He paused staring at the Area Manager's blank expression. 'Are you okay with that?'

Simon continued to look at the General Manager for Hair in stunned silence. He was about to capitulate and accede to the request, but he saw Bobby exaggeratedly shaking his head. He hesitated and then replied. 'My men are busy dealing with the situation. They're in shock but they're motivated just fine.'

Harry hesitated and then smiled at him. 'Good man!' he told the Area Manager. Harry slapped Simon's shoulder in a show of support. Simon winced as he was injured on that shoulder.

'So how about you take me to meet Lek and... what's the name of the other officer? You know. The officer that's in charge of the *Phagocytes*.'

'Fargo,' Simon answered.

'That's the one. Take me to Lek and Fargo,' Harry instructed.

'We were asked to evacuate as many from the field of engagement as possible. Only vital systems personnel were allowed to remain. It was recommended that we wait here, until its safe,' Simon advised.

'Nonsense, we'll be fine,' Harry admonished the junior man. 'I'm the General Manager for all follicles. They'll appreciate my council, wouldn't you agree?'

Simon said nothing. He simply indicated that he would take him into the field of engagement.

Harry saw Bobby with an injured worker and he kneeled down beside him. 'I'm going to the front line to get an update on the situation from the two officers' in charge of the defense. You keep an eye on things here for me.'

Harry followed Simon out of the room. As he did, he nodded sympathetically to the critically burned and injured Follicle Farmers.

Bobby stared at him blankly. He watched Harry following Simon out of the room and out of view. He then returned to interview the injured worker.

Harry hastened to keep up with Simon. As the staff room was now very full of injured workers there were now overflowing into the passageway. Some of the Follicle Farmers here had perished and a team of able workers were removing the corpses for disposal.

Harry reminded himself that there would be time to mourn the dead after the inquiry. He thought that he would summon the idiot in charge of that disease carrying digit nail here into the affected area. He badly wanted him to see first-hand the massive scale of the devastation the introduction of the *Staph* had caused.

As Harry followed Simon through the interconnecting passageways, he could see the numerous scorched follicle bulbs that were reluctantly abandoned by their Farmers. He decided he'd need to transfer temporary workers from other areas to the abdomen to assist with repair and reconstruction.

Simon stopped when they arrived within visual range of Lek's command post. There were numerous, near identical, *T-Cells* assembled. Some were distinguished by their rank and their campaign acknowledgements. *B-Cells* were scattered among them but in significantly reduced numbers.

Everything about these *T-Cells* was white. They had white shielding, white clothing, and white weapons. They moved in coordinated military precision. Some helper *T-Cells* were administering *cytokines*. New *T-Cells* were forming ranks. Harry was very impressed with the spectacle and was encouraged that they would have both the numbers and the experience to mount a strong defense against the enemy.

As Harry turned to walk towards Lek's command post he and Simon heard someone shout 'Get back!' Simon withdrew to the assembled *T-Cells* as ordered, but Harry decided to make a run to get to Lek. He hastened toward the commander and was intercepted by a group of *Staphylococcus Aureus*. Their formation consisted of bright purple spheres, and they quickly surrounded Harry and pounced on him. The *T-Cells'* from both Lek's command post and the assembled ranks opened fire with IL-2. The *T-Cells* ammunition pounded the *Staph's* invading advanced action, and they were forced to withdraw.

Harry lay alone and injured.

He struggled to hold up one hand to attract aid. Lek and two senior Follicle Farmers rushed from the command post to the weakened follicle GM as did Simon and two troupers from the *T-Cell* ranks.

Simon got to him first. 'Harry! Are you okay?' Simon asked as he knelt next Harry.

Harry attempted to smile. 'Better get me to the meeting room, son.'

A stretcher soon arrived.

Lek recognised the prone Follicle Farmers' GM. He spoke to the two Follicle Farmers. 'I want you to load Harry onto this stretcher.' They hesitated, shrugged, and proceeded to load their leader.

'Simon, you lead them back to the meeting room,' Lek ordered. His voice was low but commanding. 'You shouldn't have brought him here!' He admonished.

Simon looked at the two and nodded. The two Follicle Farmers lifted the stretcher and they dutifully carried Harry.

'I'll follow them and get a report on his condition from the triage officer,' he advised his second-in-charge. I'll have to inform his System Manager of his injury.' He paused. 'Arrange to invite Fargo to meet me there,' he ordered.

The 2 IC saluted, did an about face and barked orders to subordinates.

Lek marched hastily to catch up to the stretcher party.

They moved away from the battlefield and into the relative safety of the healthy zone of skin and follicles. Work was suspended as farmers and builders alike were in shock and awaiting leadership and direction. They were all in fear that the infection would spread to them before the battle could be won.

The stretcher party wound its way through the narrow passage-ways. Simon had led them to his office, now being used as a triage room where victims could receive initial treatment and be assessed for repair, rehabilitation or be discarded.

Before the change in policy, all damaged cells, be they workers or management were immediately ordered into *Apoptosis*. The new way of doing things meant that injured workers were given a chance to recover, and wayward workers were given an oppor-tunity to improve. Less energy was spent on removing the dead, less time was spent training replacements and there was less op-portunity to replicate bad habits, poor procedures, and negative outcomes. The new way had Head Office's full support as well as support by the management teams at system level. The Unions and the workers all embraced and espoused the change. They were all motivated to make the new way work, as they knew deep down that this could result in a longer life span for their man, and that bene-fited everyone.

When Harry was resting on the triage table the manager in-serted some clear liquid into his patient. The Triage Manager stud-ied Harry and then looked up at Simon and shook his head.

'He's our GM,' Simon explained.

'If we had stronger medication, then perhaps...,' the Triage Man-ager tried to explain.

Lek had sent a runner to get a manager from the meeting room.

The messenger returned with Bobby close behind him.

Bobby looked at Lek and they nodded their acknowledgment. 'How is he?' Bobby asked the room.

'He's wounded pretty bad...,' the Triage Manager started to explain.

'But, if we can get more sophisticated medical treatment for him, he may survive!' Simon cut the man off.

'We'll send him to George,' Bobby explained to Simon.

'How?' both Simon and Lek demanded.

'We have a Zodiac,' Bobby explained. 'We'll get him safely on board and Skip can take him to George's office. He has a massive research facility and they are always doing advanced work on the repair and healing of damaged cells.'

Simon and Lek nodded.

'It'll be his best chance,' Bobby concluded.

Lek looked out of the room and spotted the two Follicle Farmers that had carried Harry to the triage room. He was grateful that they hadn't wandered off. 'You two!' he called them to attract their attention. 'Get in here.'

The two did as they were ordered.

Bobby watched them as they came into the room. They had correctly figured out that they were required to carry Harry once more, and they assumed their previous positions at each end of the stretcher.

'Who are both of you?' Bobby demanded.

'Hello, Bobby,' said the first. 'My name is Clive and I'm from the Follicle Farmers union.'

'The Union?' Bobby was puzzled.

'And I'm Frederick,' The second Follicle Farmer explained. 'I'm from the Follicle Farmer's Network News Service. I'm here to report on the conditions from the front lines.'

'They both have formal approvals from both Marketing and George,' Lek added.

'They got here just before you did,' Simon added.

'Harry invited us,' Frederick added.

'Could you please follow me? We'll go to the Taurus and load Harry on board,' Bobby asked them and they nodded their agreement.

The two lifted the now sedated Harry and were ready to exit the room.

'Simon, please go on ahead and locate Skip. He's the Captain of the Taurus that brought us here,' Bobby ordered.

Simon nodded his acknowledgement and preceded Bobby and the stretcher bearers out of the room. Lek remained behind to wait for Fargo.

The team filed around the wounded and shocked workers, and headed toward for the boat. As they advanced toward the Taurus, Skip walked toward them. 'Simon has explained the mission to me. I'll get him there as quick as I can,' he explained to Bobby.

When they got to the boat, Skip boarded and Frederick and Clive passed the stretcher to him and he rested it on top of the bow and the first seat. Skip, under the watchful eye of the others, expertly fastened Harry and the stretcher to the boat. He tested it and was satisfied. He gave his audience the thumbs up and a half smile.

Skip sat at the helm, strapped him-self in and started the motors. Bobby loosened the tie ropes and as they automatically rewound, the Taurus drifted into the *Plasma* stream. Skip advanced the throttles and the boat accelerated away from them, steered around a bend and was gone.

Bobby turned to the others and spoke. 'Let's get back and see who we can help.'

They followed Simon back into the meeting room.

Bobby found Banjo in conference with both Lek and Fargo. He joined them as did Simon, Fredrick and Clive.

Fargo looked up at Bobby, smiled and embraced him. 'I wish we were reunited under better circumstances,' he said sincerely.

The others were respectfully quiet.

Lek had set up a diagram of the conflict area. They crowded the screen.

'This is the area of engagement,' Lek explained. 'These purple dots are the *Staph* invaders. They are multiplying at an anticipated rate. The thing to realise with *Staph* is that they use our own resources against us, which means they grow using our supply chain. It is vital we restrict their access to it as soon as we can. Time is of the essence, gentlemen.'

Lek drew in a deep breath and continued, uninterrupted. 'These white dots represent my troops. The *T-Cells* are amassing and will soon be in sufficient numbers to switch from a fortification posture into an attack posture.'

'That's good,' someone muttered. Others murmured their agreement.

'Our *B-Cells* aren't equipped to deal with penetrated cells so they are being held at the periphery to deal with strays.' Lek pointed to the blue dots on the screen.

Lek continued the briefing. 'The green dots just outside the engagement area are the *Phagocytes*. As you can see they are already in significant in strength and their numbers are rapidly increasing.'

'I was given the authority to deploy reserves from other battalions,' Fargo explained.

'Anything else you want to add?' Lek invited.

Fargo took a deep breath and addressed them. 'The *Phagocytes* will initially act as the fall-back guard and will prevent the infection from spreading beyond this current infection area.' Fargo indicated the screen. 'We'll kill any *Staph* that slips through when the *Cytotoxic T-cells* advance. *T-Cell* numbers will decrease through the campaign as they engage the enemy. I expect the casualty numbers will be quite high.' Fargo looked at Lek who nodded his acknowledgement.

'As the *T-Cells* destroy the bulk of the enemy, we will commence our own advance into the engagement zone in a mopping up engagement,' Fargo told them.

Fargo continued. 'As there is significant raw, and open to the outside world, tissue exposure we'll use our dead to form a pus barrier to reduce infection from other bacteria or viruses who will try to take advantage of our weakened, damaged *Epidermis* barrier. Others will attempt to further infect us whilst we battle the *Staph*.'

Fargo took a deep breath and looked at Lek. 'We definitely do not want a secondary infection.'

'Can the *NK's* and *B-Cells* be brought back into battle to deal with them?' Banjo asked.

'I'll arrange it with their Commander,' Fargo agreed nodding.

Lek again took up the briefing. 'These red lines indicate our supply lines. We have sent for additional *Plasma* and food to keep our troops hydrated and replenished as they battle the enemy.' Lek looked at the others in turn and calmly asked. 'Are there any questions?'

'I have a few,' Bobby spoke for the first time since the briefing began. 'Both sides are multiplying in numbers. How do you know when you have sufficient strength to commence engaging their positions?'

Lek answered. 'At the outer perimeter we currently out-number their troops by three to one. We'll engage them on that perimeter as that is where we'll win. As we defeat them, we'll only advance as fast as we can replace our own fallen numbers.' He paused. 'They are surrounded. Their troops effectively shield each other, blocking them from engaging us directly in battle.'

'Have you engaged *Staph* before?' Bobby asked. Bobby noticed that Banjo, Clive and Frederick were all busily taking notes on their e-pads.

Lek answered. 'We have, but not in such significant numbers. This is a serious infection. We have detailed files on them and we know how to kill them, but it will take time, and there will be significant pain for our body whilst we engage the enemy.'

'We quickly assessed how many *Staph* arrived from the nail source,' Fargo added.

'We also know their duplication rates given these conditions, so we have a reasonably good idea of their current numbers,' Lek reassured them.

'We know what we're doing,' Fargo added.

'I know you do,' Bobby said confidently. 'I seem to find myself being the ranking Follicle Farmer here and I know I'll be questioned after this becomes history. I need to understand what is happening and I appreciate your patience with me,' he added modestly.

'By our assessment, you're the senior ranking *Integumentary* representative,' Clive told him. He looked at Banjo and Frederick who nodded their agreement.

'I did hear about your promotion, Bobby. Congratulations,' Lek said warmly.

'Thanks, but there will be time for catching up on old news after this campaign is won,' Bobby told them.

'We'll be ready to commence in about four cycles,' Fargo explained. 'I'm waiting for one more battalion to form here.' He pointed to one side of the battle zone. 'As soon as I have word that they are ready, I'll let Lek know and his troops will commence engaging the enemy.'

'Once we start, we won't stop until the battle is won,' Lek offered encouragement to the others. He then chanted 'We'll never slow down...'

'...and we'll never surrender!' Fargo joined in the military cry.

'So from here you'll push on until the enemy is defeated?' Bobby asked calmly with a smile.

'Absolutely!' Fargo and Lek responded together.

'We'll ensure that your supply lines remain functional,' Bobby added.

'I see you three are busy taking notes of this historic meeting,' Lek said to Banjo, Frederick and Clive.

Banjo replied first. 'As Bobby's E-A it is my responsibility to record what occurred and how we dealt with it. We're QA and we need to understand the process's utilised to learn what we did badly and learn how to do it better next time...,' his voice trailed off.

'Son.' Lek spoke in fatherly tones. 'The Follicle Farmers are collateral damage here. You couldn't possibly contribute to this situation and there will be zero blame assigned to Follicle Farmers. Let me guarantee you of that much.'

'I meant it from a recovery and resumption of follicle production perspective. I'm well aware that we didn't cause this situation,' Banjo countered. 'I do wish you all the best for the campaign and add that I, for what this is worth, have every confidence that you'll win.'

'Thank you, Banjo.' Lek looked at Bobby's E-A with a smile.

'From my perspective this is significant news,' Frederick explained. 'Most of the stuff I get to report on is routine. This is exciting!' He then hastily added. 'I'm speaking from a journalistic perspective, of course. No disrespect intended.'

Lek raised an eyebrow but let the comment go unchallenged. He was about to send his troops into battle and many would die, and this reporter found it exciting.

'Speaking on behalf of the Union,' Clive spoke up. 'I'm proud to be a witness to the fine job you're all doing. You guys are amazing,' he said to Lek and Fargo.

Lek and Fargo said nothing.

'Bobby. You and Banjo are amazing also. The Union is so proud of you. All Follicle Farmers will be proud of both of you,' he gushed, 'and you too, Simon,' he added smiling at the room.

'I think we should return to our troops,' Lek suggested to Fargo.

'Agreed,' Fargo acknowledged. 'I'll send you word when my final battalion are properly in place. You'll soon be able to commence your attack.'

With a salute to the non-combatants, Lek and Fargo marched out of the room.

Simon returned to his men, sharing the updates that he had just learned of the campaign, reassuring them that the plans for repelling the *Staph* infection were going to work.

Bobby turned to Clive and Frederick.

'Let me get my facts straight,' he said to them. 'You're here at the invitation of Harry?'

'That's right,' Clive agreed.

'And you were both here before we arrived?' Bobby queried.

'Yes. We were being briefed by Lek at his command post when we saw Harry arrive,' Frederick agreed.

'So, you would have been here quite a bit earlier than us,' Bobby speculated.

'I guess,' Frederick conceded.

'So Harry sent for you whilst he was still at the pit. He had sent for both of you before he had even told us there was a problem on the *Abdomen*.' Bobby was figuring it all out.

Frederick explained. 'You don't know Harry as well as we do, you see, Harry enjoys publicity. When he sees an opportunity to look good, he calls us.'

'He wants everyone to admire and respect him,' Clive added. 'He learned a long time ago, if he can impress the Union and have us respecting him publicly, it'll go a long way to strengthen his power base with Follicle Farmers, Management and Head Office.'

'We go along with it because we get great stories to share,' Frederick explained.

'Kind of a win-win situation, we figure,' Clive added.

'We're doing our job,' Frederick said.

Bobby looked at Banjo. Banjo shrugged one shoulder.

'Now that you're the Senior Manager on site, we'll write about you. You'll be famous.'

'I'm not seeking fame or awards. Our concern here is the recovery of Follicle Farmers and *Epidermis Builders* so we can get on with the job of growing hair and re-building the *Dermis* and *Epidermis* layers back to full strength,' Bobby countered.

'Spoken like the true natural leader that you are,' Frederick complimented.

Bobby sighed.

Frederick and Clive had returned to note taking when Simon approached them.

'I've just heard from the front line. The *Cytotoxic T-Cells* have commenced their counter-attack. The battle for the abdomen has begun.'

A *Helper T-Cell* approached the desk where Bobby and the others were discussing possible outcomes of the battle. He saluted them and spoke directly to Bobby. 'I am here with commander Lek's complements sir. I'm to escort you to his command post where you and your colleagues will be able to witness the battle from a safe position.'

Bobby looked at the others. He had hesitated but Banjo spoke for them. 'We'll be right behind you.'

The *Helper T-Cell* did another salute, executed an about turn and marched to the exit. Banjo indicated to the others that they must hurry up in order to keep up with him.

They followed the *Helper T-Cell* past the evacuated injured warriors and onto the outer edges of the field of engagement.

They looked over at the battlefield from the relative safety of Lek's command post. A red hue hung over the area. Inflammation of the *Dermis* and *Epidermis* was occurring as a reaction to the infection. The wounded and shocked *Dermal Builders* were evacuated long ago. About them, follicles stood eerily erect, their Farmers also long evacuated. Everywhere there were scorched fat cells, damaged *sebaceous glands,* and lumps of white. These lumps were the remnants of the externally applied burn cream that caused the allergic reaction and provided an environment for the *Staph* to thrive.

The abundant raw nerve endings were sending strong messages of pain and discomfort to the *Central Nervous System.*

Before them they could see a swarming mass of enemy purple spheres replicating rapidly.

In an irregular ring, surrounding and containing the *Staph* infectors, were the white *T-Cells.* They were tall, heavily armed, and well equipped. They were poised for battle. There numbers were increasing as fast as the *T-Cells* could replicate themselves. The newly replicated arrivals were expediently armed by the numerous expert Helper *T-Cells* that supported the warrior *Cytotoxic T-Cells*. They aided them in growing their numbers, arming them with *Cytokines* and *Interlukin-2* and then directing toward the battle.

Behind them, the green *Phagocytes* had assembled into three ranks and were ready to pounce should the staph break through the *T-Cells* lines. These lumpy green *Phagocytes* were from the wandering *Macrophages* battalion and proudly displayed their battalion colours on their uniforms.

The *Cytotoxic T-Cells* themselves were engaging the enemy using the full force of their numbers. From a vantage point, which was Lek's command post, they could see the *Staph* being challenged and defeated by the superior strength, technology, training and discipline.

The five Follicle Farmers present to witness the campaign, felt confident that all was going well in the effort to rid the body of this aggressive infection.

Lek returned to his command post.

'The battle is not going well,' Lek informed them as he stepped up to speak to them. 'Here, where you can see the front line, you can see that we are advancing into the enemy positions. However, on the other side the *Staph* has broken through the *Cytotoxic T-Cell* perimeter and the *Phagocytes* there are now fighting a fierce battle.'

'I thought we were winning?' Bobby queried.

'My men do have them contained on this side of the infection because I'm here to guide them and inspire them. But, on the other fronts the infection is spreading rapidly. Some of the newer *Cytotoxic T-Cells* have yet to be activated. Others have shoddy aim, and they are wasting their *Perforin* and *Lymphotoxin*.' He took a deep breath and continued. 'You see the *Perforin* and *Lymphotoxin* needs to make direct contact with the *Staph* in order for it to be effective. If they miss they run the risk of being overwhelmed and defeated.'

'What of your Junior Officers?' Clive asked.

'They are inexperienced,' Lek responded gravely.

'What are you planning to do?' Bobby asked.

'I shall leave this front for Milo to command and I'll redeploy to the far side and encourage my men to do better,' he explained. 'This is a battle we must win.'

Lek paused for deep reflection and then continued. 'This infection is very virulent and will cause massive inflammation and extreme pain. The sooner we can contain the *Staph* the less likely there'll be permanent lesions.'

Lek turned and left them to watch his back as he marched away to circumnavigate the battlefield.

A burst of purple spheres rushed the *Cytotoxic T-Cells* but their attempt was thwarted by precision aiming of weaponry. The *Phagocyte* Officer had prepared his troops for a breach in the line, but on this occasion it wasn't required.

Fargo came up to them. 'Promise me you'll evacuate from here if the *Staph* break through the *T-Cells* lines.'

'We will,' Bobby agreed for the whole group.

'Why are those *T-Cells* falling back?' Frederick wanted to know. He pointed to a small group of ragged and tired looking *Cytotoxic T-Cells* that were falling backward through their own ranks.

'They're probably low on ammunition,' Fargo surmised.

Even from their relatively safe distance they could see the *Helper T-Cells* re-arming those *Cytotoxic T-Cells*. They were very efficient and expedient. The rejuvenated brave soldiers immediately returned to engage the enemy once more.

Some of the *B-Cells* were engaging the *Staph* with limited success. There casualties were high as they were outmatched by the infection.

Bobby and the others could see the purple spheres being destroyed under the crush of the superior *Cytotoxic T-Cells* in this sector. These *T-Cells* were delivering lethal hits and were continuing to the next *Staph* sphere as the previous one was still falling after receiving a fatal dose. The Follicle Farmers were smiling at each other, and Bobby realised that they were all suppressing a premature urge to cheer as their side was now clearly winning. Bobby hoped that Lek's shift in command position was having an equal effect on the other side in defeating this invading force of staph warriors.

Fargo stepped up to Bobby and explained. 'The *Cytotoxic T-Cells* are winning here but I've received an update from Lek and there have been additional breaches in the line in several places. I'm going to send half my men to reinforce other positions to the left and right of this position.'

'Oh,' Bobby looked at the others in concern.

'Do you want an escort to the recovery centre?' Fargo offered.

'No!' Banjo, Frederick, and Clive chorused.

'I guess we're staying, Fargo. Thanks for the concern,' Bobby replied for the group.

Fargo nodded, turned, and went to his men. They could hear Fargo bark orders to his troops.

The Follicle Farmers watched as the first rank executed a left turn and marched away to take up positions on the left flank. The second rank executed a right turn and headed for the right flank. The remaining rear line spread them-selves in a defensive position ready to receive invaders should they break through the *T-Cells* positions.

Milo, the *Cytotoxic T-Cell* second in command, marched up to where the Follicle Farmers were at the command post. He was followed by two *Helper T-Cells* who held a captive *Staph* prisoner . The weakened purple bacteria sphere initially struggled but eventually gave in to his captors. He looked angry and contemptuous at being taken prisoner.

'I thought you might want to meet one the enemy before we dispose of him,' the Commander offered.

They studied the *Staph*. He was a blotchy sort of purple and round shaped and had small projections that they guessed he used to deliver infection into human cells. The *Staph* spat pus at them but he was too far away to hit anyone. One of the *T-Cells* hit the prisoner and he quietened.

'Is he dangerous?' Clive asked cautiously.

'Not anymore,' the commander responded.

The *Staph* shouted unintelligibly and the *T-Cell* guards laughed.

'Do you understand his language?' Bobby asked.

'I understand some of their main words,' Milo answered. 'They have a very limited vocabulary. He said he wants to kill us and display our bodies to his friends.'

'Why is that funny?' Banjo was curious. Clive and Frederick were taking photos and taking notes of the behaviour of the superior *T-Cells* and their prisoner.

'His friends are dead and dying and he'll be joining them soon,' Milo replied.

'How do you spell your name please?' Frederick asked. He continued typing furiously into his e-pad trying to record as much detail as possible, as every journalist worth his salt must do.

'I'm Commander Milo. M-I-L-O,' the *T-Cell* replied with a confident smile.

It occurred to Bobby that this *T-Cell* was seeking fame and glory whilst his superior officer was busy leading weakened troops in another part of the battle.

Milo offered an explanation. 'This *Staph* has run out of *Exotoxins*. They are *Super Antigens* and he can't infect healthy human cells anymore and is now vulnerable to our ammunition.' Milo and the two *Helper T-Cells* laughed at the *Staph's* impending execution.

'Are you planning to interrogate this prisoner?' Clive wanted to know.

'No,' Milo answered. 'We know all about his kind and we have excellent memories.' Milo studies their faces. 'Under normal circumstances we should have been able to eliminate the *Staph* infection from its earliest onset. Our *Memory T-Cells* have detailed information on this infection and that would have allowed us to defeat it before it commenced proliferation.'

'So why…?' Bobby left the question hanging.

'The burns and then the subsequent allergic reaction to the externally applied burn cream slowed our progress. It has made it very difficult for us to group and divide into sufficient numbers,' he replied.

'It seems to be a classic case of a Head Office decision working against us,' Bobby murmured.

'Head Office may have been unaware of the MI's potency, and it may have been an unintended consequence. We've had to deal with those types of situations before,' Milo explained. 'Just, not this bad,' he conceded.

'How will the *Phagocytes* know when they need to reinforce your positions?' Frederick asked.

'You see, we do a lot of work together. We *Cytotoxic T-Cells* secrete a *Gamma-interferon*. This alerts the *Phagocytes* and they'll coming rushing in. After we weaken the enemy, the *Phagocytes* are able to literally eat them up,' Milo replied with a smile.

'It sounds disgusting,' Clive said.

'*T-Cells*, don't eat their enemy,' Milo replied without agreeing.

The *Staph* looked angry and scared at the same time. Milo made a hand slashing the throat gesture to the two guards and everyone knew what that meant.

The *Staph* was kicking furiously as it was dragged away. They didn't see it again.

'How are your supplies?' Bobby wanted to know.

'The *Cardiovascular* System is sending as many rations as needed. The problem is that they are also transporting rebuilding teams to our location,' Milo answered.

'Is that too soon?' Bobby guessed.

'If there are too many then they'll get in our way. We do need the rations, but we can't cope with the others being here at this stage,' Milo explained.

'Can we help?' Banjo asked.

'If you could ask them to keep away from the front line, it would be a tremendous help,' Milo told them.

'Simon, Banjo. Could you please organise an assembly area for the re-builders? It'll need it to be far enough away so that they are out of the way of the soldiers and close enough so that they can start rebuilding work as soon as an area is secured,' Bobby asked.

Simon nodded his acknowledgement and Banjo saluted. The two turned and left the command post to select the assembly point.

'That will also help bring the temperature down,' Milo informed them.

Bobby immediately became aware of the heat. The increases had been so gradual that he hadn't noticed it up till now. He was hot. Normally, the *epidermis* that Follicle Farmers work in is cooler than core body temperature. Bobby remembered that he had previously commented to Banjo that internal parts of the body were warmer than temperatures that they were used to. The heat being generated by the battle meant that it was even hotter.

Fargo approached the command position and he spoke directly to Milo. 'Your men are doing a fine job.'

'Thank you, sir.' Milo had stood to attention despite being from a different system. Clearly there was much respect and co-operation between the different defence forces.

'It is only my opinion, but I feel you should withdraw some of your troops from this sector and redeploy them to strengthen weaker parts of the front,' Fargo suggested.

'I'll send a runner to Lek and get his approval for that excellent advice, sir,' Milo responded tactfully.

Fargo nodded.

Milo nodded at the Follicle Farmers and turned smartly and marched away to arrange a runner.

'He's a good man and a fierce warrior in the fight against diseases and infections,' Fargo uttered the compliment.

'I sense a 'but' following that comment.' Bobby stepped up close to his friend and together they watched Milo.

'But... he likes to show off. He wants his own command. Oh he'll get it, but he's ambitious and therefore impatient,' Fargo conceded that there was more to his comment.

'Just as you were I'm sure,' Bobby teased.

'Yes, of course,' Fargo looked at him and smiled for the first time in a long time.

They shared a quiet moment.

'Growing my follicle in the beard seems like such a very long time ago,' Bobby lamented.

'How is that *Rhinovirus* working out? You know the one that you wanted for follicle growing duties,' Fargo asked.

'Last I heard he was being considered for promotion to Team Leader.' Bobby laughed at the memory of Rhino's arrival at his follicle.

'He may be dead, you know,' Fargo said sadly.

'Why do you say that?' Bobby was alarmed.

'They don't have as long a life span as us,' Fargo explained.

'Oh,' Bobby said.

'But then, with the improved nutrition and...,' He laughed '...nurturing environment that you lot furnishes workers with; it'll probably double his natural life span.' Fargo laughed again and Bobby laughed with him.

'Milo's heading our way.' Clive had alerted them to the Commander's approach.

As he drew closer, he spoke to Fargo. 'Lek agrees with your assessment, sir. Would you please engage the enemy here whilst I redeploy my men to weaker fronts?' He asked formally.

'Certainly,' Fargo agreed. 'I'll be happy to do so.'

Milo saluted Fargo who returned the salute. Bobby understood that it was a measure of respect but thought it a bit excessive when they were in an actual active battle with a virulent infection. He said nothing.

Milo did a snappy about face and marched away to assemble the troops that he was about to redeploy.

Fargo gave a casual salute to Bobby, almost in mockery of Milo and waved farewell to Frederick and Clive.

'Good luck,' Clive acknowledged.

'Stay alive,' Frederick told him.

'Be very safe my friend,' Bobby told Fargo. 'I want you present when we celebrate the victory.'

'First drink is on you,' Fargo replied as he smiled and headed towards his troops.

Bobby mused. Skip had mentioned catching up for a drink when he was with Jack from the Capricorn and now Fargo was talking about having a drink. He must investigate this drinking. Perhaps it was a ritual. He was used to consuming fluids, but this "drink" sounded like it might be something special.

Milo came up to Bobby and the others. 'I'm redeploying half my men to the other fields of engagement. The *Phagocytes* are reduced in numbers after their own re-deployment. Would you like an escort to a safer zone?' he asked with concern.

Bobby took a deep breath. 'I have every confidence in your, and in Fargo's men, that they'll hold the line here.' Bobby reassured the *T-Cell* Commander.

'Are you certain?' Milo asked feeling for their vulnerability and lack of weaponry. 'I can't spare anyone to protect you and you've had no training in self-defence,' Milo lamented.

'We'll be fine. Besides, I'll have to wait here for Banjo and Simon as we have to co-ordinate rebuilding efforts once the battle is won. I believe there is a risk of a secondary infection if we don't commence reconstruction quickly.'

'That is true, sir,' Milo agreed.

Milo did a quick salute, turned, and hastened to his men. He assigned two officers to take charge of the remaining *T-Cells* and he ordered the other to follow him. They left the area at the double march, *Helper T-Cells* following in their wake.

Fargo barked orders at the remaining *Phagocytes,* and they snapped their jaws and advanced on the remaining enemy. The

Wandering Macrophage Phagocytes performed a manoeuvre known as *Phagocytosis*. It processes the enemy via ingestion. They literally eat their enemy. They also clean up the debris on the battlefield by eating it. They are not known for their table manners.

The *T-Cells* stepped aside as the *Phagocytes* filed past them and engaged the enemy. They were grateful for a short rest from the battle as the *Phagocytes* took up the fight. Bobby and the others watched as *Phagocytosis* commenced on the hapless *Staph* infection. They begin by seeking out the *Staph's* own *Chemotaxis* which they use to hone in on when targeting the enemy. They next performed an *Adherence* in which they slowly hold the *Staph* captive. The immobilised *Staph* is then surrounded by *Pseudopods* which project around the *Staph's* body by engulfing it and then he commences ingestion in a sac known as a *Phagosome*.

During this process the *Staph* is killed with an *Oxidative Burst*. It isn't known if the process is painful to the invading infection, but no-one has been interested enough to find out. Like the *T-Cells*, this battle was also fought in relative silence. Bobby heard some of the commands by the officers from both sides, but there wasn't any screams or moans. The two sides engaged each other fiercely, but quietly. Some *Staph* slipped through the *Phagocytes* lines and the *Cytotoxic T-Cells* expediently dealt with them using a blast from their weapons. Soon the area before the command post was becoming clear of the enemy. The officers ordered their troops to attack the enemy positions to their left and right and they pursued the enemy into adjacent engagement zones.

Banjo returned to the command post. 'What did I miss?' He asked Bobby.

'We've won this part of the battle,' Bobby replied. 'There are a few *Phagocytes* mopping up the debris. The rest of the *T-Cells* and *Phagocytes* have gone to strengthen our troops over there and there.' Bobby pointed to the left and right flanks of their own position.

'Oh. I missed it,' Banjo lamented.

'I've recorded a lot of the action,' Frederick informed him holding up his camera and e-pad.

Banjo nodded.

'How many re-builders have arrived?' Bobby asked quickly changing the subject. The last thing he wanted was for Banjo to lose focus on the reconstructive process.

'Heaps,' Banjo answered non-specifically.

Simon approached them. 'Do you think it safe to start work in this area?' He asked Bobby.

'I think we'll bring the *Dermis Builders* in first. They can assemble here, and they'll deploy when I get the all clear from the *Suppressor T-Cell*,' he answered.

Simon nodded and returned to fetch a team of *Dermis Builders* and have them move themselves and their materials and supplies closer to the front.

'It's very chaotic at the assembly area,' Banjo explained. 'They're all very keen to rebuild,' he added. 'Morale is the best I have seen. The dead have been removed and many of the probable's have survived and have recovered enough to help with the reconstruction.'

'That's great news!' Bobby was excited.

'It is!' Banjo agreed.

'What a team!' Bobby was proud. He was a proud Follicle Farmer and an equally proud QA Manager for Follicles. But at this moment he was proud to be an *Integumentary* team member. The way they had collectively dealt with the situation made him proud to be a part of this wonderful body.

Bobby slapped Banjo's back in happiness. Banjo winced and wondered what he'd done wrong.

Simon approached them. 'You do realise that you're the ranking *Integumentary* System Manager here, don't you sir?

'Hasn't anyone from the *Dermis* or *Epidermis* arrived to take charge of the reconstruction?' Bobby was bewildered.

'There are plenty of workers, sir, but no managers. I guess it's all up to you,' Simon added with a smile.

'Fine then.' Bobby accepted the responsibility.

'Banjo, please ask that officer if we can commence reconstruction in this area?'

Banjo nodded and went to the *Suppressor T-Cell* and asked the question. The *T-Cell* nodded, and Banjo gave his boss the okay signal.

'Simon, lets rebuild!' Bobby ordered.

'Yes sir!' Simon agreed. He turned and hastened to issue the orders to get work started.

It took many hundreds of cycles for the re-builders to work on the *Dermis* and *Epidermis* reconstruction. They transported the building blocks of the skin into the former battlefield. They erected *Derma Papilla*, rerouted *Capillary Loops*, positioned *Sweat Pores* and *Sebaceous Glands*. Soon Follicle Farmers were arriving and were busily reactivating hair follicles. *Arrector Pili Muscles* were checked repaired and tested. Some of the *Eccrine Sweat Glands* had to be completely re-grown as they were destroyed by the allergic reactive cream. The nerve endings were pacified and they slowly returned to normal communicative duties. The *Adipose Tissue* in the *Subcutaneous Layer* that were unaffected by the battle supported the workers and soon this region was looking pink and healthy again. They started the routine feeding and management of each hair under the rigorous scrutiny of Bobby and Banjo.

Eventually, Fargo and Lek caught up with Bobby. They proudly confirmed that the *Staph* infection had been completely destroyed. They conceded that they did have some outside assistance from an external antibacterial agent that arrived in the blood. The *T-Cells* had dispersed the chemical into the *Staph* population and it hastened their demise. Lek intimated that he had the *Staph* defeated but appreciated the bonus assistance provided by Head Office. The two now had to go away and downsize their military strength. As was their custom, they'd celebrate hard and then the surplus warriors would voluntarily complete *Apoptosis*.

The re-builders now spread over the whole of the former battlefield. The remnants of the enemy, the fallen *T-Cells* and *Phagocytes* had been cleared away. Bobby toured the reconstruction area and it looked to him that there wouldn't be any scarring as a result of this infection. The *Integumentary* rebuilding team had done a remarkable job. He was proud of them and he kept telling them that at every opportunity. They appeared to appreciate his praises and they kept working hard, smart and efficiently.

The blood supply kept everyone replenished. A rebuilding program required an unlimited supply of amino acids, proteins, and sugars. Hard workers had healthy appetites, and these were properly satisfied. Bobby and Banjo worked tirelessly throughout the entire reconstruction, and both were hopeful of a lengthy rest period before recommencing their QA inspection tour.

As Bobby was instructing a recently promoted Team Leader on the correct procedure for adding chemicals to a *follicle papilla* for the third time, he was interrupted by Skip.

'Give an old friend a welcoming hug?' he suggested to Bobby as he walked up behind him.

Bobby turned to face the voice. 'Skip!' he acknowledged the Captain of the Taurus.

They embraced and Skip next embraced Banjo.

'How is Harry?' Bobby asked with concern.

'He is still recovering, and he may yet pull through. George has a wonderful, highly advanced expert medical team and they just might perform miracles on him,' Skip explained.

'I should have let him complete *Apoptosis*,' another voice said. It was George, System Manager for the *Integumentary* System, who then walked up to Bobby, his hand extended in friendship.

Bobby took the hand and returned the handshake.

'Well done on a brilliant job. I hear you were an inspirational leader and produced a healthy result,' George told him warmly.

'Thank you, sir. I just did my best,' Bobby replied modestly.

'Your excellent best,' George reiterated.

For the next few cycles Bobby gave George the tour of the affected area and pointed out the rebuilding efforts and the retraining of *Integumentary* personnel as replacements for the dead cells were put into place.

Bobby asked. 'Who have you selected to take over as Manager for the *Abdomen*?'

'Simon is the ranking Follicle Farmer. He'll be promoted to Regional Manager for the front of the *Torso*. His boss didn't survive the burns, you know?' George answered.

'I didn't know him, but I had learned that he was a casualty,' Bobby acknowledged.

George continued. 'I have also appointed new managers for the *Dermis* and *Epidermis*. They have now commenced their duties and they'll take over from you so you can get some well-earned rest.' George explained. 'I'm satisfied that you can resume your QA inspection tour, Bobby, but first, you and Banjo deserve some rest and relaxation. I've asked Skip to take you to a quiet place so that you can unwind and relax a little.'

'Thank you, sir. That would be gratefully appreciated,' Bobby responded happily.

George smiled and added. 'I have also instructed the manager for the nails to be sure they are kept trimmed. Can't have a repeat of our own system damaging itself, can we?' he asked rhetorically.

'No sir,' Bobby agreed. 'That wouldn't be good.'

George smiled.

~ 15 ~

Bobby and Banjo completed their farewells and together with Skip, departed the *Abdomen*. They were looking forward to a long rest. This was a well-earned break from their tasks, and it was fully authorised, as Banjo had reminded Bobby when he had briefly lamented the temporary suspension of their QA work. Even though they had been journeying with Skip in the Taurus for some time now, they had really only quality assessed follicle production in the left arm pit. The work and actions they had performed at the *Abdomen* was vital and personally rewarding, but as they were done under extreme circumstances, it didn't really count as far as routine QA was concerned.

They had to contend with the knowledge that they had set things up so that the *Abdomen* Follicle Team were now following QA principles and they should competently pass a QA audit when next they visited.

They were on a "whole of the body follicle tour" and just now they were going to the...

'Skip!' Where are we going?' Bobby demanded. He had to yell to be heard above the roar of the engines.

'We're going to get fuel,' Skip replied.

'Food?' Banjo queried hopefully.

'I said fuel!' Skip answered louder.

'Food is fuel,' Banjo countered. He was hungry.

Bobby smiled at him and then repeated his question to Skip, with just a little more detail. 'Where are we going after we fuel up?' Bobby yelled, as he once again asked the captain for details of their destination.

'The *Liver*,' Skip replied. He was checking the stern and his voice projected in the wrong direction.

'Deliver? What do we need to deliver?' Bobby was confused.

'What?' Skip looked confused.

'I asked. What are we going to deliver!?' Bobby re-asked the question a bit louder.

'Nothing,' Skip answered shaking his head. Then, after a thought he added. 'You two.'

'Us too... what?' Bobby was very puzzled.

'He's going to deliver the two of us to the place where we'll be resting,' Banjo concluded helpfully. 'And eating,' he added hopefully.

'I understand that, but where?' Bobby demanded from Banjo.

'Maybe he's being awkward because he wants to keep it as a nice surprise,' Banjo offered hopefully. He turned to face Skip. 'Somewhere where there is... a lot... of foooood.' He had exaggerated the food comment to reiterate his current hungry status.

Skip responded with the okay signal.

Bobby gave up. He shrugged and smiled.

As the Taurus wound its way through the body on the *Plasma* flow through the *Cardiovascular* System, the two sat back, rested, and enjoyed the ride. They had already gone through the now familiar *Heart* and *Lungs*. Skip had explained to them that each journey required a loop through these two organs.

Just to mix things up a bit Skip alternated between the left *Lung* and the right *Lung* circuit. Both Bobby and Banjo agreed that they couldn't see any difference between the two, but they were pleased that Skip cared enough to try to keep the journeying part interesting.

'We're coming up to the *Suprarenal Artery*!' Skip yelled. 'We'll now exit the *Abdominal Aorta*.'

As Skip was beginning the turn toward the exit to go to the *Adrenal Gland*, the blood pressure suddenly increased. This caught

Skip by surprise. He had the steering aimed at the *Suprarenal Artery* but ended up unintentionally being surged into the *Renal Artery*.

'Oh no!' Skip lamented.

'What?' Bobby and Banjo chorused.

'We're in the *Renal*,' Skip informed them flatly. His monotone expression told them that this wasn't a good thing. He no longer had to yell as the noise in this smaller artery was much less than the main artery.

'What does that mean?' Bobby was confused. He'd gathered this wasn't their rest and recreation destination because they were here to get fuel. Rest and recreation came after getting fuel.

'We're heading to the *Kidney*. Sorry.' Skip was down cast.

'Is that a bad thing?' Banjo asked.

'It isn't nice.' Skip took a deep breath and moaned.

'Why?' Banjo queried.

'We'll have to go through it.' Skip was being scant on details and was clearly avoiding the full explanation.

'So we go through it.' Bobby accepted the situation. 'I gather this means we'll have to go back through the veins into the *Heart* and *Lungs* and work our way back to the *Adrenal Artery*,' Bobby verbalised what he thought was happening. 'It's a small delay, so what?' He added.

'I mean we'll literally have to go through... the *Kidney*. There is no shortcut,' Skip replied.

'Oh.' Bobby was beginning to comprehend.

'That's going to be a tight fit. Isn't it?' Banjo had also begun to understand what was happening to them.

Skip nodded and took a deep breath. 'Normally, if I have to deliver someone to the *Kidney*, I drop them off at the entry, and they make their own way in.'

'Oh,' Bobby responded. He was becoming deeply aware of their predicament.

Skip manoeuvred the Taurus to the docking port in the *Segmental Artery*. The blood whooshed passed them on its way to be filtered.

It seemed to Bobby and Banjo that there was plenty of room, but they said nothing.

'Hello,' a voice greeted them.

'Hello,' Skip called back.

'Hello,' the voice reiterated.

'Where are you?' Skip demanded.

'Here,' the voice offered.

The three looked about them and saw nothing.

A face appeared from an invisible bend in the walls of the *artery*. 'Hello,' the face said again.

'We're lost!' Skip told the face.

'You're in my *Kidney*,' the face informed them.

'I mean we've lost our way.' Skip took a deep breath, restraining his exasperation in putting them all in this situation.

'I believe you,' the face agreed. Its owner moved around the corner of the wall and stepped up to them. He surveyed them and their boat. 'How do you plan to get that out of my *Kidney*?' he asked flatly.

'Are you the *Kidney* Manager?' Bobby questioned.

'I am,' he answered. 'You shouldn't be here with that... thing,' he informed them.

'My name is Skip,' Skip introduced himself. 'I'm the Captain of this boat...,' He started to explain.

'Not a very clever Captain. Are you?' The *Kidney* Manager accused.

'We were pushed into the *Renal Artery* by a surge in the *blood pressure*. I was heading for the *Adrenal Gland* to fuel up,' Skip defended. 'We didn't mean to come here.'

'Who are you two?' The *Kidney* Manager asked.

'I'm Bobby and this is my assistant Banjo.' Bobby did his own introductions. 'We're Follicle Farmers doing a...,' Bobby started to explain.

'There is no hair here!' The *Kidney* Manager exclaimed. 'Hair isn't allowed. It would be very bad for my *Kidney*.'

Bobby was becoming as exasperated as Skip. He tried to explain. 'Skip is taking us on a tour of the body to see the follicle growing regions. We're QA Managers doing an inspection of hair growing practices. We need to fuel up and we were...,'

'There is no fuel here, only urine.' The *Kidney* Manager cut Bobby off again. 'Unless your craft can run on pee, I surmise you're in the wrong place.'

'That's what we've been trying to explain.' Skip was clearly beyond exasperated. He was becoming agitated.

'What is your name, sir?' Banjo asked as he alighted from the Taurus. Banjo offered his hand in friendship which the *Kidney* Manager accepted.

'I'm known as Erik. We don't get many visitors here. They don't like the smell in the *Glomerulus Capsule*. You'll have to go through that if you want to get to the *Adrenal Gland*,' Erik added, seemingly more informative, now that he had identified himself.

It had occurred to Bobby that people were much more forthcoming with information once you knew their name. Anonymity offered a sort of immunity from responsibility.

'I've heard that from another Captain that came through the *Kidney*,' Skip agreed.

'It must have been the other *Kidney*,' Erik speculated. 'We've never had one of those here before.' Erik was pointing to the boat.

'It may have been,' Skip wasn't sure.

'That won't pass through the *Peritubular Capillaries*. It is too big,' Erik advised them pointing at the Taurus.

'That's what I thought,' Skip lamented. 'Is there another way through?'

'No.'

'Oh.'

'I can lead you three through, but you have to abandon your boat,' Erik offered. 'It's quite tricky and you don't want to end up on the wrong side of the *Glomerular Capsule*.'

'Why not?' Banjo was curious.

'You'll end up in the pee tank,' Erik replied.

Bobby and Banjo took a deep breath.

'We need the boat. What do we have to do?' Skip asked.

'Can you make this thing smaller?' Erik asked.

'We can deflate it,' Skip answered. 'Most of the bulk is just oxygen under pressure. I can also detach and separate the two inboard motors.'

'We'd better give it a try then,' Erik offered with a smile. 'I'm sure you're keen to get on with your hairy tour.'

As the blood swished passed them on its way to be filtered the Captain of the Taurus, the two Follicle Farmers and the *Kidney* Manager worked on carefully deflating the Taurus and reducing it into the smallest components possible. It took many cycles and they worked at a steady pace.

When Skip was satisfied they had done all they could, they bundled smaller components to each other so they wouldn't get separated or lost when going through the confined areas of the *Kidney*.

'It is very important that we don't get stuck,' Erik advised them. 'It would cause a blockage and that would be bad.'

'Very bad,' Skip agreed. Bobby and Banjo nodded but said nothing.

'If we do, I'll get a lot more visitors,' Erik smiled. 'But not the type we want.' He smiled some more.

'I think he means the white *B-Cells*.' Banjo whispered to Bobby. 'If we cause a blockage they'll come here to clear us away. They wouldn't be gentle.'

Bobby took a deep breath but said nothing.

They had separated the parts of the Taurus into four bundles. Bobby had one motor and the control panel. Banjo had the other motor and the seats. Erik held onto oars, ropes and some other items that were bound together. Skip had the zodiac. It was flattened, rolled, and shaped into a long narrow black tube.

Erik led the way into the blood stream, followed by Bobby. Next Skip entered and Banjo followed Skip in case the rear of the boat got caught up in anything as they passed through the *Kidney*.

In this way they passed through the ever-decreasing diameters of *Arteries*. By the time they got into the *Interlobular Artery* the passage was very cramped. In the *Afferent Arterioles* they had to lie flat and pull their way through. Strange as it felt, they were assisted somewhat by the blood pressure pushing them through.

When they passed into the *Glomerulus* the travellers witnessed the separation of urine from the blood. They saw the even narrower openings that allowed the *Kidney* to literally squeeze the super concentrated urine out of the blood into the *Convoluted Tubule* that led to the bladder. It was strong but gentle, and it functioned without hurting the blood cells or the travellers.

Bobby resisted the urge of letting go of the motor to cover his face. The stench of the urine was very overpowering. Soon they were through, and the arteries gradually expanded in size. When they reached the *renal vein*, Erik guided them to a platform where they could rest and reassemble the boat. Skip thanked and apologised again to Erik profusely. Erik was nonplussed.

After they rested, they reassembled the Taurus. 'We won't be able to inflate her,' Skip explained. 'I've arranged for a barge to meet us at the exit and take us back to the boat-yard to get her inflated and checked over.'

Bobby and Banjo said nothing. They were relieved that they had survived the experience and were looking forward to getting underway once more. After Skip confirmed that all the components of the Taurus were accounted for, they agreed to drift through the *Renal Vein* and waited for the barge at the exit into the *Inferior Vena Cava*.

FOLLICLE FARM ~ 247

After sliding back into the blood flow and drifting away from the *Kidney*, Banjo turned and called to Erik. 'Where is your team?' he called.

'They're in the dining room on their meal break!' Erik answered.

Banjo went pale. In the excitement he'd forgotten to ask for food. Bobby and Skip laughed at him.

Soon they were moored at the exit point, and they waited for the barge.

'I'm sorry for the delay boys,' Skip apologised once more.

'Forget it,' Bobby dismissed the apology. 'It was a unique experience. Wasn't it Banjo?' Banjo nodded his head. He was looking upstream for the barge.

'There it is!' he announced.

The barge eased its way to them, and they loaded the components of the Taurus and themselves on board. Skip spoke to the captain and then they found as comfortable a place as they could among the supplies that the barge was carrying. Soon all three were asleep.

After an uneventful journey, Skip roused his travelling companions. 'Wake up!' he said as he shook them. 'We're at the Zodiac's pen.'

As they pulled the deflated Taurus into the Zodiac's boat pen Phil came out of his office to greet them.

'What have you done to my beautiful Taurus?' he teased.

Mechanics arrived and aided them by moving the Taurus into the service pen and they immediately started work reinflating the craft and checking it for flow going worthiness. Banjo had led the charge into the meals room and while the three ate their fill, they shared experiences with Phil, who for some reason found it all hilarious. After a few cycles, the Taurus, apart from being low on fuel, was considered ready to go and so the travellers bid Phil farewell.

As they departed Phil called after them. 'Remember to take the *Adrenal Artery* and not the *Renal Artery*,' he bellowed and laughed.

Skip waved and accelerated. Once more they circuited the *Heart* and *Lungs* and were soon the *Adrenal Artery*. Skip completed the well-practiced manoeuvre at the *Adrenal Gland* and the attendant filled the fuel tanks with *Epinephrine* and gave Skip the okay signal. Skip thanked him. Powered the motors and headed for the exit. They were now on their way to rest and recreation. The Taurus cruised the vein, went through the *Heart* and *Lung* once more and took the exit at the *Hepatic Artery*.

'Where are we Skip?' Bobby asked.

'The *Liver*,' Skip answered. 'Finally.'

Bobby and Banjo looked at each other and wondered what they were doing here.

'Don't look so sad,' Skip said laughing at them. 'It's the greatest place in the whole body. If you don't trust me on this, trust George. It was his idea to bring you here.'

'Ah, um, what is so great about the liver, Skip?' Bobby asked cautiously.

'I'll arrange a tour and you'll soon find out,' Skip responded vaguely.

They disembarked from the boat and stepped onto a long platform that lined each side of the artery. Along the platform stood rows of green *Phagocytes* that stood guard protecting the entry to the *Liver*. They nodded at Skip and the two Follicle Farmers and let them pass by unchallenged, apparently aware of their authorised visit. As they entered the *Liver* proper, they watched on as several *Phagocytes* yanked out *Red Blood Cells* and ate them.

Bobby was concerned and turned to Skip for an explanation.

'Those are *Sentry Phagocytes*. They're permanently stationed here to remove damaged or worn out *Red* and *White Blood Cells* that come here from the *Gastrointestinal Tract*,' he continued. 'I really don't know too much about them as they aren't very talkative. It seems that they like to keep to themselves.'

Bobby and Banjo nodded their heads in semi-understanding.

A representative from the *Liver* approached them. He was very tall and wore a *Liver* coloured robe. He spoke gently and melodically. '♪ Welcome to my *Liver*. My name is Alec and I'm the First.' ♪

'The First?' Bobby queried.

'He's the First in charge,' Skip explained. He turned to Alec and responded melodically. ♪ 'Thank you for honouring us, first. You do us proud to greet us thus.' ♪

'A healthy *Liver* makes us a longer liver. We ask you to respect our *Liver* as your very lives depend on it,' ♪ Alec advised. ♪ 'In that way we can all live long and prosper.'

Skip bowed and indicated to Bobby and Banjo to follow his example which they did.

♪ 'These are Quality Assurance Managers from the Follicle Production Team.' ♪ Skip sounded weird as he attempted to almost sing the introduction. ♪ 'This is Bobby, the Manager and Banjo his Assistant.' Skip didn't have a voice for singing.

'George said that we should expect you,' ♪ Alec sang in response. 'He asked that I should personally give you the tour.' ♪

'I'm Skip, Captain of the Taurus.' ♪ Skip pointed to the zodiac.

Alec looked at the craft and faced Skip. ♪ 'Of course you are. The names and faces of all the Zodiac's Captains are well known to us here in the *Liver*. ♪ I'm just glad that you're all safe and well after your horrible ordeal in the *Kidney*,' ♪ he sang.

'You heard about that?' Bobby queried and Banjo nudged him. 'You heard about our trip through the *Kidney*?' ♪ Bobby sang. He also was off-key, but the attempt seemed to please Alec.

'♪It's such a disgusting place and all we're very glad that you all survived the experience,' ♪ Alec sang.

His voice was calming and pleasant. Bobby thought it was a beautiful voice and that he could listen to it for hours.

♪'We'd be honoured to learn more about this wonderful organ,'♪ Banjo sang enthusiastically and smiled.

'And I'd be delighted to show you.' ♪♪ Alec smiled, pleased about the request. 'Did you know we hold the record for being the largest organ within the body?' ♪ He sang.

Bobby was about to point out that the skin was technically an organ and was far bigger than the *Liver*, but he suppressed himself, not wanting to offend their host.

Alec turned and indicated that they should follow him. They did so and next Alec sang the story of the *Liver* to them.

♪'The *Liver* is made up of two sides and has four lobes. ♪They're not equal in size, but they are equal in importance. ♪We affectionately call them the left side and right side. There proper names are *Caudate* and *Quadrate* on the right and *Caudate* and *Quadrate* on the left. ♪ 'You can see here dividing the left from the right is the *Filiform*. ♪That is the very platform that we are now standing on,'♪ he sang, smiled, and bowed.

Skip smiled and bowed, and Bobby and Banjo followed doing the same.

'Here in the *Liver,* we deliver *Bile* to the *Gallbladder*. ♪The *Bile* is vile so please don't sample it or you'll die.'♪ Alec sang.

They nodded but quickly shook their heads in exaggerated agreement that they wouldn't do that.

Alec stopped by some ducts. 'These are the *Hepatocytes*.' ♪ He patted them affectionately. 'They pile the vile bile into the *Canaliculi* and down into the *Hepatic Ducts*,' ♪ Alec informed them.

'What does that do?' ♪ Banjo sang his question.

'Why, dear boy. They emulsify *Lipids*.' ♪Alec then smiled and quivered with the excitement of it all.

Banjo nodded his thanks and when Alec turned to continue walking; Banjo shrugged his shoulders in bewilderment to Bobby and Skip. He then mimicked the quiver. They stifled a laugh.

A massive bright green *Stellate Reticulo-Endothelial Cell*, also known as *Kupffer Cells* or *Fixed Phagocyte Cells* marched up to Alec, came to attention, saluted, and burped out his report. 'We have detained and eliminated 412 redundant red blood cells, fifteen white blood cells, sixty-three assorted bacteria and twelve other particles of foreign matter in the past 100 cycles.' The Commander then saluted once more and remained at attention.'

'Thank you, Commander Ricco,'♪ Alec sang his response. 'Please convey my appreciation to the troops for the excellent work they are doing,'♪ he sang. 'I see you've been doing some eliminating yourself.'♪ Alec gently patted the Sargent's fattened paunch.

'Just doing my job, sir,' Ricco belched again. He saluted, executed a snappy about face and marched off. 'Ricco and his men do such a fine job protecting the *Liver*.' ♪Alec sighed as he sang out the compliment. 'We request and they deliver.' ♪ He smiled.

Bobby now thought that he couldn't take this for much longer.

'So, you clean the blood?' Bobby asked in his normal voice. 'The *Liver* is just a fancy filter?'

Alec looked saddened. He stood erect and looked blankly at the three visitors. 'That concludes your tour,' he said as he turned and walked away.

Banjo wanted to yell out their thanks, but Skip held his arm to get his attention and shook his head.

'Was I rude?' Bobby asked.

'A little,' Skip conceded. 'But you did manage to get rid of him.' Skip smiled.

'Personally, I'm glad the tour is over,' Banjo said. 'I'm hungry, where's the food?'he added

'He's a growing lad,' Bobby laughed.

'Follow me,' Skip invited.

Skip led the way down a *Sinusoid* and found the door that he was looking for. He pressed a hidden panel and the door opened slightly.

'It's a pressure release entry,' Skip informed them. 'You need to be shown where to press to get access.'

Skip opened the door and invited Bobby and Banjo to step inside. They accepted without hesitation and entered a long room filled with tables and chairs. Along one wall was a bar shaped like a tall table with top to bottom flesh panelling and footrests beneath the high chairs that were in a line along the front of the bar. Behind the bar were three staff members dispensing coloured liquids to the numerous visitors that sat on the chairs in groups. The noise was deafening. There was laughter and yelling and someone was singing. Everyone seemed very happy.

Along one wall was a buffet of amino acids, proteins and sugars prepared in unimaginable ways. It reminded Bobby of the experimental food he'd tasted when he visited the Marketing Department.

Banjo headed for the food, but Skip called him back.

'Banjo. Not that food,' Skip told him in a whisper.

Banjo turned and looked disappointed.

Still whispering he added. 'That stuff isn't always the freshest. Follow me.'

It had looked appetising to Banjo.

Again, they followed Skip. They walked past the noisy patrons that were largely ignoring them as they were concentrating on their own partying. Laughter continued to burst out from the various groups that seemed intent on having a good time. The staff behind the bar waved and shouted hellos to Skip over the noise in the room. It was clear to Bobby and Banjo that he was well known and liked. They exchanged knowing glances.

'They came to a clearly marked door. The sign above the door read "Captains Club" and Skip pressed another hidden pressure point for the door to open slightly.

'Local knowledge,' Skip explained with a wink.

Bobby and Banjo followed Captain Skip of the Taurus, into a bar within a bar that was expressly for Captains, and their guests, private use.

As they walked into the smallish room they were greeted with applause, cheers, and hoorays.

Bobby and Banjo recognised Jack, the Captain of the Capricorn that they had met travelling through the *Heart*. Lek, Fargo and Milo were also seated as were Frederick and Clive. They all had coloured beverages in their hands and were waving and laughing happily in their direction. All three waved back in acknowledgement. Bobby and Banjo were clearly delighted with the surprise reunion. They started to head for the table, but Skip stopped them.

'Bobby, Banjo. Before we sit down and join the others, I'd like you to meet the two men that'll be looking after us whilst we're in the "Captains Club".' He led them to the bar that was a smaller version of the one they had passed.

'This is Jay, and this is Kay,' he introduced the two barmen. They had the letters K and J on their bar jackets, so Bobby was confident he'd get it right when addressing them.

Skip continued. 'Jay, Kay these are my very good friends, Bobby and Banjo.'

Kay spoke first but didn't offer his hand. Bobby therefore didn't offer his and he learned later that it wasn't customary to do so. 'We've heard a great deal about you both,' Kay said. 'We are honoured that you are visiting our bar.'

Bobby looked at the others at the table.

'Oh, they have been regaling us with your stories, and singing your praises, but mostly we learned about your deeds on the Follicle Farmer's Network News,' Jay explained.

'You get our network news here?' Bobby was impressed.

'Other than Head Office, this is the only place that receives news feeds from all the systems,' Skip informed him. 'They have a reputation for keeping up with current events.'

Bobby and Banjo were impressed.

'Have you ever been to a bar before?' Kay asked.

Bobby looked at Banjo and then at Kay. 'We've never been to the *Liver* before.'

'Then, you're both in for a treat.' Jay smiled at them and Kay joined in.

Skip laughed.

The others were calling out encouraging them to hurry up and join them.

Kay started to explain 'Behind us are quantities of liquor that the *Liver* workers have selected and saved from the filtration process. These are brought here and are reserved for our special guests.'

'We have a wide selection of spirits such as whiskey, rum, vodka and gin.' Jay pointed each one out.

'When in season, we also have red or white wine,' Kay explained.

'We sometimes have a selection of beers,' Jay added.

'The wine and beer don't stay fresh for long so we don't keep them on tap,' Kay explained.

'Our patrons are more than happy to consume the top shelf wine and beer before that happens,' Jay explained.

'Top shelf?' Banjo asked out of curiosity.

'A term we use to describe the more difficult to acquire beverages,' Kay answered the query.

'What would you like to start with?' Jay asked the travellers.

'What are you having, Skip?' Bobby asked their host.

'I'm a rum man,' Skip answered.

Bobby turned to the barmen and spoke. 'Could we have three rums please?'

'Good choice,' Kay complimented.

'We'll bring them to your table,' Jay offered. 'In the *Liver* we deliver.'

Bobby and Banjo smiled and followed Skip to the table. There was much hugging and back slapping as the abdominal defence, rescue and recovery team were once again reunited. Jack had transported the two *T-Cells*, the *Phagocyte* and the two other Follicle Farmers to the *Liver* for this surprise reunion.

Bobby and Banjo were delighted.

'We heard about your detour through the *Kidney*!' Lek roared and they all burst into laughter.

Skip blushed.

'I bet you were really pissed off,' Milo joined in the tease. There was more laughter.

'Better to be pissed off than pissed on,' Bobby countered playfully. He slapped Skip's shoulder and Skip relaxed.

'An experience I choose not to repeat,' Skip wasn't laughing.

'It didn't make the network news, Skip. And if you buy me a drink, I'll make sure it doesn't,' Frederick teased.

Skip made to get up to arrange the drink and they all burst out in laughter once more. He chuckled as he got on with the joke.

'It was the tightest squeeze you could ever imagine,' Banjo added to the conversation. 'The manager was initially annoyed we were there because we were a risk to his *Kidney*. But he ended up being really good about it.'

'He was helpful,' Skip conceded.

'His union rep told me... that despite having some strange mannerisms, he's a popular manager,' Clive shared with the others.

Bobby, Banjo and Skip burst into laughter.

As they settled Bobby explained. 'He does. And if you want to call them mannerisms then that is fine by us.' He left it at that as a new round of drinks was being supplied to the group.

They thanked Jay and Kay and resumed their conversation.

'Have any of you heard how they are managing at the *Abdomen*?' Bobby asked.

'They're almost as good as new,' Clive reported. 'Follicles are back in full production.'

'There will be no scarring,' Frederick added. 'Soon, there won't be anything to remind us of a battle at all.'

'You should get an award for what you did for them,' Clive concluded.

'That's funny,' Frederick said. 'Because, guess what arrived from the Marketing Department?' He held up two awards, one each for Bobby and Banjo.

The others cheered and got up to give celebratory slaps on shoulders and hugs to Bobby and Banjo. Frederick arranged Bobby and Banjo in a pose for the camera ensuring that the bar and the others were well out of the shot. Jay and Kay attended with re-freshed drinks and so toasts were performed.

'What about you three?' Bobby queried the three warriors at the table. 'You did all the dangerous fighting. Where are your awards?'

Lek and Milo stood up and leaned forward. 'They're on our shirts,' he told them.

Bobby and Banjo could make out the unit citation for the **'Battle of the bulge.'**

'So, they are calling it, 'Battle of the bulge?'

'Yes, and Milo has been recommended for advancement and will lead the next defence,' Lek added.

There were more cheers and drinks.

Then it was Fargo's turn. He slowly rose to his feet, feeling the effects of the whiskey he was consuming. He spoke softly and the others curbed their enthusiasm to reflect the mood he was creating. 'My friends... there comes a point in everyone's career when a man must think back and reflect on all the enemies he has eaten.'

They struggled to suppress their laughter.

'I have come to that point,' he told them with a morose expression.

No one interrupted.

'And, I have drawn a conclusion...,' he said even softer.

They looked at him with expectation.

...that they'd taste a whole heap better with a bit of salt!' he roared.

The group fell about from laughter. Even Kay and Jay were laughing. They were experienced in seeing amusing drunkards in their bar.

After they recovered Lek spoke up about his friend Fargo. 'Fargo's whole unit was awarded a merit citation for excellence. Our friend Fargo is going to take up an instructors post in George's *Integumentary* team.'

'No more eating the enemy for me.' Fargo looked almost sad but soon he was grinning. 'Food!' He exclaimed and dashed to the buffet. The others followed and piled their plates high with an array of exciting goodies.

They sat and ate and drank and shared stories for a long time.

As the evening wore on, someone thought it might be a good time to consider the QA team's future. No one can remember how the conversation started, but suddenly it became important to the others to know where Bobby and Banjo were going next.

'We haven't discussed it at all, have we Banjo?' Bobby told them swaying slightly.

Banjo could manage an exaggerated shake of his head. He used his hand to steady himself on the table.

'How about we decide for you?' Clive offered. 'I mean all of us here, now, for the two of you,' he explained.

'How?' Bobby wanted to know what he was leading up to. Where they were going was important.

'We'll do a Lottery,' Clive explained.

They all stared at him blankly.

'We draw names of places from a bowl or something like that,' he said slurring his words.

The others did a half cheer giving their approval. Clive stood up and in his politest inebriated voice requested markers and scribble pads from Jay and Kay. They efficiently materialised.

'Oh, and a bowl,' he added smiling at himself.

'Are you going to be sick?' Kay asked in concern.

'Not for me! We'll put the names of all the places you might go to, in the bowl.' Clive mocked being affronted.

In turn they wrote places for Bobby and Banjo to visit as Follicle Farmer's QA Management.

They placed the names into the bowl and asked Jay to select a name and share it with the drinkers.

'This is the third place you'll go too,' Clive announced.

'I thought it was the next place,' Bobby countered.

'We don't want to waste all this effort,' Clive defended.

'Okay,' Bobby capitulated, too drunk to argue.

'The third place you two do a QA inspection of is...,' Clive indicated to Kay that he should read from the note.

'The big toe,' Kay told them.

They all burst into laughter.

'That'll take about two cycles,' someone teased. 'There's only about a dozen hairs.'

'The second place you'll visit is the...,' Clive again motioned to Kay.

'The *Anus,*' Kay announced.

Again, they burst into laughter.

'Every follicle is important.' Someone offered.

'♪Everybody's job stinks, sometimes♪,' someone else sang.

As they recovered, Clive motioned to Kay to draw the next slip of paper and he did so.

'The next phase of the Follicle Farmer's QA department's tour will be at the...'

'Pubic hair,' Kay announced and they all burst into laughter once more.

Kay put the three bits of paper on the table in front of Bobby and returned to the bar.

Later, after even more drinks, they all quietened. Then slowly, each of the revellers gently worked their way to the floor and gradually succumbed to a deep sleep.

16

After many cycles of deep sleep, the nine revellers slowly awakened. Fargo, Lek and Milo perfunctorily straightened themselves up. They bid a cursory farewell to the others, thanked Kay and Jay for their excellent service and then marched out of the room.

The two Captains were now fully awake. They looked at each other and laughed. Then they sighed, took a deep breath, chuckled, then looked at the four docile Follicle Farmers and burst into laughter once more.

Clive gave them a wave and indicated that he wasn't well. 'Could you keep the noise down a bit please?' he asked. He was nursing his head. He found a non-alcoholic beverage and consumed it in one gulp.

'What's funny?' Frederick asked.

'You lot..., us..., everything...,' Jack had a confused response which seemed to delight him so he, and Skip laughed again.

'Bobby and Banjo seem to be the hardest hit.' Skip spoke about them, and not to them. 'Jay, Kay could we have some food for our heroes please?'

'Certainly,' Kay acknowledged.

'Absolutely, that is highly recommended after a long session of drinking rum,' Jay added.

'Not for me,' Clive said. He next looked at Jack and asked. 'Could we get going soon?' I have a Union meeting that I should prepare for, and in my current state; preparation will take me a bit longer than normal.'

Frederick coughed before speaking. 'I need to get the photo onto the network news. I'll also have to write a sober, no-alcohol based, short...,' he paused, took another deep breath and continued, '...a very short, article about our QA team receiving their awards.'

Bobby and Banjo stood up and stretched.

Clive and Frederick went up to them and gave them a big hug each.

'We'll do this again,' Clive suggested with a half-smile.

'Not too soon.' Frederick took another deep breath.

Bobby waved the suggestion away. There was an almost imperceptible shake of his head.

Banjo stood still. He barely responded, only following the others with his eyes. He didn't even shrug. Bobby restrained a chuckle at his assistant's expense.

Jack shook their hands, waved his thanks to the two barmen and led his two passengers out of the room.

Jay and Kay brought food and non-alcoholic beverages to the table.

'I'll leave you boys to fuel up and sober up,' Skip told them with a chuckle. 'I'm going to check on Taurus. When I get back, we'll head off, if you're up for it,' he suggested smiling at them.

Bobby nodded his head in acknowledgement. Banjo groaned his response.

Skip left the room with a wave to the barmen. He was comfortable leaving them with Jay and Kay as they were experienced on how to care for recovering patrons.

Bobby and Banjo sat and picked at the food and sipped their drinks. While they ate, Bobby picked up his award and tried to focus on it. Banjo copied, following his boss's lead.

Bobby then saw the three notes and picked them up with his other hand. He didn't recognise the handwriting. He laid them out on the table and read them in turn to Banjo. 'Pubic hair, anal follicles, big toe follicles.'

Banjo looked blank. He clearly didn't know anything about them.

Bobby called to the barmen and asked. 'Kay, Jay. Do you know anything about these?' He asked without turning toward them.

Kay saw Bobby and Banjo holding their awards and replied. 'Those are yours. They came for you earlier on from the marketing department by express courier.'

Bobby re-read the messages to Banjo. 'Pubic hair, anal follicles, big toe follicles. I suppose this is where they want us to go next on our inspection tour,' Bobby concluded.

'Looks that way,' Banjo agreed, speaking for the first time since waking up.

'Strange places to send heroes,' Bobby lamented.

They continued eating for a while and rested while they waited for Skip. Jay and Kay cleared up and were attentive with clear liquids and words of encouragement.

When Skip returned, he looked bright and cheerful and ready for the flow.

'You boys ready?' He asked with a smile. He looked at the barmen and Kay indicated that their patients were doing just fine.

'Certainly,' Bobby responded.

'Absolutely,' Banjo agreed.

With a wave and an appreciative thanks to the barmen, the three travellers left the bar and walked the passageways to a large vein and the tethered Taurus. 'I thought we left the boat in an artery?' Banjo queried.

'The *Liver* has a valet service. They moved our Zodiacs to the exit point whilst the captains and their visitors are at the bar,' Skip informed them. 'I guess they' learned a long time ago that it's better to move the boats themselves than risk us captains bumping and crashing through the *Liver*,' he concluded with a smile. 'The arrangement suits us very much.'

'We're going to the groin,' Bobby advised. Then he muttered under his breath. 'Apparently.'

'Okay,' Skip replied unquestioningly.

They boarded the boat and secured themselves. Skip started the motors and gently caught the flow to exit the *Liver*. They turned left into the *inferior vena cava* and headed once more for the *Heart* lung circuit. They completed the journey by exiting at the *gonadal artery* and soon they arrived at the groin.

Bobby and Banjo were both a bit woozy. The turbulence of the flow combined with their general disposition made the journey unsettling. They arrived at an unloading bay at the start of the *deep dorsal artery*. Bobby was a bit surprised that there was no one there to greet them.

Skip secured the boat and Bobby and Banjo disembarked. They decided they'd go looking to find an Area Manager or at very least a Team Supervisor. They wandered in and out of many passageways but there were no Follicle Farmers to be found growing pubic hair. In the distance they heard voices and feeling relieved they headed in that direction. They soon found, what appeared to be, the entire team of pubic hair Follicle Farmers, gathered in one place.

'I hope this isn't some form of industrial action,' Bobby mused to Banjo as they made their way to a platform where it was obvious that a senior manager for pubic hair was addressing the men.

They stopped at the base of the platform, intending to listen to what was being said, but they were recognised.

'Look, look!' a manager exclaimed excitedly. He pointed at the two of them. 'It's Bobby and Banjo. They are heroes of the battle of the bulge, and they are our Quality Assurance Managers. It looks like they've arrived just in time to sort this out!'

There was widespread cheering and yahooing as they were welcomed up onto the platform.

'What's happening here?' Bobby whispered loudly to the manager.

'I'm John, Regional Manager of the Pubic Hair. We have no follicles!' he informed them above the noise of the crowd.

Bobby was stunned. Banjo was alarmed.

'They're all gone,' John reiterated. 'It happened about fifteen cycles ago. I thought they sent you here because of my urgent communiqué.' John was clearly surprised that Bobby and Banjo didn't seem to understand what was happening. It was all explained in his report.

The crowd was becoming restless. It seemed that they were hoping for immediate and positive news from the newly arrived representatives from senior management. When Bobby didn't offer an immediate reassurance, the crowd took it as managerial capitulation to whatever had taken their follicles away. The situation was deteriorating and becoming urgent.

'Is there somewhere quiet we can go to so you can fill us in on what has been happening?' Bobby asked loudly to be heard.

'Follow me to my office,' John invited, shouting above the noise.

As he led the way off the platform, John tried to appease the farmers that they were working on a solution and asked them to be patient.

The mood of the crowd relaxed slightly.

John was accompanied by two of his Area Managers. The five filed into John's office and John introduced Richard, Area Manager for the *Scrotum* and *Penile Shaft* and Glenn the Area Manager for the *Pubis Torso*.

He next invited them all to sit down at his conference table.

'I'll begin, and by the looks on your faces, you haven't got a clue what has been happening,' John addressed Bobby and Banjo.

Bobby shook his head.

'About fifteen cycles or so ago all the follicles under our management were extracted. The process took about seven cycles. It started in Glenn's area and quickly progressed to Richards. Except for two follicles, they're all gone.'

'Two follicles?' Bobby queried.

'They were missed. I think they were spared only because they are small and immature,' John explained.

'Chemical destruction?' Bobby asked.

'No,' John replied.

Bobby was relieved as he remembered the epidermis reaction to MI on the *abdomen* and they didn't want a repeat of that.

'Were the bulbs of the follicles removed also?' Bobby asked.

'Yes.'

'So, it wasn't shaving,' Bobby surmised.

'Shaving has happened to us once before. It didn't really bother us but the epidermis manager wasn't happy about prickly re-growth,' John explained, remembering.

'It wasn't electrolysis...,' Bobby stated '...or the follicles would have died still in their place.'

John, Richard, and Glenn shook their heads.

'Bobby continued. 'Manual tweezers are a slow process and re-moval would have taken many, many cycles.'

John nodded his agreement.

'As it happened quickly, it must have been electronic tweezers,' Bobby concluded. Do you agree, Banjo?' He asked his assistant.

'I do,' Banjo agreed without adding anything.

'This order wasn't from the *Integumentary* System,' Bobby ex-plained to the management team of the pubic follicles. 'I think this might have been a marketing initiative.'

'Marketing?' John didn't understand.

'When we were managing the growth of the moustache it was the marketing department that had ordered it. They believed that a fully grown moustache would make our man more appealing to fe-males. That seems to be a marketing department preoccupation by the way.'

'They also ordered the goatee be grown,' Banjo added.

'But that's visual as the face can be seen by others. Our region is clothed,' John defended.

'Always?' Bobby asked.

'Not during washing,' explained Richard.

'Or during urination,' Glenn added.

'Or sex!' John was beginning to understand the situation.

Bobby and Banjo said nothing.

'So, you believe our pubic follicles were violently extracted in the belief that our man will get to ejaculate more often?' John asked in dismay.

'Don't you?' Bobby asked.

John, Richard, and Glenn said nothing. They looked sad, obviously concerned for their future and the future of all their workers.

'It may not be permanent,' Bobby said hopefully. 'This could have been a follicle extraction for a special event.'

'I don't know what that means,' John countered.

Bobby wasn't sure what it meant either. He then took a deep breath. 'The follicles were removed, but the mechanisms for regrowing them remain intact. I suggest you order sufficient supplies to commence regrowth immediately,' Bobby told them.

John nodded that he understood and agreed.

'Banjo, could you assist them in putting in an urgent request for growth chemicals to be sent here by barge. If they could send reinforcements to help with distribution of those chemicals, then that would also be good.'

'I'm on it,' Banjo agreed. He left the office to make the arrangements.

'Do you have contact with the penis team itself?' Bobby asked. 'Maybe they had something to do with this,' he speculated.

'They wouldn't,' John looked up.

'They might,' Richard contradicted.

'Why do you say that?' John demanded.

'Well, they're always going on about the *penis* and what an engineering marvel it is. Apart from sweating and dispelling urine, it seems its whole purpose in life is ejaculating sperm,' Richard replied.

'It's all they talk about,' Glenn agreed.

'We're bored hearing about it, but erections and ejaculations are their calling,' Richard said bluntly. 'It's what they prefer to do.'

'So, you think they'd agree to sacrifice our follicles in order to ejaculate more often?' John was serious.

'Could be,' Richard answered uncertainly.

'Makes sense to me,' Glenn agreed.

'It doesn't mean that they ordered it, or even knew about it. They may agree to it in principle, but your follicle extractions may have been a surprise to them too,' Bobby cautioned.

'We should find out,' John said.

Bobby nodded his agreement.

John turned to his two Area Managers. 'Work with Banjo to get the additional supplies to the follicle sites. Order your Team Leaders to get their teams back to their posts. Let's get them started re-growing our follicles!'

'Yes sir!' Richard and Glenn were motivated. They left the room to go find Banjo.

'I'll take you to meet Reece. He's the Fluidic Engineer in charge of the penis proper,' John explained. 'Deep down, he is a nice enough guy, just a bit obsessed with reproduction. I don't think poor chap's actually hit the target yet.'

Bobby didn't know what that meant, but he figured that if it was important enough for him to learn, he would soon find out.

John led Bobby through a maze of passageways. They passed numerous teams of Follicle Farmers returning to their posts. They didn't look happy but at least they were no longer angry.

'At least now we're doing something,' one of the Team Leader murmured as they passed.

They turned and went deep into the *dermis* and even deeper into the *torso*. They arrived at an open door and John stuck his head through the doorway.

'A voice called out. 'Come in, John. Good to see you.'

John motioned Bobby to follow him into the office.

'Reece, I'd like you to meet Bobby. He's the QA Manager for all Follicles. He works for George.'

'This is an unexpected pleasure.' Reece stood up from his chair and they shook hands.

'Can I offer you a beverage or something to eat?' Reece indicated a table with a limited ration of food and drink.

'I'm fine, thanks,' Bobby responded with a dismissive wave of his hand. He was still a bit seedy after his experience in the *Liver* and this wasn't the time, place or environment to share his stories of misadventure.

'Please take a seat,' Reece invited his guests to sit down. Both Bobby and John did so.

'I heard about your hair,' Reece volunteered. 'That's quite dramatic,' he said giving nothing away.

'I'm here to ask you, Reece...,' John said stoically. 'Did you have anything to do with it?'

'No.' John looked at them both in turn. 'I didn't ask for it and I wasn't told it was happening. I did however get a weird message from marketing when it was completed'. He pulled the note out of a drawer. 'I kept it to show you.' He offered it to John who took it, read it, and passed it to Bobby.

Bobby read the words. "Their small sacrifices should increase your chances of hitting your target." It was signed Roscoe and Ralph MD.

'I gather my follicles are the small sacrifices,' John concluded.

'I suppose so,' Reece replied. 'How do you feel about it?'

'I'm angry and confused,' he replied taking a deep breath.

'We don't know is if this is meant to be a permanent or a temporary event,' Bobby restated.

'What difference does that make? This should never have happened.' John spoke loudly. He was clearly angry.

'Have you had any orders about an impending ejaculation event?' Bobby asked the manager of the penis proper.

Reece laughed. 'Unfortunately, it rarely works that way for us. We get very little warning of a pending launch.'

'Oh,' Bobby became attentive.

'You see, we get alerted to potential activity. The optical department send us numerous green alerts and... so we ignore them. The mind sends us many green and amber alerts and they seem to be coming all the time,' Reece laughed. 'Generally, we don't take any notice on those either.'

'Anyone else?' Bobby was fascinated.

'*Olfactory* sometimes sends us an amber alert but hardly any green alerts, which is weird.'

'So, how do you know when to prepare for an ejaculation?' Bobby wanted to know.

'If we get a red signal from the *epidermis*, a red signal from the *mind* and a red from *auditory* we take that very seriously,' Reece explained. 'Typically it means that a full stream ejaculatory event will take place very soon.'

'*Auditory*?' Bobby was confused.

Reece laughed. 'Mostly, our man hears from a third party when to prepare for an ejaculatory event. Everything else just seems to be wishful thinking on Head Offices part.' Reece laughed loudly and Bobby and John even joined in though they really didn't understand.

'So you get three types of alerts and they come from the *mind, auditory, optical,* and *olfactory* and the *epidermis.* You need at least three red alerts to be able to stage an ejaculatory event.' Bobby was figuring it all out.

'We can do it with two, but three is better....'

'I see.' Bobby nodded his head.

'...and one of those red alerts must include the epidermis. Without tactile stimulation we don't or can't ejaculate,' Reece clarified.

'This message came from the marketing department.' Bobby held up the note.

'I'm certain that if they could, the marketing department would have us permanently on a red alert,' Reece explained. 'But they don't send us any signals at all. The system doesn't work that way.

'What about my follicles,' John lamented.

'The presence or removal of the follicles has no impact on the number of erections or the number of ejaculations we'll achieve,'

Reece stated. 'I'm sorry for this John. I think your follicles were re-moved without any benefit to the reproductive system.'

'Will you say as much to an enquiry?' Bobby asked Reece.

'It'll only be my opinion, but sure..., why not?' he asked rhetori-cally.

'I'd better get back to my team,' John said to Bobby.

'You get on with regrowing all the follicles, John. I'll get started on an inquiry.' Bobby agreed.

As John bid his farewell to Reece he turned to Bobby. 'Do you want me to send someone to fetch you?' he offered.

'I'll return him to you,' Reece promised and John left the room.

'I didn't want to say this in front of John, but the removal of pu-bic hair may make the whole of the groin region look more attrac-tive to a female. It may actually stimulate their red lights.'

'Oh,' Bobby was speechless.

'I could be wrong. Sorry, it must seem like I'm messing with you. It could be that marketing thought it might be visually stimulating to a female, and they're simply testing a theory. Marketing would do something like that,' Reece concluded.

'Just like growing a moustache and a goatee that was supposed to stimulate female interest.....,' Bobby mused.

'That's really funny,' Reece laughed. 'So, the marketing depart-ment decided that growing facial hair was going to increase the number of ejaculatory events, whereas that same department de-cided that removing hair from the groin might achieve the same thing?' Reece laughed loudly again.

'Those marketing boys are really messed up,' Bobby said joining in the laughter. It took some time for them to settle. They collec-tively sighed.

'Thank you, Reece. I'm really beginning to understand how these things work.' Bobby looked at him. 'What about the *medulla oblon-gata*. Do you get any instructions from Percival?'

'All the time,' Reece replied sardonically. 'They confirm a urination event when we advise him the bladder is getting full. We dispel urine when we get the "go to flow" signal from his office.'

'I learned that it can take some preparation,' Bobby conceded.

'We've come close to having an embarrassing outcome, but we've held on so far,' Reece smiled.

'I'm going to contact George and find out what he knows,' Bobby said.

'How is Harry?' Reece enquired.

'Do you know him well?' Bobby asked before answering.

'Reasonably well. He visits me as part of his regular tour. We once met in the *Liver* for a meeting.' Reece winked at Bobby.

Bobby restrained a smile. 'I've had a meeting there myself. It was a follow up to the battle of the bulge.' Bobby smiled.

Reece smiled. 'Where are my manners? Would you like the tour?'

'I'd be delighted,' Bobby responded.

'We refer to ourselves as fluidic engineers. I'm graded a Regional Manager for the *Reproductive* System and I report directly to my System Manager. My boss's focus is on the hormonal activities that occur away from the groin region, and I look after things here.'

Reece stood up and Bobby followed his lead. They noticed a green light had come on. Reece pointed to it without a word.

They walked out of Reece's office they stepped up to a massive diagram of the *penis, testis, seminal vesicles, prostrate* and *urinary bladder.*

'We're here.' He pointed to the region marked *suspensory ligament*. 'It's one of the muscles we use to hold up the penis when it gets erect.'

'How does it get erect?' Bobby was fascinated.

'When we get a triple red alert, we open up these valves here.' He pointed to the *deep dorsal artery*. 'I think you'd have arrived here on this one. The valves are only open a small fraction of their maximum diameter at present. When flaccid, we only allow enough blood to support the normal health of the shaft of the penis. It supplies oxygen, food and fluids, completes waste disposal, that sort of thing.'

Bobby understood so far.

'The triple red alert initiates these valves to open, and we flood the *tunica albuginea* with blood. In about twenty beats we can go from flaccid to fully erect,' Reece explained.

'The erection event shuts the valves of the flow of blood exiting the penis via these veins so we can maintain the high blood pressure build up for many cycles,' he said pointing them out.

'Does it hurt?' Bobby was concerned.

Reece laughed. 'A sustained maximum pressure erection event can cause some discomfort, but it's mostly regarded as a pleasurable pain.' He paused. 'There are a massive number of nerve endings in the *penis*, so the pleasure pain ratio is very unstable, particularly in the *glans penis*, there at the tip.' He pointed it out to Bobby.

Bobby nodded.

'These nerves shoot those pleasure messages right up to the spine and directly into the brain. There are numerous nerve endings in the *prostate* so when they're sufficiently stimulated to release their load, they send a message to the brain via the *hypogastric nerve* straight into here to the *amygdala*. It is so powerful that some brain functions can shut down for a short time.' He smiled. 'When we ejaculate, they party.'

'I'm beginning to think that some of the Mind Managers live there,' Bobby speculated.

Reece pretended to ignore him. 'You see this valve here?' He pointed at the chart.

Bobby nodded.

'This cuts out the urine flow from the bladder when there is an erection. Urine kills sperm so we don't want any flowing through the penis during an ejaculatory event.' Reece next pointed out the small gland under the prostate. 'This is *the bulbo-urethral gland*. It neutralises the effect of any residual urine in the *urethra* during an erection as well as pumping out some *mucus* to moisten the *exter-*

nal urethral orifice.' He pointed to the furthest end of the shaft. 'It's a useful penetration lubrication aid.'

Bobby nodded his head in understanding.

'Some of the workers here call it the "sticky dicky" aid, but I prefer to discuss it in technical terms.' Reece chuckled.

'What does the *prostate* do?' Bobby asked.

'It's a gland that manufactures the sticky fluid that collects the sperm and carries them from the *seminal vestibules* into the *urethra* for ejaculation.' Reece pointed to the centre of the *prostate*. 'This is the orifice of the ejaculatory duct. Some of the guys here call ejaculation "coming". Again, I don't encourage the use of incorrect terminology.'

'It's all about reproduction for you guys, isn't it?' Bobby mused. 'You think females are there to make more babies, and for those babies to grow up and reproduce and make even more babies.' Bobby wasn't hostile or derogative. He was just saying it the way he understood it.

'Biologically that is true. It was how we were designed. After all, why would we manufacture hundred million sperm for each ejaculation when it only needs one to reach a human female egg to start the new life process? The truth however is very different.'

'I'd like to learn more about the female,' Bobby said.

'Well done you. Less than point one of a percent of us have,' Reece informed Bobby. 'And why would we, we're too busy maintaining this body. The brain uses the body to support it, but the mind is primarily thinking about leisure and pleasure.'

'I'd like to see one, one day,' Bobby mused.

'I've seen them,' Reece boasted.

'Have you?' Bobby was impressed.

'I did a visit to the *optical* department when I last meet with my boss. Mostly he comes here, but on that occasion, I got summonsed to go visit him. His office is very close to the *optical* department,' Reece explained.

'I'd like to go there myself,' Bobby replied nodding his head.

'I thoroughly recommend it,' Reece agreed.

'So, what is the truth?' Bobby asked.

Reece stared at him and then answered dryly. 'As a man we like it. In fact, I'd go as far to say that we love it. Orgasms are intensely pleasurable, and some mind managers crave them.' He went quiet for a moment. 'Men love to orgasm. Some Mind Managers demand them so much they'll order the Marketing Department to orchestrate situations that make orgasms more probable to achieve.'

'The only downside is that our orgasm releases a hormone called *prolactin* that reduces sexual desire for about four hundred cycles. After then we're ready to go again!'

Bobby found himself really liking Reece. He was always positive, and he was an interesting and well informed manager. They performed a very important role in male activities here in the groin. He had a lot of responsibilities and he seemed to manage them well.

'Would you like to see the sperm factory?' Reece interrupted Bobby's thoughts.

'Could I?' Bobby was impressed.

'Of course,' Reece laughed.

They set off for the *scrotum* in single file as the passageways were very narrow. Bobby could hear the flow of blood and the noise levels here were higher than he was used to.

'The *testes* require a lot of blood and a lot of manufacturing supplies. They get their own blood supply from the *testicular arteries* which branch off from the *aorta* just below the *Kidneys*. Their blood must be fully independent from the blood flowing in the penis as an erection would mess with factory's quality and volume,' said Reece explaining.

Bobby nodded.

'There are actually two sperm factories.' Reece stopped and looked at Bobby to see if he understood the implications.

'You have two factories producing millions of sperms every day that go no-where,' Bobby concluded.

'One day, we may hit the target and actually make a baby,' Reece smiled. He wasn't lamenting as he was a realist about these things.

'We take reproduction very seriously, don't we?' Bobby mused again.

'I guess, to us, it makes many of the other human functions seem less important,' Reece speculated.

They continued down a shaft and arrived at the left *teste*. Reece opened several secure doors and Bobby followed him into the inner workings of the factory. There were many workers and managers supervising them. They were attentive to the tasks they were performing and largely ignored the two visitors. Bobby figured Reece had brought many visitors here, given the relative high priority that this place had.

'Each teste has about two hundred and fifty *lobules* and each *lobule* has approximately two coils called *seminiferous tubules*,' Reece explained.

'Is it cold here?' Bobby was shivering.

Reece laughed. 'It's about five degrees colder here than anyway else,' he replied. 'Except for maybe the toes.' He laughed again.

Bobby smiled. That had to be a coincidence.

'They make about a thousand sperm every cycle in each *teste...*,' Reece stated, completely absorbed in what he was explaining. 'The process is called *spermatogenesis...*'

Reece continued explaining but Bobby was just fascinated to watch the factory in operation. The sperm were so small that he couldn't make any individuals out. The whole thing looked like an enormous white puddle being churned about. He interrupted Reece's monologue. 'Do they talk?' he asked.

Reece paused, unconcerned at being interrupted. 'We think so,' he replied. 'But we've concluded that it is at a frequency that we can't hear.'

'Have you ever seen one close up? What do they look like?' Bobby was fascinated.

'We don't have that technology here, but from the research department we've been shown that they look like this.' Reece headed into to a meeting room and found a white board and using a marker he drew. It had a narrow pointy head, a slender body, and a very long tail.

'Is that what they look like?' Bobby was amazed.

'That's what we've been shown,' Reece agreed. 'They're really tiny. In fact, the smallest thing we have…,'

'Where do you put them all?' Bobby was confused. 'If we don't ejaculate very often then what do you do with all this factory output?'

'We can store a lot of sperm in the *ampulla* of the *ductus deferens*.' He laughed. 'I should have pointed that out when we were at the chart. They are just above the *prostate*. Sperm aren't very big and don't take up much room. They can survive for a very long time, but after about seventy-four days they'll die and are reabsorbed as raw materials within the factory.'

'That's sad.' Bobby looked sad.

'That's life,' Reece concluded. 'When we pump them out of the penis, they die much quicker than that.'

'How quick?' Bobby asked.

'I don't know.' Reece said dryly. 'That is beyond our control, and I don't even know if our research department has looked into that question.'

They stood in silence for a few moments.

'I think you'd better take me back to John, please Reece,' Bobby asked his host.

'Seen enough?' Reece asked.

'I think so,' Bobby nodded his head. 'It has been a very humbling experience, thank you.'

'You're very welcome,' Reece replied smiling.

Reece set off leading Bobby through many security doors and many lengthy passages. They passed numerous workers who ignored them, and they arrived at the *epidermis* at John's empty office.

Bobby turned to shake Reece's hand.

'I think I now know enough about your workplace to be confusing when I explain it to others,' Bobby told him with a smile. 'Thank you for everything you've shown me.'

'I'm glad you enjoyed the tour.' Reece smiled but then frowned. 'I never once offered you some food or a beverage. I'm so sorry.' He was clearly embarrassed.

'Yes, you did,' Bobby assured him. 'It's all right, I wasn't hungry. I'll grab something to eat with the Follicle Farmers.'

'Are you okay to find them?' Reece was concerned. They hadn't seen any Follicle Farmers since they returned.

Bobby smiled. 'The *epidermis* is my part of the body, Reece. I'll find them.'

They shook hands. 'You'll come and say hello next time you're in the groin?' Reece asked.

'Of course... I look forward to it,' Bobby agreed.

Reece waved a farewell and headed toward his office.

Bobby decided he'd help himself to some of the food and drink that was in John's office. He realised that he was very hungry and ate till he was content.

'Boss!'

Bobby heard Banjo's voice behind him, and he turned to face him, wiping his face.

'You were gone a long time!' Banjo gently admonished him.

'Sorry,' Bobby smiled politely. 'I kind of left everything to you.'

'John said you'd be gone a long time. He said the Penis Manager likes to talk,' Banjo said.

'He certainly does.' Bobby took a deep breath. 'How are things going here?'

'All follicles have recommenced growing. I heard from George and apparently, he wasn't consulted about their removal. He's very angry about it, but also pleased that regrowth is proceeding smoothly.'

'Thanks for covering for me,' Bobby said.

'My pleasure.' Banjo smiled.

'You'd better show me around,' Bobby instructed. 'I've seen how the penis works, so I'd better see how well we can grow pubic hair.'

Banjo took his boss to find John and together they did a tour of the regrowing efforts. After many cycles they were completely satisfied that everything was growing to the highest standards.

Bobby enlisted Banjo's assistance to write a detailed report to George and an even more detailed report to Percival.

His report included details of the QA training and its implementation. He described current workers morale and managerial efficiency. They even included some recommendations for advancement. Bobby concluded with the fact that he felt the management team for follicle production was efficient and professional.

Bobby next sent Banjo to find Skip. He'd neglected the captain having been distracted by the reproductive system and follicle regrowth of the pubic hair.

As Bobby waited for Banjo, he reflected on some of his earlier experiences. He thought of Curly, and that he had come to him from the pubic hair. His reports of the behaviour of the Follicle Farmers in the groin were very different from the way they found it. He was both glad and relieved that this team were proud of being Follicle Farmers and they conducted themselves both professionally and efficiently.

Banjo returned with Skip. They were both glum.

'I've been up to visit Harry,' Skip explained.

Banjo was clearly upset and teary.

'Harry passed away. He died in George's arms.'

17

FOLLICLE FARMERS NETWORK NEWS REPORT - By Frederick.

WE SADLY REPORT THAT HARRY – GENERAL MANAGER FOR
FOLLICLE PRODUCTION, HAS PASSED AWAY. HARRY DIED AS A
RESULT OF THE WOUNDS THAT HE SUSTAINED DURING HIS
HEROIC ACTIONS DURING THE BATTLE OF THE BULGE.
THE *INTEGUMENTARY* SYSTEM MANAGER'S DEPARTMENT HAS
DECLINED TO COMMENT ON THIS GREAT LOSS. SYSTEMS
MANAGER GEORGE IS REPORTED TO BE DEEPLY SADDENED BY
THIS EVENT. HIS OFFICE IS CLOSED FOR A BRIEF PERIOD OF
MOURNING.
HARRY WAS CONSUMED BY A CLOSE PERSONAL FRIEND.

* * *

Banjo reread the news report.

'The bit I don't understand is that Frederick reports that Harry died because of his injuries during his heroic actions. But he didn't do anything heroic!' Banjo bemoaned. 'Frederick knows that. He was there. He saw it happen.'

'They're expected to write nice things about important Follicle Farmers that die tragically,' Bobby explained.

'I've known Harry for a very long time.' Skip spoke for the first time after returning to the groin with the news. He'd been very sullen and withdrawn.

'I know,' Bobby replied, not sure of what to say to him.

'He deserved to be well thought of,' Skip added.

'Who's going to be the new General Manager?' Banjo asked Bobby.

'I guess they're still figuring that out,' Bobby replied.

'It should be you, boss,' Banjo told Bobby.

'I don't think now...,' Bobby started but Skip cut him off.

'That's true, Bobby,' Skip agreed with Banjo. 'You already know more about hair growing and the different regional needs of follicle production, than any other Follicle Farmer's I've heard about.'

'It's too soon to contemplate such matters. Bobby told them. 'We should focus on doing our jobs and not concern ourselves with who is going to be Harry's replacement. George will want to talk with me at some point about our successes as a QA department. That's our focus.'

'Sorry boss,' Banjo apologised.

'And don't call me boss. Call me Bobby like you always have.' Bobby chastised.

'Sorry Bobby,' Banjo apologised again.

Bobby gave him that look that warned Banjo not to apologise again.

Banjo said nothing.

Skip ventured a change of topic. 'So... the anus hair isn't far from here. Did you want to get going?'

The three were standing on a loading bay adjacent to the Taurus and were at the exit point of the *deep dorsal vein*. The pubic hair Follicle Farmers were now progressing satisfactorily with regrowing the extracted follicles. They had said their good byes to that team.

It had occurred to Bobby that the investigation into the temporary loss of hair in the pubic region would have to be delayed. He realised that mourning Harry's death and the need to promote, and then induct his replacement, would be a bigger priority for their System Manager.

'No.' Bobby looked at Skip. 'The very thought of spending time in that place depresses me.'

Banjo looked at him with that look.

280 ~ STEPHAN DE JONGHE

'I know we have to go there, but seriously...,' Bobby groaned. 'It's the place where Follicle Farmers that aren't liked, get transfer to.'

Skip smiled at him.

'I know we have to go there, but I don't think George, or anyone else, is going to care if we swap the order in which we complete these regions,' Bobby concluded.

Banjo shrugged, still not speaking.

Skip said nothing.

'Let's do the boring visit to the big toe before we get depressed in the anus,' Bobby had made it sound like a suggestion, but both Banjo and Skip knew that that was what they were going to do.

'Sure,' Skip agreed.

'We could visit some follicles on the leg on our way, just to break up the journey,' Bobby added.

Banjo nodded his head, agreeing.

They exited the *vein* and sped along the *inferior vena cava*, through the *Heart* and *Lungs* and back down the *aorta* to the *iliac*, then into the *femoral* where they stopped for a while. Skip moored the boat and Bobby and Banjo met with the Area Managers of the *thigh* follicles. They performed QA tasks and training and assessed that those tasks were being performed at a satisfactory level. After the reports were written and sent, Bobby and Banjo returned to the Taurus and they continued through the *femoral artery*, into the *popliteal*. The farmers on the kneecap were having a tough time and Bobby told them he'd request some external assistance in moisturising the thick and tough *epidermis* in their region. They exited the knee and continued along the anterior tibial.

They stopped at the shin and performed the same QA tasks and training and were again satisfied that everything was procedurally correct. They wrote a near identical report to the one they wrote on the thigh and to send to George's office. The more detailed one they sent to Percival's office. Banjo was clever and knew how to change some of the wording in order to freshen up reports that were routine and repetitive in nature. Bobby and Banjo were comfortable with the routine nature of their work. The banter was returning to normal, and they readily agreed that they made a great team.

Skip was content to wait for them. They weren't staying long at any of the locations where they worked, and he was happy doing small maintenance jobs on the Zodiac. He spent the rest of the time keeping up with news reports from the many systems news services that he had access to via his screen on the Taurus. Skip still marvelled at the improved technologies that the body now employed, and the speed and clarity of communications continued too impressive him. Skip had previously commented that Phil had left them to their own tasks. He had made no additional demands on Skip, or the Taurus since they had left the boat yard for the second time after the *Kidney* incident.

Bobby's morale was improving. 'Once we complete our quick visit the toe, I'll be ready to deal with the *anus* hair,' Bobby concluded lamenting this less desirable aspect of their mission.

'It'll be okay, Bobby,' Banjo assured him.

Skip smiled at Banjo and gave him the customary imperceptible nod.

Banjo nodded back conspiratorially. 'We'll just sniff things out for a bit; write down what we smell, and then get going,' Banjo suggested to his manager whilst managing to maintain a straight face.

'Wha...?' Bobby looked at his assistant, puzzled by the unusual choice of words.

'We shouldn't get browned off about it,' Skip informed them.

Bobby looked at Skip.

'It's definitely the place to go... you know... err, when you got to go,' Banjo chided.

♪ 'And you'll never never know, if you never never go!' ♪ Skip sang.

'What are you two on about?' Bobby asked perplexed.

'I'm sure they'll have turdied the place up for us before we get there.' Skip grinned at him.

'How crappy can it be?' Banjo queried.

'I'm confident it'll be a real gassy experience,' Skip added trying hard not to smile.

'And they'll have numerous unpredictable explosive methane discharges,' Banjo chuckled.

'They really should get that looked into,' Skip said laughing and Banjo joined in.

Then Bobby laughed also when he realized what they were doing. He was smiling and shaking his head in bemused wonder. 'You guys are the best,' he told them and they had a group hug.

'Let's go to the toe,' Bobby said and took a deep breath.

Once more they boarded the Taurus and proceeded farther along the *tibial artery* and into the foot at the *dorsalis pedis artery*, and then straight to the *dorsal digital artery*.

They secured the boat, disembarked, stretched and looked about.

'What do you want?' a voice demanded.

'Oh, hello. Is there a representative from the Follicle Farmers available? We are from...,' Bobby started to explain.

'Pus off,' the voice told him.

'I beg your pardon.'

'I said 'pus off',' the voice repeated without malice. Its owner rounded the corner and looked at them. The Follicle Farmer looked unkempt.

'Look. I'll be as plain and simple as I can be,' the farmer offered. 'Go away!' He motioned with the back of his hands in a shooing motion urging them to leave.

'Err,' Bobby wasn't sure how to proceed. They hadn't dealt with hostility from a Follicle Farmer before. He looked to Banjo for inspiration.

'We're from the QA department,' Banjo offered nodding his head.

'QA, Quite Awful, I'm sure I don't care,' the worker replied.

'Who are you?' Bobby demanded.

'I'm a worker,' He answered.

'A Follicle Farm worker?' Bobby clarified.

'Sad, but true.'

'And your name...?' Bobby wanted more details.

'Noneovya,' he replied.

Banjo started to write it down.

'Noneovya business,' the face informed them and laughed.

Skip walked up to the Follicle Farmer and punched him hard in the mid-section. The worker doubled over in pain.

Bobby and Banjo were very surprised by Skip's actions.

'He fell onto my hand,' Skip complained. He held it up, shaking it, as if in pain.

'That's true,' Bobby agreed and looked at Banjo who slowly nodded his agreement accepting the situation.

'Okay. Don't hit. My name is Greg.' He took a breath and winced as if still in pain. 'I recognise you two from the moustache.'

'Greg!' Bobby declared. He looked again at Banjo who nodded and confirmed he also recognised their former boss. They were very surprised to find him at the big toe.

It transpired that the former AM from the moustache had been demoted and sent to the left arm pit. As he was a bad fit, they transferred him to the anus to grow hair there. Apparently, that didn't work out either and he found himself transferred here.

'I suppose you're surprised to find me working at the toes?' Greg told them.

'Last we heard you were working on the anal hairs,' Bobby agreed.

'I was, for a short while. Then they transferred me out of there and sent me here as punishment.' Greg laughed at them sardonically.

'The big toe is punishment?' Banjo was confused.

'They thought it was.' Greg looked about him. 'It's not so bad. I like the isolation. You get left alone and I like that.'

The others said nothing.

Greg continued. 'Anal hair growing was terrible for me.' He looked at them and then decided to continue explaining. 'They wanted to "rehabilitate me" and "indoctrinate me" into their weird rituals.'

The others said nothing.

'It was horrible,' Greg concluded.

'We haven't been there yet,' Bobby told him.

'Don't!' Greg responded. 'Save yourself from a truly horrible experience.'

'It's part of our job,' Bobby started to explain.

'Where-ever a hair grows, we goes,' Banjo said forcing a smile.

Greg said nothing.

'Do you have a Team Supervisor we could speak to?' Bobby asked.

'Yeah,' Greg nodded his head slowly.

Bobby took a deep breath. 'Could we meet him?'

'Sure,' Greg replied not moving.

Bobby took another deep breath. 'Could you take us to meet him now?' he asked. Next he added. 'Please.'

Greg looked at the three of them.

Skip was exercising a fist by rotating it in the air in Greg's general direction.

'Follow me,' Greg capitulated and he turned and walked away.

Bobby and Banjo gathered their things and started to follow.

'I'll stay with the Taurus,' Skip called out to them and they waved back in acknowledgement.

Greg led them down a short path and into a shabby office. Here they found a Follicle Farmer sound asleep at his desk.

Greg shook him awake. 'Scott! We've been invaded.'

Scott opened bleary eyes and slowly became aware of the two strangers in his office.

'I'm Bobby and this is Banjo. We're Follicle Farmers.' Bobby started to explain. 'I'm the QA manager and we're here to...'

Scott cut him off. 'I'm very happy for you both. Check out a follicle and pus off,' Scott invited.

Greg smiled.

'We're here to do a full QA audit and...,' Bobby had started to explain.

'Look at all our follicles if you must. We have eight on the big toe, two each on the three middle toes and we gave up growing hair on the small toe.' He looked very annoyed at their intrusion.

'Fourteen hairs,' Banjo said.

'Well done, son,' Scott applauded sarcastically. 'Give him an award for counting. He can add it to his others.'

'I gather you've heard of us?' Bobby enquired.

'We do get some titbits of news.' Scott smiled. 'We may be at the furthest point from the brain but we're still part of the body.'

'A very important part,' Banjo agreed.

'The toes are... Mr mathematical genius,' Scott replied. 'But the hairs on them aren't.'

Banjo said nothing.

Greg started to explain. 'We're on the toes and the toes get ordered to do a lot of undesirable tasks.'

'We're the first to be immersed into hot or cold water!' Scott lamented. 'Why is that?' he asked. 'Are we expendable?' he asked rhetorically.

'They cramp toes in shoes for extended periods. Feet sweat, toes stink, *epidermis* rots and we're out here stuck to them.'

'They use toes to kick things!' Scott explained.

'That pain shoots through all of us,' Greg added taking a deep breath.

'Toes are stabilisers and propellers. The human couldn't walk comfortably without them yet we're used to test the water, kicked about and cramped in hot sweaty conditions.' Scott was angry.

'Unless we're freezing.' Greg looked sinister.

'We're often left out in the cold,' Scott complained. 'The Toe Manager sends messages to the brain. "We're all cold!" he tells them. But does anything get done?' he asked. 'No. It doesn't. It's normal to ignore messages from the toes,' he lamented.

Bobby said nothing. It didn't seem appropriate and so Bobby didn't promise to investigate. These issues were beyond him.

'Look. I get it,' Scott softened his tone. 'You're Follicle Farmers, just like we are,' he sighed. 'You're just doing your job and you can't do anything for the toes,' he concluded waving his hands in the air as a demonstration of his exasperation.

Bobby drew in a deep breath and was trying to say something re-assuring. He didn't.

Scott regarded him. He snorted. 'Greg, take them on the tour of all the follicles on our toes,' he ordered.

'Sure, boss,' Greg answered.

Scott made himself comfortable once again and closed his eyes.

Bobby looked at Scott is dismay. He'd never met a Follicle Farmer with such a poor attitude before. He felt dismissed, and in one way he was relieved that they could leave his negativity. But on the other hand, he'd felt intimidated. He was graded a Regional Manager and this Team Supervisor was totally disrespectful and should be disciplined.

Bobby saw Greg motioning to him and so he ended up saying nothing. He followed the others out of the room. They started at the big toe and worked their way from toe to toe in descending size. They met with the Team Leaders and their workers. They discussed follicle growing techniques and QA initiatives. For the most, the teams were responsive, after initially being surprised that someone from the System Manager's office would show any interest in them at all. After Scott's rebuke, they were glad that this part of their experience was routine.

Greg next took them to a small, ill equipped, staff room to discuss what they had seen. 'So, now you've seen toe hairs,' Greg concluded.

'Which follicle are you assigned to?' Banjo had his e-pad ready to record the response.

'I'm sort of a floater worker,' Greg replied. 'I sort of help out where needed,' he smirked. 'Scott takes advantage of my experience to take care of things whilst he does paperwork.' Greg smiled broadly and winked at them.

'Thanks for showing us around, Greg. I wish you all the best.' Bobby paused and then added. 'We'll write up our report and get going. No need for you to hang around.'

Greg left the room.

The resulting report that they wrote about the follicles on the left foot toes was neither scathing nor exemplary.

'This is the shortest report I've prepared since we started,' Banjo commented.

'There are only fourteen hairs to report on,' Bobby reminded him.

'What should I put in about Scott and Greg?' Banjo was concerned. 'Scott was very disrespectful.'

'I suggest we don't put anything down at all. Morale here is low enough without us pushing it down any lower,' Bobby replied. 'Hair grows slowly on the toes, and they do seem to be very isolated,' Bobby added.

'But?' Banjo started to contradict.

'But nothing,' Bobby cut him off. 'Fourteen hairs!' Bobby paused to marshal his thoughts. 'Even if we worked really hard here to improve follicle quality and improve morale, it's still only fourteen hairs!'

Banjo said nothing.

'What if we complained about Scott and he got transferred, he'd contaminate another region with his attitude. Plus..! Plus..! Whoever replaced him here would feel they were being punished,' Bobby concluded.

Banjo studied his boss's face.

'It's only fourteen hairs and they are growing,' Bobby reiterated.

'Should we recommend rotational transfers for any of the Team Leaders or workers?' Banjo was very concerned.

'Are they likely to want it?' Bobby countered.

'No.'

'You have your answer.' Bobby gave Banjo that look he used to end a discussion.

Banjo knew that look.

'Look who I found.' Skip came up to the two of them.

Bobby turned to see Skip.

'Hi Skip,' Bobby said. 'This place is depressing us and we're ready to get going.'

The captain of the Zodiac Capricorn moved passed Skip and came into Bobby's and Banjo's view. 'Hi boys!' Jack greeted them.

'Jack!' Bobby and Banjo choroused, delighted to see their drinking buddy.

'I have a surprise for you,' Jack announced. He dragged another person into the room. 'This is Neil,' he told them.

Neil seemed hesitant to come into the room. He nodded at Bobby and Banjo but said nothing. Despite the relatively cool temperature, he seemed hot and fidgety.

'Hello, Neil.' Bobby approached the newcomer extending his hand in friendship. 'My name is Bobby, and this is Banjo my assistant. We're QA Managers for the follicles.'

'Yes. I have heard of you both. I'm Neil,' he added unnecessarily.

'What brings you to the toes?' Bobby asked trying to make conversation. 'You must be important to warrant travel by Zodiac,' Bobby concluded.

'Ahh..,yes. I'm a General Manager,' Neil confirmed.

'Oh, well then, you out rank me.' Bobby smiled. 'Which system?' Bobby asked pleasantly.

'*Integumentary,*' Neil answered.

Bobby looked at Banjo. Were they being introduced to their new boss in a grotty staff room in the big toe of the left foot?

Banjo understood the look and shrugged.

'Follicles?' Bobby asked cautiously.

'No,' Neil replied.

'*Dermis* or *Epidermis*?'

'No.'

'Oh..., so you're the GM for the nails?'

Neil took a deep breath. 'Yes.'

The room went deathly quiet.

'Oh,' Bobby eventually said.

'I was on my way to the right foot to do an inspection of the nails, but somehow we came here,' Neil started to account for his being there.

'I must have taken a wrong turn,' Jack explained. 'Sorry.' He winked at Bobby.

'Neil.' Bobby looked squarely at him. 'You've got some explaining to do.'

'I was told not to discuss the *Staph* infection with anyone until the formal inquiry,' Neil said defensively.

'That'll be a long time coming,' Bobby said.

'I'm sorry for your losses. I knew Harry and we liked each other. I didn't have, don't have, much to do with follicles, despite us being in the same system,' Neil informed them.

'I don't suppose you need to,' Bobby agreed.

Skip and Jack had been standing around awkwardly. Jack spoke. 'I have to check a relay switch on the Capricorn. Skip, I could use your expertise if you're not too busy?' he asked.

'Ah,' he looked at Bobby and Banjo. 'I'm only too happy to help,' he said and the two turned and hastened out of the room.

'When Jack told me, he had taken the wrong *artery*, I should have been suspicious,' Neil said dryly. 'He's been travelling the *cardio-vascular* system all his life. It's what he does.'

'You think you were set up?' Bobby asked.

'It feels that way,' Neil agreed.

Bobby looked at Banjo. 'We didn't know anything about it, did we Banjo?'

Banjo shook his head.

'We do want to hear the nail department's perspective about what happened at the *abdomen,* but we were resolved that it would have to wait until the formal inquiry,' Bobby explained.

'I read your report,' Neil told them.

'And?'

'I respected the way it was written. It was full of details, without being encumbered with emotions or conclusions.'

'Did you agree with it?' Bobby asked.

'We're not supposed to...,' Neil wailed.

'Off the record! Did you agree?' Bobby insisted.

'Yes!' Neil capitulated. 'Off the record..., I agree,' he looked solemn.

'And?'

'There were numerous extenuating circumstances,' Neil defended.

'There always are,' Bobby sighed.

'From your perspective, what were they?' Banjo asked.

'Well,' Neil started. 'How much do you know about the duties of the fingers?'

'I know they do a lot.'

'A lot is an understatement,' Neil said to them. 'They participate in almost every external activity.' He paused. 'Considering how slender they are, they are remarkably strong and work perfectly together as a team.

'Go on,' Bobby encouraged.

'Unlike the toes, whose only functions are stability, propulsion and manoeuvring, the fingers are masters. The thumb grasps. The index finger is strong and precise. The middle finger is primarily used to push things. The fourth is supportive, and the fifth, the small finger, is the cleaner.'

'Cleaner?' Banjo was confused.

'Any perceived blockage in the nasal passage or the ear canal, the brain commands the small finger to go in and unblock.

Neil was warming up to his audience. 'The digits play musical instruments; they carry things, press things that need pressing. They put food in the mouth and they're used to wash things. They test for heat, cold, roughness, smoothness, count things, rub things. They even provide tactile contact with the...'

'Enough!' Bobby believed he knew where this was going. 'What about your nails?' He demanded.

'Toenails are mostly redundant. They come from a time when we needed nails to climb things like trees,' Neil explained.

'Hair is going the same way,' Bobby lamented.

'You used hair to climb trees?' Neil was confused.

'No, I mean hair is becoming redundant,' Bobby corrected.

'It is?' Banjo was concerned.

'Not in our lifetime, don't worry,' Bobby assured Banjo.

Banjo looked worried.

'Please continue, Neil,' Bobby requested.

'The fingernails are beneficial in opening things and for scratching things. They're quite effective during cleaning,' Neil seemed proud of this. 'Fingernails are what my department focuses on. We wouldn't be much of a department without them.'

'How big is the nail department?' Banjo asked out of curiosity.

'There are fifteen workers and one Team Leader for each fingernail, only twelve on the small finger. There are twenty workers on the big toes but only ten on the other toes, except for the small toe, they have seven workers each. Toenails grow slower than finger nails,' Neil replied.

Banjo was using his e-pad to work it out. 'That's ten Team Leaders and 228 workers.'

'Plus, my executive assistant and I make 230 in my department,' Neil confirmed.

'We have over one and a half million in the follicle department,' Bobby told him.

'The *dermis* and *epidermis* builders have many times more than us. We're small by department standards so your 230 is statistically non-existent,' Banjo explained apologetically.

'I'm not offended,' Neil brushed aside the diminutive conclusion. 'I know we're small and that's why we're attached to the *Integumentary* system.'

'I always thought you should be part of the *Skeletal* System,' Bobby told him.

'A common misconception.' Neil smiled. 'Nails aren't made of bone. They are made of tightly packed *keratinized epidermal cells*.'

'*Keratinized*? You mean like our hair?' Banjo was concerned.

'Exactly, nails and hair are made from the same material.' Neil smiled victoriously. 'However, we process ours differently.'

'I never knew,' Bobby said looking at Banjo who agreed that he didn't either.

'Not many do.' Neil was smiling proudly. Then an idea sprang to mind. 'Hey, how about a tour? The big toenail team is very close by. I could show you how we do it.'

Bobby had done enough tours and was about to decline when Banjo spoke for the two of them. 'That'd be fantastic. We'd love to see how nails are formed. Thanks.'

Bobby sighed and then chuckled.

Neil led the way out of the follicle staff room with Bobby and Banjo following. The toes follicle team were entering the room for a meal and rest break, so the timing was perfect. Neil led them down a short passageway and into a long narrow room.

'This is the nail root. It is where the nail is still under the skin. Here we strengthen the nail,' Neil explained. 'And then we push it out towards the end of the toe.'

They followed him around the corner of the room, and they were adjacent to the side of the nail. There they found the toenail team hard at work. They were liberally applying *keratin* from large vessels onto the nail.

'That's the nail bed.' He pointed to the nail. 'Here we thicken the nail. The *epidermis* provides us with specialised skin called a *cuticle* that prevents invasive forces from entering where the nail comes out to the outside world.'

They stood there watching the team at work for a while.

'It takes us 260,000 cycles to get the nail from the start of the nail root up to the tip of the toe.' He smiled. 'It's slow going, slow growing but we make it from really strong and tough stuff.'

'It's quite an engineering marvel,' Banjo concluded looking at Bobby who nodded.

'Yes, we're proud of them.' Neil smiled and he looked proud.

Neil excused himself and went to the Team Leader and they spoke in hushed tones for a brief period. He then returned. 'He said we could use his office. I told him the follicle staff room is being used by the hair growers and he said his office was free for a while.' He offered to follow them indicating the path they should take.

'What about the rest of the tour?' Banjo queried, concerned they were missing something.

'No, that's all of it,' Neil explained.

They entered the Team Leader's office. The room was modestly furnished. It had growth charts that were manually updated.

'Don't you use electronic charting?' Banjo queried.

'Technology hasn't reached here yet. As I said, toe nails are a low priority,' Neil lamented.

'What about the finger nails?' Bobby asked, speaking for the first time in a while.

'Yes, we do have electronic charting for the finger nails,' Neil answered.

'Did you record the scratch you made on the damaged *epidermis* layer of the abdomen?' Bobby wanted to know.

Neil was disappointed. 'I'd hoped we'd moved on from that.'

'It'll all come out in the inquiry,' Bobby reminded him.

'The brain ordered us into the *nasal cavity*. The brain ordered us to scratch the *abdomen*. I'm not saying they deliberately wanted the

infection transferred, but the evidence will prove we were innocent and merely an unknowing carrier for the *Staph*,' Neil told them
bluntly. 'Let's see how well the brain takes responsibility for its actions, huh!'

Bobby was shocked. Banjo was speechless.

'If you ask me...,' he started to explain but shook his head. 'And I
realize you haven't, but if you did, I'd bet there won't be an inquiry
at all. For one, the Marketing Department won't like it. They don't
want bad publicity and they'll block anything that reduces morale.
Secondly, the Head Office hates, I mean really hates, loathes, admitting it did anything wrong.'

'That's true,' Bobby capitulated.

They sat in silence contemplating the reality of what had just
been said. After a while they talked at length, and they agreed not
to pursue an inquiry. They would participate in one only if ordered
to do so. They'd stick with the indisputable facts and not offer opinion or conjecture. They shook hands in agreement and friendship.

Bobby and Banjo left Neil to complete his work at the toenail and
went up the passage to find Skip.

They found him talking to Jack. 'Take us to the bum hole please,
Skip,' Bobby requested. 'We both need cheering up.'

18

Skip looked thoughtfully at his two passengers. 'We could always say that we've been to the anus, and that we looked about, and that there wasn't much to report on,' he paused. 'All is well with *anal* hair!' he added as if making an announcement.

Banjo looked concerned.

Bobby considered the suggestion as he studied Skip's face. He wasn't being funny, he was serious. On the one hand, he had signed up to be the QA Manager for all follicles, regardless of where they are growing. Therefore they should go. Besides, it would displease Banjo if he asked him to fake the report. On the other hand, the Follicle Farmers at the anus did have an undesirable reputation. It was where management sent you when you were a misfit. It was regarded by many as being the region of the damned. Bobby slowly became aware that Skip and Banjo were staring at him expectantly.

'That's an idea...,' he replied, stalling whilst remaining uncommitted.

'You're not seriously considering it?' Banjo was aghast.

'I know you want to go,' Bobby smiled. 'You'll probably want the tour!'

Banjo said nothing.

Bobby took a deep breath. He'd come to a decision. He said to Skip 'Your suggestion is appreciated, but I believe I need to know the truth about them. I think we...,' he indicated Banjo and himself. 'Need to spend time there, and learn what it is about them that got them the reputation they have.'

Banjo looked relieved.

'Furthermore, I'm curious as to why they wouldn't keep Greg. I'd like to find out why they thought that sending him to the big toe was a bigger punishment compared to keeping him in the *anus*.'

'That's fine with me,' Skip agreed.

'You don't have to stay... if you don't want to?' Bobby offered Skip an out.

'No, no. Being at the anus doesn't bother me. I recently took the *Digestive* System Manager on a tour of the *colon*. Let me tell you, any experience I have with the Follicle Farmers at the *anus* will have nothing on that adventure,' Skip snorted.

'So you'll join us?' Banjo queried hopefully.

'Sure, why not?' He replied. 'I'll be able tell the others that I've been to the arse end of the body and survived the experience.' Skip smiled at them both and chuckled. 'I've never understood why they grow hair there anyway.' He shook his head in disbelief.

'Percival explained it to me. *Anal* hair comes from a time, long ago, when the *anus* needed protection from other life forms. Now our man wears clothing, which has kind of taken the place of bulky body hair. From what I understand, clothing will one day making follicle growing a redundant activity, for many regions of the body.' Bobby explained.

'Interesting,' Skip responded

'I don't like it,' Banjo told them.

Bobby couldn't help that. He responded with a half-smile and shrugged his shoulders. He then looked about. 'I'm a bit surprised that no one has come out here to meet us,' he lamented.

They'd departed the left foot some time ago and had travelled the circuitous route to get to the anus. The three of them were now standing on a platform adjacent to the anus follicle growing region, when Skip had made the suggestion.

'Maybe they're not expecting us?' Banjo speculated.

'It's a bit strange. They weren't expecting us at the pubic hair or the toe hair either,' Bobby agreed. 'I had thought that as we were specifically sent to these places, that the managers would have been informed.'

Skip said nothing. He was to embarrassed to remind them of their drinking session in the *Liver* and how these destinations had come about.

'Maybe it's because they're expecting us to make our own way..., to them,' Banjo speculated.

'Maybe...,' Bobby agreed uncertainly.

'Do you want me to go looking for someone?' Banjo offered.

'Let's all go. Let's see who we can find,' Banjo concluded.

The others nodded in agreement.

Bobby led them to a passageway which they entered. He sniffed about thinking that the legendary odour would guide them to the *anal* Follicle Farmers. The odour was pleasant, and his *olfactory* senses told him nothing. They continued for quite some time and soon found themselves in a large room filled with modern tables and chairs, food dispensing units and multiple giant computer screens on the walls populated with growth information about the hair under the *anal* Follicle Farmer's management. The three travellers stood and stared in wonder. This was clearly the staff amenities room. It was state of the art and by far the best equipped staff room they had seen since leaving the head. The room had a pleasant clean odour and sparkled with cleanliness.

'Oh, hello,' a voice greeted them.

They turned to see a tall Follicle Farmer that had entered the staff room. He was holding a cleaning cloth.

'Hello,' Bobby responded for the team.

'Are we expecting you?' The Follicle Farmer inquired politely.

'Actually, I was hoping that you were,' Bobby replied.

'I'll get our manager,' the Follicle Farmer concluded. 'Please make yourself comfortable and help yourself to fresh food and refreshments.' He waved in the direction of the self-service meal and drink dispensers. He then bowed and exited the room.

Banjo was about to start helping himself to the food, but Bobby restrained him. 'Let's not get caught with food in our mouths,' Bobby suggested.

Banjo said nothing.

They stood together staring at the door the Follicle Farmer had used to go get his manager.

The manager appeared at the door and walked to them. 'Hello, I'm Gary,' Gary introduced himself. 'I'm the AMAF, Area Manager Anal Follicles,' he said offering his hand in greeting.

'I'm very pleased to meet you, Gary. Bobby was smiling as he returned the handshake as he was very pleased at the professional greeting. 'My name is Bobby and I'm the QAMF, Quality Assurance Manager for Follicles. This is Banjo my EA and this is Skip. Skip is the Captain of the Taurus and he is our Transport Manager.'

'I gather that your visit to us is part of your role as QA Manager?' Gary inquired.

'Yes. I was hoping you'd say that you we're expecting us,' Bobby queried.

'Not specifically,' Gary replied. He took a deep breath. 'When we learned of your promotion to QA Manager we naturally assumed that you would eventually visit us in the course of doing your job.'

'Yes, that's right,' Bobby agreed. He hid his confusion.

'Please be seated,' Gary invited. 'Make yourselves comfortable.'

They selected a group of chairs around a table near the centre of the room. The chairs were good quality, padded and were very clean. The surface of the table sparkled with cleanliness. They sat and made themselves comfortable.

'You honour us with your visit, so early in your new role.' Gary smiled. 'Many would think us to be a low priority.'

'No! Not at all. We've all been looking forward to coming here for some time,' Bobby smiled cordially. 'The incident at the *abdomen* did occupy us for quite some time, but we're only too pleased to be here now.'

'We heard about the infection,' Gary nodded solemnly. 'It was a nasty business, from the sound of it,' He concluded. He looked at them pensively. 'It makes you think just how vulnerable to infection we all are.'

'Especially here,' Bobby agreed.

'We're deemed a high-risk area given the nature of the prolific *bacteria* that can grow here,' Gary conceded. 'We therefore practice the very highest levels of hygiene and risk management,' Gary beamed proudly.

'As part of our QA roll, we'd like to do an audit of your current practices and then recommend improvements, should they be necessary,' Bobby explained how it worked.

'Of course,' Gary agreed. 'We welcome outside observation as we strive for continual improvement. Your inspection is welcomed, and your input appreciated.'

Bobby was relieved. He smiled at Banjo, and he apparently shared his relief.

'I suggest I bring my Team Supervisors in to meet you. Perhaps you could give us all an overview of how you'll conduct the audit before starting. My team will of course assist that process in every way.'

'That would be most acceptable,' Bobby agreed nodding his head.

'Please help yourself to food and beverages, whilst I assemble the team.' Gary gestured to food and drink stations as he stood up to leave the room. 'It's all fresh,' he added.

'Thank you. We are parched and peckish.' Bobby smiled his appreciation.

Gary left the room.

'So far so good,' Bobby said looking at Banjo and Skip in turn.

'It almost seems too good to me,' Banjo was suspicious.

Skip shrugged his shoulders the way Banjo did when he doesn't have an opinion to share. Banjo gave him a look.

'Let's eat,' Bobby suggested.

They all got up and helped themselves to the amino acids, sugars and proteins on offer and piled them onto spotlessly clean serving platters. Banjo next dispensed beverages for the three of them and they sat and ate hungrily.

As they finished their meal the tall Follicle Farmer returned to the staff room. He nodded and smiled his greeting and cleared the remnants of the meal. He cleaned everything, returning the room to its spotless condition. Bobby, Banjo and Skip watched him in fascinated silence. The Follicle Farmer never spoke. He finished cleaning and then bowed as he left the room.

Gary returned to the staff room with two other Follicle Farmers. Clearly, they were the Team Leaders. Bobby, Banjo and Skip arose from their chairs to greet them.

'This is Larry, and this is Terry. They are my two TM's Larry is TMALS Team Manager Anus left side. Terry is TMARS, Team Manager Anus right side.' Gary next introduced their visitors and they all sat down.

'Side of what?' Banjo queried.

'The area is divided into the left side and the right side of the *anal* opening,' Gary explained.

'How many follicles do you have growing here?' Bobby asked.

'We have 120 under our management.' Gary answered.

'With only two Team Managers?' Bobby queried.

Larry and Terry smiled proudly as Gary continued to explain. 'I've learned that these two do an excellent job and that the separation of the workers into two teams makes for friendly rivalry and healthy competition,' Gary explained.

'If we don't grow, we don't grow!' Larry and Terry chorused unexpectedly.

Skip wasn't impressed. 'How did you work out the left side from the right?' he asked.

'We align our teams to the left and right butt cheeks,' Gary answered.

Bobby stood up. He had their attention. 'We'll do a random audit on five follicles on each side. That is sufficient for us to make an assessment and to make any recommendations for improvement.'

'What specifically are you looking at?' Terry asked.

'That you're managing follicle growth efficiently, that they're following procedures on trolley replenishment, chemical applications, hygiene and cleaning routines and that they are following good growth practices,' Bobby explained.

'Very good,' Gary acknowledged.

'We'll also be looking at your records management,' Banjo added.

'If it doesn't get recorded, then it didn't happen,' Bobby added.

'We look forward to your assessment,' Gary acknowledged them with a slight bow.

'Before we start, do you remember a Follicle Farmer named Greg? He came to you from the Arm Pit, and you transferred him to the Anus,' Bobby queried.

'We do,' Gary acknowledged. 'What about him?'

'Why did you transfer him?'

'He wasn't a team player. He was too disruptive to the others, and he affected negatively on morale. He said we were weird and did bizarre things. We offered him the toes and he left immediately,' Greg was monotone. 'Do you think...?'

'No!' Bobby acknowledged. 'I appreciate you explaining it.'

They all stood and filed out of the room.

There was a very brief rumbling sound, almost musical in its nature that echoed about them. Bobby looked at his companions but couldn't figure the noise. The three *anal* Follicle Farmer Managers laughed briefly but said nothing. There was a hint of an unpleasant odour, but it passed so quickly that it was easily forgotten.

For the next 250 cycles Bobby and Banjo were first escorted by Terry and then Larry to the teams growing hair. They were very impressed with the record management and growth achieved. Hygiene standards were at the highest levels they had seen since beginning their tour as the QA team. Both Bobby and Banjo were very pleased. The only thing of curious note was that whenever that rumbling, musical sound occurred, the Follicle Farmers that they were with, had a brief chuckle. The noise made them laugh. The louder the noise, the louder they laughed. Their mirth didn't affect hair growth, or their professional standards.

When they had completed the inspections, Larry took them to meet up with Gary and Terry. They were standing expectantly outside of the staff room. Skip had been with them the whole time. He followed them about, looking, but saying nothing.

'Skip's been very bored,' Banjo whispered to his boss as they walked.

'We'll be leaving soon,' Bobby replied.

'Thank you for your hospitality,' he said to Gary and his two Team Supervisors.

'How did we go?' Gary asked unconcerned.

'Very well,' Bobby replied. 'We're very impressed,' he assured him.

'I'm very pleased that you are,' Gary replied with a slight bow.

'We'll just go to the staff room and write up the report,' he told him.

'It might be better if you use my office,' Gary suggested. The team will be having a meal break soon and the green light is on.'

There was another rumbling musical sound. The *anal* Follicle Farmers laughed.

'Green light?' Bobby was confused. He'd experienced the green lights references before and wasn't sure he liked where this conversation was heading.

Gary pointed to a green light above the entrance to the staff room. It was brightly lit and there was an unlit amber light and unlit red light adjacent to the lit green light.

Bobby was very concerned. He was frightened to ask. Fortunately, Gary was ready to explain it to them.

'The green light indicates that a *defecation* event is about to take place,' Gary informed them.

'Oh,' Bobby was relieved.

'When the green light comes on it give us time to get ready. We mostly meet in the staff room during a *defecation* event and have a bit of fun,' Gary smiled. 'You're welcome to join us, or you can use my office to write up your report,' Gary suggested.

'We'd be delighted to join in the fun,' Skip responded for the three of them. Bobby and Banjo looked at him in surprise.

There was another, much louder rumbling musical sound. The gathered *anal* Follicle Farmers laughed very loudly. It confirmed that the louder the rumbling musical noise the louder the farmers laughed.

'What is that noise?' Bobby demanded to know.

'That's a methane gas expulsion,' Gary replied smiling. 'Please don't ask me why we think they're funny, but we just do,' He chuckled and then sighed.

'Oh,' Bobby responded.

'I thought they were called *flatulence*?' Banjo queried.

'That is a technical name for them, and I have heard that there are a few others,' Gary smiled.

'In the colon they call *intestinal* rumblings "*Borborygumus,*"' Skip added helpfully.

'We've heard talk about them,' Banjo conceded.

'And now you've actually heard them,' Gary laughed.

'I assume the unexpected nature of *flatulence* makes funny because it's a surprise,' Bobby speculated dryly.

'Something like that,' Gary agreed smiling.

The green light turned off and the amber light came on. 'Let's go inside,' Gary invited. 'That means that we don't have much time.'

They followed Gary into the staff room. The workers and their leaders were noisily gathered about two giant and very long tables. At each of the tables, there were two workers wearing weird head wear, assigned to manage the activities. The politeness and respectfulness they had observed during the inspection was replaced with laughter and banter as the *anal* Follicle Farmers jostled to and from the tables.

'I'll explain what's happening,' Gary offered. He had to shout above the noise.

Bobby. Banjo and Skip nodded their interest and appreciation.

'There's about to be a *defecation* event. The *Sphincter* Master sends us an alert when the pressure reaches a certain level. We all gather in the staff room and place bets.' Gary pointed to the monitors on the walls. 'We're wired to the *rectum* and *anal canal* to receive data on volume and duration.'

'Wow!' Skip was impressed. Bobby and Banjo were bewildered.

Gary offered them some complementary betting tokens which the three accepted. Gary led them to the two tables and the workers parted respectfully allowing the boss and his guest's access to the table.

The tables were divided into marked segments. The first table had markings indicating time graduations. The largest area was marked with one beat. The table was further divided into additional beats, so it read from one to ten. Workers had placed their betting tokens on the table under the watchful eye of the hat wearing, Table Supervisor.

'On this table they're betting on the time duration the longest stool takes to exit through the *anus*. It's not an exact science and the betting is fierce and a lot of fun.'

'What are the mitigating factors?' Banjo asked intrigued.

'Typically, the higher the pressure and length of time between *defecation* events has an impact on the result. Many of the long term workers here are quite expert at predicating the outcome,' he replied. 'I also suspect that the type of material that has been processed by the digestive tract has a bearing on the nature of the output.'

'What about the other table?' Skip asked. 'What's happening there?'

They turned to face the other table. 'This is the table where they bet on volume,' Gary replied. 'The *Sphincter* Master Controller sends us a volume report at the end of the defection event. The Follicle Farmers bet on how much the total volume of *faeces* is going to be pushed through before the clean-up is completed.'

'Wouldn't you know the result when clean up starts?' Skip was very interested.

Gary laughed. 'Sometimes the order for the clean-up comes prematurely,' Gary explained. 'It doesn't happen often, but sometimes the clean-up is requested before the *Sphincter* Master has completed the purge.' He chuckled. 'I can only speculate on the expression on the Finger Manager's face when that happens!' He laughed very loudly as did his fellow workers, who thought it extremely funny.

They settled and looked at the table. Bobby was intrigued at the range of increments displayed. They ranged from twenty units right up to twelve hundred units. It seemed the workers felt this was going to be about nine hundred units as that's where the betting tokens were mostly positioned. Bobby put his token on the seven hundred unit line and looked at the others as if seeking some reassurance that he'd done the smart thing. Skip put his on the one thousand unit line and Banjo put his on the four hundred. The light changed from amber to red and workers pulled away from the betting tables and looked up expectantly at the score boards.

Defecation was a relatively quiet event. The three visitors were aware that motions were being passed but they were more fascinated by the expectant looks on the faces of the *anal* Follicle Farmers. Some of the workers were counting in hushed tones. The highest number Bobby heard someone utter was a four. There were interspersed methane discharges and the workers responded in mirth. The red light went off and the numbers came up on the screen. The first screen showed a four. This meant that the longest turd took four beats to exit. The Follicle Farmers that bet on four were cheering and happily collecting their winnings. The remainder groaned in disappointment.

'It takes a bit longer to calculate the volume,' Gary explained.

Presently the number 1034 came up on the screen and Skip and a few others whooped in delight. The table controller paid the winners their tokens. Presently, the *anal* Follicle Farmers filed out of the room. The table managers and the cleaning crew waited respectfully for their Area Manager to finish with his guests before tidying up.

'I can now proudly tell everyone that I made a crap bet and won!' Skip couldn't help himself. He laughed at his own joke.

Bobby and Banjo groaned but Gary was happy for him and gave him a gentle pat on the back.

'It's good of the *Sphincter* Manager to provide you with that information. It certainly seems that your team has quite a bit of fun,' Bobby said to Gary.

'He is a very accommodating man. He's very new to the role having replaced Adam when Adam got promoted to manager of the *Liver*.' He paused. 'We see him socially and we share a few laughs about working here, given our undesirable location,' Gary added.

'He has a big responsibility,' Bobby agreed.

'Would you like the tour?' Gary offered enthusiastically. 'He'd be only too pleased to show you about...'

'NO THANKS!' Banjo replied with finality. He then returned his voice to normal. 'We do appreciate the offer, but we're on a tight schedule and we really must press on with our QA responsibilities.'

Gary looked very disappointed.

Bobby said nothing and there was an awkward silence.

'What else do you do for fun around here?' Skip asked Gary changing the subject.

'We'll...um, how would you like to be the judge of that?' Gary asked speculatively.

'Huh?' Skip was confused.

Bobby was about to say they were ready to leave, but he became intrigued that there may be more to see and learn about this place. He shared a look with Banjo but he said nothing.

'We're preparing for a contest,' Gary informed them. 'It's quite a big deal and our performers have been practicing a lot.' Gary nodded agreeing with his own assessment.

'A contest?' Skip was curious.

'We have a song and dance team entered in the annual Pelvic Floor Variety Show contest,' Gary informed the three bewildered guests. 'They'd be so pleased to perform for you and get your opinion.'

'Did you say the pelvic floor region has an annual entertainment contest?' Bobby was amazed, but wanted confirmation of what Gary was telling them.

'Yes. We compete every 10,000 cycles,' Gary explained. 'This will be the fourth time we've entered and we're very hopeful of winning this one.'

'How many entries are there?' Banjo queried.

'Oh, there are a lot of teams, but only four Follicle Farmer teams. The rest are from the *Muscular Skeletal* System and the *Digestive* System. None from *Reproductive* or *Cardio-vascular* but we do keep sending them invitations,' Gary explained.

'Which Follicle Areas are represented?' Bobby demanded. This was bigger than he originally feared and he was surprised he'd never heard of it.

'The left buttock have entered the 'Cheeky boys.' The right buttock now has a team called 'Bum Fluff', they're very good by the way and they won the previous contest,' Gary informed them.

Skip laughed but Bobby and Banjo didn't.

'This is the first time the Pubic Hair Region hasn't entered a team. They said they were too busy to enter this time for some reason.'

'What do they call themselves?' Skip was curious.

'Originally they were called the "Pubic rhythm and blues",' Gary answered. 'But for the last contest they changed it to "Puberty Blues".'

'That's a great name,' Skip concluded.

'It's a pity they're not entering this year. We'd really liked to have beaten them.'

'What sort of songs do your performers sing?' Bobby was concerned given their location.

'Oh, they make up their own lyrics,' Gary answered. 'Originality is a factor in the judging.'

'Bring them on,' Skip requested gesturing that they should set up and perform. Clearly he was intrigued.

Gary left them standing there and went to assemble the performers.

'I should really find a quiet place and work on the report,' Banjo muttered.

'You should stay. What we see next may become a part of the report,' Bobby said smiling.

Banjo looked down and said nothing.

Presently Gary returned with eight assorted Team Leaders and workers. They were smiling happily at the prospect of performing well-practiced routine before these distinguished visitors. Gary stepped back and indicated that they should commence. After a group huddle they looked and then bowed at the guests. Next one of the Team Leaders stepped forward and began dancing, swaying and slowly twisting his way toward the floor clicking his fingers rhythmically. When his knees were slightly bent, he maintained the sway and started to sing, softly at first, and then his voice level grew imperceptibly.

He sang in a deep voice. ♪'Ate, ate, ate, ate♪.' Next another two performers copied the first and they sang the word 'ate' repeatedly also clicking their fingers. Then the other five joined in until all eight were swinging, clicking, swaying, and singing 'ate' repeatedly.

The lead performer led the others into the chorus of the song.

'♪We hydrate to urinate, we masticate to defecate, we stimulate to sali-vate and we nauseate to regurgitate♪.'

'♪We all rotate♪'

They did a full 360 degree on the spot turn.'

'♪Ate, ate, ate, ate♪.'

'♪We commiserate to compensate, we dictate to domesticate, we humiliate to infuriate, and we fumigate to obliterate♪.'

'♪We all rotate♪'

They all did another 360-degree turn.'

'♪Ate, ate, ate, ate♪.'

'♪We masturbate to stimulate, we fornicate to inseminate, we penetrate to impregnate, and we ejaculate to populate♪.'

'♪We all rotate♪'

They did another 360-degree turn.'

'♪Ate, ate, ate, ate♪.'

'♪We exaggerate to illustrate, we articulate to...♪'

Bobby pulled Gary's arm and guided him away from the performance 'You're not seriously going to let them present this? Are you?' Bobby demanded. The singers continued unaffected by Bobby's manoeuvre.

'I think they're very entertaining.' Gary was clearly surprised at the intensity of Bobby's response.

'I know you're away from the mainstream, but you will be representing all Follicle Farmers at this event.' Bobby was aghast.

'But...,' Gary started.

'Couldn't they come up with something a little more... dignified?' Bobby demanded.

Gary drew in a deep breath. 'We're working in-between two butt cheeks next to the *anus*. The sun never shines on us Bobby. How dignified do you think we should be!?' Gary demanded angrily.

Bobby said nothing. They stared angrily at each other.

'I'm sorry, Gary,' Bobby capitulated. 'You're their Area Manager and from my perspective you're doing an excellent job at growing hair. How you spend your spare time shouldn't be any of my business.'

'Damn straight it isn't,' Gary was now angry.

'We have a report to prepare. I wish you all the best with your contest,' Bobby told him. He turned to walk away.

'Are you putting the details of our entry into the contest in your report?' Gary stared at him coldly.

Bobby stopped. He turned and stared back at him. He wasn't sure how to respond to that.

Skip approached, interrupting their silence. 'Hey! These guys are really good! This event has a lot of merit. We should do this in other parts of the body. Go body-wide.' Skip was very excited.

Gary smiled and Bobby held up his hands in capitulation.

'What do you call these guys?' Skip asked.

'Someone, I forget who, named them the "The Anal Retentives". The name sort of stuck so we ended up using it.'

A runner hastily approached Banjo and passed him a note. Banjo thanked him and read it.

He turned to the others and got their attention.

'We have an urgent message from George,' he explained. 'We're to proceed immediately to the upper back. There is a massive, fast growing, anomalous growth that he wants us to check out.' Banjo took a deep breath. 'They think it might be skin cancer.'

~ 19 ~

Bobby, Banjo and Skip left the *anus* after hurried "Good-bye's" and hastily made promises to visit again soon. The seriousness of the report from George was immediately felt by those that had heard Banjo's reading of it.

Melanoma was the worst thing that could happen to the *Integumentary* System. *Melanoma* could readily spread to other systems and attack them also. Melanoma wasn't caused by an outside bacterium or a virus. *Melanoma* was the *Integumentary* System attacking itself. *Melanoma* could kill them all and all would, quite rightly, blame the *epidermis* and *dermis* managers, under George's management, for allowing that to happen. This wasn't just a war. This could be a fight for their very survival.

Skip steered the Taurus into the vein and sped up the *Torso* to the *Heart*, went through the left *Lung* through the *Heart* and into the *aorta*. From there he took them out of the main artery into the *right subclavian* and they exited into the *intercostal posterior artery* just before the *right auxiliary* that would have taken them into the arm. After navigating the smaller *arteries* and *capillaries* they ended up at the shoulder blade *dermis* near the region George had described.

They exited the Taurus and were promptly greeted by a Follicle Farmer.

'Hello sir. Thank you for coming. You don't know how much this means to us.'

'Hello,' Bobby replied with a sigh. The toll of their constant travelling and visits to numerous parts of the body was becoming evident. Bobby was exhausted and hungry.

'Forgive me,' he added unnecessarily. 'My name is Alan. I'm the AMFTBLSB,' Alan told them proudly.

Bobby thought back to the time he had spent in marketing, but he said nothing.

'That's short for the Area Manager Follicles Torso Back Left Shoulder Blade,' Alan clarified its meaning.

Skip suppressed a laugh under the stern gaze of Banjo who knew how their Transport Captain would respond to such a title.

'I'm Bobby, QA Manager Follicles and this is Banjo, my EA,' Bobby did the introductions.

Banjo nodded his head.

Bobby completed the introduction. 'And this ruffian is Skip, he's our guide.' He yawned and stretched and smiled when he noticed Banjo and Skip were doing the same.

'Well I'm very glad you've arrived. I hear you're a bit of a marvel when it comes to problem solving, and as it is, we seem to have quite a predicament,' Alan gushed.

'Where is it?' Bobby asked.

'Pardon,' Alan responded hesitantly.

'The *melanoma*?' Bobby told him.

'Oh,' Alan responded. 'Do you...err... want to see it?' he asked cautiously.

Bobby was becoming impatient. 'That's why we're here.' Bobby smiled briefly. He took a deep breath and sighed. 'Look Alan, we're here to help. The quicker you help us, the quicker we can get started helping you. Do you follow me?'

Alan stepped up to Bobby. 'I think it should be you that follows me,' Alan replied stiffly. 'I'm the one that knows where it is, after all,' Alan retorted huffily.

This time it was Banjo that suppressed a giggle and it was Bobby that gave him the look. Skip just rolled his eyes and shrugged his shoulders.

Bobby decided he'd change his approach. 'Perhaps we could follow you to your office?' Bobby requested. 'I'd like to send some messages to George and perhaps arrange a Head Office perspective on what's happening.'

'Oh they sent someone already,' Alan suddenly remembered. 'But he's not one of us,' he added whispering loudly.

'He's a *virus*?' Bobby queried sarcastically.

'No,' Alan replied. He was confused by the question.

'So he's a *bacterium*?' Bobby asked triumphantly.

'No!' Alan was agitated. 'I mean he's one of us, but not one of us Follicle Farmers. You know. He's from the *Immune* System.'

Bobby sighed. 'Good. We'll need them. Does "he" have a name?' Bobby asked hoping it was Lek. It would be nice to see him again and at least Lek was someone they knew they could work with.

'I think he said his name was, Milo,' Alan replied helpfully nodding his head as if agreeing with himself. 'He said he knew you,' he added with a smile.

'That's good. Yes, we know Milo.' Bobby turned to Banjo and Skip who nodded their agreement.

Alan said nothing.

After a lengthy silence Bobby asked. 'Could you... please lead the way to Milo?'

'Yes,' Alan replied looking at them with a perplexed expression. He then decided what to do. He bowed. 'Follow me please.'

They followed Alan all the way to the edge of the *melanoma*. Milo was supervising the troop build-up. He seemed satisfied and looked in control of the situation.

Milo smiled when he saw them coming. He held up a hand in a halting signal. 'Please don't get too close,' Milo warned. 'The infection is highly virulent, and we wouldn't want a celebrity such as your fine self, being turned into a malignant tumour.' Milo burst into a deep hearty laughter and then hugged Bobby, Banjo and Skip in turn.

Alan stood back and said nothing. He was in awe of the familiarity exhibited by these very important personages.

'I'm glad you're here,' Milo told them. 'But I have noted that there aren't a lot of follicles in this region.'

'We're representing the *Integumentary* System. I gather our experience on the *abdomen* gives us an advantage when dealing with this type of multi system problem,' Bobby surmised.

'Well. From what we have learned so far, we're in for a rough ride,' Milo told them gravely.

'Have you seen much of Lek, recently?' Bobby asked.

'He's on patrol,' Milo explained. They don't give out much information about the activities of *T-Cells* and Bobby accepted that. He was just glad that they turned up where and when you needed them.

'Do you have any prior training or information on this type of condition?' Banjo inquired pointing at the *melanoma*. The *T-Cells* have extensive files on these types of encounters, and they have the ability to access and share information between themselves and their *Immune* System headquarters.

'No,' Milo replied.

'Oh,' Banjo was surprised.

'This is a first for us,' Milo told them. 'How's that for my first command?' he asked rhetorically. 'There's no experience as valuable as being responsible for dealing with an unknown enemy,' he smirked. 'If I survive this one, they'll sing songs in my honour. If I don't, they'll sing at my funeral service, either way it'll be memorable,' he laughed.

They were quiet for a moment as they each, in their own way, reflected on the seriousness of the situation.

Then Milo's second in command approached him and saluted smartly. 'The troops are now fully deployed, and they have completely surrounded the *melanoma*. The *Cardio-vascular* System has increased the blood supply as you requested, and our additional supplies have arrived. They're being distributed.' He then saluted and stepped back one step, did a left turn, took another one step back and stood fast at attention while waiting for further orders.

'Thank you.' Milo acknowledged the junior officer. He turned to Bobby, Banjo and Skip. 'Let me bring you up to date, because I'm sure bozo here hasn't,' he said looking at Alan.

'Excuse me, sir. My name is Alan,' he explained with a smile, evidently not understanding the insult.

'Like I said,' Milo took a deep breath. 'The Follicle Farmers in this area have been evacuated. There are no casualties. The *epidermis* and *dermis* have been impacted. When all this is resolved they'll need assistance with reconstruction.'

Bobby nodded his head in understanding.

Milo continued. 'Have you heard how we came to find out about it?' Milo pointed to the *melanoma*.

'No,' Bobby answered for them all. 'How did we learn about the *melanoma*?' he asked with a smile.

'Well, it had nothing to do with bozo or his *epidermis* counterparts.' Milo looked at Alan.

'It's Alan,' Alan's voice was strained from always having to correct Milo.

'The builders and farmers in this region didn't have the wherewithal to report the problem. You see this area is in a blind spot to the *optical* sensory department. Even the fingers can't reach here properly so there was no digital sensory detection. These things...,' He indicated the *melanoma*. '...do give off an odour, but it is too faint for the *Olfactory* Department to detect it, so we couldn't even have sniffed it out.'

'So how did we find out about it?' Bobby queried.

'*Auditory*.' Milo smiled.

Skip laughed. 'Did the *melanoma* call out 'Cooee? I'm here! Come and get me!" He laughed so much that the others, apart from Alan, joined in.

They evidently needed to break the tension.

'We were told about it by another human,' Milo explained after they'd settled.

'Oh,' Bobby acknowledged. They were all quiet for a moment contemplating the enormity of that statement.

Milo continued. 'Head Office acted swiftly on the advice given and sought outside specialised assistance. After a lengthy process of examination, the diagnosis was declared.'

'Makes you think,' Skip said to no one in particular.

'We're trained to believe that we're a self-sufficient body with all the resources to grow, build, rebuild, clean and defend our body,' Milo stated. 'The sad truth is that there are more enemies to our way of life than we defenders of the body can defend against.'

'At least we're not alone,' Banjo added.

'What do you mean by that?' Milo asked.

'What if there wasn't an outside body. A body that was available, willing and able to detect this problem and say something about it? Or, what if they did detect it and didn't tell *auditory* about it. This *melanoma* would have grown rapidly beyond ours, and any other outsider's ability to deal with it.' Banjo took a deep breath. 'I think we're lucky we found out about this when we did.'

'You make a good point, Banjo. Well done,' Bobby told him.

'So do we know what we're up against?' Skip asked.

Milo held up an e-pad. 'This is the official report. It seems like everyone who's anyone has been copied in on it.' Milo seemed impressed. 'I guess that reflects how seriously we're all taking it.'

'And so look at us. We're at the front line representing our body's fight against these traitors,' Bobby lamented.

Alan spoke for the first time in a while. 'Excuse me sir. I knew these *epidermis* cells before they went black. They wouldn't hurt anyone. They were really nice, and we Follicle Farmers liked them.'

'So why now? Why did they change from *melanocytes* into *melanoma*?' Bobby demanded.

'They weren't feeling well after a severe ultraviolet radiation burn. They didn't get better, and they slowly changed. We thought they'd get better because we were all burnt and we got better, but they didn't get better. Then they turned black.' Alan suppressed a tear and sniffed. 'Can you make them better?' He asked hopefully.

'We can't.' Milo turned on Alan. He was angry. 'The outside specialist is going to get a sharp tool and dig it all out. It'll leave a giant hole in the dermis that will have to be pulled closed and aggressively held together,' he informed them.

Alan wailed. Bobby, Banjo and Skip went pale.

'What is it that the *melanocytes* do that makes them more vulnerable to sun burn damage than other *epidermis, dermis* cells?' Skip wanted to learn more.

Banjo explained. 'The *melanocytes* are responsible for skin colour. They release *melanin granules* that colour the skin. When they get sun exposure, they release more granules that turn the skin brown. It looks red from the increased blood flow feeding the cells during excessive sun exposure but that fades after the blood supply returns to normal. The *melanocytes* stability the sun damage with colour pigments. It puts them in the firing line for sun damage.'

'Well put,' Milo complimented.

'What exactly are we dealing with?' Bobby indicated the report in Milo's hand.

'Oh, Sorry.' He consulted the screen. 'We have a *malignant melanoma* in *situ.*'

Banjo explained it to Skip. 'That means it has the potential to spread but it hasn't started to spread yet.'

'In *situ* is a good start,' Bobby agreed.

'It hasn't penetrated very far into the *dermis* yet either,' Milo explained.

Banjo opened his mouth, but Skip forestalled him. 'I understood that bit,' Skip confirmed.

'The report believes there isn't any sign of *mitosis* at this stage,' Milo continued.

'That's cell division,' Skip said smiling.

Banjo smiled in reply.

'There is no ulceration at this point,' Milo said and he lowered the e-pad. 'It looks like we got here early in its growth stage so that's lucky, if you can call dealing with this thing being lucky.'

'Okay.' Bobby nodded at Milo. 'I gather your role is containment until the outside specialist can remove the cancerous tissue?'

'That's right,' Milo confirmed. 'We've been sent a supply of *alpha interferons* to boost our weaponry.' He drew a deep breath. 'We can't win a fight against it, but we can slow it down.'

'Good.' Bobby was pleased the *T-Cells* were organised as best they could be under the circumstances.

Bobby turned to Banjo. 'Our role will be to co-ordinate the evacuation of as many mobile builders and workers as possible.' He turned to ask Milo. 'How many cycles is it to the removal of the *melanoma*?'

'I'll see if I can find out,' Milo replied holding up his e-pad. He indicated to his second in command to follow him and check on the troops surrounding the *melanoma*.

Bobby watched the two brave officers inspect their soldiers. The *T-Cells* were very brave in his opinion, and he had developed a lot of respect for them.

Bobby turned to Skip, Banjo and Alan. 'We'll have little to do whilst we wait for the removal event.'

'What do I do?' Alan asked worriedly. He was clearly overwhelmed by the unfolding events.

'Go to your Follicle Farmers and explain what is happening. Give them assurances that they'll be okay and that they'll return to growing duties as soon as this crisis is over. Perhaps you could meet in your staff room and do some team building exercises or staff training,' Bobby suggested calmly and confidently.

'Okay,' Alan agreed. He stared at Bobby and Banjo seemingly considering something. He nodded slowly at Skip and Banjo and then with slow deliberate steps, left the area.

'We'll need to prepare everyone for a numbness that will accompany the removal event,' Bobby explained.

Banjo and Skip nodded in agreement. Such chemicals being introduced into the body wasn't new but none of them had experienced it personally.

'Do you want me here for that?' Skip asked sounding a bit concerned.

'Would you like to check things out on the boat?' Bobby asked with a half-smile.

'Whilst you're waiting, I thought I'd go fuel Taurus up. It's good to be fuelled up in case we need to get somewhere else in a hurry,' He told them.

'Off you go.' Bobby indicated the passage way from which they had arrived.

'I won't be long,' he assured them as he hastened from the area.

Bobby spoke to Banjo. 'We'll need to set up a command post, allocate duties to *epidermis* and *dermis* reconstruction crews, and conduct pain management exercises...'

'Won't the specialist do that after the removal event?' Banjo interrupted.

'I guess so, but it's our responsibility to be prepared,' Bobby replied.

'I've never been involved in a tissue removal event before,' Banjo lamented.

'Neither have I,' Bobby confirmed. 'Let's avoid being in the tissue that gets cut,' he smiled.

Banjo nodded his agreement. 'I wonder how long it'll be before they start,' Banjo pondered.

'I think it'll be soon. *Melanoma* has a dramatic reputation. I think the quicker they remove it, the better off we'll all be,' Bobby speculated.

They stood in silence and watched Milo and his second in command patrol the circumference of the *melanoma*. The area it occupied was small compared to the infection on the *abdomen*. The number of *T-Cells* replicated for this encounter was much less than the *abdomen* event. Bobby was surprised by the absence of the *phagocytes.* This was an *Integumentary* event and he was confused by their non-participation. The soldiers were adjusting their uniforms, checking weaponry, sharing a joke, which was their way of releasing tension prior to an enemy engagement. One began singing a military hymn and was soon joined by others. Singing and joking were a feature of soldiering that kept them close, and united, in the lead up to a battle.

Bobby looked again at the *melanoma.* He was scared and felt he had every right to be. *Melanomas* sprang up from nowhere and they were potentially lethal to everyone in the body. Bobby was also angry. He was angry at these traitorous skin cells that had allowed themselves to be transformed from cells that gave skin it's colour to cells that gave us the worry of a potential death sentence. How, why, he didn't know. He shook his head in dismay. He said nothing to Banjo but looked at his assistant who was also in quiet contemplation.

Bobby turned and looked at the menacing melanoma once more when he thought he saw movement. Initially he was alarmed. Was the *melanoma* growing, was it attempting to exert its transformation on its neighbouring cells. Bobby stared in earnest and concluded that it wasn't. It was a trick of the light emanating from the outside world. It was a shadow. Then Bobby saw it again. This time he took hurried steps closer to the movement so that he wouldn't lose sight of it.

'Ahoy, sir!' one of the soldiers shouted. 'It's too dangerous for you to be so close to the prisoner.'

'He's hardly a prisoner,' Bobby admonished the soldier. 'Parts of it can leave here anytime it wants. That's the whole problem.'

The *T-Cell* said nothing.

Bobby returned his attention to the *melanoma.* It was still moving and Bobby recognised the gesture as a "come to me" signal.

After glaring at the soldier, he stepped up to the *melanoma.*

'I'm scared,' it said to Bobby.

'You're a *melanoma*,' Bobby informed it. He was using his calming voice. 'We're scared of you.'

'I'm not a *melanoma*,' it declared in a meek voice.

'How come you can speak?' Bobby demanded in a hoarse whisper. '*Melanoma's* are supposed to be the silent killer.'

'I'm not a *melanoma*,' it repeated.

'Okay... what are you?' Bobby demanded.

'I'm scared,' it explained.

Bobby was patient. 'Why are you scared?'

'There are a lot of heavily armed soldiers surrounding me, and they have nasty looking weapons pointed in my direction,' it explained.

It occurred to Bobby that if he were the target of a *T-Cells* planned engagement then he'd be pretty scared too. Bobby sat down next to the black cell. 'How did you get to be this way?' he asked kindly.

'Bobby! What are you doing so close to the *melanoma*? It's dangerous to be so close,' Milo cautioned.

Bobby waved him away. He motioned for the black cell to be patient and he stood up to see Milo and a large quantity of *T-Cells* that were aiming their weapons toward him and the black cell. 'He says he's not a *melanoma*.' Bobby explained.

'A deception,' someone said.

'Don't trust it,' someone else said.'

'Cut first, ask questions later,' someone else added.

'What do you think it is?' Milo asked calmly.

'The fact it can speak and express fear, gives me cause for doubt,' Bobby explained.

'*Melanomas* aren't known to speak. This one may be an exception.' Milo was cautious.

'I don't think so,' Bobby countered.

'What do we do?' Milo asked.

'Move your troops back a bit. Don't stand them down, just give us a bit of space and time to explore this development,' Bobby requested.

Milo nodded to his second in command who immediately hand signalled a minor withdrawal. The troops moved back and took up a defensive position slightly farther away.

Bobby turned back to the black cell. 'Is that better?' He asked soothingly.

'Only a little,' it squeaked.

'Now I'm going to ask my friend to come and meet you,' Bobby started to explain. 'He's not armed and he's not a soldier. He's a Follicle Farmer like me.' Bobby smiled at the black cell reassuringly.

'Okay,' it squeaked. 'I like Follicle Farmers. Some of my friends grow hair near here.' It smiled.

Bobby smiled and gestured for the black cell to wait.

'Banjo, come here and meet... I'm sorry, but I don't know your name?' Bobby asked invitingly.

'I don't have one,' it told Bobby.

'That's okay, not many *epidermis* cells do until they get promoted into management.' Bobby said to the black cell. 'Can we call you "Blackie", whilst we work out how best to help you?' Bobby asked the black cell hopefully.

'Oh, yes please,' it gushed. 'That'd be wonderful. Blackie is such a nice name, thank you.'

'That's fine,' Bobby reassured the cell now known as Blackie. 'Blackie this is my friend, Banjo.'

'Hello, Banjo.'

'Hello, Blackie.'

'My name begins with a B just like yours and Bobby's,' Blackie declared.

'I'm sure we'll "B" good friends because of that,' Banjo agreed with a smile.

Bobby turned and looked seriously at Banjo. 'Blackie needs our help. Would you send an urgent signal to everyone, George, Percival, Jeremiah, and anyone else you can think of that may be able to help us here?'

'Sure,' Banjo agreed. 'What do I put in the signal?'

'Let them know that we have the situation contained. We have made friends with Blackie and we're helping him through this situation.' Bobby turned and smiled reassuringly at Blackie. 'Also tell them we need a second expert professional opinion from an outside specialist. Tell them we think that Blackie isn't a *melanoma,* and we'd like a second opinion before drastic action is taken,' Bobby concluded with a reassuring smile to both of them.

'I'd be only too happy to do that,' Banjo nodded his head enthusiastically. 'I'll do anything to help our new friend. I'll ask Alan if I can use his office,' Banjo then added jovially. 'Hey, Blackie. I'll see you soon.'

'Hey, Banjo,' Blackie responded happily.

Banjo stood up and left the area to communicate with management about the developing situation.

'Now I'm going to tell those soldiers to relax, Blackie,' Bobby explained. 'Okay?'

'Can't you tell them to go away?' Blackie pleaded.

'I'm sorry, but I can't,' Bobby apologised. 'They are from the *Immune System* and they won't take orders from me.'

'From the *Immune* System?' Blackie was confused. 'Is there an infection?' He asked meekly.

'We thought there might be, but now I think we're okay. They'll stay and protect us just in case.' He nodded his head reassuringly and Blackie seemed to relax knowing they were being protected.

Milo waved to Bobby and then Bobby excused himself from Blackie with a promise to be back as soon as he could. He stood up and walked to the gathering of soldiers who were now in a more relaxed posture.

'So, any idea what it is?' Milo asked.

'No.' He drew a deep breath. 'But I don't think he's a *melanoma.*'

'Best to wait until we know for sure, I guess,' Milo speculated.

'An un-required invasive event would remove a great deal of tissue. Cell lives will be lost and we'd have a lot of pain generated from this area, all for nothing,' Bobby explained.

'And some follicles will be lost,' Milo added with a half-smile.

'That too,' Bobby agreed. 'But at least no Follicle Farmers.' He grinned.

They stood in silence for a moment. Bobby was about to excuse himself and return to Blackie when Milo spoke.

'I'm glad you're here, Bobby,' he said with added sincerity.

Bobby nodded in understanding. He walked over and sat beside Blackie and they talked about anything and everything for many cycles. Quite sometime later Banjo returned. He was hurrying but slowed to a relaxed walk as he drew nearer to Bobby and Blackie.

'Good news, Blackie. The second specialist has confirmed it. Apparently you're a late developing *Pagetiod Spitz Nevus!*' Banjo told him. 'A PSN'

'A wha...? Bobby demanded.

Banjo laughed. 'Blackie is a late developing *Pagetiod Spitz Nevus!*'

'Is that good news?' Bobby was cautious.

'That's fantastic news!' Banjo was clearly very happy. 'He presents just like a *melanoma* but he's totally benign and he's just an unusual skin growth.' Banjo laughed. 'We're all in the clear!'

'Well I'll be.' Bobby was relieved.

'They're regarded as neat, orderly and very polite,' Banjo added.

'That's you!' Bobby exclaimed excitedly to Blackie.

'It's true,' Blackie agreed happily. 'I am!'

'You'd better go and explain it all to Milo,' Bobby suggested to Banjo nodding in Milo's direction.

Banjo did as he was bade and went to explain the situation to the concerned looking warriors.

'You gave us quite a scare, Blackie,' Bobby said.

'But I was the one that was truly scared,' Blackie stammered.

'Yes,' Bobby agreed. 'I'm sorry we scared you, but I'm glad you're not a *melanoma*. You do understand that we had to take precautions?' Bobby asked showing concern.

'I guess so,' Blackie agreed sheepishly.

'So, you're no longer scared or upset now that we know that you're harmless?' Bobby asked.

'Oh no!' Blackie replied. 'I'm very happy!'

'That's good,' Bobby acknowledged. Then after a pause he asked, 'Why are you happy?'

'I now have a name,' Blackie answered with a generous smile. 'I've always wanted a name.'

~ 20 ~

Bobby was finishing up with Blackie when he heard a voice mumble behind him.

'Excuse me, sir,' Alan stammered, uncomfortable about interrupting.

Bobby looked away from Blackie and saw Alan bowing profusely.

'Why do you bow so much, Alan?' Bobby demanded. 'Please stop.' And he did.

'You're a hero. You saved all of us from the *melanoma*,' Alan gushed and resumed bowing.

'But he wasn't a...,' Bobby started to explain but then abandoned that approach. 'Stand still please!' He demanded.

Alan stood rigid.

'What did you want to tell me?' Bobby asked patiently.

'Yes sir. You see sir,' he effused and became animated. 'You got a..., you received..., that is I received a message to..., no, no, that's not correct. It's your message. It's a message addressed to you, but it came to you..., via my computer?' He took a deep breath and half smiled to himself.

'Let's keep this moving forward,' Bobby suggested adding rolling hand gestures to encourage more information.

Alan looked at him. He initially wondered where they were going. Then he realised that Bobby meant the message. 'Oh,' he blurted. 'I err..., George! He wants you to report to him. The big boss, you know. George.' He pointed one hand at Bobby and the other in the air. He then realised that he was doing that, and promptly returned to a rigid posture.

'Alan. Thank you, for giving me my message,' Bobby responded. He hoped the AM would go away. How did he ever get promoted to AM he pondered? Perhaps he should schedule a follow up visit to this region focusing on management advancement practices and full QA assessment.

Bobby turned to Blackie and spoke with a congenial assurance. 'You'll be fine, Blackie. I promise. You'll soon have some new friends, and they'll look out for you.'

Blackie nodded his understanding and he smiled appreciatively.

'I have to go now,' Bobby said as he patted Blackie on what he thought was his shoulder. He hoped it was his shoulder. 'Take care of yourself,' he suggested kindly.

Bobby walked over to Banjo and Milo.

'George wants to see us. We're going to Head Office,' he added with a wry smile.

Banjo nodded in understanding.

'Good-bye, Milo. It was a pleasure, as always,' Bobby said to the military commander.

'We're just doing our job.' Milo smiled. 'We protect and we serve,' he said and saluted.

'And fight the good fight,' Bobby added.

'Shall we adjourn to the *Liver* for a quiet celebration before you head off to Head Office?' Milo suggested.

'Tempting, but when it's George that summons us...,' Bobby explained without completing the sentence.

Milo understood. He stepped forward and shook Bobby's and Banjo's hands in turn. He bowed his head as a further mark of respect and returned to his men.

Bobby motioned for Alan to lead the way. Alan led Bobby and Banjo back to his office where Bobby read the message for himself.

TO BOBBY. QAMF: PLEASE REPORT TO ME AT MY OFFICE AT YOUR EARLIEST POSSIBLE CONVENIENCE. GEORGE. ISM

'Do either of you have any idea where Skip is?' Bobby asked Banjo and Alan.

Banjo shook his head, but Alan knew. 'He's with your boat at the landing. He returned with the boat just before this message came, arrived, got sent, for..., to you,' Alan explained nervously.

'Thank you,' Bobby acknowledged the response. 'Just out of curiosity, how long have you been an AM?' Bobby asked showing some interest.

He thought about it with his eyes looking up. 'I think it was approximately ten cycles before you arrived,' Alan replied looking at them. 'I got promoted from Team Leader when both my Team Supervisor and Area Manager transferred themselves away from here at once when they saw the *melanoma*.'

Bobby looked at Banjo. Banjo shrugged.

Alan next led them to Skip and the Taurus. He turned to Bobby and said softly. 'Thank you again, sir. We'll honour your deeds and sing your praises,' he paused and added with a smile. 'I bid you safe travels,' he turned and walked away.

'Did you sort it out?' Skip asked showing concern.

'It was a "*Spitz Nevus*," Skip. He's a harmless *melanoma* doppelganger,' Banjo informed him.

'And he now has a name,' Bobby sighed.

'What did you name him?' Skip asked.

'Blackie.'

'Good name,' Skip acknowledged nodding his head. 'Where are we going now?' He asked without curiosity.

'George wants to see us,' Bobby answered. 'The ISM awaits our arrival with eager anticipation, and we proceed with trepidation.'

Banjo laughed.

Skip said nothing.

Wordlessly the three boarded the craft and with practiced routine they made ready to cast off and re-join the stream and start the journey to the head. They travelled via the *Heart, Lung Heart* route and into the *carotid artery* and then into the *Superficial Temporal* which was near the *Integumentary* System Headquarters and George's offices.

As they docked, Ramus, the *Integumentary* assistant they had met before, approached them. He wordlessly watched them disembark the Taurus.

Bobby and Banjo waved in his direction in recognition and Ramus nodded in response.

'How long will you be here?' Skip asked.

'I don't know,' Bobby answered. He turned to look at the EA. 'Ramus. Should Skip wait here for us, or will we be here for a while?'

Ramus nodded his head accepting the relevance of the question. 'I believe you'll be here for quite some time. It may be appropriate for the transport captain to return to his station.'

'I've been dismissed,' Skip concluded.

'I'll send word when we're ready to travel again,' Bobby advised.

'It could be that I'll already have been assigned a new passenger by the time you're ready. This current policy of management types visiting workplaces, has kept us Zodiac Captains very busy,' Skip replied.

'I hope we meet again. You've been very good to us and I'm sure I speak for Banjo also, that we consider you to be a close friend.' Bobby looked sad at their imminent separation.

'Aw shucks,' Skip wailed. He stepped forward and gave Bobby a big hug. He then turned to Banjo, and he got one also.

Skip boarded and released the docking ropes. As the Taurus drifted into the stream he stood to attention and saluted. Bobby, Banjo, and Ramus watched the craft gathering speed in the flow of the blood vessel. As it approached the bend, they gave Skip a final farewell wave and he was gone from view.

'George suggested that you freshen up before meeting with him,' Ramus explained. 'Follow me.'

They followed Ramus down familiar passageways and they soon entered the reception area. Erastus was at his usual place and looked up as they entered his workspace. Erastus nodded in acknowledgement and returned to his E-pad and continued doing what he was doing. Ramus led them into the staff dining room. They were experienced with the room and how it functioned. They felt comfortable and joined a slow-moving queue of *Integumentary* Head Office staff, lining up for platefuls of food and refreshments. Surprisingly, it turned out that Ramus was joining them. They looked at him in mild surprise.

'I'm hungry,' Ramus informed them deducing their curiosity.

They sat together and ate in relative silence. After they'd eaten, Banjo brazenly asked the obvious question. 'Do you have any idea why we're here?'

Ramus smiled. He clearly anticipated the question and was amused that they had waited this long for one of them to ask it. 'No,' he answered as he pushed his empty plate forward.

'Oh,' Banjo responded.

'I'm presuming that we'll be reviewing our progress as QA Managers and discussing where we've been and what we've learnt and what we have achieved,' Bobby surmised.

'I find its best not to presume,' Ramus responded.

'But that's...,' Bobby was about to justify himself, but Ramus held up a hand to forestall him.

'I'll take you to George now and he'll tell you for himself,' he informed them.

A senior researcher approached them and sat on a chair at their table before they had moved. Bobby remembered that his name was Earl. He acknowledged the three of them in turn with a nod. 'Bobby, Banjo, Ramus.'

'Hello, Earl. How have you been?'

'Busy,' Earl replied. He hesitated and then added. 'We're doing follow up research on the *Merkel Cell carcinoma* or MCC, also known as a *neuroendocrine* cancer. It attacks skin and hair cells.'

'We just left a *spitz nevus* on the back. It caused a bit of a scare,' Bobby informed him.

'Yes, we heard about that, and we we're very glad that, that was all it was,' Earl replied. He next looked about the room conspiratorially. He seemed unconcerned that Ramus was present. He spoke softly. 'We've double checked your research on the fat stem cells,' he informed them.

'Oh,' Bobby was unsure how to respond.

'It's official. Your discovery works. We've documented it as a practical solution to alopecia and premature follicle colour loss.'

'That's good!' Bobby was pleased and then hesitated. 'If this is meant to be good news, then why are we speaking with hushed voices?' Bobby whispered.

'A decision about actually using it hasn't been reached yet,' Earl explained. 'We have all the data, but there seems to be some contention.'

'About its effectiveness?' Bobby was defensive.

'No, no. It works. The data and all the field tests prove that.' Earl leaned back. 'The issue is whether or not to implement it,' he said, looking relieved to get it out into the open. He looked about the room.

'Why wouldn't they?' Bobby was confused.

'I don't know. It's a no brainer to me,' Earl responded.

Bobby started to smile but stopped when he realised that Earl was unaware of his own pun.

'So, are they going to use Bobby's discovery?' Banjo spoke for the first time since Earl sat down. 'What's going to happen now?'

'There's going to be a debate by the Mind Managers about it,' Ramus answered for Earl.

'Your discovery is important, and it works, but the marketing department has been preparing for a future "distinguished gentleman" image. They are campaigning against implementing your new proven techniques.'

'But they gave you an award for that!' Banjo was getting agitated, defending his boss's honour.

'How does this debate work?' Bobby asked Ramus.

'Volunteers from the managers in the mind are invited to participate. Only six are selected by a random draw. A secondary draw determines if they'll oppose, or if they'll support the proposal. Each side has a turn to present its case. At the conclusion there is a vote, and the decision is announced.'

'So, there are three debaters per side,' Bobby nodded in understanding.

'What if a debater ends up on the side they initially opposed?' Banjo asked.

'Experience suggests that actually improves the quality of the debate. Delegates have to work harder to win when they are ideologically opposed to the position they'd normally represent.' Ramus obviously enjoys the process and was happy to share with them what he knew. 'Winning the debate becomes more important to them than their personal viewpoint,' he added.

'Experience also shows that this process is less likely to produce a favourable decision,' Earl lamented.

'The mind can't make up its mind?' Banjo intended it to be funny.

'I have to go,' Earl said as he rose from the chair. 'I hope you have a pleasant time here at *Integumentary* Headquarters,' he added loudly for anyone to hear.

Bobby looked about them and noted that no-one was even slightly interested in them. He smiled to himself as he shook Earl's hand before he left them.

'We'd really better get going,' Ramus suggested. 'George doesn't like to be kept waiting.'

They stood and followed Ramus out of the room and walked past Erastus, who didn't look up. They came to a panel in the wall. Ramus indicated they should wait and as they did, he stepped into George's office. A moment later he returned and motioned them both to proceed into the room. As they entered, Ramus bowed slightly and left them with George. They then realised that Dan was in the room waiting for them also.

They approached each other and the four greeted each other warmly.

'Please gentlemen, sit down, relax,' George said inviting them to a lounging area with comfortable chairs that Bobby believed were new since his last visit. The chairs surrounded a rectangular table that held refreshments.

Bobby sat opposite George at the long ends of the table.

'Please help yourself to food or a beverage,' George invited.

Dan spoke. 'I've been following your exploits with some fascination,' he told Bobby and Banjo.

'Yes,' George affirmed. 'Quite the travellers aren't they?' he asked rhetorically.

Bobby and Banjo smiled, but said nothing. Bobby was beginning to think that this was an ambush and Banjo was worried that they may be in trouble.

'Firstly, let me bring you up to date,' George said cordially. He indicated Dan who was seated to his left. 'Dan is now the acting General Manager for Follicle Production. His promotion will be made permanent as soon as Percival is able to meet with him, and sign off on Dan's appointment.'

'Congratulations,' Bobby and Banjo murmured.

'Thank you,' Dan beamed happily.

'Dan has been invaluable to me since Harry's passing.'

'A great loss,' Bobby agreed.

'He was my friend,' George lamented. 'But we have a massive organisation and every department deserves quality leadership. I believe Dan is the man for the job. After Dan meets with Percival, he'll be embarking on a whole of body follicle tour.'

Bobby hoped it wasn't being presumptuous in assuming that Percival would endorse Dan's rapid advancement from Area Manager to General Manager. But then, like himself, Dan was at the right place at the right time and in the right circumstances. It also helped that George liked him, and he made that fact very apparent.

'Ask for Skip. He's the Captain of the Zodiac, Taurus. He's very experienced and will look after you,' Bobby suggested amiably.

Dan nodded his thanks.

George began to outline why they had been summoned. 'I'd like to talk with you about your experiences since you completed your training and commenced your tour.'

'We have been sending in reports...,' Bobby started to explain.

'And they have been quite detailed, that's not the issue,' George interrupted.

'Are there issues with our work?' Bobby was concerned.

'Some of the choices you have made are questionable, yes,' George confirmed.

Banjo and Dan were following the exchange with swift turns of their heads.

'I see,' Bobby was miffed.

'Let's review where you have been, and I'll ask you to fill in some of the gaps that I have in my understanding of the reports that you sent me,' George suggested, intending to keep it cordial and friendly. His tone however, indicated that he was in charge, and that this was a command.

'Is this an official review?' Bobby was suddenly very tense. 'Should I have a Union representative with me?'

'You forget Banjo.'

'Banjo was following my orders. I'm the one responsible for what Banjo did or does.'

George took a deep breath. This was escalating quickly, and he didn't intend for the meeting to be this formal.

George leaned forward as he spoke. 'I am the *Integumentary* System Manager, and you are the Follicle Quality Assurance Regional Manager,' he said stating facts. 'This is a meeting between senior managers of a very large system. I'm not intending to brawl with you Bobby. I'm simply reviewing where you have been. I also want to discuss how well you have performed as a QA Manager.' He paused. 'We should be able to do that without Union involvement.'

Bobby wasn't yet convinced, but thought he'd try and co-operate despite sensing hostility. He looked at Dan to gauge his former bosses' attitude to what was happening, but he only received a neutral stare.

Bobby turned to Banjo for support. He replied with his customary capitulatory shrug.

Bobby took a deep breath and turned back to George. 'We started in the left arm pit.'

'Why?' George asked.

'I decided to go there because one of my former team workers had been transferred to me from the arm pit and I was curious about the comments he had made about his professional experiences in the pit,' he paused. 'Harry agreed to that suggestion.'

'Your report indicated a dependency on the...,' George picked up an e-pad and read from it. 'Sweetness,' he looked at Bobby.

Bobby delivered a monotone report. 'It's a chemical that the brain requests for the *epidermis* within the pit. It masks the urine odour from the *bacteria* that live on the *dermis*. The chemical is known as a deodorant. Earlier versions that were used contained the mineral called "aluminium" and that effectively blocks sweat pores. It's the sweat that encourages bacteria numbers to multiply rapidly, so by blocking the sweat pores they discourage bacterial growth.'

'Yes. I'm aware of the problems that that caused, and we have already switched to a non-aluminium deodorant,' George countered.

'The damage to the Follicle Farmers working in the pits is already done. They are producing lengthy follicles, but the Pit Managers are not as responsive to new techniques as we'd like them to be,' Bobby concluded.

'This dependency they have on the sweetness. Is it a concern?' Dan asked.

Banjo took the opportunity to contribute. 'I think it's a sad, but yet in some ways funny, but mostly a harmless pleasure,' he looked at Bobby.

'They are doing the job, but we won't get much more out of them,' Bobby concluded.

'Should we implement staff rotations? Relocate the staff and integrate them into other teams. Start with fresh Follicle Farmers working the pits.' Dan was sounding efficient.

Bobby hesitated.

'Bobby?' George invited him to respond.

'Most Follicle Farmers would consider a transfer to the pits to be a backward career move. The pits are only secondary to working on anal follicles, as the least desirable workplaces, within the Follicle Farmers work environments.'

'They are successfully growing hair,' Banjo reiterated.

'They're happy,' Bobby was sounding a little exasperated. 'Leave them alone to grow hair and enjoy the sweetness.'

'They wouldn't cope well with being broken up as a team,' Banjo agreed.

George nodded and addressed Dan. 'From what we understand, the situation in the right pit is the same.'

Dan nodded in understanding.

'From there, you went to the *abdomen*,' George was reading off his e-pad.

'There was an infection...,' Bobby started to explain but George held up his hand.

'We all know the details of the battle of the bulge,' George told him.

'I heard that they were calling it that,' Bobby confirmed.

'Congratulations on your awards, by the way,' Dan said to both Bobby and Banjo encouragingly.

'The consequences of the campaign were far reaching. It also resulted in the death of my close friend, Harry.' George said sadly.

'We were sorry about Harry,' Bobby agreed. 'We never imagined his injuries were fatal when we sent him to you by the Taurus.'

'He...,' It was apparent that George was going to add details but seemed to not know how to.

Banjo was about to speak, but Bobby's warning glare told him not to.

George took a deep breath and summarised. 'You did a fine job with the reconstruction of the *dermis* and *epidermis* after the infection was destroyed. We were grateful that the two of you were on hand in a senior capacity, and that you skillfully took charge of the reconstruction efforts.' He then added. 'The area is healing nicely. Well done.'

'Thank you, sir,' Bobby responded.

'But...you didn't submit a report on follicle growing activities,' George challenged.

'Sir?' Bobby questioned.

'You didn't submit a report on follicle growing activities on the *abdomen*,' George repeated.

'We worked extensively with the Senior Follicle Farmer on the recommencement of Follicle Farming teams for the entire region.' Bobby was confused. 'It was in our report!' he was becoming agitated.

'The rebuilding is well documented,' George agreed. 'But your assessment on follicle growing practices is vague and non-specific.'

'Sir! Under the circumstances I felt it best to do the QA review only after they had a chance to recover from the infection.' Bobby was disappointed by George's assertion that he and Banjo had failed because they hadn't completed a QA assessment whilst at the *abdomen*. 'They had suffered great losses and needed time to rebuild and heal as a team. We respectfully decided to wait before we fine-tuned the quality control aspects of their work duties.' Bobby was incredulous.

George looked at Dan and Dan nodded in acceptance of the explanation.

George continued with the review. 'After your rest and recreation at the *Liver*, you set out to recommence your tour of the body.'

'Yes,' Bobby agreed.

'You went to the groin, but you couldn't do a proper inspection because all the follicles had been removed.' George looked up from his notes and directly at Bobby.

'That's correct,' Bobby agreed.

'You wanted to learn why they had been removed,' George said.

'Yes,' Bobby agreed.

'The manager...,' George referred to his notes. 'John.' He returned to look at Bobby. 'Was upset and you felt the need to assist him in understanding what had happened to the hair in the groin region.'

'It was quite a shock to him and his team.'

'It was a surprise to me also.'

'John wanted to know if it was going to become a permanent condition or if it was a once only occurrence. Should he expect to lose follicles as part of an ongoing image change?'

'And you were curious as to who gave the order.'

'Yes, I was,' Bobby agreed.

'You spent a lot of time in the penis,' George observed looking at his notes.

'I was offered a tour, which I accepted because I thought I'd have the opportunity to find out if the *Reproductive* System was behind the follicles extraction order,' Bobby defended.

'A tour of the workings of the *penis* isn't part of your job description,' George explained.

Bobby said nothing.

George took a deep breath. 'After growth on pubic hair recommenced, you departed for the leg and the toes,' George stated, as if for the record.

'Yes,' Bobby agreed.

'You did some routine inspections on leg hair, and then you spent a lot of time at the toes.' George was reading from his report. 'In fact, you spent more time on the five toes than you did on the whole of the left leg,' he said looking at Bobby questioningly. 'And you achieved nothing in the way of improvements.'

'Yes sir,' Bobby agreed, unwilling to add reasons to why they had spent extra time there. He didn't want to reveal their conversation with the nail's manager.

'It wasn't a productive use of your time,' George accused.

'No sir,' Bobby felt it best to agree.

'You next went to inspect *anal* hair,' George didn't have to refer to his notes for that question.

'Yes sir,' Bobby agreed.

'The report you submitted on the follicle farming there is very detailed, and they are obviously performing exemplary work, despite the circumstances in which they are working.' George studied Bobby. 'At least, that's what it says in your report.'

Bobby nodded in agreement. 'Yes sir,' Bobby confirmed. 'They're doing a thorough job of growing hair.'

'A well written report I agree, but I wish it was written for a follicle region of more significance, as opposed to one about growing hair around the anus,' George lamented.

'Sir?' Bobby wanted clarification.

'Such as arm hair or chest hair even beard hair.' He paused for effect. 'You haven't even been to the scalp.' George wailed. 'I'm sure you'd consider scalp hair a bigger priority than anal hair?' George was becoming very agitated.

Bobby was about to speak but decided to sit quietly and contemplate his response. He reflected on their reasoning for visiting the groin, the toes, and the anus. He then felt that the notes of the three written destinations were still in his pocket.

'I need to get something to eat,' he said despite there being ample refreshments on the small table that separated them. He stood and looked about the room.

'Let's adjourn for a moment,' George agreed. 'Why don't you boy's go to the staff room and help yourselves to a meal. Perhaps we can reconvene in fifteen cycles?' George asked it in such a way as if they had a choice, but Bobby knew they didn't.

All four stood up and briefly stared at each other. Next Bobby and Banjo left the room and headed for the staff room. There, they joined the queue to get a platter of food each. They found a relatively quiet place to sit and talk whilst they ate.

'Are we in trouble?' Banjo was confused and concerned.

'I'm not sure.' Bobby was equally confused and concerned.

'Why is this happening to us?' Banjo was upset.

'Originally we were supposed to be with Harry on his tour. After he became injured, he was taken to George for medical treatment,' Bobby recounted their experiences after Harry was wounded.

'That's right,' Banjo agreed between mouthfuls. Stress wasn't going to impinge his appetite.

'Next, George met us at the *Abdomen* and thanked us for our work. He next sent us to the *Liver* so we could have a rest and some fun as a reward.'

'And we got drunk,' Banjo winced remembering.

'When we woke up we had messages to go to the pubic hair, toe hair and anal hair,' Bobby recalled.

'The barmen remembered us getting them,' Banjo agreed. He had finished eating.

'Jay and Kay,' Bobby said remembering their names. Bobby pushed his half-eaten food aside.

'Do you still have those messages? Do they say who they came from?' Banjo asked.

Bobby dove into a deep pocket and retrieved the three bits of paper with the destinations on them. He spread them out on the table to examine.

'Pubic hair, toe hair and anal hair,' Bobby read them out loud unnecessarily.

'Routinely, an official notification has who it was from and who it was too, written on them. These just have hand written regions where follicle growth happens,' Banjo observed.

'But I checked with Jay and Kay.' Bobby was puzzled. 'They said they came from Head Office.'

'Weren't we looking at our awards at the time, remember? Maybe they thought we were referring to those?' Banjo speculated.

'Oh no,' Bobby wailed realising their predicament. 'So where did these come from?' He indicated the three slips of paper before them.

'We were drunk,' Banjo said blankly.

'Very drunk,' Bobby agreed. He was puzzled.

'Do you think someone played a joke on us?' speculated Banjo.

Bobby went pale. 'Now I think that maybe they did.'

'Who?' Banjo asked.

'Maybe it was all of them. Maybe we were part of it also. Maybe we were in on the joke but can't remember it because we were so very drunk,' Bobby speculated.

'That's a lot of maybes.'

'Oh dear,' Bobby lamented again.

'Do we tell George?' Banjo was worried.

'I don't think any good would come from doing that,' Bobby replied.

'Do we lie?'

'No!'

'So how do we explain why we chose those areas instead of the important ones like the one's he just spoke about?' Banjo wanted to know.

'Let's let him think it was poor judgement on our part and not say anything,' Bobby suggested.

'Bobby. I really like being your EA. But if you're determined to put us on a path of self-destruction, well boss..., I hate to say it, but you are on your own.'

'Banjo! Don't be like that.'

'Can you think of something better?'

'How about we say that we thought we should work up to the bigger, more important regions. We decided to...that we should hone our skills on less important areas, before committing our-selves to the more high-profile regions.'

'That could work,' Banjo smiled relived. He liked the strategy.

'We felt out of our depth..., without Harry being with us..., and thought that smaller challenges...'

'Hang on!' Banjo disagreed sternly. 'We were never out of our depth. Harry was slowing us down. We did better without him.'

'True. But we'd better not say that to George or Dan,' Bobby capitulated.

'Just stick to what you just said about honing our skills on less important stuff before tackling the major growing regions,' Banjo advised.

'Knowing that in the major regions we'd be under closer public scrutiny as we are representing all Follicle Farmers...'

'The entire..., err..., all of the *Integumentary* System,' Banjo suggested.

'We're representing all Follicle Farmers, the *epidermis* and *dermis* departments of George's system.'

'Also, the nails! Go on,' Banjo encouraged.

'We wanted to be sure we're able to perform our responsibilities professionally when we did so before Percival, and Georges' counterparts.'

'Impressive,' Banjo told him. 'Leave out the Percival bit.'

'Do you think he'll accept that?' Bobby asked hopefully.

'Gentlemen!' Ramus interrupted their flow of their strategising.

'Oh,' Bobby responded looking up at Georges' EA. 'Are we late?'

'George is waiting for you and he's a very busy man,' Ramus admonished them.

Hastily they left the staff room and followed Ramus to George's office.

After they were seated, George started with the obvious question. 'Did you get enough to eat?' He asked feigning concern.

'Yes, thank you,' Bobby replied, answering for both of them. He patted his stomach appreciatively.

'And I presume you have been working on improving your story?' He stated it as an invitation for them to start explaining recent discussions.

Bobby and Banjo alternatively stared at each other, George, and Dan, unsure as to how they should proceed.

Erastus quietly entered the room and made his way to the table. He leaned toward George and gave him a message.

George silently read the message and then passed it on to Dan.

Dan smiled broadly at Bobby and Banjo. He drew in a deep breath and leaned forward. 'Apparently, Percival is very impressed with you both and is ordering you to return to work at once.' He stared at the wall behind them and chuckled. 'Apparently an eye lash has dislodged and it is now annoying the right eye.' He paused. 'Percival has ordered that the two of you to go there as a matter of urgency and deal with it.'

21

Bobby looked at Banjo.

Banjo looked at Bobby.

Bobby and Banjo both looked at George.

George smiled and looked at Dan.

Dan smiled at George and then looked at Bobby and Banjo, and he smiled at them.

Bobby and Banjo returned his smile, with a smile.

Bobby and Banjo stood up.

George and Dan stood up.

'I'll arrange for someone to escort you both to the eye,' George offered.

'Thank you.' Bobby was appreciative as he had no idea how they would get there.

'There will be a Mind Managers debate about your discovery, and I would like both of you to be present,' he added, as if it were an invitation. 'Until then, I'd like you to focus your attention on work within the head region,' George requested graciously.

'Should we prepare for the debate?' Bobby offered.

'No. Earl has made available the final reports and all the data he collated during the trials. Any potential delegates have access to all the relevant information.'

'I don't understand why they don't just apply the knowledge.' Bobby was confused. 'It works.'

'The mind doesn't think that way Bobby. It isn't logical in the way the rest of the body is.' George tried explaining as best he could, but in his experience, it wasn't easy to teach someone how to understand the complexities of mind rationalising.

'I think I understand,' Bobby explained. 'Jeremiah said that the mind was about weighing up the benefits of the variable options and then calculating the possible consequences of decisions that may, or may not, be made.' Bobby paused but then added, 'he said it was a lengthy process and it can often appear that the mind is procrastinating..,' he paused again. 'And that they are also very easily distracted,' he laughed.

'Well put.' George was clearly impressed. 'The mind has much to consider.'

'Where should we go after we're finished with the eye?' Bobby wanted to be sure he understood their orders correctly.

'There are numerous hairs in the nose and the ears. I want you to gain a solid working knowledge of them and spend time learning about the very important roles these follicles perform.' George sounded very intense.

'The scalp?' Dan reminded George.

'Ah yes, the scalp. Thank you for reminding me, Dan. The Regional Manager for the scalp will be retiring soon. We need to decide on his replacement.'

'How can we help?' Bobby asked enthusiastically. He deliberately demonstrated that he was keen to assist.

'Meet all the Area Managers and do the full QA report on them. Asses their strengths and weaknesses and then make a recommendation to me as to which one will be best suited for promotion.'

'I understand.' Bobby looked at Banjo who shrugged in reply.

'This isn't about who you like either,' George added. 'It's about who impresses you as a future Regional Manager.'

'Remember, in management, it's not about performing actual tasks. It's about leading others to perform those tasks efficiently and professionally for you.'

Bobby wondered why Dan wasn't making this decision as he was the acting General Manager. He would discuss these thoughts with Banjo when they next got the opportunity.

'I understand,' Bobby nodded and then asked. 'Do we go to the scalp before the nose and the ears?'

'The eyes, nose and one ear shouldn't take you too long. Complete them, and then go to the scalp. Work there until you're summonsed to observe the debate.' He paused and drew in a deep breath before continuing. 'We'll meet again after the debate to discuss the outcome, and then review all your QA work, and your management recommendations for the scalp.'

Dan nodded his support.

Bobby nodded in understanding.

Ramus entered the room and waited by the door. He looked at George for instructions.

'Ramus, please escort Bobby and Banjo to the eye,' he requested.

'Which eye?' Ramus queried.

George burst into laughter. 'The one with the eye lash problem, of course.'

Bobby and Banjo each waved a modest goodbye as they left the room. As the door closed behind them, Banjo was about to speak. Bobby held up a cautionary hand stopping him, and he pointed to Ramus's back. The ISMEA was leading them down a passageway to the departure point.

Banjo nodded in understanding.

They entered the blood stream tethered to avoid separation. Ramus guided them expertly to an exit point behind the eye. There was a workstation with two operators who were busy with keyboards. Ramus approached them confidently with Bobby and Banjo following.

Above the workstation Bobby and Banjo read the large sign.

WELCOME TO THE OPTICAL INPUT SENSORY RECEIVER.

THIS AREA IS RESTRICTED. AUTHORISED ACCESS ONLY.

There were smaller signs describing visitor registrations, visitor clothing requirements and visitor behaviour and protocols.

Ramus found that he had to speak before the operators would acknowledge them. 'My name is Ramus. My manager, George, manager of the *Integumentary* System, has sent these specialists to assist you.'

One of the two looked up and he spoke without greeting.

'Do you have an appointment?' He asked.

Bobby stepped forward as did Banjo following in his boss's lead. 'I'm the QA Manager for Follicles. Percival sent us to investigate the dislodged eyelash that is causing a problem.

'Which ones?' The operator asked.

'Sorry?' Bobby was confused. He thought there was only one.

'Which follicles are you the QA Manager for?' The operator clarified his question.

Ramus knew from experience that this was going to be a lengthy process, so he interrupted the exchange and spoke to Bobby. 'I'll leave you gentlemen here with these two. Good luck with your assignments.' He waved goodbye and re-entered the plasma flow.

Bobby returned to the operator.

'Which follicles are you the QA Manager for?' The operator repeated the question.

'Err, all of them.' He smiled. 'Banjo is my EA. Banjo, and I are here to assist with an eyelash problem,' he smiled. 'Percival sent us.'

'The Operations Manager?'

'Yes.'

'From the *medulla oblongata?*'

'Yes.'

'I've never met him.'

'Oh.'

The operator turned to his colleague.

'The right eye,' the colleague informed him without looking up.

'The surface of the right eye currently has an detached eyelash on it,' the first operator repeated to Bobby and Banjo.

'How do we get to it?' Bobby asked.

The operator looked irritated. 'You can't get to a dislodged eyelash,' he sighed. 'You can only get to eyelashes that are firmly in place.'

'Perhaps you could lead us to them?' Bobby asked. He looked at Banjo for support.

'Or point us in the right direction,' Banjo suggested.

'No unescorted visitors allowed.' The operator bluntly denied the request.

'So how do we...,'

The second operator stood up and looked at them. 'I can ask the on-duty QA Manager, or the PR Manager, to assist you. Which would you prefer?'

Bobby looked at Banjo. This was promising. He returned is attention to the operator and smiled. 'The QA Manager would seem to be the most appropriate.'

Banjo murmured his agreement.

The first operator typed something into his computer terminal and spoke without looking up. 'He's not available. He is currently recalibrating a lens and can't be disturbed,' he informed them without adding an apology.

'I'll see if the PR Manager is available to see you,' the second operator suggested. He typed a message into his computer and after a short pause the computer responded with a musical ping. 'He's on his way, please take a seat,' the second operator informed Bobby and Banjo.

'Where do we...err?' Bobby started to ask.

The operator pointed to two chairs that weren't previously there.

'Thank you,' Bobby had directed his gratitude to the top of the operator's head. He looked at Banjo who shrugged.

Presently a previously unseen door opened and a tall man, dressed in blue coveralls sporting a cheerful disposition walked through it entering the reception area.

'Hello, I'm Travis. May I ask your names?' he effused. He offered a welcoming handshake to both Bobby and Banjo.

'I'm Bobby and this is my EA Banjo,' Bobby replied returning the handshake.

'My word, it seems everyone has an EA these cycles. I'm going to have to get one for myself.' He then laughed and slapped Bobby on the shoulder conspiratorially. 'He must save you a lot of the drudgery?' He smiled broadly.

'Err... we're more of a team than a traditional boss and assistant,' Bobby explained and Banjo smiled happily. 'In fact...,' Bobby continued looking at Banjo. 'We really should update your title from Executive Assistant to Quality Assurance Assistant Manager.' Bobby smiled at Banjo.'

'I like it. I like it a lot.' Banjo looked like he did. He hadn't realised his boss felt that way, but was very pleased that he did.

Travis stepped back and looked at his two visitors serenely. 'Do Follicle Farmers have a team motto?' Travis enquired in semi hushed tones.

'As a matter of fact, we do.' Bobby replied. 'But it isn't a good one and I'd like to think I can influence a revision of it one day.'

'May I ask what it presently is?' Travis asked hopefully.

'If we don't grow, we don't grow.' Bobby and Banjo chorused in reply without enthusiasm.

'Fabulous!' Travis responded. His broad smile masked his desire to laugh. 'I completely understand why you'd want to improve on that.'

Banjo looked at his boss quizzically. That was the second thing he'd learnt about his boss today.

'Here, the team motto is "There is no me, in eye," he paused for impact. 'We're all very positive here in the optical department and you'll hear that spoken a lot by team members during your tour of the eye. Everyone that works here, is proud of how we're providing clear and accurate visual information to the brain.'

Bobby thought Travis was overdoing it just a little. He then remembered that he was a Public Relations Manager, and they tended to do that.

'We're not actually here for the tour..., even though it has been recommended to us that we do..., we're here because one of our lashes has dislodged and is in the...,' he looked at Banjo questioningly.

'Right.'

'Right eye,' Bobby completed his explanation. He looked at Travis expectantly.

'Oh,' Travis paused considering, 'That lash has impacted the lens,' he said flatly. His earlier enthusiasm was now replaced with a normal voice. 'Fortunately, our QA Manager knows how to fix the lens but the lash has been very irritating for the eye.'

'We'd like to visit the Follicle Farmers responsible for the eyelashes and see if we can assist them with some training to reduce the instances of eyelash loss.'

'Yes, of course,' Travis agreed. 'I'll take you to them.' He nodded his head as if agreeing with himself.

Travis walked up to the two operators. 'I'll take responsibility for these guests,' he informed them. 'Log them in as maintenance contractors from the *Integumentary* System's Follicles QA Department. We're going to the lashes and if they have time, they'll do the tour and then perhaps they can even watch a live feed.' He turned and looked at the visitors as if to see that they were impressed.

Banjo wanted to ask who they fed as he was feeling quite peckish himself, but he said nothing.

Travis led them through a door marked "Visitors assembly area." He instructed them on what to do before they proceeded. 'You'll need to replace your coveralls with these blue ones,' he said offering them a choice of sizes to put on. 'We wear blue as it doesn't distort the vision signals from the eyes.' He started to undress, swapping his clean old blue suit for a new clean one. 'I have to refresh my clothing every time I re-enter the optical area,' Travis informed them as they too were swapping out their clothing.

'That must get annoying,' Bobby observed.

'It's just a part of the job,' Travis replied. He didn't seem annoyed.

When they had completed dressing, Travis placed the Follicle Farmers clothing into lockers and instructed Bobby and Banjo on how to palm print the door locks. He took them to a hygiene station and demonstrated the application of moist disinfectant hand towels. They followed his example and wiped down all surfaces that weren't covered by the blue clothing. They disposed of the soiled towels into an open receptacle.

'When did you last eat?' Travis asked.

'It's been forever,' Banjo replied. He was hungry and hoped that the dining room as part of the tour. He was wondering what optical workers got to eat.

'Good,' Travis replied, 'The *Optical* Department has a minimal food consumption protocol, prior to entry. We have to eat outside the *optical* area, and we do so only after our shift.' He smiled at them. 'If it has been some time since you last ate, then you won't need to perform an oral rinse.'

Banjo looked sadly at Bobby and Bobby returned the look with a knowing smile. His assistant was hungry again.

'Which eye do you want to visit first?' Travis asked.

'The right eye has the eyelash problem,' Bobby replied.

'Yes, of course.' Travis smiled and then frowned. 'Err... do we go to the upper or lower eyelashes?'

Bobby looked at Banjo and he acknowledged with a shrug. He turned to Travis. 'We don't know.'

'Typically, a lost lash on the eye is from the upper. Lower lashes tend to just fall away.'

'Upper it is,' Bobby agreed.

'We'll be journeying on the outer edge of the *levator palpebrae superior muscle*,' Travis informed them. 'I don't go that way very often. It can get a bit bumpy if the eye is active and rapidly changing its visual direction.' He smiled to reassure them that they'd be all right.

Banjo looked concerned.

'We've been experiencing some unusual privileges, my young friend.' Bobby then gave his assistant a rare, one armed, comforting hug.

Banjo smiled his appreciation. He took some deep breaths and nodded his head that he was ready.

They followed Travis along a lengthy path. There was little to see, and their journey was smoother and gentler than they had been led to believe. They presently arrived at the upper eye lid and found the manager's office of the TSURE Team Supervisor for the Upper Right Eyelashes.

'My name is Paul,' he said offering his hand as they arrived. 'I've been expecting both of you.'

'I'm Bobby and this is Banjo.' Bobby indicated toward his assistant who nodded.

'Yes,' Paul replied. 'We have heard of the two of you and your exploits.' He smiled at Travis. 'Hello Travis. It's been a while.' He gestured that the three of them sit and make themselves comfortable.

'We're here because of an eyelash that has found its way into the right eye,' Bobby started the process of explaining.

'Yeah,' Paul lamented. 'Nigel told us.'

'Nigel?'

'The QA Manager for the right eye.' Travis explained.

'Nigel gets upset with us when that happens.'

'Percival has a particular interest in it also.'

'Who's Percival?'

'The Operations Manager for the *Medulla Oblongata*.'

'Sound's important.'

'Very. All the System Managers report to him.'

'Super important,' Paul agreed. He looked sad and obviously felt responsible. 'We don't mean to lose them.' He looked downcast. 'We grow them and sometimes they get dislodged and occasionally one goes into the eye.'

'So, you've lost more lashes than what actually falls into the eye?' Banjo asked.

'Look, about one in ten lost lashes ends up on the eye. We lose eyelashes the same way as you lose any follicles. Our losses just seem to get more attention than yours.'

'You'd be surprised just how topical hair loss is,' Bobby told him.

'Because we lost one eyelash into the eye?' Paul was worried.

'No. Sorry. I meant for the whole of the body,' Bobby clarified. 'It's a long story. Let's focus on helping you.'

'Focus. That's a good one,' Travis said to no-one in particular.

'There are many reasons why eye lashes fall out,' Paul began to explain. 'Mostly, they just get old. You see, a newly grown lash pushes out an old one.' He demonstrated with a hand movement. 'Often they get dislodged by the fingers rubbing the eye or picking at the *rheum*.'

'*Rheum?*'

'It's the mucus that crusts in the corner of the eye during sleep,' Travis explained.

'They are supposed to use warm clean water to wash it out, but oh no, the fingers come diving in with long fingernails to gouge it out. That's when follicles can get pushed onto the eye.'

'By the fingers,' Bobby had stated it without it being a question.

Bobby and Banjo looked at each other acknowledging a deeper understanding.

'Yes,' Paul confirmed. 'The main function of the eyelashes is to reduce the volume of perspiration that drops from the brow into the eye. The lashes flick the sweat away from the eye reducing the sweat volume that could impair visual clarity. When the sweat volume exceeds the lashes protective capability the fingers come in to wipe away the sweat, creating yet another risk of pushing a lash onto the eyeball.'

'What about the Demons?' Travis asked Paul.

'Sure,' Paul agreed, 'they occasionally dislodge eyelash follicles, but it's the fingers that push them into the eyes.' Paul was determined to blame the fingers again.

'Demons?' Bobby queried.

'Yeah. We have them. They're harmless. They're our friends. They're okay.' Paul seemed impassive.

'You have friendly demons here, in your eyelashes?' Banjo was incredulous.

'Yes,' Paul replied hesitantly. 'We always have.' He was confused. 'Why do you ask? Don't you know about them?' Paul looked at Travis for support.

'Yes. Tell us about them Travis,' Bobby invited.

'The technical name for them is *demodex folliculrum*, or demons for short.' He drew in a deep breath and continued. 'They are *arthropod ectoparisites* that live with the Follicle Farmers here at the base of each eyelash. Sometimes they live in pairs,' he paused, 'it's truly a fascinating relationship.'

'Between the Demons, or between the Follicle Farmers and the Demons?' Bobby questioned.

'Err..., both.' Travis replied.

'We've never heard of them.' Banjo was amazed.

'Few people have,' Travis agreed. 'The *optical* sensors have a special protective status. Consider these Follicle Farmers that grow the eyelashes, technically they come under your management as they are part of the *Integumentary* System, but in reality, as they are a part of the eye they are under *optical* management.'

'Once an eyelash farmer, always an eyelash farmer,' Paul told them.

'Transfers to and from the eyelashes are problematic, so they just don't happen,' Travis agreed. 'So, eyelash news, working conditions and routine procedures remain as optical department functions.'

'Tell us more about these Demons?' Banjo asked.

'They are *arthropod ectoparisites*,' Travis repeated and added, 'they have a long cylindrical body with eight stubby legs nearer to their head.'

'What do they feed on? You said they were parasites,' Bobby queried.

'*Ectoparisites.*' Travis clarified. 'They feed on dead skin, bacteria and clean up excess oil from the *sebaceous glands.* They're actually beneficial to the optical area and are quite pleasant to associate with.'

'You like them, these *ectoparisites*?' Bobby was confused.

'We play cards with them. They're very good,' Paul explained.

'So, you socialise with them, and they work alongside your Team Leaders and workers?'

'Yes.'

'In both upper and lower eyelids?'

'Yes.'

'Both eyes?'

'Yes.'

'Do they breed?'

'Yes. Their babies are born about three quarters the size of the parent,' Paul happily explained. 'I've witnessed numerous births. It's really very fascinating,' He smiled.

'Do they poop?' How do you deal with their waste?' Banjo asked.

'No.' Paul shook his head and looked at Travis for confirmation.

Travis nodded. 'They don't poop at all. They eat, breed, sleep and play cards.'

'We should meet one of them while we are here,' Bobby concluded. 'Do they have a leader or manager...?'

'They seem to operate as a co-operative. They function well and are abiding to our unique optical rules of behaviour,' Travis explained.

Bobby looked at Banjo. 'Send a message to Fargo and ask him if he knows anything about these Demons,' he instructed his assistant. 'I'll go and meet one of them.'

Banjo looked at his e-pad. 'I don't have a signal.'

Bobby pulled out and looked at his own e-pad. 'Same.' He looked at Paul. 'Can we use your computer?'

Paul immediately vacated his chair and offered it to the visitors. Bobby indicated to Banjo to sit and log into this communication channel. Banjo logged on to send the message to Fargo as Bobby, Paul and Travis left the office to go meet one of the Demons.

Bobby met the Team Leader of the follicle adjacent to Paul's office. 'Hello, my name is Bobby. I'm the QA Manager for all follicles.'

'Are we doing something wrong?' The Team Leader looked worried. He stared at Paul hopeful of an explanation.

'Bobby and his colleague are here to investigate eyelashes falling into the eyes,' Paul explained to him.

'It's the fingers you should investigate,' the Team Leader suggested.

'Yes,' Bobby agreed. 'But first I'd like to meet one of the Demons please.'

The Team Leader appeared to kick the follicle. A protruding Demon tail moved startling Bobby. He hadn't noticed the Demon before as it slowly reversed out of its position by the base of the follicle, its head and eight stumpy legs eventually appearing.

'Why did you wake me?' It asked indignantly blinking rapidly.

'This big boss wants to meet you,' the Team Leader informed the green mite.

'Who are you?' It asked Bobby with a yawn.

'My name is Bobby and I'm a QA Manager for follicle production and we...,' Bobby started to explain.

'Did you want to play cards?' The Demon interrupted him.

'Err..., no.' Bobby shook his head.

Banjo came up to him and showed him he had a message that he'd written down. 'It's incomplete, Bobby, the signal from *Integumentary* System Office just dropped out.'

'It does that. Our internal signals work perfectly but the outside channels have an intermittent problem,' Paul agreed.

'There's a dampening field that protects the electrical impulses from the eyes all the way into the brain. It has a slight detrimental effect on external communications,' Travis added.

Bobby leaned over to Banjo and read the message from Fargo. 'Beware of the Demons. Don't trust them as they...,' the message ended.

Bobby looked at Banjo and they shared a blank stare.

'I think you should try again,' Bobby suggested.

Banjo looked at the green mite and recoiled slightly. 'I agree,' he said nodding his head.

Banjo returned to Paul's office and Bobby tried to resume his conversation with the demon. He was too late; its head was already buried below the base of the follicle.

The Team Leader explained. 'I told him you didn't play cards.'

'So, these Demons are no hindrance to follicle growth?' he asked, concerned.

'No.' The three optical men chorused. 'Well, not to us,' Paul added.

'And they don't impact negatively on eye function?'

'We're agreed that they provide us with a service in a janitorial sort of way. You see the blood supply is a bit limited given the thinness of the eye lid and they seem to enjoy keeping the place clean,' Travis explained. He was neither defensive nor assertive. He was a PR man doing his job.

Banjo returned sporting a generous smile. He showed Bobby the full message from Fargo. "Beware of the Demons. Don't trust them as they sometimes cheat at cards. Keep up the good work. Best wishes. Fargo."

Bobby sighed in relief. He decided not to share the message with the others.

'I think we've seen enough.' He looked at Banjo who nodded his agreement.

'Did you want to do a QA assessment while you're here?' Travis suggested trying to avoid a second visit from the follicle QA manager.

'No,' he replied flatly. 'We have seen and heard enough to do a comprehensive report.'

Banjo nodded his agreement.

'Would you like the tour?' Travis offered.

'Just the short version, if that is possible?' Bobby replied trying to sound grateful.

'Certainly,' Travis replied trying not to sound offended by their lack of interest or enthusiasm.

'We should meet with your QA Manager, if that is possible?' Bobby asked hopefully.

'Sure,' Travis agreed trying to sound as if it were possible.

'Paul. Thanks for your hospitality. It was a pleasure to meet you.' Bobby shook the manager's hand.

Banjo followed suit. 'Thanks for letting me use your office,' he said to Paul.

'You're very welcome,' he replied. He watched Travis lead Bobby and Banjo back the way they had come. 'I'm surprised they've never seen a Demon before. They're all over the body,' he muttered to himself.

Travis referred to his e-pad as he turned to face Bobby and Banjo.

'It seems that Nigel, our on-duty QA Manager, is actually close by. The lens is now re-aligned and so he can speak with you both, but only for a brief moment,' Travis informed them.

'Good,' Bobby replied.

Travis led them away from the *rectus muscle* into the *ciliary muscle* and through to the *ciliary process*. Nigel was cleaning some newly installed *scleral venous sinus's* that were used to anchor the lens. He stood up to greet them as they approached.

'I'm Nigel,' he told them without offering his hand. 'Sorry, I don't shake hands when I'm on duty. With the work I do the risks of contamination are too high.'

'Thank you for agreeing to see us,' Bobby was gracious.

'I didn't realise the Follicle Team had a QA manager,' Nigel said.

'We're a relatively new department and we're still finding our way, learning what there is to learn,' Bobby harboured a desire to explain the challenges they faced to someone who'd understand.

'I'd love to share my experiences and insights with you, but I'm very pressed for time here.' Nigel was doing his best at being polite and cordial.

'I understand,' Bobby agreed. 'We're sorry for the eyelash in the eye and the extra work that causes you.'

'Percival sent you.' It wasn't a question. 'Eyelashes irritating the eye are a personal lament of his,' Nigel told them.

Bobby said nothing. He looked at Banjo who shrugged.

'I've explained to him that it's not the follicle teams' fault. It's those damned fingers that need to be kept away from the eyes. It was one of them that pushed my lens out of alignment.' Nigel sounded frustrated.

'I have to do a report for my boss, George, as well as for Percival,' Bobby started to explain. 'I'll write that it is our conclusion that the fingers are mostly responsible for the dislodgement of eyelashes and their prevalence on the eyes.'

'Two QA reports will be better than one.' Nigel nodded his head. 'I sure hope it'll help.' He smiled.

'Do you really think so?' Bobby asked.

'No.' Nigel looked downcast. 'The Fingers Controller knows how we feel. He sends the fingers all over the body seemingly on impulse. Ooh, there's rheum in the eye, send a fingernail. Ooh, I have an itch, send a fingernail. He doesn't stop to think about what may have caused that itch to occur. The Fingers Operations Controller is the most reckless manager in the whole body.'

Bobby secretly agreed, but it was a dangerous assertion to make, so he said nothing.

'I don't know who he even reports to,' Nigel lamented.

Bobby hesitated as he wasn't sure if he had an answer to that question. 'Someone in the brain, I guess.'

'They move to quickly for a committee to be running them,' Nigel sniggered.

'Do you need our assistance to locate and remove the rogue eye lash?' Bobby offered unsure of how they'd be of any help.

'That is sweet of you,' Nigel smiled. 'It'll work itself out. We've dealt with them before. It's all good.'

'Did you want to see a live-feed before you leave us?' Travis offered, trying to get them out of the QA manager's way.

'There isn't much to see at the moment,' Nigel informed them.

'Are we sleeping?' Travis asked.

'I wouldn't have been able to work the lens adjustment if we were awake, Travis.'

Travis nodded his head but said nothing.

'We don't have long to spare so..., perhaps another time.' Bobby was gracious.

'No. You'll get busy with your new responsibilities, and you may never get another chance. We should go to the live-feed room and see what's happening. You'll be able to say you have had a look,' Nigel suggested.

'This way gents,' Travis invited.

Travis led Bobby and Banjo back to the main path that led them back to the visitor's reception area. Nigel followed them for a short while but then headed in another direction.

'The live-feed room is manned by only one operator during sleep time,' Travis explained. 'You can talk normally. Some visitors feel they have to whisper, but that's only true in the visitors' room in the ears.'

'*Optics* is a silent world,' Banjo said to no-one in particular.

They entered the room and Travis informed the operator who the visitors were. There was apparently no need for introductions.

'You're in luck,' the operator informed them with a welcoming smile. 'He's awake as Bladder Control has been sending a series of urgent signals and he's finally responding.'

The operator pointed to a bladder fluid level monitor on one of the adjacent walls to the main viewing screens.

Bobby and Banjo watched in fascinated silence as the images on the screen started to make sense. They saw shades of grey with blurs of faint light streaming into view.

'He doesn't use artificial light when purging at night-time,' the operator informed them.

'That's actually better on the eyes,' Travis added. 'Going from dark to bright light strains them a little and it takes a while for the *iris* to properly adjust to the sudden increase in light volume entering the eye.'

They saw a brief dull yellowy glow.

'That's called a door handle,' the operator told them.

The vision stabilised.

'When he's without light, he sits still to urinate,' the operator explained.

'Better directional control,' Travis added.

After a moment the light levels alternated from very dark to several shades lighter.

'He's finished and has left the toilet,' the operator informed them.

The faint light levels suddenly waved violently across their screens. There appeared to be rapid blinking. They settled after a moment and a foot came into the field of vision.

'I think he kicked something he wasn't expecting,' the operator informed them. He was sporting a big smile.

'I didn't feel a thing,' Travis added. He was also grinning.

Then there was a flash of dull light drawing closer to the eye and Bobby and Banjo instinctively ducked.

'He's having a drink of water. He has a glass next to where he sleeps, and that light is the reflection off the water,' the operator seemed quite happy to give them the commentary.

The image was now dark.

He'll be trying to get back to sleep now,' the operator told them. 'I'd be surprised if there is anything more to see before he awakes again. There is heaps to see during daytime activity.'

'We have to leave.' Bobby replied. 'Thanks for showing and sharing.'

'Um, you're welcome,' the operator waved a farewell.

Travis waved his thanks to the operator and escorted the visitors from the room.

They returned to the change room and swapped their clothes to the ones they were wearing when they arrived. Travis led them out of the secure area and into the visitors' centre.

'Thank you for your hospitality. Sorry we didn't do the full tour, maybe next time,' Bobby said to Travis.

'You actually saw more than most of our visitors do. Most of the time I just show them the scaled down models in our interactive display centre,' Travis smiled.

'We're honoured.' Bobby thanked him.

'And no one ever gets to meet the demons. I'd prefer you keep that knowledge to as few people as possible. Knowledge of demons residing near the eyes may freak some people out,' Travis looked concerned.

'I agree. They're not the cause of the problem, so we won't reveal their presence.'

'Safe journeys my new friends,' Travis said and he turned to the two operators to inform them that the two guests had officially left the vision centre.

Bobby's and Banjo's e-pads beeped excitedly. They both had switched them on and read the displayed messages.

'Mine is from George,' Bobby informed Banjo.

'Mine is from Earl,' Banjo replied. 'They have selected the six debaters,' They chorused.

Bobby and Banjo walked returning to the blood vessel that they had used to get there. 'Err..., how do we get to the nose?' Banjo asked his boss.

22

Bobby and Banjo found themselves fascinated with their e-pads. They were waiting patiently to obtain permission to visit the olfactory receptors, and they were occupied with a news article posted by the Follicle Farmer's network news.

Often, one read the news and then shared what they had learned with the other. On this occasion however, the news was worthy of simultaneous reading.

A FOLLICLE FARMERS' NETWORK NEWS REPORT – By Frederick

THE MIND HAS ANNOUNCED THAT SIX DEBATERS HAVE BEEN SELECTED FOR THE FORTHCOMING PUBLIC DEBATE ON THE PROPOSAL TO MAKE USE OF A NEW DISCOVERY IN FOLLICLE REJUVENATION AND COLOUR RECOVERY.

THEY INCLUDE

1. THE MANAGER FOR TRANSPORT.
2. THE MANAGER FOR ARTS AND COLLECTABLES.
3. THE MANAGER FOR REPLENISHMENT.
4. THE MANAGER FOR PLANTS AND GARDENS.
5. THE MANAGER FOR PAINTING AND DECORATING.
6. THE MANAGER FOR FILING AND GENERAL STORAGE.

The finalists were selected from a record number of seventeen managers that had volunteered to take part in this debate.

Interestingly, this reporter has learned that none of the managers from the Work Employee clique have offered to participate. This reporter finds this fact newsworthy, as in my opinion the personal, external appearance of the body would improve with the application of this discovery, and when at work, a youthful image would be a positive contributing factor to success. Representatives from the clique have refused to be interviewed on the topic.

The only dissenter to the announcement was the Manager for Marketing. He argued that as external appearances are a marketing function, he should have an automatic right to predetermine the outcome and that there shouldn't even be a debate. Jeremiah informed me that the objection was noted and had been discussed and now subsequently rejected by a committee of managers. They were unanimous that no-one manager ever had an automatic right to take part in any debate, regardless of the topic. All voting managers had an automatic right to join in the discussion and had the right to vote.

The six debaters will soon attend a detailed briefing on the science and application of the new discovery which will be presented by the research and development team of the office of the *Integumentary* System. Shortly after the presentation the debaters will learn if they are to speak for, or against, the proposal.

It was signed by Frederick.

-

'We should be at that presentation,' Banjo suggested He had completed his reading just before Bobby.

Bobby finished and lowered his own E-pad. He drew a deep breath but said nothing.

Banjo could tell that Bobby was disappointed. He pressed the matter forward. 'At least you should be there,' Banjo concluded. 'It's your discovery after all.'

'Maybe they think I'll be biased towards its benefits and exaggerate the success rates,' Bobby speculated. 'Perhaps the independent investigation and scientific assessment has greater credibility.' He laughed. 'It could be that they think we're too busy with our QA duties to make such a presentation.'

'Maybe...,' Banjo conceded unconvincingly.

'Speaking of QA duties, we should try again to get access to the *Olfactory* System,' Bobby suggested pointing at the closed door. They had arrive earlier after being guided to the nose by a passerby.

Banjo took the hint and stood up from the visitors' chair and knocked once more on the door marked "*Olfactory* System Reception."

'At least the vision reception centre was staffed,' Bobby lamented.

They heard footfalls. The door finally swung open and a short, very stocky, green clad olfactory system person looked at them. 'Sorry. No visitor's today as my manager is away.'

'Technically we're not visitors!' Banjo blurted before the person could close the door on them.

'Who are you?' he demanded.

'We're inspectors,' Bobby answered as he stood up and walked up to the man. 'My name is Bobby, and this is Banjo. We're Follicle QA Managers from the *Integumentary* system and we're here to inspect the *cilia* hairs.'

'Oh,' the person mumbled. He appeared uncertain how to continue. He looked at the floor while he pondered. He hesitantly reached a decision. 'You'd better come in.'

He stood aside showing that Bobby and Banjo should enter the visitor's reception area. They looked about the room and found it to be sparsely furnished, with only a diagram of the nose for decoration. It did have a functional table and several mismatched chairs that didn't look too comfortable. There were two doors in the wall opposite to the one they had used to enter the room. There were more unmarked doors set into each side wall.

'If you could wait here and please read these visitors regulations.' He handed them each a set of spiral bound visitor's regulations. 'I'll go and see if I can get approval from the boss to show you around.' He headed for one of the doors.

'What is your name please?' Bobby asked before the man could leave the room.

'I'm Dwayne,' the man replied without expression. He went through the door on the left.

Bobby and Banjo sat down to read the visitor's regulations.

Welcome to the olfactory system.

For avoidance of obvious questions, we have prepared the following official visitors notes for you.

A. The nose holds nearly 100 million olfaction receptors. Do not touch them.

B. The receptors cover the inferior surface of the *cribriform plate* (bone) and it extends along the *superior nasal concha* and upper part of the *middle nasal concha*. See the diagram on the wall behind you.

C. The *epitelium* has three types of cells. *Receptors, supporters,* and *basal stems.*

D. The receptors have the *cilia* (hairs) that project from the *dendrite* and they detect the odours for conversion into electrical impulses for transmission via the holes in the *cribriform plate* (bone) and into the *limbic system* for interpretation.

E. Warning – Certain odours can trigger emotional responses such as disgust, appetite, or sexual excitement. **All** Visitors entering the operational area must at all times be always odour neutral. No exceptions!

F. We can presently detect approximately 10,000 different odours. Please refer to the *hypothalamus* department for a detailed list of emotional responses to detectable odours. Don't ask our staff for a list as our refusal may offend.

G. Damage to the *orbitofrontal* area may cause a disruption to the identification of different odours. Refer to the brain for more information as we just manage the receptors and the mucus.

H. It's the *olfactory* gland that produces mucus and any build up disrupts the odour receptors. Expulsion of the mucus can, and

often will, damage the *cilia*. We are at high risk of nasal infections and your participation in prevention management is
mandatory.

    I. Do **not** touch or consume the mucus.

    J. Blank stares are free, and our staff members are proficiently
willing to provide them.

All visitors must

    A. Wear the green clothing provided.

    B. Place all personal items, including recording equipment and
communication devices into the secure locker which we'll
provide.

    C. Be scrutinised for infectious agents and you will be sanitised
by our staff.

    D. Always follow the instructions of our staff.

    E. Leave the *olfactory* system when told to do so.

    F. Never offer advice or suggestions on how we can improve
things or perform our functions better.

    G. Never touch anything unless invited to do so.

    H. Never say "it doesn't make sense to me," or offer us any jokes,
puns, witticisms, related humour, comic references, banter,
wisecracks, satirical offerings, ridicules, jests, jibes, or sarcas-
tic commentary.

    I. Immediately leave the *Olfactory* system when told to do so.

Duncan - Manger of *Olfactory* Sensory Department. (Nose)

Bobby put his copy down on the table and looked up at Banjo who
now was looking intensely at the diagram on the wall.

'Interestingly that he twice wrote, "Leave the olfactory system
when told to do so,"' Bobby observed.

'Three times, if you count the following staff instructions at all
times,' Banjo agreed.

'I wonder if we'll get to meet Duncan,' Bobby mused.

'I'd rather not, given the way he writes.' Banjo pointed at the welcome guide. 'It should say visitors are tolerated instead of welcomed.'

The door opened and Dwayne re-entered the room and forced a smile.

'Duncan said you can visit the *cilia's* and ask the *Cilia* Follicle Farmers Area Manager any questions that you have about them,' Dwayne explained. 'All your other questions should be addressed to him when he returns.'

'When will that be?' Bobby asked.

'Soon.'

'Where do we get changed?' Banjo asked.

'In the next room there are green gowns for visitors and temporary lockers for your stuff. Help yourself to refreshments and snacks as there is no eating or drinking in the *olfactory* chamber,' he offered.

Bobby and Banjo walked into the staff room, disrobed, and stowed all their items into the secured lockers. Dwayne sprayed them with an odour neutralizing agent before they redressed into the gowns. They didn't touch the unappealing food.

'Do you have a dedicated QA Manager for the Olfactory System?' Bobby asked hopefully.

'Duncan does our QA for everything but the little hairs,' Dwayne replied.

'What about a PR manager?' Banjo asked looking at Bobby and shrugging.

'A pee-are manager...?' Dwayne was very confused.

'A Public Relations Manager,' Banjo explained trying to be helpful.

'All our relations are private, not public,' Dwayne replied in earnest. 'You should really be asking Duncan.'

When Dwayne was satisfied that they were ready, he led them through yet another door and then down a short passageway and into the *olfactory epithelium*. All around them were millions of tiny follicles that appeared to be waving at them.

'It's quite a sight, isn't it?' someone called to them.

Bobby and Banjo turned to see a fellow Follicle Farmer approach them. Dwayne did the introductions.

'This is Cornelius,' Dwayne explained. 'Cornelius is the Area Manager in charge of growing the *cilia follicles*.'

'How do you do, Cornelius?' Bobby asked, remembering not to offer his hand in greeting. 'I'm Bobby and this is Banjo. We're from the *Integumentary* System and we perform Follicle Quality Assurance inspections, training, and management.'

'Bobby, Banjo,' Cornelius acknowledged. 'Have you come to check up on me personally or on the hairs that we manage?'

'Actually,' Bobby countered. 'We're here to learn.'

Cornelius studied the two visitors for a long moment. 'I'll be okay, Dwayne.' Cornelius dismissed the *Olfactory* Assistant Manager.

Dwayne nodded his head in acknowledgement and turned and walked away without comment.

'Dwayne is technically second in charge, but the ability gap between manager and assistant manager is extremely wide,' Cornelius explained.

'For us the gap between manager and assistant is barely discernible,' Bobby explained his relationship with Banjo.

'I have plans to replace him one day,' Banjo joked.

'Make jokes about yourselves, but please don't make fun of this place,' Cornelius warned.

'Sorry,' Banjo drew back and apologised. 'We won't.'

'Oh, it doesn't bother me,' Cornelius explained. 'It's Duncan.' He paused. 'He's been sniffing out agitators for a long time now and he really doesn't like them.' He maintained a stolid expression.

Bobby thought that was a very funny thing to say but refrained from laughing due to the local policy. Cornelius could see the struggle on Bobby's face, and he winked at him. Bobby smiled. He looked at Banjo who responded with a shrug.

'You have more hair growing here, than we have on the entire surface of the body. How do you manage it?' Bobby wanted to know.

'I have a hundred Team Supervisors managing ten teams each. Each team manages approximately 100,000 olfactory follicles. It sounds like a lot, but these follicles are perfectly capable of looking after themselves. We lose many with each sneeze. A bad cold or influenza can almost decimate the receptors. They are not very strong, but fortunately they grow very fast.' Cornelius explained.

'How do you take temperature readings?' Banjo asked.

'We take a field average.'

'What about growth rate statistics?' Bobby asked

'Again, we take an average,' Cornelius answered, and then he added. 'The hair grows at a constant rate. We have a fully automated feeding system which works very well and requires very little maintenance.'

'How do you cope with smell overload?' Banjo was curious.

'The technical name for smells is 'odorants,' Cornelius corrected. 'We don't have that information here; you'd have to inquire to the managers within the *frontal lobe*.'

'Do you get much information from them?' Bobby asked. 'Is there any feedback on your performance?'

'We only get notification if our data stream seems inconsistent when compared to visual or auditory information,' Cornelius explained. 'This is away from my area of expertise, but from my understanding, the *olfactory* system works in conjunction with *optical*, *gustatory*, *auditory* and *tactile* gathering information, and can often anticipate the odorants that are expected from the information provided by the other senses.'

'Wow,' Banjo was impressed.

'We're part of the body's early warning system. If the *olfactory* measurements are different to the expected *olfactory* readings, it triggers an alert requiring investigation.'

'How do you...?'

'We sniff some more and see if we can contribute to an answer.'

'You have a big responsibility,' Bobby told him.

'According to Duncan we're somewhat undervalued.'

'Do you have a standard for operating the....,' Bobby indicated the area of hairs that stretched out before them.

'It's called the *epithelium*,' Cornelius told him. 'But we're Follicle Farmers and so we call it a field.' He smiled happily.

'What does Duncan call it?'

'He calls it the *epithelium*.'

'So, do you have a SOP for the field?'

'I can forward you the electronic version directly to your e-pad when we get back to the visitors centre,' Cornelius offered.

'Thank you,' Banjo replied for the two of them.

'What other functions does the nose perform besides detecting odours?' Bobby looked about them.

'Well, we are an important conduit for air into the *Lungs*.' Cornelius smiled.

Bobby slapped his head in mock self-flagellation. 'Of course, you are. Sorry,' he apologised.

'Don't apologise. Everyone thinks of the nose, and they think of smelling. Breathing is often taken for granted... until you can't.' Cornelius smiled.

'Can't breathe?' Banjo was concerned.

'A serious infection can make the *olfactory* glands produce more mucus than the nose is able to clear. It can get very stuffy up in here,' Cornelius explained putting on a sad face.

'Mostly, it's either one side or the other that gets blocked, and as we can breathe through either side, it's rarely too serious.'

'I'm just asking this out of curiosity,' Bobby explained. 'But how often do you get visited by a finger?'

Cornelius snorted. 'It seems like it's all the time,' Cornelius replied dryly. 'Duncan loves visits from a finger. They perform cleaning and unblocking functions.' He looked sad. 'I don't agree with it personally as most of the infections we suffer are as a direct result of digital presentations.'

Bobby and Banjo looked horrified.

'If only the Finger Manager could have the fingers sterilised before shoving them up here, we'd be so much better off.'

'Have you said anything to Duncan?' Bobby was querulous.

'Here's a touch of irony..., if you like that sort of thing...,' he explained 'You both had to be sanitised before you could visit here and I assume you were clean to begin with.' He laughed 'Duncan doesn't like visitors.' He shook his head in bewilderment. 'The fingers are nearly always dirty, but Duncan welcomes them!'

They stood silently watching the Follicle Farmer Teams work the field considering what had just been spoken about. Bobby's thoughts shifted to how much he liked Cornelius. He looked at him and smiled imperceptibly. He reflected that he was able to spend this time observing the process of smelling..., or was it called aromatising; he wasn't sure, all without having to maintain a conversation.

Finally, Cornelius spoke, interrupting his thoughts. 'I've heard about your restorative work on external follicles,' Cornelius said looking at Bobby.

'They're debating its future use soon,' Bobby replied nodding his head.

'I think it's very important that they make the right decision.' Cornelius looked serious.

'I'm inclined to think that from an external perspective, follicle colour and hair density is purely about vanity,' Bobby said dryly. 'I guess it'll come down to how youthful the mind thinks our external appearance should try to be.'

'I was wondering if it could apply to our follicles as well,' Cornelius explained. 'After we experience an extreme infection, the nose loses *olfactory* capability, and our effectiveness suffers.' He paused. 'I also believe that diminished *olfactory* capacity is going to be a part of the aging process. It's something that we should plan for,' Cornelius explained.

'Do you really think my discovery will assist *olfactory* recovery after an infection?'

Cornelius nodded his head confirming that he did.

'And that it may minimise diminished olfactory performance that may occur due to aging?'

'I do.'

'You'd better talk to mind management on that one. Banjo and I are relegated to being observers during the whole assessment and evaluation period. I think we were only just lucky enough to get invited to observe the debate.' He paused, thinking. 'If it gets approved, we should at least get involved in its application,' Bobby sighed.

'Bobby was told he just had to be happy with receiving an award and being promoted to Quality Assurance Manager,' Banjo added.

They returned to watching the Follicle Farmer teams work the field. No one spoke for some time.

'You know, I believe the hairs in the ears could benefit from your research also,' Cornelius spoke, breaking the silence.

'We have yet to visit the ears,' Bobby told him.

They stood watching the Follicle Farmer teams work the field some more. No one spoke.

'Cornelius!' a voice shouted over the silence.

They turned to see a giant of a man striding rapidly towards them. His hands were huge, and his arms pumped as he sped across the field toward them.

The Follicle Farmers ignored him as he brushed by them. As he got closer to them, he slowed to a comfortable walking pace.

'I'm Duncan,' The green cladded giant introduced himself.

'Bobby.' He nodded his hello. 'And this is Banjo, my assistant.'

'Dwayne told me where I could find you,' he explained to no one in particular.

'I've finished explaining to Bobby and Banjo about the follicles under our management,' Cornelius informed his boss.

'Have you two been sent to check up on us?' Duncan demanded defensively.

'No,' Bobby replied. 'We're here to learn.'

'Don't you know how to grow hairs?' Duncan teased.

Bobby sensed a trap and avoided it. 'We do, but nose follicles are a unique type of hair requiring a specialised approach, which...,' Bobby looked about them. 'You obviously perform very well.'

'Humph,' Duncan responded.

Undaunted, Bobby continued. 'As Quality Assurance Manager for Follicles for the whole body, it's our responsibility to understand all regional needs on how to grow follicles to their optimum efficiency.'

'Fancy words,' Duncan concluded.

Bobby felt baited but resisted. 'We enjoy doing our job,' he concluded dryly.

'Have you finished here?' Duncan eyes flashed and he seemed to be willing them to answer yes.

'Yes,' Bobby took the hint. 'Thank you, Cornelius, for providing us with an understanding of how things work here.'

'What does he mean by that?' Duncan demanded looking sternly at Cornelius.

'It means, he appreciates the professional way I have replied to his questions, and he now feels enriched by the experience.'

Duncan looked sour. Bobby thought his face betrayed a look of confusion. Finally, he responded. 'Good.'

'I'll take Bobby and Banjo back to the visitor centre and see them off,' Cornelius offered. He walked in the direction of the visitors centre.

'I can do that,' Duncan informed the Follicle Manager stopping him in his tracks. 'You have a field to manage,' he reminded Cornelius. 'It looks to me like they have wasted enough of your time.'

Cornelius gave him a cold stare. 'I did promise them a printout of temperature checks and growth statistics,' Cornelius added trying to sound pleasant.

'I can give them that,' Duncan countered angrily.

'It was a pleasure meeting you both,' Cornelius had turned to Bobby and Banjo. He was capitulating to his boss and abandoning the plan to escort them.

Duncan turned and marched away leading the group back to the visitors centre.

As Bobby and Banjo waved farewell to Cornelius and mumbled their thanks, Cornelius indicated that he'd send the promised information later on, by miming typing on a computer keyboard mid-air.

Bobby smiled and nodded his understanding and thanks.

As they walked Duncan asked his questions.

'Are you happy working as the QA Manager for Follicles?'

'Yes,' Bobby replied. 'It has been most satisfying. Hasn't it Banjo?'

'We get to visit a lot of places about the body that most others wouldn't get to see,' Banjo agreed.

'Where have you been?' He asked showing genuine interest.

'The *Heart, Lungs, Liver, Kidney...*'

'No hairs growing there, I hope,' Duncan observed.

'No, there isn't,' Bobby agreed, refraining from laughing. 'But they were on our way to where hair is growing.'

'And?'

'Oh..., we've been to the armpit, abdomen, legs, toes, groin, anus and the left shoulder blade,' Bobby replied listing their experiences.

'I have heard about you, you know?' Duncan stopped and stared directly into Bobby's face.

'I didn't know that,' Bobby replied with a half-smile.

'You're the finger hater,' Duncan declared accusingly.

'I don't hate the fingers!' Bobby was shocked by the accusation.

'Word is, you want to make trouble for the Finger Manager.'

'I do not. I just want...'

'No one cares what you want,' Duncan said cutting him off.

Bobby looked at Banjo. Banjo shrugged. Bobby got the message. Bobby said nothing.

'Typical,' Duncan murmured. He turned and resumed walking toward the visitors centre.

Bobby and Banjo followed cautiously.

'So where did your Follicle Farming career start from?' He asked casually as they slowed as they neared the visitors centre.

'I started in the beard on the left side of the face. I later met Banjo whilst we were working in the moustache,' Bobby answered relieved that the subject had changed.

'Hey! I remember now. I do know all about you!' Duncan roared. 'You're that *Rhino-virus* lover! You gave that *Rhino-virus* sanctuary. Do you realise just how much damage they can do in the nose!' he demanded without it really being a question.

Bobby was shocked and frightened. He kicked himself. He should have seen this coming. He'd forgotten about Rhino and his threat to the nose. It all seemed like such a long time ago.

'I was so angry when I'd heard that you'd saved that pest,' Duncan spoke loudly with restrained anger. 'Do you realise how infectious they are? They can wipe out our entire *olfactory receptors* with one attack.' Duncan was very hostile, and it was all directed at Bobby.

Banjo tried to defend his boss. 'Now just you wait a beat,' he started. 'You can't talk to Bobby like that.'

'Puss and snot on you, you... virus lover!' Duncan turned his aggression onto Banjo. He raised a fist.

They'd stepped into the visitor's centre and Duncan slammed the door behind them. Dwayne looked up from his platter of food in startled confusion.

'Let us sit down and discuss this calmly,' Bobby suggested, trying to sound calm and was indicating they should sit on the chairs.

'No!' He replied angrily. 'I want you both to get out.' Duncan opened a door and urged Bobby and Banjo through it.

Bobby quickly seized the opportunity to escape. He led Banjo through the door, but they realised too late that they had been led into a small, one way room. The door slammed and they heard the door being locked behind them.

The room contained janitorial items. They looked about them in panicked confusion. They looked at each other. They could see a worried shocked expressed in each other's faces, just before the light went off.

They heard themselves breathing heavily. It took a long time before one of them spoke. Bobby said in a comforting voice. 'I think we should sit down and catch our breath.'

'Yes.'

They heard another door slam.

In the darkness they felt for each other's hands, and they held on to each other as they slowly lowered themselves to the floor. The darkness was absolute. Bobby had hoped that as their eyes adjusted, they'd be able to make out something about the room.

They heard Duncan's voice boom through the locked door.

'Stay here and don't let those two out,' he yelled.

'But boss, we shouldn't lock visitors in the cupboard,' Dwayne countered.

'I can and I have!' he relied still yelling.

'What did they do? Should I call someone?'

'No!' Then more calmly he added. 'Look they are bad people. They harbour our enemies. Do you understand?'

'No!' Dwayne sounded scared and confused.

'We have to teach them a lesson. They have to realise how wrong they were and that they need to learn.'

'Learn what?' Dwayne yelled his question.

'Listen. It doesn't matter. Leave this to me. I'll deal with them.'

'What are you going to do to them?'

'It's best you don't know,' he replied and then added, 'but if you don't keep them locked securely, the same will happen to you,' Duncan warned him, and they heard a door slam again.

Silence ensued. 'It's very dark,' Banjo said calmly after a while.

'Yes,' Bobby agreed.

'Do you think we can reason with him?' Banjo sounded scared.

'No.'

'Oh.'

'What do we do?' Banjo was lost.

'It'll take a while before anyone realises that we're missing,' Bobby was thinking out aloud.

'I suppose.'

'Cornelius might realise our predicament and try to help us,' Bobby spoke encouragingly.

'Do you think so?'

'No.'

'Oh.'

'It's a pity we don't have our e-pads,' Bobby lamented. 'We could summon help.'

'I have mine,' Banjo informed him.

'You do?' Bobby was surprised. 'But I saw you put it into the locker.'

'I held it in the locker but pulled it back out again and I put it onto the chair when Dwayne was assisting you. I snuck it into my clothing when Dwayne headed for the door.'

'I'm very proud of you, Banjo,' Bobby told him. 'You deserve an award.'

'I'm hungry so I'll settle for a meal.'

'No jokes, remember,' Bobby chuckled as he chided his assistant.

'I'm not joking. I really am very hungry,' Banjo defended.

'Well, why don't you order some food to be delivered to us here while you arrange our rescue?' Bobby suggested.

'I will.' Banjo liked the idea. He pulled out the e-pad and checked they had a signal.

'We have a strong signal,' he said happily.

'That's good.'

'Who should we contact?'

'Either Lek or Fargo.'

'I think Lek,' Banjo suggested. 'Fargo may think it's a prank, whereas Lek is more likely to take this seriously.'

'I agree.'

Banjo typed onto the screen. The backlit screen seemed to brighten up the whole room. Bobby looked about him for a weapon should Duncan return with harmful intent. He found a bottle of cleaning spray and decided he'd attack the giant by spraying it into his face as he opened the door.

'This is what I wrote,' Banjo spoke when he'd finished composing an appeal for assistance. 'Lek. Bobby and I are being held captive in a janitorial cupboard in the visitor's centre in the nose. The Manager, Duncan has imprisoned us for Bobby's kind treatment toward Rhino when he was a Team Leader in the beard. He is angry. He is a big person, and we feel threatened and we urgently require rescuing. Can you please help us! Bobby and Banjo.' He looked at Bobby. 'What do you think?' he asked hopefully.

'Perfect,' Bobby assured him. 'Can you get a read and receive confirmation?'

'Sure.' Banjo clicked onto two check squares on the screen. 'I'd better send it now as it's using up a lot of its stored power.'

'Send it on its way,' Bobby agreed.

The e-pad was switched off and the room returned to complete darkness.

'We should rest,' Bobby suggested. 'Save our energy also.'

Banjo said nothing.

They slept despite their predicament. They slept for what seemed an eternity.

They woke to the sounds of crashing doors and of men yelling. They heard Dwayne defending his involvement and busily explaining it wasn't him and that he was ordered to do so.

The cupboard door swung open and Lek was standing there smiling at them.

'Hello boys. Your message said you needed rescuing?'

'Thank you. We're so very glad you're here,' Bobby said struggling to get up. They were cramped from sitting on a hard floor for all that time.

'I forgot to ask for food,' Banjo lamented.

'Don't worry.' Lek laughed at his perpetually hungry friend. 'I remembered to bring some of your favourite ration packs with me.'

They entered the staff room. Lek's troops held onto Dwayne and he didn't look happy.

'Where's Duncan?' Bobby asked. 'What will happen to them?'

'My men are bringing him in now,' Lek replied. 'They'll both be held pending an inquiry.' They heard chatter on the two way communicators that Lek and his men carried. Lek spoke into his microphone. 'Understood.'

Bobby and Banjo collected their possessions from the lockers and walked out into the main foyer outside of the *olfactory* reception area.

'Did you want to say anything to Duncan before we haul him away?' Lek offered.

'No,' Bobby replied.

'Dwayne.' Banjo looked at his boss and Bobby considered for a moment.

'Dwayne isn't really a part of this problem and he objected strongly to Duncan. Duncan is the one who acted inappropriately. We think you should let Dwayne go,' Bobby explained it as he believed it, to Lek.

'Besides, he'll be needed to run things here,' Banjo added.

'That sounds reasonable enough to me,' Lek agreed and he returned to his troops and ordered that Dwayne be released.

'What do we do now?' Banjo asked Bobby.

'We go to the ears, Banjo.' He gave him a comforting shoulder hug. 'But first we'll have a meal, a banquet at the biggest buffet we can find.'

Banjo smiled happily, he liked the sound of that.

~ 23 ~

A FOLLICLE FARMERS' NETWORK NEWS REPORT - By Frederick

THE MIND HAS ANNOUNCED THAT THE SIX DEBATERS' FOR
THE DEBATE ON THE FUTURE OF FOLLICLES HAVE NOW BEEN
DIVIDED INTO TWO TEAMS.

The participants that will argue in favour of implementing follicle colour recovery and follicle rejuvenation include:

1. Alphonso - The Manager for Painting and Decorating. Captain and first speaker.
2. Fabian - The Manager for Arts and Collectibles. Third speaker
3. Manny - The Manager for Replenishment. Fifth speaker

The participants that will argue against implementing follicle colour recovery and follicle rejuvenation include:

1. Sandy – The Manager for Plants and Gardens. Captain and second speaker.
2. Ford - The Manager for Transport. Fourth speaker
3. Leo - The Manager for Filing and Storage. Final speaker.

Jeremiah has confirmed he will be the host.

The six are being assisted by the Research and Development team of the office of the *Integumentary* System as they prepare for the debate.

Detailed profiles on the participants are available by clicking **here.**

Frederick

Bobby and Banjo were reading the news and researching participant profiles on their e-pads. They had had their fill of food and refreshments and were now seated comfortably in a rear corner of the
Head Office staff dining-room.

'I'm disappointed that Sandy is speaking for the "against" team.'
Bobby lamented.

'I was thinking that also,' Banjo agreed. 'A love of plants and
gardening would suggest that he's a man that that would support
growing abundant, vibrant, colour rich hair.'

'At least Alphonso and Fabian will have a flair for what looks
good. I think they'd have to be personally supporting the implementation argument. It's good that they are on our side,' Bobby
speculated.

'How do you feel about Manny?' Banjo queried.

'Good, I think.' He paused. 'Replenishment is a positive activity,'
he added. 'Our side needs positive thinking people.'

'I don't understand Ford or Leo's interest,' Banjo said sounding
confused.

'Maybe it's just that they enjoy the challenge of debating,' Bobby
speculated.

They sat in silent contemplation.

Banjo looked at Bobby in concern. 'How will you feel if the "For
implementation" team loses?'

Bobby took a deep breath and considered the question. 'I really
don't know,' he eventually answered. 'At first I thought my contribution was just about reducing the size of bald patches and having
less grey hairs...,' his voice trailed off. He sighed. 'Who'd have imagined it could come to all this?' He gestured toward Frederick's press
release.

Banjo said nothing.

The e-pads pinged as another news article was received. This one was from Richard, the journalist from the Marketing Department.

THE MARKETING DEPARTMENT PRESS RELEASE – By Richard

Roderick – The Manager for Marketing has announced that he'll be personally assisting the debating team speaking against implementation of the proposal for follicle colour recovery and follicle rejuvenation.

I quote, "This proposal goes against the natural progression of aging. Regardless of the outcome of the debate, I'll be supporting the "NO" vote and, I'll urge all voting Mind Managers to vote "NO" also,' Roderick had stated.

Roderick has scheduled meetings with several groups of Mind Managers to discuss his views on why the "NO" vote should succeed. If you wish to attend a "NO" vote briefing, please contact the department of the Marketing Manager to register your interest by clicking **here.**

Richard

'He's not particularly reserved about his views, is he?' Bobby murmured after reading the press release.

'Do you get the impression he's against your discovery?' Banjo smiled.

'Just a bit,' Bobby nodded, grinning.

'Do you think it may be personal?' Banjo queried.

'Oh,' he paused considering. 'I guess..., it certainly feels that way.'

They sat in silence for a while.

'Shall we go into the ear, my friend?' Bobby suggested.

'Absolutely. I believe that's a sound motion,' Banjo agreed. They switched off their e-pads and stood up and made their way out of the busy room. In the foyer they looked about them in shared confusion. They both realised their dilemma and spoke over each other.

'How do we...,?' Banjo started to ask.

'Which way do we...,' Bobby was about to say.

They laughed.

'I don't know.' Bobby laughed again. He examined the walls. 'They really should have signs.'

As they looked about for assistance, they saw a man watching them. He stepped toward them and casually approached.

'You look lost,' he guessed.

'Oh, we know where we are.' Bobby smiled, bemused at their situation. 'But we don't know how to get to where we're going.'

'Perhaps, I can assist?' The man offered. 'Where are you headed?'

'The ear.'

'There are two ears my friend. Each is in an opposite direction from here.' The man crossed his arms and pointed in opposite directions. 'Which ear are you planning to visit?'

'Um...we don't know.' Bobby felt foolish. 'We don't have an appointment and they are both the same, so I guess it really doesn't matter which one. Which ear is the closest?'

'From my understanding, the ears are regarded as off-limits to most people,' the man explained, sounding doubtful if he could help them.

'Oh, it's okay. I'm sure we're expected,' Banjo added. 'It's just that we weren't told to visit a specific ear or to do so at a specified time.'

'I'm intrigued. What work do you do?' The man inquired.

'We're QA Managers for Follicles from the *Integumentary* System,' Bobby explained. 'I'm Bobby and this is Banjo.'

'Yes..., I've heard of you both,' the man explained nodding his head. 'You're doing the tour of the body and your examining follicle growing in various regions.'

'That's us,' Bobby agreed. He was impressed.

'And now the mind is preparing to debate a discovery that you made...,' he pointed at Bobby. '...to determine its potential and suitability for use.'

'Yep. That's me,' Bobby confirmed nodding his head.

'Let me introduce myself,' the man suggested. 'I'm Horace, and I manage the communication signals from the ears into the brain.'

'That's extremely fortuitous for us.' Bobby accepted Horace's outstretched hand.

He shook Banjo's hand also.

They became aware that they were being watched by a growing gathering of curious onlookers.

'I suggest you visit the left ear,' Horace told them. 'I'm on my way there now and I'd be happy to escort you both.'

'Much appreciated,' Bobby thanked him.

They talked as they walked. 'Are you pleased to be the focus of so much attention?' Horace questioned.

'No. Not really,' Bobby confided. 'I discovered the relationship between fat stem cells and hair rejuvenation purely by accident. I applied it in order to resolve a difficult situation in the moustache. It then became the focus of an inquiry, so I had to explain it all to my System Manager. I never expected it to be taken seriously, or that it would become such a contentious issue.'

'Your discovery is only one part of the story. The fact that you successfully applied your discovery is what makes it worthy of notoriety,' Horace contended. 'The significant aspect in this case is that you applied your discovery where and when its result would come to the attention of decision makers.'

Banjo had been silent up to now, but he wanted to know something. 'Are there many discoveries like the one that Bobby made? I mean this sort of thing must be happening all the time, surely?'

'My young friend,' Horace smiled as he started to explain. 'You must understand that nearly all of the discoveries of this nature are made by Mind Managers. They mostly apply to topics external to the body.' He paused. 'This is a very significant discovery and it was made by, at the time, a very junior team member of a semi-redundant part of the *Integumentary* system.' He looked at Bobby. 'No offence intended,' he smiled indicating that Bobby should understand that.

'Oh, um, none taken,' Bobby assured him. He was fascinated by Horace.

'You see, Banjo. Human evolution is an extremely slow process. Yet Bobby has discovered a way for hair follicles to maintain their youth. We can anticipate that our human now has an extended life span, but we are also conditioned into accepting that there will be deterioration aspects to aging.'

'Oh,' Banjo murmured.

'Like alopecia and greying hair,' Bobby confirmed.

'That is only a very small part of it,' Horace agreed. 'As you know from discussing it with Cornelius, your discovery may also extend the effective life span of sensory follicles.'

'Cornelius thought so.' Bobby nodded his head. 'How well do you know, Cornelius?'

'Very well,' he confirmed.

'He was going to ask that it be included in the debate on the list of probable benefits. It's an argument for the "FOR" side.'

'We are preparing for that now. The problem is that sensory benefits are just speculation as we haven't had time to field test the discovery on sensory follicles. There just isn't any supporting data for it yet,' Horace lamented.

'Can't we delay the debate?' Banjo suggested.

'I doubt it. Roderick has made it clear that he'll block any delay and he has a lot of influence. He seems to be in a hurry to rush through the debate and to have it fail.'

'But...why?' Bobby was taken back. He couldn't understand. 'Wouldn't looking youthful be a good position for the body to be in? Wouldn't it make our human more appealing to other people?' He asked rhetorically.

'Maybe that's what concerns him.' Horace looked saddened.

Bobby and Banjo looked haplessly at each other. They didn't understand. This was politics and they weren't equipped to deal with these types of conflicts and hidden political agendas.

'The fact is that this benefit may apply to other types of cells also. Not just follicles,' Horace added. 'That is why this is such really big news.'

'I'm humbled,' Bobby said hiding the fact that he didn't really understand.

'No need to be,' Horace told him.

'How come you know so much?' Banjo asked.

'My friend, Nigel and I have been discussing the topic extensively,' Horace replied.

'Nigel. You mean the QA Manager for the eyes?' Bobby queried.

'That's the one,' Horace confirmed. 'He contacted me, and we discussed the benefits of your discovery in relation to all the senses. He's been talking to Cornelius also. He is bursting to send a sensory deputation to the debate teams and argue our case before the debate begins.'

'You were waiting for us outside of the staff canteen, weren't you?' Bobby questioned.

'I was,' Horace confirmed.

'And you do more than manage the communication signals from the ears to the brain, don't you?' Bobby added.

'I do manage the communication signals, as well as a few other things.'

'What other things?' Bobby pressed.

'When it comes to our senses, I manage almost all of them. I'm the Sensory Manager for *optical, auditory, olfactory* and *gastronomy.*' He smiled. 'The only ones I'm not responsible for are the *somatic* sensations. Those ones I leave to my very good friend, George.'

Bobby started to laugh at his own realisation of how small their world actually was. Banjo looked confused. Bobby saw his confusion and found that funny also and so he laughed even louder. Banjo realised what was funny and so he started to laugh with him. Then

Horace joined in and the three found themselves roaring with laughter.

After they settled, they recommenced their journey to the left ear. There were numerous passages to take, and the two QA Managers were grateful to have an experienced guide. Banjo held Bobby's arm to slow their pace and they gradually fell back away from Horace who was maintaining his quick pace. He asked in a whisper. 'What are *somatic* sensations?'

Bobby whispered his reply, respectful of his assistant's embarrassment of not knowing. 'In the *Integumentary* system the *epidermis* and *dermis* are also responsible for the transmission signals to the brain such as touch, texture, irritation, temperature and pain.'

'Oh,' he uttered in realisation. 'Of course.'

'But it doesn't include muscle or joint pain,' Bobby added as they hastened to catch up to Horace.

When they arrived at the reception centre for the ear, they found it very beneficial to be escorted by such esteemed company. A few words from Horace to the reception staff and they became immediately co-operative and welcoming. This was despite all the cautionary signs alerting visitors that their desire to visit the ear was likely to be refused.

Horace turned to Bobby and Banjo. 'We're in luck. Both Reggie and Arnold are close by.' He looked at them and smiled. 'Unless we co-ordinate our movements, we're often in different locations.'

'What are they responsible for?' Bobby queried.

'Reggie is our PR Manager for ears,' Horace explained. 'And Arnold is the Music Manager, or music maestro, as he prefers to refer to himself.' He looked about him. 'They'll be here shortly.'

'Music Manager?' Bobby queried. 'Is he a mind manager?'

'Not really. You see...,' Horace started to explain but cut himself short when he was interrupted by Reggie's arrival and a generous arm hug.

'Reggie. This is Bobby and Banjo. They're VIP's from the *Integumentary* System.'

Reggie extended his hand in greeting and appeared to be studying their guests.

'So you're the Follicle QA Managers that everyone is talking about?' Reggie surmised.

'They'll want the tour,' Horace explained. 'And I'd also like them to meet Arnold. I believe he's been asked to provide music during the debate.'

Bobby had never actually heard internal music. 'Will we be able to hear it also?' He queried.

'It's best that Arnold explain the answer to that question my friend. But simply put, without a decoder, you can't. The input is at a frequency that only the mind can translate and interpret,' Horace informed them.

'I'll tell you more about that during the tour,' Reggie promised.

'The only music I've ever heard was when we were at the anus,' Banjo offered innocently.

Horace and Reggie gave him a disgusted look. Bobby restrained laughter realising that Banjo was referring to the song and dance contests that the Follicle Farmers at the anus held. He said nothing.

Horace cleared his throat and announced. 'I'll leave you in Reggie's capable hands.' He waved a quick farewell and turned to leave.

'This way gentlemen,' Reggie invited gesturing to the visitor's reception room.

Horace stopped and turned and spoke loudly to the three of them. 'I've arrange some front row seats for us at the debate.'

The three turned and gave him a wave in appreciation of the offer.

'Horace seems very casual for a manager of such importance,' Bobby observed.

'Horace is a great guy. Everyone loves him. He's the sort of guy that inspires everyone to do their best for him, without him ever appearing to be trying to do so.'

'Bobby's like that,' Banjo gushed.

'Well thank you, Banjo,' Bobby blushed.

'It's true,' Banjo defended.

'Anyhow,' Reggie resumed the explanation. 'You're probably unaware, but you've solved a big problem for Horace.'

'We have?'

Reggie stopped walking and turned to smile at them. 'Duncan has been causing him grief for a long time.'

'Duncan. The *Olfactory* Manager?' Bobby clarified.

Reggie nodded his head in confirmation. 'He's now the former *Olfactory* Manager.'

'Oh,' Banjo replied.

Bobby was concerned. 'What happened to him? Was he ordered to apoptosis?'

'No. No!' Reggie took a deep breath and sighed. 'New rules, new ways.' He smiled. 'I hear he's now pushing a food trolley for Percival.'

Bobby and Banjo laughed and Reggie joined in.

They continued walking to the visitors reception centre for entry into the ear. The two duty reception managers were very friendly and assisted Bobby and Banjo to slip into clean red one piece clothing for entry into the ear itself. They washed their face and hands with a sanitiser and followed Reggie into a briefing room.

'I'll give you a quick overview and that'll help you understand what you are about to see.' Reggie led them to diagrams that hung from the briefing room walls. Bobby and Banjo also noticed the small scale replicas on display tables.

'You seem very well set up for visitors,' Bobby murmured.

'After the eyes, we're the second most popular destination for curious managers.' He smiled. 'And we're a bit easier to get into.'

Bobby and Banjo said nothing.

'These diagrams are soon being replaced with electronic display units,' Reggie explained apologetically. 'Our display department is busy putting the finishing touches on simulators that demonstrate the movement of sound waves through the ear.' He paused. 'Sorry, but they aren't ready yet.'

Bobby nodded his head in understanding and Banjo shrugged his shoulders.

'This diagram shows the basic anatomy of the ear.' He pointed up to the diagram. 'Sound enters here via the *auricle*. It funnels sound vibrations into the external *auditory canal*. They vibrate onto the *tympanic membrane*, commonly referred to as the ear drum.' He looked at his visitors.

Bobby and Banjo nodded indicating they were keeping up.

'Over here you can see that the drum is attached on the inside by ligaments to three small bones called the *malleus*, the *incus* and the *stapes*. They are sometimes called the *hammer, anvil* and *stirrup*, so please don't be too confused if you have heard them referred to by their other names.' He smiled knowingly. 'Ear drum vibration causes these bones to vibrate into the *perilymph*. By this time the *stapes* are vibrating about twenty times faster than the rate of the ear drum.' He pointed. 'The *peri*, as we call it, vibrates through the *cochlea* into a fluid filled tube called the *scala*.' He paused studying their faces. 'Have I lost you?'

'Sort of,' Bobby conceded. Banjo nodded his head.

'That's fine. We'll soon go into the actual ear, and you'll see it all in more detail for yourself,' Reggie explained to them.

'Thanks.'

'This is one of two areas that'll really interest you.' Reggie pointed to the diagram. 'I won't bore you with the nature of sound waves, but this is where the vibration hits the follicles in the spiral organ named the *corti*.'

'Follicles,' Banjo perked up.

'The *tectorial membrane* vibrates on these follicles, which converts those vibrations into electrical pulses and sends them via these fibres in the *cochlear* branch of the *vestibulocochlear* nerve which carries them to the *superior temporal gyrus* via the *thalamus*. Without these follicles our human wouldn't hear a thing.'

'Wow.' Bobby drew a deep breath. 'That's easy for you to say.' He smiled.

Reggie laughed. 'I really have lost you, haven't I?' Reggie smiled knowingly.

'Totally,' Bobby conceded. Banjo nodded.

'It must seem like I'm trying to impress you with my knowledge of the ear,' Reggie said apologetically.

'It's important that you're knowledgeable,' Bobby countered. He added, 'and..., well we're impressed.'

'You should be, according to the *Thalamus* Manager, they can now distinguish 400,000 different sounds.'

'Wow!' Banjo exclaimed. He did the sums in his head. 'That's forty times more than the number of odours the brain can identify.'

'We were told about the data matching protocols when we visited the *olfactory* senses,' Bobby explained to Reggie.

'When we hear flatulence, the brain predicts the smell before the nose detects it. If the smell doesn't match the sound, the brain asks why.' Reggie laughed. 'It's a common observation.' He paused and then added. 'So far as I know the eyes are still trying to detect flatulence, (he cupped his ear and squinted) but I think it's just because they want to know who to blame.' He laughed at his own joke.

'Is there much rivalry between the senses?' Bobby asked.

'A bit,' Reggie confirmed. 'We don't let it get in the way of being professional. Besides, Horace wouldn't allow that.'

'Who manages those follicles?' Banjo pointed to the diagram.

'I can take you to meet our QA Manager that's responsible for them if you'd like,' Reggie offered.

Bobby nodded his head in reply. He thought for a moment and asked. 'You have a QA Manager just for the follicles in this ear?'

'We have two dedicated follicle QA Managers in each ear.'

'Wow.' Bobby was impressed.

'What does the other one do?' Banjo queried.

'Over here is a diagram of the *maculae*.' Reggie led them across the room. 'Follicle bundles support the *otiliths*'

'What are they?'

'Crystalline rocks.' Reggie smiled. 'There's a joke circulating between the mind and us auditory specialists. Apparently, our human was once told that he had rocks in his head.' He laughed. 'Ironically, it's true!' He laughed again louder.

'Why would we have... rocks in the ear?' Banjo was curious but hesitant. He studied the diagram.

'The supporting follicles are formed into bundles of about seventy or more. At the centre of the bundle is one specialised follicle called a *kinocilium*. That hair is connected to the basal body. They have motor fibres and sensory fibres that detect the attitude of the head and advise the brain of the heads motions.' Reggie demonstrated by leaning forward and then sideways. 'The rocks pull the follicles into that particular downward trajectory alerting the sensors to advise the brain as to which way the head is leaning. They are called *proprioceptive sensations.*'

'Oh, of course. My boss has mentioned them.' Bobby nodded his head in understanding.

Banjo frowned at Bobby in disbelief. Bobby nodded rapidly to indicate that it was true.

'An infection in here can cause our human to lose control and over balance.' Reggie pointed to the diagram unaware of their non-verbal exchange.

'I believe inner ear infections can be very painful to our human,' Bobby asked rhetorically.

'Mostly the bacterium and viruses that cause ear infections enter via this tube here.' He pointed to a lengthy tube on the diagram. 'It has several names including the *Auditory* tube, the *Pharyngo-tympanic* tube and the *Eustachian* tube.' Reggie smiled. 'It connects the ear to the throat.'

'Why do we have it if infections can travel along it?' Banjo asked. 'Is it a design fault?' He smiled bleakly.

'Not really. We need it to equalise the air pressure on both sides of the ear drum,' Reggie answered. 'Otherwise, it wouldn't vibrate properly and we end up with diminished auditory input.' He paused. 'A greater presence of the Immune System at the throat end of the tube might be an improvement,' he added.

'The ears are very important,' Bobby concluded.

'All the senses are important,' Reggie agreed. 'But so are all the organs.'

'We're not that important,' Bobby lamented.

'Without follicles we couldn't hear or smell,' Reggie countered.

'I'm talking about the follicles that we grow. The one's that we push through the skin and out into the world.' Bobby was suddenly downcast.

'Music will cheer you up!' A voice behind them said.

They turned away from the wall charts to see a tall individual wearing a multi-coloured one-piece suit. He looked very colourful and smiled happily.

'This is, Arnold,' Reggie introduced.

After they completed the introductions and customary hand-shakes, they stood looking at each other. Finally, Arnold spoke.

'How are you going with the tour?' Arnold asked Reggie.

'We're about to go into the ear itself,' Reggie answered. 'They're mostly interested in the follicles and I'm hoping our two QA managers are available to answer any of the technical questions that Bobby or Banjo may have.'

'Do you have a moment before you go in?'

'Sure.'

'Perhaps we could sit in the dining room and chat. I'd like to explain about the music I'm preparing for the debate.'

'The dining room sounds like the perfect venue to me.' Banjo readily accepted for the three of them. He was hungry.

Reggie led them through a door and along a lengthy passageway. They entered the dining area that was filled with auditory workers. Banjo led the charge to get to the food and refreshments and Bobby and their two hosts joined the queue behind him. After they loaded their plates, they followed Reggie to the quietest corner of the noisy room where they sat to eat.

'Arnold spoke first. 'Have you explained anything to the boys about music?' He asked Reggie.

'Not yet,' Reggie answered. 'I thought it better to leave it up to you, actually.'

'I'm the Music Manager,' Arnold explained to Bobby and Banjo. 'I work in the mind, but I don't have voting rights.'

'I don't understand,' Bobby said.

'It's a bit complicated,' Arnold apologised. 'There are two types of Mind Managers. 'The common type that everyone knows about, is those Managers that are responsible for external functions and external activities. They get to debate topics that affect them or that they are interested in. They also get to vote on topics where and when a vote is called for.'

Bobby and Banjo nodded their heads in understanding.

'There is a smaller group of managers who do debate, but don't vote. We're internally specialised and we don't need a consensus to do things or make decisions.' He paused. 'I'm one of them.' He smiled, pleased with himself.

'You manage music.' Bobby queried.

'I do indeed,' Arnold confirmed. 'Over the years the mind has heard a lot of music via the ears. The mind stores music tracks in its memory banks. I have direct access to those music tracks, and I decide which ones the Mind Managers get to listen to.'

'It's very different to a live feed,' Reggie added.

'A live-feed? You mean music from the outside world via the ear and into the brain?'

'That's right,' Arnold confirmed. 'As the Music Manager I can influence the decision to select and play external music. I can influence the decision as to which music is played. I can store music tracks for later use.' He paused. 'That music I can't control, but I can influence it, as I know what Mind Managers enjoy listening to.'

'So, what music do you control?' Bobby asked. He was puzzled.

'I control the music the Mind Managers think they can hear when there isn't a live-feed. That music is random to everyone who can hear it, except to me,' he said proudly.

'Some Mind Managers get annoyed with the songs or music rifts that Arnold selects.' Reggie smiled knowingly.

'They can switch off if they want to,' Arnold defended. 'You see, the internal music is optional. A Mind Manager can either opt in, or opt out, of hearing it. They just can't choose it. Sometimes I play TV jingles or TV show theme music.'

Bobby and Banjo looked at each other, totally bewildered.

'And sometimes I play music that hasn't been played in a long time and the managers who like listening to my selections get into a tizz trying to remember the recording artists name or where they heard it.' He laughed. 'I sometimes use it to tease the Entertainment Managers.'

'That is funny,' Reggie said.

'They often engage the research department to do a search trying to identify it.' Arnold laughed.

'You can do all that from recorded live-feeds?' Bobby questioned.

'Absolutely,' Arnold confirmed.

'How many Entertainment Mind Managers do we have?' Banjo was curious.

'A lot. Entertainment is very important to the mind,' he replied.

'Can we...,?' Bobby looked at Banjo who nodded his head vigorously.

Arnold and Reggie looked at them with anticipation.

'Err..., get to hear the music too?' Bobby finished his question.

'Yes,' Arnold answered. He drew out two boxes containing earpieces. 'Put these into your ears.' He offered them one set each. 'One in each side will allow you to hear the music in stereo,' he explained by demonstrating where to insert the devices.

Bobby and Banjo inserted them into their *auditory* receptors.

'You use your mind to turn them on or off,' Arnold explained. 'You'll get used to it, soon enough.'

'Should we be hearing something now?' Bobby queried looking at Banjo to see if he was getting anything.

Banjo shook his head.

'The music isn't always on,' Arnold explained.

'You'll hear it soon enough,' Reggie assured.

'The internal tracks are rarely on if there is a live-feed in progress,' Arnold explained. 'It creates too much confusion. I also discourage multiple music sources during live music feeds. Again, it's just too confusing.'

'Tell them about singing,' Reggie suggested.

'Oh yes,' Arnold nodded his head. 'When the Mind Managers are agreeable, we can have the music redirected into vocalised singing, whistling and humming. That mostly happens when there is a pre-vailing mood of happiness.'

'We've established a feedback loop as the vocal output is reheard by the ears for quality control and training purposes,' Reggie explained.

'We're actually pretty good,' Arnold smiled.

'So, how does all this affect the debate?' Bobby wanted to know.

'Horace and I were thinking that if I select the right music to play during the debate it may help us achieve a positive vote,' Arnold answered.

'How would that work?' Bobby was confused.

'Music can excite or relax Mind Mangers,' Arnold explained. 'That's one of the reasons why it's so popular.' He smiled and looked about the room conspiratorially. 'I've selected the non-operatic version of Mozart's "Marriage of Figaro" during the lead up to the debate. It has a great tempo and Mind Managers love it as it has a positive affirming feel to it.'

'Great,' Bobby agreed without knowing why.

'When the "for the motion" speakers are speaking I'll have some soft Johann Strauss Junior music playing. I was going to use the

"Blue Danube" track because that's always popular, but I've decided to use the "Die Fledermaus" instead.'

'Is that good?'

'It's perfect.'

'What about the music for the 'against' team?' Banjo asked.

'"Mars, bringer of war," by Gustav Holst.' Arnold explained smiling

'Sounds aggressive,' Reggie offered.

'It is. Horace and I agree that it may sway the result of the debate and it may also have a subliminal positive influence on how everyone ultimately votes.'

'I... really appreciate the way, so many of you, are so supportive of my discovery,' Bobby sounded humble. 'I can't help but feel that with so much support, that it will be implemented.'

'We hope so too, Bobby,' Arnold agreed. 'Your discovery is beneficial in so many ways and has so much potential, that every intelligent manager should be one hundred percent behind it.'

'You represent the ordinary workers dream to make practical contributions to the human body.' Reggie was suddenly solemn. 'You're an inspiration to others.'

'Aw shucks,' Bobby was very embarrassed.

'You've truly inspired me,' Reggie told him.

'I have? How,' Bobby was curious.

'Not that ear wax thing?' Arnold questioned sighing.

'Yes, that ear wax thing,' Reggie defended. 'I have an idea about the *cerumen* that is produced in the outer ear external auditory canal by the *ceruminous glands*. Its main purpose is to prevent the penetration of external objects reaching the *tympanic membrane*. I believe that the ear wax is a perfect substance for determining the exact perfect formula for maintaining the *epidermis*. I've had numerous positive reports from the Fingers Manager after they extract surplus ear wax and rubbed it into the *epidermis* on the fingertips.'

'Reggie thinks it's the missing ingredient for *epidermis* and *dermis* rejuvenation,' Arnold added.

'It is!' Reggie exclaimed. 'And we make it ourselves.' He was excited. 'We'd reduce our dependency on unnecessary external body lotions.'

'We could mention your idea to our System Manager,' Banjo offered.

Bobby hesitantly nodded in agreement. He was wondering how George would perceive the notion of the whole body being rubbed with ear wax.

'I'd really appreciate it,' Reggie seemed happy to be taken seriously.

Arnold smiled cordially at his friend. 'You never know. One day, I might be preparing music for a debate about your ear wax discovery.'

Reggie smiled happily.

'I'm looking forward to hearing the music you've selected,' Bobby said.

'I'm sorry, but I'll need those back after the debate,' Arnold referred to the music listening devices he'd supplied them.

'Oh,' Bobby was disappointed.

'Only Mind Managers are authorised to have them. I did get permission for the two of you to have them temporarily as you are invitees to the debate.'

'Actually you'd better return them to Arnold now,' Reggie advised. 'You won't be allowed to wear them during the tour.'

Bobby and Banjo removed the devices and returned them to Arnold.

'Right.' Reggie stood up from the table. 'Let's tour the ear,' he suggested.

The three others were rising from their chairs also when they noticed that one of the ear reception staff members was approaching them.

'I've been looking for you everywhere,' he complained. 'We have been advised that the debate has been moved forward and it's about to start. Horace is waiting for you in the great hall.'

~ 24 ~

Bobby and Banjo followed Reggie and Arnold through the various passageways that led to the great hall where the debate was being contested.

They met a group of Mind Managers who were walking toward them. Bobby hoped that they were favourable to his discovery as he didn't think he'd be able to cope with negative or condescending comments.

Arnold greeted the group with affection.

'Bobby, Banjo. These are some of my colleagues,' he indicated the group smiling happily. 'Like me, they are Mind Managers that are without voting privileges.'

'How do you do?' Bobby asked politely extending his hand in friendship.

'We do very well, and we thank you for your interest,' one replied happily accepting the offer to shake hands.

'This is Isadore, Mind Manager for Sleep Dreams,' Arnold pointed to each in turn. 'This is Josh, Manager for Superstitions and Rituals, Algernon; he's the Manager for Trivia and Kenny, Manager for Daydreaming and Fantasies.'

Arnold continued, 'this is Bobby and his 2IC Banjo. They are Follicle QA Managers from the *Integumentary* System.'

'I often include hair in our dreams,' Isadore explained. 'I think there is a link between dreaming of hair loss and the actual loss of virility.'

'That wouldn't be popular,' Arnold countered.

'I sometimes speculate that a full face of moustache and beard would look great on us and give us a ruggedly handsome persona,' Kenny sighed.

'Wasn't there a musical about hair?' Algernon asked.

'There was, but it wasn't popular with our Mind Managers, so I don't play it much,' Arnold replied.

'Bald men are unrepresented in public office,' Algernon informed the group.

His colleagues groaned audibly.

'It's true!' Algernon defended. 'We have over five million follicles growing on our body, and they have the nerve to refer to us as the "naked ape".'

'We'll,' Josh interceded, 'We all know that there's link between long healthy hair and its power over others. I do a lot of research and I once read about a suitor, a wizard, who arranged for three pubic hairs to be obtained from the woman he secretly loved. As a joke they supplied him with three hairs from the udder of a cow. He made his magic potion and the love-struck cow followed him everywhere all over town.'

The five managers burst into laughter. Bobby, Banjo and Reggie looked about themselves uncertain of what to think.

They were quiet for a moment.

Banjo came to the rescue. 'How many non-voting Mind Managers are there?' Banjo queried.

'Lots!' They chorused and laughed some more.

'Not as many as there are voting managers but there are quite a few of us that rarely debate and don't have a vote or have a say in any actual decision making,' Arnold started to explain.

'You see, we also have the naughty and not so nice managers on the "not allowed to vote" side of Mind Management,' Isadore added.

Bobby and Banjo looked confused.

'Imagine if the Manager for Illicit Drugs and Alcohol or the Manager for Illegal, Corrupt and Nefarious Activities got permission to debate or vote? They could corrupt others and the consequences would be dire.'

'Or the Manager for Immoral behaviour,' Kenny said it as a statement.

'Yeah,' the others chorused their agreement.

Bobby was about to ask a question, but Arnold cut him off.

'Bobby, these guys are fascinating, but we don't want to miss the start of the debate.' Arnold indicated that they should proceed to the great hall.

Bobby nodded in agreement. He was relieved to leave these managers behind. There was so much he still didn't understand.

They waved their farewells and continued walking toward the great hall.

'Good luck!' Josh yelled over his shoulder and the four burst into laughter.

Arnold chuckled and sighed. 'Those guys...'

As they got close to the main entry Arnold stopped them and spoke. 'Here are your earpieces.' He handed a receiving audio device to each of them including Reggie. 'Reggie will teach you how to use them.'

Bobby nodded his appreciation.

'I've got to get to work.' He shook Bobby and Banjo's hands. 'I hope that our side do well today and that they reach an affirmative conclusion,' he sounded very sincere.

Arnold waved his farewell leaving Reggie to explain how to hear the music.

'Put these into your ear, one on each side and I'll let you know when the music is being transmitted.' Bobby and Banjo followed his example.

Reggie led his guests into the great debating hall. Its design was aesthetically pleasing and supported comfortable seating and a good view of the proceedings for all that attended. Both Bobby and Banjo were amazed at the high level of interest. They looked at each other nodding and smiling at the crowd. As they studied the faces, they sensed a high level of anticipation among the throng.

Bobby turned when someone placed a hand on his shoulder.

'Dan!' Bobby exclaimed. 'I wasn't sure you'd be here.'

'George is here too,' Dan said. 'This is a significant event for all Farmers, and we wanted to be here for it.'

'It is, but I'm not so confident that it'll be a positive outcome.' Bobby looked slightly disappointed.

'George and I agree. Roderick has been assertively campaigning for the "NO" vote.' Dan looked sad also.

'Where is George?' Bobby looked about the room. He spotted George sitting with Earl. They gave him a cheery wave. Bobby waved back.

'Should we be sitting with you?' Bobby queried.

'We tried to save you some seats near us, but they were already allocated when we got here,' Dan explained.

Bobby turned to Banjo who'd been standing behind them unobtrusively. 'Horace has organised seats near the front for Banjo and me.' Banjo had been watching and listening to their conversation.

'Hi Banjo, exciting times,' Dan said by way of acknowledgement.

'And it's a big honour for all of us,' Banjo added.

'Sure is,' Dan agreed. 'George would like a word with you after the debate.'

'Of course,' Bobby accepted the invitation.

'This place is filling up fast,' Dan observed. 'I'd better get to my seat.' He waved his goodbye and headed off to re-join George.

Bobby and Banjo walked over to a cluster of chairs near the debating arena where Reggie and Horace were already seated.

'I'm impressed by the turn out,' Reggie spoke, expressing his own thoughts as Bobby sat down.

'Is this a lot of people for a debate audience?' Bobby asked Horace.

'I don't get to come to many, but I gather that usually there are only a few observers,' Horace replied. 'Mostly, they are the immediate colleagues of those that are actually debating and they're here to provide morale support.' Horace paused. 'Or they are managers who are planning to participate in a debate and want to study form and technique.'

Bobby nodded.

Horace pointed to a group of people to the rear and right of them. 'Have you seen your boss?'

Bobby and Banjo looked to where Horace was pointing and saw George, Dan and Earl waving at them, which Bobby and Banjo returned.

'Yes. We spoke with Dan and we're meeting with George after the debate,' Bobby replied.

'Did Dan tell you that he's now officially General Manager for Follicles?' Horace smiled. 'We heard that Percival approved his promotion.'

'I will congratulate him after the debate.' Bobby faked a smile, unsure as to how he felt about Dan's rapid advancement.

'Ooh!' Reggie exclaimed. 'The music is on. Can you hear it?' He asked Bobby and Banjo.

At first, they couldn't, but as Reggie started humming to the music and soon, they were able to hear it for themselves.

Their introduction to music was Mozart's, 'The Marriage of Figaro.' They didn't know they were only getting the music score and that this managerial preferred version was without the accompanying operatic singing.

Bobby and Banjo looked at each other. They were smiling happily as the orchestral notes sounded in their ears. It was sublime, invigorating and truly amazing. They found themselves moving to the rhythm of the notes.

Bobby felt that regardless of the debate's outcome, the fact that he was able to hear this music, made the journey to this point in his life, all worthwhile.

'Do you like the music that Arnold selected?' Reggie asked.

'Oh yes, very much,' Bobby answered and Banjo nodded in agreement.

Reggie smiled. It was good to be the PR Manager for audio. He loved these special moments when other outsiders could share the pleasures.

'Who are those people?' Bobby pointed to a group of official looking uniformed people.

'They provide security and show people to seating if needed. Mostly there is only one or two on duty, but today I count six,' Horace replied.

One of the security persons sensed they were being referred to, and he came over to where they were seated.

'Are you all comfortable?' He asked cordially.

They all nodded that they were.

'Just a reminder that you won't need to record this debate as it is being recorded for future review. It is also being screened live to all voting Mind Managers,' the security person informed them. 'The recording will be accessible until the conclusion of voting on this topic.'

'Oh.' Bobby was surprised.

'Yes.' The security person smiled. 'Roderick arranged it.'

'Thank you for your attendance,' a voice announced cutting off Bobby's next question to the security person who had since turned and walked away.

Bobby and the others stopped talking and listened. The voice belonged to Jeremiah.

'It's so good to see so many visitors attending this debate. It's certainly an important topic and from the rumblings that I have heard and a contentious one.' Jeremiah smiled.

'I believe that the last time we saw so many people in attendance was when we debated the practicalities of do-it-yourself bathroom renovations.'

The audience chuckled. There was numerous yes's being murmured as they recalled that heated debate.

Jeremiah continued, 'This debate is to discuss the merits for and against the proposition that given that we now have the knowledge on how to reverse the inevitable aging effects of follicle colour loss and alopecia, that should we use it.'

Mumblings were heard in the great hall.

One person rose from his chair and yelled at Jeremiah. 'My name is Terrance and I'm the *dihydrotestosterone* controller. I manufacture *follicle-stimulating hormones* and I can't understand why we are having this debate at all.' At Jeremiahs signal, two security personnel stood either side of Terrance. 'My department has been stimulating follicle growth for a very long time and we...,' his voice trailed as he looked at the two security guards who suddenly appeared at each side of him.

Jeremiah tried to sound patient, despite being interrupted, 'Terrance, whilst we respect the work your department does, we have noted that *dihydrotestosterone* production is falling because of aging...'

'We're doing everything we can. We need more time to do more research...'

'And that will happen, but this debate isn't about your hormone output. Now, please, be seated or you'll be escorted from the room.' Jeremiah was very firm.

Terrance sat down. The two security persons remained in proximity and in full view of Terrance. He remained quiet.

The room was very still.

Jeremiah cleared his throat. 'Our human is entering the life cycle stage when we will begin to experience the effects of aging. In regard to the growth cycle of hair follicles we have transitioned through the *anagen* stage, and we are now well into the *catagen* stage. We have proven statistics to confirm this. Before we enter the *telogen* stage we have an opportunity to minimize the impact of follicle death and permanent loss of colour.'

'A discovery by a remarkable young man, who I see is present as an observer to this debate, was made to facilitate the growth of a perfect moustache when a moustache was requested by the Marketing Department. He has since been promoted to Quality Assurance Manager for Follicles. Please welcome Bobby.' Jeremiah indicated to Bobby that he should stand up and be acknowledged. He did and the audience gave him a smattering of applause.

'From the start, there were some inconsistencies in the length, shape and colour of the follicles in the moustache during the growing event. Bobby applied his discovery which resulted in a perfect moustache being produced.' Jeremiah then drew in a deep breath before continuing.

'Since then, the science behind his discovery has been tested, trialed and proven. The fact that it works is not on debate. This debate is philosophical and will focus on whether or not we should apply the discovery to our hair follicles.'

Some loud murmurs threaten to interrupt Jeremiah's introduction, but he held up one hand and they abated. 'The team that will argue in favour of implementing the follicle colour recovery and follicle rejuvenation include Alphonso as Team Leader, Fabian and Manny.' Jeremiah started to give a clap as each team member stood up and was acknowledged, others joined in giving mild applause.

Jeremiah continued. 'The team that will argue against implementing follicle colour recovery and follicle rejuvenation include Sandy as Team Leader, Ford and Leo.' Jeremiah again led the applause as each team member stood up to be recognised.

Bobby noticed that the applause was slightly more enthusiastic for the "not in favour" team than when the "in favour off" team were introduced.

'Without any further delay we shall now start the debate. Please welcome Alphonso from the YES team' Jeremiah announced.

The opening music faded and was replaced with Johann Strauss Junior's music the "Die Fledermaus".

Alphonso rose from his chair in the centre of the great hall and walked to the dais. He nodded his thanks and then started his presentation.

'The quest for youth is universal. To look good is to feel good. We consistently live out our life by being positive and by being stylish. We have noted on so many occasions that we receive external compliments when our scalp hair has been recently cut and styled. We ensure that it is at all times neatly trimmed, combed, washed and shaped to present ourselves in public to our fullest advantage.'

Alphonso continued, 'When meeting others, we get one chance to make a great first impression. We note that baldness is unfairly associated with diminished brain ability through reduced reasoning and analytical skills. Bald men are rarely elected leaders and those that are, are often rely on artificial hair or external clothing called "hats" to cover their baldness.'

'The presence of greying hair should indicate that our man is distinguished and experienced and therefore wise. The truth is that greying hair is associated with decreased stamina and diminished virility and therefore it will reduce our sex appeal.'

There were gasps of horror from parts of the audience. Alphonso waited for them to settle before continuing.

'The discovery that the application of follicle stimulating hormones released from fat cells can lead to follicle rejuvenation is the most significant event in the management of anti-aging practices. We should embrace this discovery. We should be grateful that we have the intelligence and foresight to apply it now, before baldness and graying hairs become our reality.'

'I say we utilise this discovery. I say we restore our good youthful looks, that we will be a confident leader and a positive role model. I say we remain a great man among all men.'

Alphonso sat down to a smattering of applause.

Jeremiah rose from his seat and announced. 'Please welcome, Sandy from the "No" team.'

The music faded and was replaced with "Mars, Bringer of war."

Sandy approached the dais with arms stretched up above him to increase everyone's attention with the anticipation that something unusual was about to happen. He slowly lowered his arms. The room was silent in anticipation.

'Rogue hairs are a serious blight on our human exterior! The application of Bobby's discovery would only lead to an increase in the number of unsightly hairs proliferating from ears, nose, and other parts of the body. They will appear on us as weeds appear in a garden. They will require more work, more time, and more effort to find and remove them. They'll therefore discourage human interaction and therefore reduce our sex appeal.'

There were more gasps from the audience and Sandy held up his arms again until they settled.

'I have recently received a report of rogue hairs having to be forcibly removed from the groin!' He held up a sheaf of papers as evidence. 'Can you imagine what detrimental effect this could have had on the frequency of *coital* encounters?' Sandy challenged his audience.

The audience was very still.

'Furthermore, that event coincided with Bobby's visit to the groin!' Sandy was pointing accusingly at Bobby.

There were serious objections from the audience and Sandy had to hold his arms up once more to settle them.

Bobby blushed at the implication. Banjo was very angry and restless in his chair. Bobby had to put a hand on Banjo's arm to settle him. They exchanged a knowing look.

'Coincidence...! I think not,' Sandy concluded.

'I say 'No' to Bobby's discovery. I say it is foolish to tamper with nature and to inflict ourselves to the unnecessary stresses of managing excessive and unwanted hairs.'

'Furthermore, I say you should say No!'

Sandy sat down and the applause he received was significantly more than Alphonso's.

Jeremiah rose from his seat and announced. 'Next, please welcome, Fabian.'

The music faded and was again replaced with Johann Strauss Junior's music the "Die Fledermaus."

Fabian spoke with strength and determination. 'In all my research I have never heard or read that rogue hairs have affected our ability to mate, or our desire to mate, or influence the probability that it will happen. All knowledgeable managers know that the intricacies involved with finding, seducing, and proceeding to a coitus event with a willing participant go far beyond the impediments of a few rogue hairs!'

'We need to focus on the broader benefits of this discovery. We should always set a good example to others. We need to advance our self-sufficiency and reward internal effort by praise and application. If we ignore the advances we make in our own understanding of our human, our home, we devalue that contribution.'

'Bobby has made that contribution. His discovery advances our knowledge of anti-aging practices. They are revolutionary. We should be grateful. We should be respectful. We should do more than simply acknowledge and reward him as utilisation of his discovery is itself the greatest exultation.'

'We need to consistently acknowledge the efforts of our own, and their contributions, to the advancement of our physical body.'

'By popularising this discovery, we give approval to each worker with a great idea for human physiological advancement, the encouragement they need to advance that idea.'

'I say "Yes." I say let's have strong rich natural coloured hair. I say "Yes" to invite others to equally contribute to our body and our home. I say, "Yes" and you also should say "Yes!"

Fabian sat down and to a smattering of applause.

Jeremiah rose from his seat and announced. 'Next, please welcome, Ford.'

The music faded and was again replaced with, "Mars, Bringer of War."

Ford approached the dais and made numerous engine revving noises. He earned chuckles of approval from the audience and got a smattering of applause.

'I agree,' he said and looked about the room. 'I agree,' he said again and smiled at the confusion. 'I'll say it again, in order to remove any doubt. I agree!' he said it louder on the third occasion.

The room was silent.

'We do need to encourage our workers to contribute. We should always reward them. We should set a good example and facilitate a working environment that inspires innovation and enhances our lifestyle.'

'But not in this case. This is different. This is fraught with complications. This discovery of Bobby's comes at too high a risk. Consider this my friends. If Bobby's discovery were so good and so positive, then why would we feel the need to debate it? Wouldn't we just unanimously agree that this is worthy of inclusion into human maintenance practices?'

'I mentioned risk.' Ford paused for effect. 'In an age where conformity is the norm, to look youthful as others are aging is to attract unwanted attention. How do we explain our youthful exterior when others are showing their age with dignity and finesse?' Ford asked the audience.

'I say we vote "No".' He paused. 'I won't repeat it. You're all intelligent managers you wouldn't be a manager if you weren't. You'll know the right decision to make.' He paused and looked at the opposition team. 'I won't beg like some do.' He smiled and left the dais.

Ford sat down and the applause he received was significantly more than Fabian's.

Jeremiah rose from his seat and announced. 'Next, please welcome, Manny.'

The Die Fledermaus music played then faded as Manny approached the dais. He waved jovially to everyone. 'I think Ford just drove his argument off a cliff,' he stated.

There were some chuckles in the audience.

'The fountain of youth has been a popular legend among humans for an eternity. Why is that? It's because we crave looking good to others. We ache for youthfulness. Industry makes billions of dollars marketing youthful products that basically do the very job that Bobby's discovery will allow us to do for ourselves.'

'Bobby's discovery will be bad for the economy!' Ford yelled.

The room erupted with laughter.

Jeremiah came up to the dais, his arms rose to calm the audience and was about to protest Fords unprofessional interjection when Ford stood up and spoke first. 'I apologise unconditionally for my interruption of my esteemed colleagues presentation. It won't happen again.' He sat down.

Manny drew in a deep breath. He looked at Jeremiah and nodded. Jeremiah returned to his seat.

'This discovery has the broader support of the *Adipose* community. They want to contribute in a more meaningful way than just as fat storage cells. They have been storing these reserves long enough and they now want to see some action. They want you to say, "yes".'

Manny sat down and there was a smattering of applause.

Jeremiah rose from his seat and announced. 'Next, please welcome, Leo.'

The music of Mars, Bringer of War swelled in their ears.

Leo growled at the audience, and they chuckled in amusement. He spoke boldly and confidently. 'How will the *adipose* cells react to the continual demands placed on them to supply their stem cells that will be used to rejuvenate the hair? Some may think we can afford to lose a little weight, but how zealous will the follicle team be when applying this discovery. How many *adipose* cells must suffer for hair growing vanity? The *adipose* cells store energy for when there's a genuine food supply issue. They are our insurance. They are for the tough times that may well lie ahead, and they mustn't be squandered on vanity. I say the "No" vote wins. So should you.'

Leo sat down and received significant applause.

Jeremiah rose from his seat and shushed the audience.

The music returned to Die Fledermaus.

'This concludes the debate. Thank you to both teams for the work which you have done in preparing your arguments, and for the professional way you presented them.' Jeremiah nodded his respect to the six that were now standing in the centre of the great hall.

Jeremiah continued. 'The determination of which team has presented the strongest argument is now up to voting managers within this audience. In this case that includes those that have watched the live feeds from the comfort of their own offices. Electronic voting has now commenced and will close in five cycles.'

'Five cycles! That isn't very long.' Bobby lamented. He was standing with the others in front of his seat stretching himself after being seated for so long.

'It's a 'for' or 'against' decision, Bobby,' Reggie explained. 'They either do, or they don't.'

'How do you think we went?' Bobby asked Horace.

'I think you know the answer that question, Bobby.' Horace looked sullen.

Bobby looked at Banjo. Banjo shrugged in reply.

Bobby drew a deep breath and sighed.

Arnold returned to the great hall. He didn't look happy.

Roderick intercepted Arnold before he could reach the others. 'Arnold! Thank you very much for the music.'

Arnold stopped and looked at him but said nothing.

'Mars! God of War! Inspired! I believe it gave the 'against' side the edge. It's strong and commanding. I'm surprised I didn't think of it myself. Truly, a great choice. Well done.'

Arnold continued to say nothing.

Roderick reached for Arnold's hand and shook it firmly. 'Anytime I can return the favour, just let me know. I owe you one my friend.' He smiled and waved a cheery hello to Horace, Reggie, Bobby, and Banjo turned and walked back to resume his seat.

Jeremiah's voice boomed above the animated discussions in the room. 'Gentlemen please, the voting has closed, and we have a result.'

Everyone hastily returned to their seats and became quiet.

'I will remind all voting managers that the outcome of the debate is not the outcome of the vote. The purpose of the debate is to educate voting managers about the broader issues surrounding the topic. I therefore encourage all voting managers to continue to do research so that they can give their best consideration to the actual vote.'

Jeremiah drew in a deep breath. 'In regard to the proposition, that as we now have the knowledge on how to reverse the inevitable aging effects on follicle colour loss and alopecia, should we use it. The result is 68% against and 32% in favour, therefore the 'against' team wins this debate.'

Bobby and Banjo were seated in the now, almost empty, great hall dining room. The reveller's that were celebrating their debate victory had long since departed for a planned reception now being held within the marketing department.

To add insult to injury Roderick had made an exaggerated effort to invite Bobby and his other 'Losers" to his party. He also boasted that he'd arranged a special shipment of carbonated wine to be delivered to his soirée by the manager of the *Liver*, who when invited, seemed overly excited to attend.

Seated at the table opposite Bobby and Banjo were George, Dan, and Earl. Horace sat to Bobby's left and Reggie and Arnold sat to Banjo's right.

They had said very little.

The dining room staff, and the two remaining security personnel seemed familiar with the sight of patrons lamenting outcomes. They kept away at a respectful distance. Bobby sniffed the air and cleared his throat. He looked up at George. 'We haven't been to the scalp yet.'

'I'm aware of that.'

'We've submitted reports on our visit to the eyes, nose and ears.'

'Yes, we got them. They are very good,' George nodded his head agreeing.

'How long do we have to wait for an announcement on the formal vote?'

'Horace?' George asked his friend.

'Not long.'

George looked at Bobby and Banjo. 'Go to the scalp and complete your mission. When the result is ready to be announced, I'll send for both of you and we can decide how to proceed once we know the outcome.'

Bobby and Banjo nodded their heads in understanding and agreement.

'I gather the formal vote will go the same way as the debate?' Banjo asked the obvious question.

Horace drew in a deep breath. 'Typically, it does.'

'We can't do any more until we know the official outcome,' George added. He stood and Dan and Earl followed his lead. 'We've all got our jobs to do and now we must resume doing them.'

Horace, Reggie, and Arnold also stood up.

'Bobby. I'm sorry my music plan didn't work,' Arnold apologised again.

'We got to hear that music, Arnold. Banjo and I agreed that they are truly the most beautiful things we have ever heard. We felt the music and it was good,' he paused and added hopefully, 'I only wish we could have kept our decoders.' Bobby lamented looking at Banjo who nodded his agreement.

They had already returned the equipment as per Head Office policy.

Arnold nodded in understanding. 'I'll be playing angry music for a while as that's the mood I'm in. I expect I won't get too many managers tuning in, but it'll make me feel better.' He smiled.

'You'll get complaints,' Horace cautioned.

'I hope so,' Arnold countered.

They all shook hands, and the three groups left the dining room for their various destinations.

This time, George had thoughtfully arranged a guide to lead the QA team to the scalp and their meeting with the Regional Manager. The journey to the scalp felt like an uphill climb. Bobby knew that wasn't possible as from any perspective all pathways were relatively flat. Bobby wondered if there was a psychological sensation experienced when visitors journeyed to what was regarded as the highest part of the human body. True that this was only accurate from the human's perspective, but after so many cycles of data collecting and data processing, it seemed to have ingrained itself into mitochondria culture.

Their guide stopped outside the office of the Regional Manager of the Scalp. They thanked him and he departed. The RMS had three aides guarding his office door.

Without looking up from a computer display unit, the aid on the left of the other two asked wearily, 'Do you have an appointment?'

'Yes,' Bobby answered.

He looked up. 'Your name?' he demanded.

'Bobby,' he replied. 'I'm the RMQAF and this is Banjo my AM.'

'Oh.' He stood up and the other two looked up.

'Is Alvin available?' Bobby asked.

'He should be. I'll check,' the aide offered. He turned and walked through a door into what was presumably Alvin's office.

An elderly man immediately appeared with the aide peering close behind.

'Bobby?' He queried.

'That's me,' Bobby confirmed.

'Don't just stand there like a petulant miscreant, come in and bring your young friend with you.' Alvin disappeared into his office. The aide indicated they should follow and so Bobby and Banjo did.

The office was well appointed by Regional Manager of Follicle Farmers standards. It reminded Bobby of Steven's office in the beard. It occurred to Bobby that this was the first time he'd thought of Steven since leaving the moustache.

Alvin interrupted his thoughts. 'Have you come to replace me?' Alvin asked hopefully.

'Err, No.' Bobby looked at Banjo in confusion. He was surprised by the question.

'Have you come to audit me?' Alvin asked mischievously.

'Well, yes we have,' Bobby replied.

'You're aware that I'm retiring soon and really don't care?' Alvin was flippant.

'Yes, we do know that you're retiring, and I also know that you do care very much,' Bobby replied.

'Oh darn,' Alvin conceded.

Alvin reached down to an antiquated internal communications system and spoke to an aide. 'Please invite my five Area Managers to attend my office. I need them now, please,' he said into the device.

'You can't be too polite to these aides,' Alvin explained. 'All three are Union orientated.' He forced a smile as he sat down, inviting Bobby and Banjo do so.

'My new young friends....,' Alvin addressed them. 'George assures me that you'll assist me in selecting which one of my Area Managers will replace me when I finally do retire.' He then nodded as if agreeing with himself. 'Given your reputation Bobby, I was hoping that you'd present yourself as the man for the job.' He looked at Bobby hopefully.

Bobby said nothing. He looked about the room.

'I suppose you believe QA is your thing? The two of you have been busily gallivanting about the body with all care and no responsibility.' He had said it in such a way so as to provoke a reaction.

Bobby laughed and Banjo looked confused.

'I suppose you've upset many heads of departments on your travels?' He queried

'One or two,' Bobby conceded grinning.

'You don't say much. Maybe you're not the inspired leader we want for this prestigious post,' Alvin concluded.

Banjo was bursting. He twisted in his chair and looked set to counterattack and defend his boss.

Bobby gave him a look of reassurance. 'Alvin was my Area Manager when I first started as a worker in the beard. It was Alvin who promoted me to Team Leader,' Bobby explained to Banjo with a smile. 'Ever since then he's been tormenting me at every opportunity.'

Banjo relaxed.

'And since that time you've had a meteoric rise in both position and power.' Alvin smiled proudly at his young protégée. 'Well done, Bobby.'

'Thank you, sir,' Bobby responded gratefully.

'Sir? I haven't been knighted, have I?' Alvin queried. 'Someone should have told me.'

Bobby laughed at the old joke. Alvin had aged, but he was still the jovial person he fondly remembered.

'Now, while we wait for the others to arrive, introduce me to your young friend,' Alvin suggested.

'Banjo is my assistant,' Bobby started to explain. 'Actually, he's so much more than that. He's become a trusted friend.' He smiled at Banjo.

'Aw shucks boss,' Banjo blushed.

'We've been together since I was a promoted to Team Leader for the moustache.'

'Team Leaders for the moustache get an EA?' Alvin was querulous.

'It was meant to be a temporary appointment. We were given unlimited resources during a moustache growing event and it was thought that we would do it faster and better if we had skilled assistance...'

'From the briefing George gave me, I understand that you ended up taking charge of that project which resulted in producing a magnificent moustache,' he complimented.

'Thank you,' Bobby replied smiling proudly.

'And when they changed their decision from growing the moustache to shaving the moustache you went to George and complained.'

'That's right,' Bobby confirmed.

'And by complaining, you ended up being promoted to Quality Assurance Manager, most extraordinary,' Alvin concluded.

'When we first started to complain we didn't even know we had an *Integumentary* System Manager. It came as a bit of a surprise to me to learn just how many levels of management there are.'

'We're a very big organisation. It requires a solid structure and strong leadership.' Alvin nodded his head again agreeing with himself.

'Banjo was initially my assistant, but he's been promoted to second in charge. He does the job very well and I expect he'll replace me as QA Manager when I retire.' Bobby smiled.

'Not too soon I trust.' Alvin feigned concern. 'You look fit. Travel suits you.'

'It's been fascinating. We've learned a lot about the body and how it interacts.'

'Good,' Alvin concluded. 'Now let me tell you a little about our scalp hair,' he suggested.

Banjo leaned forward and Bobby relaxed into his chair.

'We have a work force of a little over 300,000 to manage the 99,612 follicles on the scalp. That includes the eyebrows,' Alvin explained.

'That's a lot of follicles,' Banjo murmured.

'It's an approximate figure. We lose so many and we're constantly initiating replacements.' Alvin made it sound like a routine function. He studied his guests' reactions.

Bobby and Banjo nodded their understanding.

Alvin continued, 'Scalp hair can grow extraordinary long in comparison to follicles in other parts of the body. Our follicles are more exposed to the sun which causes them damage. They get dirtier with dust contaminating them and require specialised chemicals that are arranged by a Mind Manager. Are you familiar with dandruff?' he asked.

Bobby and Banjo looked at each other.

'Dandruff is scales of dead *epidermis* from the scalp and it's caused by *seborrheic dermatitis*. It is cured with a steroid scalp lotion. We've not been afflicted for a long time, but it was once a recurrent problem that I had to remedy when I first arrived and took charge as the scalp RM.'

'You must be glad to be rid of that problem,' Bobby mused.

'Uniquely, the *epidermis* manager for the scalp reports to me also,' Alvin explained. He again studied his guest's reaction.

Bobby and Banjo looked up in surprise but said nothing.

'Are you familiar with nits?' Alvin asked hopefully.

Bobby and Banjo shook their heads.

'Lice are small parasites that feed on the blood of the scalp. They infest the hair and lay tiny white eggs called nits which are small enough to stick to individual hair strands. There hasn't been a problem with lice for a very long time and the last infestation happened long before I arrived. We still look for the signs of them and we do practice drills on what to do in case of an infestation. Our researchers have found that an external application of Carbaryl lotion works the best.'

'It's good that you don't have that problem anymore also,' Banjo added to the conversation.

'We remain vigilant,' Alvin agreed. 'We do have early signs of alopecia at the crown apex and hair colour loss particularly near the two temples. We could use your help with that. Perhaps you could guide us on what to do while doing your audits?' Alvin suggested.

'Those procedures haven't been approved yet. I think we should wait,' Bobby countered and Banjo nodded his head in agreement.

'We don't want to cause any problems,' Banjo added.

'I don't agree,' Alvin responded kindly. 'Your discovery may not get approval for body wide use, but as I see it, wherever Bobby goes, his procedures and practices go with him. You're the Quality Managers, aren't you? You're graded a Regional Manager. When it comes to hair, wherever you are, you can do what ever you like!'

Bobby and Banjo smiled. They looked at each other and nodded. 'We'd be happy to assist you with your alopecia issues and reduce the numbers of greying hairs.'

'Good.' Alvin smiled. He pressed a button on the intercom. 'Let me introduce you to my management team.'

The practiced cue resulted in the door opening and the five Area Managers filed into the room. Alvin stood up as did Bobby and Banjo. Alvin walked to a long narrow conference table and the others followed him to it.

Alvin introduced his guests. 'Gentlemen, please welcome Bobby and Banjo to the scalp. Bobby is the QA Manager for all follicles and Banjo is his second in command.'

The five AM's stood in a semi-circle uncertain how to proceed.

Alvin indicated that all present should be seated.

'Bobby's purpose is to audit our procedures, and protocols, and advise us on how to reduce alopecia and prevent colour loss occurring in our hairs,' Alvin explained.

'Could you please now individually introduce yourselves to Bobby and Banjo,' Alvin commanded.

The first manager stood up and bowed almost imperceptibly to the guests. 'My name is Peter and I manage the follicle growth on the left side of the head. Our team's name is the "Saints".' He sat.

The second manager stood and smiled. 'Hello, my name is Lance and I manage the follicle growth on the right side of the head. Our team's name is the "Knights".' He resumed his seat.

The third manager stood. 'I'm Willie. We grow on the top of the *scalp*, and we're called the "Mitts".'

The fourth rose and spoke quickly. 'I'm Nelson, we grow the hair at the rear of the head, and we're called the "Rear Admirals".'

The last manager stood up and introduced himself. 'Sylvester..., Eyebrows..., "Eyebrows".' He sat.

Bobby stood up and gave an address to the managers that he'd been preparing for some time. He felt confident. 'Our System Manger, George, sent Banjo and I to do an inspection on how well you all perform your tasks in growing scalp follicles. We'll be meeting with you individually to measure your output to learn if you're meeting or exceeding growth output expectations. We'll also examine your documentation on how you record each stage of follicle growth. We'll next look at your maintenance procedures.' He drew in a deep breath and continued after delivering a reassuring smile. 'We'd also like to get to know you a little better, so please tell us about yourselves and what your plans are for the workers under your management.'

'Before you leave to do your QA stuff, perhaps you should learn a little about what we do for recreation,' Alvin suggested. He was smiling mischievously.

Bobby and Banjo looked expectantly as four of the five Area Managers smiled excitedly. Only Sylvester seemed disinterested.

'Sure,' Bobby agreed. 'That's always a good way to start. During our travels we have met other Follicle Farmers who have interesting social activities. We have found that they make for a more cohesive workplace and reduce the tedium of growing hair.'

'Those areas performed the best in relation to follicle growth, strength and documentation,' Banjo added.

'May I be excused?' Sylvester asked.

'Sure,' Alvin agreed.

'I'll be in the eyebrows when you want to check out my area,' Sylvester explained.

'We look forward to seeing you there,' Bobby acknowledged.

Sylvester left the room.

'Sylvester doesn't like games,' Peter explained.

'Games?' Bobby queried. 'Are they part of your social activity?' They all laughed.

Alvin explained. 'A while ago we had a visit from some of the Mind Managers; one of them was from the entertainment group. He was the Mind Manager for Games and Strategies. He didn't have any games with him, but he told us all about his favourite game, a game he called Chest.'

'Despite promising to send us the game and a rule book, he never did,' Lance added.

'I wrote down as much as I could remember and we've had to make up some of the rules for ourselves, but I'm quite sure I got it close enough in the end,' Peter explained.

'Peter has a good memory and a fantastic imagination,' Alvin uttered the compliment and Peter beamed appreciatively.

'It works and everyone understands and plays by the rules,' Willie added.

'It's become very popular,' Nelson agreed.

'We've estimated that at any one time there are over 12,000 games of Chest being played somewhere on the scalp,' Lance boasted.

'The top ten players from each area get to represent their areas in a team competition. There are four teams, and each team has their own competitions in order to determine their top ten players,' Peter enthused. 'It's a really big honour.'

'Those top ten players are treated like celebrities by their teams,' Alvin confirmed.

'The player ranked number one wins ten points for his team for each game that he wins. The second earns nine points and so on, all the way to one point for the tenth ranked person. Each player competes against their opposite number in each of the other teams.'

'If one team won every game, at every level, then that team would score 165 points.' Willie was obviously good at the calculations. 'So far, the highest score that any team has achieved is ninety-two.'

'That was my team, The Saints,' Peter beamed.

'Everyone seems to think that a score of a hundred is the ultimate goal and I must admit the enthusiasm levels to achieve that remain extraordinarily high,' Alvin added.

'Does it distract you from growing hair properly?' Bobby queried.

'Oh no!' They chorused.

'Then it's a good thing,' Bobby accepted smiling.

'And a significant morale boost,' Alvin confirmed.

'Can you demonstrate the game to us?' Banjo asked.

'Certainly,' Peter enthused. He looked at Alvin for confirmation who nodded his approval. Peter crossed to a cupboard, opened the door, and removed a chest set from the shelf. He then placed it on the conference table.

'May I?' Peter looked at Alvin again. He nodded yes.

'The board is divided into sixty-four squares in an eight-by-eight configuration. They alternate in colour to delineate them from each other. The colour of the square doesn't actually mean anything, but it does make it easier to perform a move. Each side has the same sixteen pieces. To separate them, one player has white pieces, and the other player has black pieces, but again, that is just a way to separate the pieces and tell which pieces are whose. There is no colour advantage.' He smiled as he placed the pieces on the correct squares.

'Some sets have white and red pieces, and some have white and brown.' Alvin added.

'It's a personal preference,' Larry chipped in.

Peter resumed explaining. 'For some reason, which we haven't worked out, the white always starts first, but after that each player takes it in turn to move one piece.'

'Why is it called, Chest?' Banjo queried.

'We think it is because the pieces are stored in a chest when not being used,' Alvin nodded as he explained as if to reaffirm this logic to himself.

Peter continued, pointing out and positioning pieces as he explained. 'Each side has a royal family comprising of a king and a queen. They have eight children called prawns. They are the short ones in the row in front of the king and the queen. The prawns must cross the board into enemy territory and earn the right to succeed their parents in the event that the parents are captured. Prawns have short legs so they can only move forward or backwards on the board one square at a time. Also, prawns have to stay in their own line unless they are attacking an opposition piece. They can only attack diagonally, forwards or backwards.'

He looked at the board and touched the two pieces indicating the king and the queen. 'The king is very old and can only move slowly, moving one square in any direction at a time. The queen however is young, fit and very powerful and she can move upward and downwards and diagonally across the board for great distances striking fear into her enemies and protecting her old husband and her eight children. The royal family are everything. Once they are gone from the board that player has lost.'

'They also have these six special pieces to help attack the opposition royal family and protect their own royal family. Two fortresses on each corner provide a safe place for the king, queen, or their prawns to shelter if they are threatened. There can only be a maximum of one other piece on the same square with a fortress piece. The fortresses can move up and down and across the board and they can take out any of the opposition royal family or other fortresses or pieces, but only if they don't have anyone sheltering on their square. You see, fortresses can't be captured when they are protecting.' He smiled happily.

'These two pieces are ells. They are called ells because they can move in an L configuration on the board doing surprise attacks on any unwary pieces. They move two squares along and one square sideways. They're surprisingly agile. They can be removed from the board by an opposition royal family member, an ell, a fortress or one of these.'

Peter pointed to two tall pieces next to the king and queen pieces. 'These are called priests and they can move diagonally across the board and can provide sanctuary to a threatened royal family member by sharing the square with them. If the priest is with another piece, then neither piece can be removed from the board. Either of them can launch an attack from the shared square.'

'If a priest or a fortress is protecting another piece and they move off, then they are no longer protecting that piece.' Peter looked as if he may be confusing himself. 'Have I said that already?' he looked at the others.

'You already explained that,' Nelson admonished.

'This is fascinating.' Bobby was mesmerised. He had never seen anything like it.

'Can you teach us how to play?' Banjo asked. He also was clearly intrigued by the game.

'I'd be proud to teach you,' Peter agreed.

'You'd better complete the explanation first,' Lance suggested.

'What did I miss...?' Peter looked confused.

'You can't have a fortress protect another fortress and you can't have a priest protect another priest. There not compatible,' Alvin offered this as a contribution.

'And you forgot to explain the laws of succession,' Lance informed him.

'Oh yeah. If a queen or a king is removed from the game, then a prawn can be crowned as their successor, but only if they reach the front line uncaptured,' Willie chipped in.

'They have to prove themselves worthy,' Lance added.

'You can only have one king, or one queen, on your side at any one time,' Nelson added.

'How do you know when a prawn is now a king or a queen?' Bobby asked.

'We swap the pieces with the captured king or queen in a prisoner exchange,' Willie answered for the group.

'When all ten members of a player's royal family are removed from the game, then that player has lost the game and the other wins and scores the points for his team.'

'So, the royal family is the king, queen and their eight children?' Bobby clarified.

'Yes. They're the prawns,' Peter confirmed touching one of them.

'During the official tournaments we have Visual Display Units all over the scalp so that supporters can watch the action,' Alvin explained.

'Do you like to place bets on who is going to win?' Banjo asked innocently.

'What's a bet?' Lance asked.

Bobby gave him the urgent silent 'NO!' signal and so Banjo said nothing.

'Would you like to give it a try?' Alvin offered.

'Against one of you?' Bobby queried. He was hesitant.

'Why don't you have a go against each other?' Alvin suggested. 'Watching you challenging each other would be a good way for us to get to know just a bit better.'

Banjo cautiously nodded his agreement. 'Okay Banjo. Do you want black or white?'

~ 26 ~

Bobby and Banjo sat opposite each other for their first ever game of Chest. Peter aided Bobby and Nelson assisted Banjo. They cautiously tried moves and received some chuckles from their avid audience. This was a teaching game and Bobby and Banjo responded to the advice and direction being offered by their respective mentors. The game soon progressed to a point where Bobby and Banjo were taking charge and confidently moving their own pieces.

Their audience was appreciative. 'You're both doing very well,' Alvin offered the compliment.

The two players and the five observers failed to notice George's arrival. He walked stealthily up to the conference table and observed that his two QA Follicle Managers were in a desperate duel, so he cleared his throat. Everyone ignored him.

'Hello,' he spoke affirmatively in order to get their attention.

Nelson looked at the interloper. 'Who are you?' he challenged. He was upset that his enjoyment of the game was being disturbed.

'I'm Alvin's boss,' the person responded.

Everyone looked up at George.

'Hello, George,' Alvin greeted George from across the table.

'Who's winning?'

'Banjo, but he's only slightly in front,' Alvin replied.

'Do carry on,' George suggested.

Bobby looked at Banjo. They silently questioned each other on their vulnerability and asked each other if they thought this was a potential managerial trap. Banjo shrugged ever so slightly. Bobby drew a deep breath and moved a priest to assault one of Bobby's prawns.

'Banjo,' Bobby broke the silence.

'Yes, Bobby.'

'Which area do you think we should start our audit in?'

'I think we should visit the eyebrows first, Bobby,' Banjo replied moving his prawn out of harm's way.

'I do too,' Bobby agreed. Moving his fortress and taking the prawn that Banjo had just moved into its path.

'Should we finish the game, or do you think we should put the game on hold until we've completed the audits?' Banjo queried. He took Bobby's fortress with his ell that was sheltering with one of his own fortresses.

'I like your moves, Banjo.' Bobby responded. He moved his queen to take a priest.

'Thank you, Bobby. I think we should return to the game after our audit is completed,' Banjo suggested. He stood up and Bobby followed his example.

'Aw.' There was a collective complaint uttered by the observers who clearly were enjoying the fast pace of a novice's game.

'Banjo is right. We really should be getting on with the audit,' Bobby explained to the others. 'The results of the vote will be known soon, and I feel it would be better if we had finished our tasks here before they announce the results.'

George and Alvin said nothing.

The four Area Managers instantly offered to be the first and show them to their areas of responsibility.

'Thanks, but no, could you please arrange a guide to take us to the eyebrows, that would be most appreciated.' Bobby curbed protests with downward hand gestures.

Alvin walked to his desk and spoke to an aide via his intercom. 'Please organise for a guide to take our visitors to the eyebrows.'

A young Follicle Farmer entered the room, he stood waiting patiently.

Bobby and Banjo nodded politely to the others and left the room proceeded by their guide.

Alvin spoke to his four Area Managers. 'I suggest you men return to your areas and prepare to be audited.'

Silently the four filed out of the room.

When Alvin and George were finally alone and the room was silent, George asked his question. 'Does he know?'

'No.'

'I'll tell him after the audit.'

'How will he take it?'

'Well, I believe.' George drew a deep breath. 'It's the result he's been expecting.'

'I told him regardless of the vote that he could still use his discovery wherever he was working.'

'That's true,' George agreed.

'I invited him to take over from me as Regional Manager for the Scalp,' Alvin informed his boss with a mischievous grin.

George gave him a blank stare.

Undaunted Alvin continued. 'I think he'd like it here. Also by being here, he can reduce the alopecia impact and attend to our greying hairs with impunity.'

'That's true,' George observed. 'How did he respond?'

'Unfavourably. He sees himself as a QA Manager.'

'That's a pity..., because I don't.' George said flatly.

***

Bobby and Banjo followed their guide along the pathways that connected the scalp to the eyebrows. It was an uneventful journey and they were aware of warmth penetrating the *epidermis* from the external heat source.

Bobby and Banjo were comfortable in each other's company. They appreciated that they didn't have to fill their time together with idle conversation. They respectively gave each other time to collect thoughts, reflect on outcomes, remember the places they had been to, and the people they'd met. They were good friends and they both felt lucky to have such a strong bond. They had a bond which provided them both with support, trust and mutual respect.

The guide abruptly stopped and pointed to Sylvester. He performed a small bow and walked back the way they had come.

'Talkative. Wasn't he?' Banjo grinned.

'And he was very knowledgeable and informative about local current events,' Bobby agreed smiling.

'You're here earlier than I imagined,' Sylvester approached them. 'Are your audits such a brief undertaking?'

'No, they are actually very detailed,' Bobby corrected.

Sylvester said nothing.

'This is the first area in the scalp that we're auditing,' Banjo added.

'Oh.'

'Do you play Chest with the others?'

'No,' Sylvester snorted. 'I can't be bothered with it. None of my team has ever shown any interest. Maybe it's because we're so far away from mainstream scalp Follicle Farmers.'

'You don't approve of the game?' Bobby queried.

'I'm indifferent,' Sylvester replied. 'As long as it doesn't affect their work, I couldn't care either way.'

'What do you do for fun in the eye brows?' Bobby goaded.

'Look,' Sylvester sighed. 'I'm a Follicle Farmer. I grow hair. I follow the Union mantra when it suits me. I follow procedures. I mentor my workers into exceeding growth objectives,' he paused considering; 'I'll admit that occasionally we grow a rogue hair for a bit of fun.' Sylvester went quiet waiting for a response.

Bobby smiled and looked at Banjo.

Banjo smiled and looked to Sylvester.

Sylvester saw the smiles that bordered on laughter and asked 'What?'

'Rogue hairs!' Bobby laughed. Banjo joined in.

'Yeah..., so what?' Sylvester demanded joining in the mirth.

'So... that's great,' Bobby replied laughing even louder.

By this time all three were laughing merrily.

After they settled, Bobby and Banjo set out what the audit was going to entail. Sylvester clearly understood and was happy and willing to participate. He said that he'd made time available to show them follicle growing in both eyebrows. They visited numerous follicles and met the workers and Team Leaders that managed them. They documented the results and offered tips and suggestions on how to improve yield and neaten up the paperwork.

The team at the eyebrows were doing well. They responded positively to the constructive feedback that they were given. They saw the benefits of the slight changes that the QA Managers issued and all agreed that they had collectively benefited from the experience.

Sylvester was impressed. 'Thank you for visiting us and for the respectful way you treated my team.'

'You're very welcome,' Bobby replied.

Sylvester held out a hand in friendship.

Bobby accepted it. He smiled inwardly as this ritual was absent when they'd arrived.

'Before we go back to the scalp, I'd like your opinion on one more thing about the eyebrows.'

Sylvester became suspicious. 'What would you like to know?' He asked curtly.

'What do you consider to be the eyebrows most important function?' Bobby asked.

'Some people suggest our role is to keep sweat out of the eyes,' Sylvester replied.

'You don't agree,' Bobby countered. Banjo looked on, curious as to where Bobby was leading this conversation.

'No,' Sylvester snorted.

'Why? What do you feel is your primary purpose?' Bobby pressed for more information.

'Our eyebrows are an integral part of non-verbal communication. They add significant strength to the words the mind chooses the mouth to utter to other humans. Often, they can convey meaning or expression without the need to vocalise words. This is an important role, and we take it seriously.'

'Good for you,' Banjo congratulated Sylvester for his conviction.

'Goodbye and all the best,' Bobby said as he offered his hand as a farewell gesture.

'Thank you,' Sylvester acknowledged as he returned the handshake. 'Do you need a guide to take you back to the scalp?'

'We'll be fine, thank you,' Banjo told him.

Bobby and Banjo returned to the scalp. The journey was undertaken in relative silence and the only thing that Banjo impressed on his boss was the urgent need to find the staff canteen. He was very hungry.

Bobby laughed at him but agreed.

They sought out the dining room and served themselves a meal. The dining room was filled with workers. Many were playing Chest during their meal break and some of the games attracted observers.

'I like Chest,' Banjo commented between mouthfuls.

'I agree it's a good game. I think we should add an electronic version of it to our kit.'

'I'd prefer not to have observers about when we play our next game,' Banjo lamented their earlier experience.

'I agree,' Bobby confirmed. 'It puts unnecessary pressure on us, when clearly it should be a recreational activity.'

'An audience implies that it is competitive,' Banjo added.

After their meal, they freshened up, and then looked for the other Area Managers. In turn they visited each area. At the temples they demonstrated how to massage the region of the follicle to stimulate the release of extra colour into the shaft. At the top of the forehead they demonstrated how to tap fat cells into releasing their hair restorative properties.

They stopped briefly to observe a Chest game between two of the best from the Saints team. They were impressed by their speed as the pieces appeared to be chasing each other across the board. Clearly, at this senior level of play, the combatants knew what they were doing. For Bobby and Banjo it reaffirmed their decision to keep their Chest games recreational. They agreed to play to win, but they wouldn't care if they lost, and they definitely wouldn't be keeping a tally of the scores.

After many cycles, Bobby and Banjo had completed their scalp audits. They were happy with the outcomes and impressed with the scalps region's ability to grow a fine head of hair. As they completed each audit, they recorded their results and observations.

They approached Alvin's office feeling weary but nonetheless fulfilled. They promised themselves a well-earned rest and relaxation period after they had completed their report. At the aide's desk, they were told to sit and wait.

So they did as instructed and sat and waited.

Then they waited some more.

They were getting restless. Banjo was very hungry. Bobby was tired and hungry. He planned to get some quality sleep after they had secured a hearty meal.

The aide informed them that they shouldn't have to wait much longer.

Bobby was about to verbalise his intense displeasure when the door opened and Alvin stepped out.

'Bobby, Banjo,' he looked serious as he spoke.

Bobby and Banjo stood up to follow Alvin into his office, but Alvin held up his hand and they stopped mid-way to the door.

'Only Banjo for now, thanks Bobby,' he said firmly. 'Could you please return to your seat and wait until you're required.'

Banjo looked at Bobby in confusion. Bobby nodded his head indicating that Banjo should do as he was told. Banjo held up a hand and gave a half-wave as he followed Alvin into his office.

Bobby didn't understand. Had they done something wrong? He reflected on their performance since arriving at the scalp. He couldn't think of anything that they might have done to attract a negative outcome.

He sat and stared at the aides seated behind their desks. All three were working on computer terminals and were completely disinterested in him.

He began to speculate what was going on with Banjo. Maybe they were offering him the job of being the next Scalp Regional Manager. He didn't think that Banjo would be interested. QA was more his scene. He was good at it. His reporting skills were better than Bobby's and Bobby had allowed him to do most of it because he enjoyed it, and...

Bobby paused his thinking.

Maybe they were asking Banjo to report on his weaknesses. Maybe they were setting him up. Senior managers sometimes did that. Banjo would be loyal to the highest degree, but senior managers were skilled at manipulating questions to illicit specific targeted responses.

Banjo would never maliciously get either of them into trouble, but in his inexperience, he might be led into a trap that could entangle both of them. He should be in that room. He should be in there to protect their reputations. He was needed to defend their actions and expound on improved skill sets and promote virtues.

It occurred to him that if it were bad, really bad, then exhibiting that type of behaviour would be too little and probably too late.

Bobby once again paused in his thinking.

It night be good news. They may be asking Banjo's opinion about expanding the QA team. They might be examining his input so they can compare it to his responses when they asked him the same questions. He'd learned that *T-Cells* used these technique when questioning suspects.

Was he a suspect?

Bobby again paused his thinking.

Nah. He shook his head.

An expanded QA department would require a QA Manager for every regional manager. They would oversee the activities, but report to the QA manager in order to retain independence with QA functions. They'd have to be carefully selected and trained so that they become a vital part of each region, but still have the necessary recourse should a conflict arise between the Regional Manager and the QA Manager.

They wouldn't be talking to Banjo about that.

Nah.

That would happen in a team building meeting. The Head Office QA trainers would be involved in any expansion planning of the Follicle QA department.

It wouldn't be that. He shook his head.

The door opened and Alvin stepped through.

'We're ready for you Bobby,' he told him.

He said we're ready. We're. There was more than just Alvin in that room. How many were ready for him? Was it a surprise party? Did the yes vote win for hair rejuvenation and colour restoration. Was this a celebratory gathering for him in his honour?

Bobby hesitantly stood up. He walked to Alvin who stood aside to let Bobby into the room. Bobby slowly walked in and saw George waiting for him. Banjo wasn't in the room. No one else was in the room. Alvin closed the door gently behind him.

George motioned for Bobby to take a seat on some comfortable furniture. They sat in a triangle configuration.

George smiled reassuringly, but Bobby tried to remain impassive.

Bobby cleared his throat. 'Where's Banjo?' he asked casually.

'Banjo has been sent to my offices,' George replied.

'Oh.' Bobby was trying to formulate his next action.

'Well done on your scalp audit,' Alvin ventured. 'Very thorough.'

'Thank you,' Bobby replied looking at Alvin. 'Why has Banjo gone to your office?' he demanded.

'He's getting things ready for a whole of body tour that he'll be doing with Dan.'

'Oh.'

'I imagine you'll be wondering why you're not getting ready to do that yourself.'

'It did occur to me,' Bobby agreed. His tone was slightly shaky.

'You see, Bobby. You're not the QA Manager anymore. I'm officially relieving you of that title and its incumbent responsibility.'

'Oh.' Bobby looked at his feet.

'Percival and I believe that Banjo will make a better QA Manager than you have been. We're confident that he'll lead an expanded team to achieve better QA outcomes for all follicles.'

'I didn't even get to say goodbye.' Bobby was upset.

'Oh, you will,' George assured him. 'You'll get to see both Dan and Banjo before they depart. Banjo has to interview candidates for his old position. He'll need an effective 2IC and he has many to choose from. We've had numerous applications. I guess travelling and exploring the body is seen as an appealing aspect of the role.'

'So, you've known about these changes for a long time?' Bobby was restrained in showing his disappointment.

'I have, but I wanted you to spend time at the scalp to see if you'd like to be its new Regional Manager?' George asked smiling.

'It wasn't my original plan, but under the circumstances, I'd gladly accept the role.'

'I wouldn't want my replacement to see this role as one he's been forced into. This is a prestigious post, and you should feel honoured to be offered it,' Alvin admonished Bobby for his lack of gratitude.

'I'm sorry.' He drew in a deep breath. I'd be honoured to be the Regional Manager for the Scalp.' Bobby stood up and offered his hand to accept the post.

'Sit down, Bobby,' George instructed kindly.

'Just out of curiosity, which of my five Area Managers do you believe would be the best choice as my replacement?' Alvin asked.

Bobby gave him a confused look. He shrugged. 'Sylvester,' he answered as he returned to his chair.

'We agree,' George confirmed. 'Sylvester is going to be offered the role of the Regional Manager for the Scalp.'

'Oh.' Bobby was really confused. 'Have I done something wrong?' he wailed.

'Oh no, Bobby,' George grinned. 'You've done everything right.'

'I don't understand?' Bobby restrained himself from an emotional outburst.

'I'm retiring,' George informed him. 'Percival and I want you to be the next *Integumentary* System Manager. You're getting my job, Bobby,' he said proudly. He beamed an enormous smile at a very worried and perplexed Bobby.

Alvin stood up and offered his hand in congratulations. Bobby stood up. He was shaking. He nimbly returned the handshake.

'Well done, boss,' Alvin pumped his hand. 'But you won't be my boss for very long.'

'Wha...,?' Bobby was even more confused.

'I'm retiring very soon too, remember?'

'Oh yeah, of course,' Bobby laughed in relief.

George stood up and gave Bobby a congratulatory hug. 'Well done Bobby. I'm very proud of you,' George told him after letting go.

Bobby looked about the room. He forced a smile. 'I'm not sure what to say,' he wailed.

George and Alvin laughed.

'How about "I accept"?' George suggested.

'Accept! Accept! Of course I accept. It's just come as a big shock, that's all.'

George and Alvin laughed some more.

'What will you two be doing? I mean, as you're retiring...,' Bobby started to ask.

'Initially we'll be on hand to train you and Sylvester into your new roles.'

Bobby nodded a 'Thank you'.

'After that I'm taking up a role as the Mind Manager for Camping,' George explained

'And I've accepted the role as Mind Manager for Fishing,' Alvin added.

'But we don't like fishing,' Bobby was confused.

George and Alvin burst into laughter once more. 'That's why it's so perfect for our retirement,' George explained to a startled Bobby.

They sat and enjoyed some celebratory refreshments.

'What will be some of the things you think you'll be implementing when you're formally the *Integumentary* Manager, Bobby?' George asked out of curiosity.

'I think it's important that I spend as much time as I can learning the role before I talk about any changes I'd be making. The *Integumentary* system has been growing hair, skin and nails for a long time now, and I'd want to be confident that I know what I'm talking about before I change anything,' Bobby replied thoughtfully.

'Well answered,' George agreed.

'I do think the Follicle Farmer's motto needs to be improved. "If we don't grow, we don't grow," does sound weak,' Bobby spoke candidly.

'We agree,' Alvin replied. 'I forbade its use here in the *scalp*.'

'Now that you mention it, I don't recall hearing it since we got here,' Bobby agreed.

'You can ask Dan to work on a new slogan before he departs on his tour,' George suggested.

'I will,' Bobby nodded his head. 'I won't give him any suggestions as I believe he should take full ownership of the new slogan.'

'A sentiment of true leadership, Bobby.' George smiled. 'Well done.'

Bobby smiled gratefully.

'Oh, by the way, Percival wants your input on an idea he's been working on. After reading all your reports from different parts of the body, he feels it would be beneficial if the System Managers got together for a conference. Perhaps you could conduct a series of workshops designed for greater inter-system co-operation.' George explained.

Bobby nodded his head imperceptibly.

'Percival is very impressed with your leadership style. Will you help him arrange it?' George queried.

'Yes. Of course,' Bobby agreed. He then knew what would be occupying the bulk of his future.

* * *

This is the end of Follicle Farm.

Bobby will return in **'Follicle Farm – The convention.'**

TRANSCRIPT OF BOBBY'S INTERVIEW

The following is part of the transcript of Bobby's interview with Frederick from the Follicle Farmers News, conducted at the conclusion of this story.

Frederick: Bobby, tell me a little about the novel "Follicle Farm."

Bobby: Some might call it a biography about my growth and development as a Follicle Farmer, but really it is a fascinating account of my adventure in human physiology and psychology, with a comic twist on organisational behaviour, worker dynamics and organisational structure.

Frederick: You mentioned comic twist. Would you describe your adventure as a comedy?

Bobby: Humour is a very personal choice. The story has numerous comic moments that should amuse most readers. In truth, no-one can tell you what is funny.

Frederick: How did you feel when they asked to be the hero of your own story?

Bobby: Initially I was overwhelmed. As the book progressed, I began to feel some ownership over my destiny. Let's be truthful. I did have a lot of help for which I'm very grateful.

Frederick: Do you have a favourite moment you'd like to share with the readers?

Bobby: Waiting outside Alvin's office is my most memorable, but I'd have to say zooming through the blood stream in the Taurus with Skip was the most fun.

Frederick: I believe your story continues?

Bobby: A sequel is being planned, yes. Sorry, but I'm not at liberty to discuss it.

Frederick: It'll be something to look forward too.

Bobby: Yes.

Frederick: Thank you for your time Bobby. I realise you are a very busy Mitochondria.

Bobby: It's always a pleasure to promote the book. Thank you for having me.